EHOSHUA

BOOK TWO
CONFLAGRATION

GARRETT GLASS

JEHOSHUA: CONFLAGRATION

GARRETT GLASS - AUTHOR

Copyright © 2014

I S B N 13 : 978-0991110629

First Printing

Cover Image: *Shadrach, Meshach, and Abednego escape the Fiery Furnace* (Book of Daniel), 4th century fresco from the Catacomb on Via Latina, Rome

Cover Design and Print Layout: Pamela Trush, Graphic Designer, Delaney-Designs, info@delaney-designs.com

Map Designs: Bob Nagel, Duck Feet Design, bnagel@duckfeetdesigns.com

Editorial Assistance: Bob Trezevant

Cover Image: Shadrach, Meshach, and Abednego escape the Fiery Furnace (Book of Daniel), late 3rd century or early 4th century fresco from the Catacomb on Via Latina, Rome. This passage in Daniel tells of three Hebrews who refused to disavow the Lord God even when threatened with death, and it became a meaningful story for Christians experiencing successive waves of persecution under the Roman Empire. In this fresco, the martyrs are surrounded by flames, their hands upraised in the orant position (which is how early Christians prayed). An eagle above holds a crown symbolizing martyrdom. The modernistic costume of the martyrs seems to represent a third-century Christian artist's interpretation of the type of robe worn by an ancient Hebrew male.

Printed in the United States of America

Glass, Garrett
Jehoshua
Book Two: Conflagration
www.whocutgodshair.com

For Marisa,
my little Alligator.

From her Crocodile Afterwhile

Color and enlarged versions of the maps in Appendix D
can be found at: **www.whocutgodshair.com**

How to pronounce Jehoshua – the original name of Jesus

    In English: JOSH-yew-ah (as in Josh'-ua)

    In Hebrew: Yo-SHEW-ah

TABLE OF CONTENTS

FOREWORD

ooking back over the long arc of history, it is obvious that a defining event in Western civilization – and indeed the most significant event of the entire first century after the death of Jesus Christ - was the siege and destruction of Jerusalem by the Romans. The Romans, however, would not have thought so, because for them the fall of Jerusalem was nothing more than the restoration of the natural order, an order which required that Roman military might and political control over the Empire remained unchallenged.

By 73 CE (Common Era, or Anno Domini), when the last Jewish resistance at the fortress of Masada had been stamped out, the Romans could look back with reasonable satisfaction at the results. True, the cost to them had been high. Many thousands of Roman soldiers and auxiliaries had been killed or wounded, and the retaking of the Jewish provinces of Galilee, Samaria, and Judea had consumed seven years of hard fighting. But the Jews had been vanquished once and for all (or so Rome thought). Hundreds of thousands of Jews had died in the war, and all remaining adults in Jerusalem had been sold off into slavery or certain death in the major arenas around the Empire. Rome had confiscated unimaginable wealth in gold, silver, and jewels from the Jewish Temple in Jerusalem, which had been destroyed along with the rest of the city as a lesson not just to the Jews, but to anyone else in the Empire foolish enough to challenge Rome's dominion.

As the decade of the 70s came to an end, Rome was forced to deal with the unexpected destruction of major resort towns and villages surrounding Mount Vesuvius, which underwent a cataclysmic volcanic explosion in 79. Rome's attention was diverted from the smoldering rubble that constituted what was left of Jerusalem. Even further from their mind was the fate of a small sect of Jews which worshipped a crucified prophet named Jehoshua, also called the Christos, or Anointed One.

We can see from our vantage point how this small sect carried on after Jerusalem fell, and how it began to thrive and eventually challenge the Empire in a completely unexpected way. The Romans can be excused for ignoring these Christos followers. Initially, the Christians had been troublesome, if not a bit perplexing. The Roman Emperor Claudius had found it necessary to expel the Christians from Rome, and this policy was more than anything else a response to complaints from Jews in Rome who found the Christians heretical. The complaints were backed up by hard evidence that the Christians were disruptive, because there had been so many street riots in Rome between Jews and Christians.

As this second volume of the *Jehoshua* series shows, the Emperor Nero was forced to grapple with the Christians as well. They had been quietly reestablishing themselves in the city of Rome, and they had founded communities in other parts of the Empire. Nero heard all sorts of vile insinuations about the Christians – that they engaged in cannibalistic rituals, and believed that the world was coming to an end soon. It was this particular belief that gave credence to the rumors that the Christians had set fire to Rome in the year 64 in order to hasten the Last Judgment.

The first extensive comment about the Christians in Roman literature was written by the historian Tacitus around 116, who described Nero's attempt to blame the Christians for the Great Fire in 64. Nero had Christians dragged to the arena to suffer what Tacitus described as "the most exquisite tortures." So gruesome was this spectacle that Tacitus said the crowds turned against Nero and began to develop some sympathy for the Christians.

This situation is significant on several levels. For Christians to have an active community in Rome just 30 years after Christ's death, their expansion across the Empire must have been explosive. Second, the Romans were reasonably tolerant of all religions, and they had come to an accommodation with the Jews because their priests agreed to offer up part of the daily meat sacrifice at the Jerusalem Temple to the Emperor. Going to the extreme of torturing the Christians certainly confirms one of Tacitus' observations, that they were a "class hated for their abominations." Third, following this persecution in 64, Christians were again forced to practice their religion underground. Finally, according to legend the persecution ensnared two of the most prominent Christians – St. Peter and St.

Paul. There is good historical evidence that St. Peter died as a martyr in the Roman arena in 64 or 65. There is far less evidence for a martyrdom of St. Paul, and different legends rose up as to whether he was beheaded on a road leading out of Rome, or whether he managed to escape all the way to Hispania (Spain), where he was then beheaded. For someone of Paul's stature in Christianity, it was only natural that early Christians developed theories about his martyrdom, but we simply don't know what happened to him.

You can begin to see some of the questions I was grappling with as I put *Jehoshua: Conflagration* together. What was it about Christianity that made it so immediately attractive? Why were Christian practices considered so odious by the pagans? What was it about Peter and Paul that commanded so much respect in the Christian communities, and what was the nature of the doctrinal disputes these two men had (and which are mentioned briefly in the Bible)?

It turns out this is but half the story that needs to be told here. The other half involves the growing social and political unrest in Judea and Galilee during the reign of Nero and beyond. A time came when this unrest boiled over into outright rebellion against Rome, and Nero was forced to act, if only to take vengeance on the Jews for destroying one of Rome's legions. That vengeance came at the hands of a retired general and provincial governor, Vespasianus, who with his son Titus besieged Jerusalem and destroyed the city.

This is an exciting story to tell, because we have a detailed account of these events in a book by Flavius Josephus, *The Wars of the Jews*. Josephus (Jo-SEE-fus) was a prominent Jewish Pharisee who initially came to the defense of his country, by taking command of the Galilean city of Jotapata when it was besieged by Vespasianus. Josephus put up a stubborn defense, but after a forty-seven day siege, Jotapata fell to Vespasianus, opening the way for the Roman legions to advance to Jerusalem, their main objective. Apparently, from this experience Josephus concluded that the Jews could in no way defeat the Romans or withstand a siege. He therefore switched sides, and joined the Roman army at Jerusalem. Josephus addressed the citizens of Jerusalem from the siege works, and expostulated them to give up their resistance and allow the Romans to retake the city peaceably.

Unsurprisingly, the Jews looked at Josephus as a traitor and paid him no heed. Even to this day it is somewhat difficult for Jewish scholars to accept Josephus' account of what happened during the war, since he spent the rest of his life living in Rome under the patronage of the Flavius family (Vespasianus, Titus, and Domitianus). Setting aside whatever interpretation Josephus puts on the events he describes, his facts continue to be validated. Even as recently as a few years ago, excavations at Jotapata identified the signs of the siege works exactly as Josephus described them.

Josephus wrote his history of the wars 25 years after the events, from his self-imposed exile in Rome. He no doubt used the *Wars of the Jews* to exonerate himself of the charge of being a traitor, by painting the Jewish insurrectionists in the worst light possible. On the other hand, it seems clear that many other Jewish leaders at the time found the behavior of these rebels execrable when they took over Jerusalem as its supposed defenders against the Romans. On this basis, I generally follow the description of events provided by Josephus.

Even with the distance of 2,000 years, the suffering of the Jews during and after the siege stands out in its horror. This is the beginning of the Diaspora – the dispersion of the Jews from their homeland across the Near East and eventually the world, though it must be noted there were substantial populations of Jews in all the major Roman cities before Jerusalem fell (100,000 in Alexandria alone). There was also a very small group of Christos-worshippers in Jerusalem who eventually disappeared with all the other Jews in the Diaspora.

The disappearance of the Christian community in Jerusalem is a critical point, and I have woven into this tale some questions for the reader that lay out the historical importance of the Jewish wars. We know that Peter and Paul did not agree on many matters. Peter knew Jehoshua; Paul did not, yet he claimed to be as important as any other apostle based on a vision he asserted he received from Jehoshua. Peter wanted to keep the Christian community anchored to its Jewish roots, religion, practices, and culture. Paul was a Jew and a Pharisee, but he was far less interested in Judaism because he was deliberately preaching to Greeks and other Gentiles. Paul created a theology around the bodily resurrection of Jesus and his "blood sacrifice" for all mankind, a theology that Peter must have found odd and unacceptable. While Peter and possibly Paul met their deaths in Rome and never returned to the Jerusalem community, we have to wonder what would have happened to Christianity if this dispute had continued in intensity. What did it mean, in other words, for the Jewish form of Christianity to be wiped out with the fall of Jerusalem?

Very early in its development, Christianity lost its "home base" so to speak – the city where its founder was executed, and the shrines that pilgrims had just begun to visit – places like Golgotha, the supposed tomb of Jehoshua, and the scene of his trial. Worse still, all the people who knew him or knew someone who knew him were dying out or died during the siege. The religion was essentially unmoored. What does the loss of its center mean for its development? Related to this loss is the fact that the main opposition to this young cult of the Christos was the Jewish establishment. Now that establishment was gone as well, opening the door for the expansion of Christianity elsewhere, and especially in Rome. If these things had not happened, would Christianity have survived?

The reader will find questions like these interspersed within *Jehoshua: Conflagration*. They will also find an exciting – in fact astounding – tale that deserves to be told, because most people know little about these events. If you had to pick an essential moment in Western history where you could say – "This is it. This is the point where Western civilization takes a decisive turn in its development." – this is that moment. Judaism, Christianity, Roman civilization – they all interacted at this critical time and begin a remarkable, and sometimes tragic, journey together. I believe you will find this story extraordinary and intellectually illuminating. I certainly did, as I was researching and writing it.

Use of Terms and the Appendixes

In this novel, for proper names I use the original name of historical characters where possible. Jesus Christ is therefore referred to as Jehoshua the Christos, and the Emperor Vespasian is referred to as Vespasianus. Modern scholars no longer use BC (Before Christ) and AD (Anno Domini) when dating events in the Roman era. The preference is instead to use BCE (Before Common Era) and CE (Common Era). All events in this novel occur in the Common Era.

The writing style in this novel is formal. Characters speak in complete sentences, if not whole paragraphs, which is certainly not how people speak in real life. I make few attempts to have my characters speak in slang, because we don't know what that would sound like in the ancient world. Writers of that time used formal language, so I am consistent in that sense. Another advantage to this formal style is that everybody appears intelligent and thoughtful, and I happen to like drawing characters – historical or fictional – who have those qualities. This does not mean they were formally educated; few people in the ancient world could read or write. But I find it hard to believe that someone like Miriam of Magdala (Mary Magdalen) was simply an ignorant peasant woman. Early Christianity was already marked by intense philosophical and doctrinal disputes, and I prefer to think that the apostles and early followers of Jehoshua had the intelligence to comprehend and discuss his message.

The appendixes at the back of the book are an important component to understanding the events in the novel. The first appendix explains which events in each chapter are historical and which are fictional. The Timeline is an important tool for understanding which historical characters were contemporaries to each other. Many readers of my first book have appreciated the maps as important helps in understanding the location of certain cities, and their relative distance from each other.

In any novel of historical fiction, the author usually has only a skeletal framework of historic fact available that can contribute to plot, characters, and structure. Beyond that, it is necessary to rely on imagination to fill in the blanks and create a believable story. In a story such as *Jehoshua: Conflagration*, in which so many of the characters and circumstances have some reference to historical people and events, the most important thing I can contribute as an author is believability. Whatever my personal opinions about the likelihood of a physical resurrection for Jehoshua, I want someone like Paulus to appear as a firm believer in the resurrection, just as the rational and fact-based Roman administrators must be convincing in their skepticism.

I wrote in Book One that, in my opinion, a physical resurrection of Jehoshua did not occur. The task in Book Two is to show that despite this fact, stories arose about a resurrection and the miracles Jehoshua performed, and many people joined the cult of the Christos with a firm belief in these circumstances. Why they did so, is a core question not simply about the development of Christianity, but about the future of Western civilization. It relates to why a billion or more Christians today have a sincere belief in these circumstances just as much as the early Christos followers.

This is a story ultimately about faith, a word Paulus introduced to Christianity. Our story begins with Paulus and his trial in Rome for insurrection. Paulus disappears toward the middle of the book, just as he disappears with no explanation in *Acts of the Apostles*. His presence, however, is felt in the last chapter of the book, when Christians had to make the decision to follow Paulus' teachings or that of other Christian leaders. As you read the story, you will begin to see how Paulus of Tarsus shaped not only the world of the early Christians, but of our world as well.

Garrett Glass
February 2014

PART ONE

Aristarchus

From Corinth to Rome
Year 57

Chapter One

"Pull hard left, men! Harder!" Aristarchus felt his arm and leg muscles strain to the limit as he and the others dragged the ropes to the port side, trying to give the sail some tautness and a semblance of shape that would allow the winds to billow the cloth rather than whip it about uselessly. The rip had begun in the bottom center and by now had spread a third of the way up the right side of the sail. All of them – Aristarchus, Paulus, the two Roman soldiers, and what crew members could be spared – were ordered to grab hold of whatever bit of rope or sail they could reach. Collectively, they had the strength to hold the sail together and prevent further damage, giving Captain Tychon room to maneuver the rudder and keep the ship moving forward to the island ahead.

Every so often a gust of wind tested their stamina, and one or two of them lost their grip. The others were able to hold on, giving the team time to recover. The trickiness with the wind wasn't its strength; it was the fact that you couldn't predict where the gales would come from. They flung the ship to and fro capriciously and unpredictably, very much as this storm has risen out of the east without notice on what had been a calm sea under clear skies.

The rain came down hard with the gales, but it was not like the sideways, stabbing rain that sometimes endangered ships on the open sea. This intermittent rain left time for the remaining crew members to swab the deck as much as possible, keeping the water away from the wheat in the hold. As a corbita hauling grain from Egypt to Rome, the ship had been specially built to keep its cargo dry, with the deck planks heavily sealed with pitch, and the hold covered with two doors, the top one larger than the bottom one. Still,

Captain Tychon ordered his crew to work ceaselessly to keep the decks clear of standing water; the last thing he wanted was for his cargo to become water-sodden. The weight of a cargo of soaked and bloated wheat would probably doom the ship in this storm, making it impossible to steer forward.

Neither Aristarchus nor Paulus had taken much confidence from their first encounter with Captain Tychon. They had been escorted on to the ship at Corinth, where it had off-loaded some boxes of cloth it had picked up along the Syrian coast, on its way ultimately to Ostia, the port of Rome. They found their new captain to be uninspiring. He appeared to be twenty-five years old – one of those Greek youths who had a feminine look about him and would have been of better service as a model for the statuary that made Greek artisans famous around the known world. Other than his sun-weathered skin, one would not have guessed he had the slightest maritime experience. In truth, as Aristarchus was to learn, Tychon was thirty-six, with a wife and four children in Thessaly. His crew respected him, and his quiet demeanor had suddenly become a source of strength during this storm. No one wanted a panicky captain at a time like this.

"There's a reef ahead, men!" Tychon shouted over the wind, which had picked up again, this time from the south, pushing them away from the island which lay dead ahead west of them. "Don't worry. I know exactly where the opening is. It's tight, but it's manageable, even in these conditions. Just keep up your positions, and do as you are told!"

His orders now came with greater frequency-- a bit to the right, a bit to the center, or to the left. He had surprising strength in his wiry body, and was able to command the rudder and the ship to the one spot ahead that prevented a break-up on the rocks. It seemed to everyone that the ship wasn't making any progress, but the captain knew it was inching forward. When the sound of the surf bashing the reef became audible, Aristarchus could sense a combination of relief yet added tension among crew and passengers.

He was surprised at the sudden change in their condition once they slipped by the reef. The wind whistled about them as unpredictably as ever, and the rain picked up and stopped, just as before, but the sea felt shockingly calm. What happened to the waves, he wondered? A large bay lay ahead of them, and an extensive area of sandy beach stretched along the center of the island. The captain steered them directly ahead, and it took little more than 20 minutes to run the corbita aground on the sand. There was a wrenching sound as the ship wedged itself into the beach. Everyone wanted to jump off ship immediately, to run for safety, but Tychon would have none of this. He ordered his crew to stay aboard and continue protecting the hold until the rain stopped. He himself led the passengers ashore.

Those manning the mangled sail flopped immediately on the sand, their muscles aching from over an hour of non-stop work. One of the soldiers was sobbing with relief. Tychon, meanwhile, had gone off into an area of trees and bushes. At length, Paulus felt it was necessary for someone to go thank him for saving their lives and his ship. Paulus stirred up the strength to rise to his feet, and walked unsteadily to find the captain. He was surprised to discover Tychon on his knees in front of a small statue he apparently carried in a pocket.

"Thank you, O Poseidon, for our deliverance!" said Tychon. "I will fulfill my vow to offer you a ram at your temple when next I return home." Tychon was speaking with a tremble in his voice, and he was obviously more profoundly moved by the experience than he was willing to admit publicly. Paulus thought for a second to leave him to his prayers, and he certainly had no intention of revealing what he had witnessed to anyone else. A man's communion with his gods should be a private thing, thought Paulus – that is what the Christos had always preached. Nevertheless, Paulus had long since learned that he was unable to leave anyone alone who worshipped false gods.

Paulus therefore raised his hands and face to heaven, and in a voice just loud enough for only Tychon to hear, said "Thank you, O Lord, for our safe passage. Thank you for allowing me to continue on to my trial in Rome. Provide me, I pray, with the strength to endure whatever is in store for me. In the name of your Son, Jehoshua the Christos, I praise you for the blessings and love you provide all men who serve and worship you, Heavenly Father, with whom we desire eternal life through the sacrifice of your only Son!"

Tychon was naturally startled by this interruption of his private prayers. He realized instantly it could only be the Christian who was rude enough to disturb a man's worship to the gods. Paulus had been roaming about the ship throughout the entire voyage, boring everyone with stories about Jehoshua the Christos, and the eternal life that awaited those who swore allegiance to him. Tychon realized it was a mistake to have unshackled this prisoner. He seemed polite and innocent enough – a harmless old man, really – and where was he going to go anyway? Overboard? Tychon was at the point where he was going to clasp the irons back on Paulus, when the storm hit.

Paulus carried on with his prayers. "Most importantly, Heavenly Father, we give thanks for the protection provided us by Captain Tychon. It is only by his seamanship, his courage, and his steadfast calm, that any of us are alive after this ordeal. May you provide him and his family eternal blessings. Keep his wife and children safe always, as he has kept us safe. Amen."

Paulus felt he had accomplished what he set out to do. Tychon was mollified, somewhat, with these words. He rose to his feet, placing his statue back in his pocket. "Come, let us get back to the others," he said to Paulus.

The storm was beginning to abate. There were patches of open sky visible across the sea to the east. The captain proceeded to join his crew aboard ship, examining the vessel for damage. It appeared the rip in the sail was the only major damage, but it was enough to make the ship unseaworthy until it was repaired. Tychon ordered the crew to begin bringing a portion of the ship's provisions ashore. He rummaged around his quarters and found the chains that had bound Paulus. He brought these with him to the shore and approached the two soldiers.

"Gentlemen, I can no longer allow the prisoner to roam free while we are on land. It is your responsibility as well as mine to make sure he is delivered safely to Rome." As he handed the chains to one of the soldiers, Paulus joined the group. He offered no resistance or complaint to being constrained hand and foot yet again. Tychon felt he owed the prisoner something of an apology. "I am sorry we have to bind you again while we are on shore. This is regulation, you understand. Should there be any danger, or once we are back on ship, you will be unshackled." Tychon made a mental note that when they set sail again, he would have a word with Paulus about his proselytizing.

It was not a question in the captain's mind as to whether they would set sail again. He knew they would. He called the entire assembly together on the shore to explain the situation.

"First, let me say we are in no danger here. I know this island. There is a small fishing settlement on the other side of the island, about a day's walk from here. There are skilled shipwrights there who can help us repair the sail, and then we will be on our way.

Early tomorrow morning I will lead a small group of my crew to this settlement; we will return by nightfall of the second day."

"The rest of you will stay ashore here and await our return. My first officer will be in charge and has all of my authority in my absence. I expect your full cooperation with his orders. Your first priority will be to make temporary shelters from the palm branches all around you before it gets dark; it is easy enough to do and we will teach you how to do it if you do not know. I have already had several days of provisions brought ashore, and there is an ample supply for your needs. Tomorrow I expect you, with the exception of the prisoner Paulus and one of his guards, to assist in refilling the ship's supply of fresh water – but in that circumstance only are you to be allowed back on board the ship. The ship is listing too heavily to the right and I don't want any more weight added than necessary. I repeat – in no circumstance are you to board the ship without the permission of the first mate."

Paulus ambled over to Aristarchus to express his frustration, his chains clanking along the way. "I suppose it is regulation to keep me chained, but I feel perfectly useless at a time like this," said Paulus to his colleague. "I can certainly make a quick shelter, cook, fetch water, search for food – whatever is necessary. Maybe if they took off the hand chains but kept my legs bound, I could contribute in some way."

Aristarchus didn't see any sense in giving his master false hope. "I am sorry, Paulus, for your condition. You have said before it is just one more tribulation to bear. I will come join you for some conversation at meal time; at least at dinner you will be a contributor equal to any man here."

Aristarchus went to work with the others, pondering what lay in store for the two of them. He had volunteered for this mission because he had come to genuinely admire Paulus. He and his older brother, Gaius Nicomedes, had accompanied Paulus three years ago on a tour of the provinces of Anatolia, visiting prominent cities such as Antioch and Ephesus. True, they had gotten into some trouble at Ephesus when a public disturbance erupted at one of Paulus' speeches, and Gaius had been injured somewhat. Gaius had healed well enough, and Aristarchus had sufficiently improved his Greek writing skills that Paulus had asked him to accompany him to Rome as an amanuensis, taking dictation and copying his letters, while making sure that the correspondence was sent to the right communities and Assemblies.

His father had been opposed. "Paulus is a prisoner of the Romans!" his father had exclaimed at his mother. "What fit place is a prison ship for a young boy? Besides, I need help here on the farm, and what happens to us if Aristarchus is injured on this trip? We've already seen that Paulus is not a fit chaperon, and he'll be even less able to look after Aristarchus locked up in chains on this trip."

At age fourteen, Aristarchus had become an important resource for the farm outside of Athens, and sowing season was not yet over. His father's opposition did not surprise him, but his mother's support was a genuine astonishment. "This is not an opportunity he will ever get again," she told his father. "Once the ship is underway I am sure they will let Paulus free during the voyage – it's a grain transport, not a prison ship. In Rome, Simon Petros will be able to take care of him. Besides, the Assembly is paying all the expenses." Quietly, she told Aristarchus that this mission was important to the Christos in heaven – that Paulus was his apostle on earth, and as such, a holy man. Their family should do whatever it reasonably could to support him in this coming trial. His mother had been the first to turn Christian, and she had always felt her beliefs much more strongly than anyone else in the family.

Aristarchus had accepted the teachings of his church because they were all he had known. He learned to read because of the church's educational program for talented young people. This gave him a skill other than simple farming or a common trade; it was the reason he had developed a relationship with a man as eminent in the church as Paulus. Now it was the reason he had just passed through a terrifying trial where he had feared for his very life. His mother was right – he was going to return home a different person – a man.

A fire had been lit, and bread was being prepared on a large round, metal disc. The ship's provisions included olives and some hard cheese, and fresh fruit was added from the island; but it was the cool fresh water from a nearby spring that caused Aristarchus to declare this a feast. Everyone was tired of the near-stagnant water in the ship's casks. Paulus said a quiet prayer of thanks to the Father for providing this food, but otherwise he kept silent. The mood of the group was somber and nervous. Despite the captain's assurances, no one was certain what the future might hold.

The next two days passed quickly, and true to his word, Tychon returned in the evening of the second day with his crew and several villagers, who brought with them supplies for repairing the sail.

The heaviest of these supplies – several coils of rope in different thicknesses – were attached to a donkey. It took them nearly a week to complete these repairs and then a day more to prepare logs that could be used to lever the ship back into the water at high tide, but at long last they were ready to set sail. The captain paid the villagers as handsomely as he could out of the ship's strongbox, without digging too deeply into the ship's profits. Aristarchus and Paulus stood at the rear of the ship, watching the disappearing shoreline, with Paulus enjoying his restored freedom. "I never doubted that we would survive this," said Paulus to his aide, "though I must admit I had my share of fear. I have always felt God the Father is sending me to Rome as part of a greater plan to spread the message of the Christos. He has directed the Holy Spirit to accompany me, and I feel her reassuring presence inside my soul. God the Father will see you and me safely through this test, Aristarchus." It was the same message Paulus had delivered at the start of their journey at Corinth. Then it sounded convincing; now Aristarchus was not so sure.

Chapter Two

The rest of the trip was uneventful, if not a bit disappointing. Aristarchus was expecting some excitement when the ship passed through the strait that separated Italia from Sicily; he recalled all the tales of Scylla and Charybdis from the ancient literature. There was, alas, no whirlpool and no sirens luring the sailors with songs of enchantment. Several days later the ship berthed at the great port of Ostia, itself a major city in Italia and the port for Rome. Aristarchus was not to be given a chance to see it, however. Paulus was chained up again and had been passed over to the authorities in Ostia, where he was kept in a cell overnight, awaiting a trip up the Tiber. Aristarchus was obliged to bunk on the floor in the cell.

The very next day they were packed on a scow with several other prisoners and delivered to a prison barracks outside the walls of Rome. Aristarchus was to learn later that this was the Campus Martius. Looking back across the Tiber, Aristarchus could see the Vatican Hill, dotted with endless funerary monuments. It was Rome's cemetery. Aristarchus was eager to cross through the city gates and explore the capital of the empire, but Paulus was reluctant to let him go. "You should wait a few days until we meet up with members of the community in Rome. Kefas is sure to come visit – that is Simon Petros – and there are many here I know from correspondence over the years. It will be much safer for you then."

The look of disappointment in the eyes of Aristarchus was so pitiful that Paulus relented. He admitted to himself he wanted to keep the boy around, mostly to take dictation, but maybe he should stop thinking of him as a boy. He was fourteen years old now. Paulus gave him careful instructions regarding which neighborhoods to avoid and told him to take twenty denarii from the purse. He would need to eat, after all, and perhaps buy some better quill pens and ink.

Aristarchus eagerly headed out, promising to be back at the prison by nightfall. He passed through the western gate and was immediately immersed in a world of dark and light, of wondrous and not-so-welcome smells, of strange languages, and strange-looking people. He had seen cramped living quarters before, in several Greek cities, but nothing like this. Buildings towered four stories or higher, and people every so often appeared from windows as if they had been squeezed out by the buildings themselves.

Just as if it seemed the passageways could not get any narrower and darker, he would emerge into a great public square, with a majestic temple at one end dedicated to some Roman god or goddess. Aristarchus spoke no Latin, but he could read the script and decipher the meanings of the words on the buildings or on the posters pasted on the sides of so many buildings. Though he felt lost or confused, he was surprised at how many storekeepers spoke Greek, as did the officials who looked like policemen guarding the public buildings or shopping areas. For the first time he realized how lucky he was to have been born a Greek; Greek was spoken everywhere in the civilized world, even in Rome itself.

He found himself slowly ascending a hill – he knew there were seven of them in Rome – and at the top a series of food stalls reminded him he had eaten no breakfast. He chose a selection of fried fish with some sauce that proved to be too spicy at first, but grew on him. He discovered no one in Rome was lacking for fresh water – there were fountains and cisterns almost everywhere. When finished, he decided to explore a small garden at the very top of the hill, and having reached the summit, he realized that before him was a panoramic view of the entire city. He could spot the wall that surrounded the city and the great Roman roads that fed in from the countryside, and he saw that they all led to one point. That must be the Forum itself! Temple after temple lay before him, dappled gold and white and pink in the morning sunlight. Some were small and circular, others as enormous as the Temple to Zeus in Greece. There were long colonnaded buildings as well, where public business was done. The Forum was very near to him – maybe he could reach it in twenty minutes if he didn't get lost.

He hurried down the hill in the direction of the Forum and found himself once again in darkness, even worse than before. This area was the infamous Subura – Rome's most squalid and dangerous slum – and Aristarchus knew instinctively that it was high on the list of places he was told to avoid. He didn't see any reason to panic, as there were police on most corners, and if he stopped to ask for directions to the Forum, he was invariably pointed in the right direction. In less time than he expected, he found himself at a major road into the Forum, which he considered might be the famous Via Sacra. Before him was an arch in gleaming white marble. Surely this gateway must be where the public processions of triumph entered the Forum, he thought.

The place was certainly busy. People walked here and there with a purpose, and occasionally an important official would stride by in a dazzling white toga, some of them hemmed in purple stripes. This was a robe no one else in the world wore, and Aristarchus thought to himself that only a Roman could truly look distinguished in such a gown. There were palanquins carrying important men and women who seemed too indolent or too wealthy to walk on their own two feet; and once he saw a person in a toga with a guard of six men, who carried what appeared to be useless weapons – axes bound up in reeds. It struck Aristarchus that he saw very few military or police officials here in the Forum. Somehow these important men and women felt it was perfectly safe for them to saunter about the Forum without armed guards. It was an attitude he noticed in Romans elsewhere - these were people who acted as if they owned the world, and for that matter, they did.

Aristarchus reached the end of the Via Sacra. He did not understand the importance of what he was seeing; important, that is, from a Roman perspective. He walked by the small temple and dwelling that housed the Vestal Virgins, ignorant of the historical significance of these select women. He did not understand the purpose of the Rostra that stood before him – the platform from which great men such as Julius Caesar and Cicero and Marcus Antonius had given speeches -- though he recognized the beaks of warships that adorned the platform and that surely must have been taken as trophies in sea battles.

To the right was a large brick building, one of the few unadorned in marble. He wandered up the steps and saw inside dozens of men sitting or walking about, clad in togas. An unseen Roman soldier stepped out of the colonnade and confronted Aristarchus. "Sorry son, the Senate is in session. You have to stay off the steps." Aristarchus understood none of the Latin the soldier spoke, except for one word – "Senatus". In his best Greek he asked, "You mean, sir, this is the Senate?"

The soldier switched instantly to Greek. He had been selected for this duty in part because he spoke six basic languages, such as everyday Egyptian and a Germanic language, useful in dealing with the growing number of visitors to Rome from all parts of the world. Visitors like this boy. "Yes, boy, this is the Curia and that is the Senate."

"And you mean," stammered Aristarchus – and here he pointed to the far end of the building at a small man slumped in a chair, wearing a toga entirely of purple and sporting a golden diadem – "do you mean that man is the...?"

"Yes, boy, that is the Emperor." The soldier gently put his hand on Aristarchus's shoulder and turned the young man with mouth agape around, guiding him down the first few steps. Aristarchus found himself at the bottom of the stairs, dazed at the thought that the Emperor himself was there a short distance from him, presiding over the Senate. Who did he know had ever seen the Emperor – any emperor, for that matter? Well, now he had! He was in the presence of the great Nero, Caesar Augustus, a man Aristarchus felt he had grown up with. He had watched Nero age on the coins that circulated throughout Greece. Nero had been a young man who had turned into a corpulent figure with at least two chins. Aristarchus had often wondered why a man as powerful as Nero allowed himself to be portrayed that way, since people did say that Nero was very vain.

Wait until Mother and Father hear about this, Aristarchus said to himself. He began to elaborate on the tale ever so slightly. "Nero walked right by me," soon turned into "The Emperor stopped to speak to me!" Maybe he would save that story for his friends; his parents could always see through his exaggerations.

While concocting these fantasies, he had wandered absently across to the other side of the Forum, to the foot of a sharp, rocky incline that was dotted with villas and gardens. A young man his age approached him. "Do you want a tour of the palaces?" he asked in Greek. Aristarchus didn't really know what to say. Whose palaces were these, he wondered, and should he trust this man? "All the emperors have lived here, except, that is, Nero, who has now moved to a garden in the hills." This man seemed to read Aristarchus' mind.

Aristarchus felt he had come to no harm today, even when walking in much more dangerous places; so he put his trust in this guide, having agreed to the terms of a one denarius fee, which Aristarchus felt was steep. He was told he only had to pay it at the end of the tour if he was happy with the service. Off they went up the hill, reaching first the gardens and palace of Tiberius (when he was alive), and then of Augustus himself and his wife Livia. These were people very familiar to almost anyone in the Roman world – again from the coins that featured their faces – and Aristarchus was surprised how relatively modest these palaces were. They were villas, really, with wonderfully painted walls and considerable marble – but palaces? Hardly big enough, he thought.

His guide, who identified himself only as Porcius, expected a reaction such as this. "The Palatine hill is becoming too crowded, which is why Nero has moved elsewhere," he explained. "He lives in a villa he has 'borrowed' from a rich nobleman. You can barely see it off in the distance, in that garden atop that hill." When they reached an opening further up the hill, Porcius pointed out the Forum and then off in the distance the Subura, which looked so dense that Aristarchus could barely make out the buildings. "There's talk," said Porcius, "that a good part of that area of Rome is going to be demolished. People say Nero has his eye on the Subura in order to erect an enormous palace just for himself. That rumor is making him none too popular."

Porcius gave Aristarchus a few minutes to take in the scene. He next pointed out the aqueducts that fed water to over a million people, and he identified which roads led to Gaul or to Sicily or to Greece. "But this is nothing. Wait until you see the other side of the Palatine." They strolled through pleasant gardens, Aristarchus marveling that the general public was allowed to wander around these private gardens as if they were their own. When they reached the top of a knoll, Porcius pulled Aristarchus up a steep path, and there at the bottom of a cliff lay a structure Aristarchus recognized instantly – the Circus Maximus.

He let out a slow whistle. The immensity of the structure stunned him, even though he had known that the world's greatest chariot races took place here. "Over 200,000 people can be seated there," said Porcius. "You should stay around until the end of the week. There are two straight days of chariot races scheduled. The upper seats are free and are reserved for plebs like you." Aristarchus wasn't sure if he was being insulted by being called a pleb, but he certainly would like to see a chariot race. By then Paulus would be through with his trial and have paid his fine, so the two of them could do whatever they wanted.

"As for today," added Porcius, "try the baths near the Forum." He dutifully pointed them out to Aristarchus. "There's nothing like them in the world." Aristarchus was certainly familiar with the routine of Roman baths, and he had time to spare, so the idea appealed to him considerably.

They headed down the hill back to the Forum, and at the bottom Porcius indicated the tour was over. He waited patiently for his fee, which Aristarchus had entirely forgotten about. Aristarchus pulled out a denarius from his purse and handed it over to Porcius, thanking him for an excellent tour. Porcius accepted his fee but still did not leave, shifting back and forth on his feet. This clue Aristarchus comprehended instantly, and he felt lucky that he had some small change left over from his breakfast. He handed a bronze coin to Porcius, who sniffed in an obvious sign of disappointment but decided not to attempt to squeeze any more money out of this man. He trotted off looking for some other tourist to entertain.

Aristarchus could see the baths that had been pointed out to him from the Palatine hill. He strolled in that direction, wondering if he could afford such a luxury in an expensive city such as Rome. The building was much taller than he expected, once he reached it. It had been improved by Augustus, with pink, white, and green marble on the outside surface. Aristarchus was astounded to discover that the entrance cost was only two denarii, which covered all services with the exception of massages, which were extra. That amount was less than the citizens of Athens paid at their baths. Once inside, Aristarchus was greeted with an expanse of red, blue, green, white, and other marbles, along with different colored glass used in the roof. The sunlight through these glass panels shimmered on the walls and floors, creating the effect of a rainbow of rippling pools of water moving about the building. Aristarchus had never seen anything like it; surely no emperor could live in any finer palace.

Placed along the walls and in niches were statues of gods and goddesses, and other figures from the tales of men like Perseus and Herakles. Aristarchus liked the traditional sequence of a swim in tepid water first, followed by the steam bath, and then a final plunge in a cold pool of water. It was in the steam room that he dozed off on the warm marble. He was asleep for at least a half hour, and no one bothered him. When he awoke, the room was filling up with portly older gentlemen – the businessmen, store managers, bankers, judges, and occasional senators who had decided to finish their day early. Perhaps it was the languor induced by the steam, but Aristarchus noticed how relaxed the customers were, and how rich and powerful people easily mingled with the lowest workers. He appreciated that he was only seeing the social surface, and that no doubt people segregated themselves to be with those of their own class. The baths were certainly big enough to allow for such stratifications. Nonetheless, Aristarchus decided, laying in such palatial splendor for only the price of two denarii, that Rome was justified in boasting about the civilized advantages it offered the world.

He was about to doze off again, when he remembered he had a chore to complete. He shocked himself into action and alertness with a plunge in the cold bath, and when he retrieved his tunic and turned in his towel, he asked the attendant if there were any stores nearby that sold writing supplies. There were stalls assigned to scribes in the northern section of the Forum just before the Subura; the attendant felt sure he would find inks and pens there. Aristarchus was feeling generous. The attendant had done nothing but help him put his tunic on, but that certainly deserved a denarius tip, didn't it? Aristarchus rationalized his extravagance by remembering that the entrance fee for such a splendid experience was remarkably low.

He quickly found among the business stalls at least two stores that sold writing material. He thought that Paulus ought to try a distinctive brown ink, which he bought for four denarii. There were pages and scrolls of papyrus that Paulus would no doubt appreciate, but they were much too expensive for Aristarchus' dwindling purse. Paulus would have to look for himself after his trial.

The sun was beginning to disappear behind the roofs of the taller temples. Aristarchus headed into the Subura with renewed confidence. He decided that if he followed the occasional glimpses of the sun and kept heading west, eventually he would come to one of the large parks that led to the Tiber and then the military barracks. The tenements were even darker than he remembered from the morning. There was a noticeable quiet about the city; perhaps people slept during the hottest part of the day. He stumbled occasionally along the Subura walkways.

As he stood looking for any glimpse of the sun, he noticed on one of the buildings the sign of a phallus. He hadn't been paying much attention to the stores along the way, but as he walked along this street and the next, he saw further evidence that the shops had turned into brothels. He stopped and listened closely, with heightened nerves. He could hear the muffled squeals of delight from a woman's voice and the grunts that told him exactly what was going on. He had never had sex with a woman before. How could he, spending all his time with Paulus, a man who wrote in his letters how much better it was for someone never to marry and to abstain from sex altogether?

Aristarchus had thought about this moment the minute he had heard about the journey. He would be alone in big cities. No one would know what he did. Many of his friends bragged about the sex they were having with girls; even some of the boys from Christian families claimed to have had sex, and they were younger than him. He was certainly old enough. It was time for him to become a real man.

Yet, availing himself of this opportunity was wrong – terribly wrong. It went against all the moral teaching of his faith. Hadn't he made a silent vow to God to refrain from sex until he was married? How could he recover from such a sin? To whom could he confess? Certainly not to Paulus.

His body was tingling. As he walked along yet another street, he was greeted by elderly women in garish costumes, beckoning him to come in, showing him glimpses of nearly-naked girls standing in the background. His nerves were tingling. He feared that the lust that was mounting inside him was becoming too strong to resist, but he must resist. He was a Christian. The Christos promised eternal salvation, but not without sacrifice, and here he must be willing to sacrifice his own selfish pleasure for the possibility of life with the Heavenly Father.

A young girl stepped in front of him, halting his progress. She spoke to him in Greek. "I like boys with blond hair. You're cute." Her eyes were like those of a girl he often thought about back home. They glowed with happiness. She was a girl of his age, and her Greek had no accent. She might have been from his own village. Her hands were fingering his tunic and then running down his chest. He allowed her to kiss him, and a whole new world opened up to him -- a world of passion and delight, offering him a road to manhood.

She edged him quietly through the door, kissing him all the while. There was no madam standing about; no other girls. Just he and this girl who could have been from his own village, someone he might have known all his life, someone familiar and warm and inviting. They were behind a curtain now and she was removing his tunic; at the same time her robe fell to the floor. He had no time to admire her body. They were now on the bed as she guided him in, his mind racing with a strange mixture of thoughts. So this is what it feels like! Am I doing it right? Can she tell this is my first time? Do I have enough money to pay for this? Those sounds she is making – am I really giving her that much pleasure?"

Suddenly, his orgasm was upon him. He couldn't stop it, and he didn't know why it happened so quickly. He allowed the sensations to wash over him as he collapsed on top of her. His mind suddenly veered off in a different direction. "Is that all there was to it? Is this what everyone has been bragging about? I've had better orgasms by myself!"

He rolled off to her side, as a wave of fear and disgust welled up inside of him. "What have I done? Why couldn't I have waited? Can I ever wash away this sin?" She ran her fingers through his hair, telling him how good he was, asking him what his name was, and telling him hers was Eumilia. "Normally I like to take my time with my clients, even though with most of them I have no desire at all. But you – you are so attractive, I could not hold back. You were wonderful! Perhaps we should wait a short while and have another go. I would like that very much. It will be free, of course."

Aristarchus's mind shifted back again just as quickly. He liked being told he was good at it. Maybe she couldn't tell it was his first time. He had done it! He had finally done it! He felt like bragging about it to someone. But that could wait. He liked even more lying naked next to this girl, talking to her naturally, taking in her smells, letting his hands cup her breasts. This is what life was really about, or what it should really be about. He would deal with sin and sacrifice later.

Just then there was a rustling outside the curtain. "Ah! It is Renita. I thought she would be back much later." Eumilia sat up and looked about for her robe. A woman twice her age peeked behind the curtain. "If you are done, Eumilia, collect your two denarii. There is another gentleman waiting outside."

Eumilia rose from the bed and put on her robe. She picked up Aristarchus's tunic and placed it over his head. He fumbled around with his undergarments as she straightened out his hair. "Don't listen to her. Pay me one denarius. Don't worry, I will make up the difference with other clients. I meant what I said; you were very good. Maybe I should pay you!" With that she laughed and pulled back the curtain.

"Don't forget your package," she said, as she handed him his ink purchase and kissed him on the cheek. He headed back out down the street. He had never felt such a sense of exhilaration and fear at the same time. He had a desperate desire to tell somebody, but not Paulus. Certainly not Paulus.

It was nightfall as Aristarchus finally found his way back to the military camp. He sought out the jail cells and discovered Paulus sitting near the door, trying to read one of his manuscripts by the moonlight. "Aristarchus! I was beginning to worry about you. In a city as big as Rome there would be no way to find you if you had gotten into any trouble."

"There was no reason to worry, Paulus. I'm a man; I can handle myself. But I saw the most marvelous things, including the Emperor!" Aristarchus proceeded to regale Paulus with the highlights of his day's adventures, with the exception of his intimate encounter with Eumilia. That still weighed on his conscience, but his exuberance over the other events of the day overwhelmed any misgivings on that score. Paulus detected in himself a sense of envy. Here he was confined to a barracks cell while his secretary was out enjoying some of the greatest sights in the civilized world.

Paulus thought back to his own youth and remembered the excitement he used to have when visiting a city for the first time. Whatever happened to that feeling? Now when he came to a new city or town, he would focus on the most advantageous place from which to preach sermons about the Christos. He thought it important, but maybe what people said about him was correct. Maybe he was too absorbed in his preaching, and had lost some important things in his own life. He had long since given up the thought of marrying and having a family; a man needed to be free of such distractions if he was dedicated to serving God. But giving up even the happiness in life that can come from travel – travel that was after all necessary for spreading word about The Way – was that truly necessary?

"Look what I have brought you, Paulus!" Aristarchus pulled out from his leather bag a half chicken and a flask of wine. "We are going to have a feast, even if the chicken is cold." Paulus couldn't disagree at all. The two of them sat in the cell eating their chicken, with Paulus wondering if the guards would confiscate such a bounty if they discovered it. Aristarchus pushed that thought away by revealing his gift of ink and describing the variety of papyrus and animal skin parchments available in the city.

"You know, Aristarchus, that I have spent my adult life preaching to people about faith, love, and generosity. I even remind people that Jehoshua promised eternal life to those who followed the law and obeyed his new covenant, paid for by the blood he shed on Golgotha. Remember, he even said that visiting those in prison is more important to your salvation than the number of times you are seen praying in public."

"Yet, I think that I am as blind today as I was years ago in Damascus. I cannot see in front of me the very example of that faith, love, and generosity that is the essence of Jehoshua's message: love your neighbor as you love yourself. I fail to recognize or acknowledge that a young man of fourteen can have all those qualities in abundance, and that someone like you is more worthy of God's grace than I am. Promise me you will never lose those qualities, that you will continue to live a life of purity in thought and action, and that you won't forget that the little things – the small gestures of kindness such as this meal tonight for a lonely and forsaken man – are the stones that pave your road to salvation."

Aristarchus blushed. He didn't know what to say to this, other than a quiet, "Thank you, Paulus." He especially felt unworthy of such praise after his act of sin that afternoon, an act that loomed as something heinous when placed against the admonition of Paulus to live a life of purity in thought and action. But confusion set in as well. "Was it that bad?" he thought. What if it turned out he loved Eumilia or someone like her? Wouldn't intimacy smooth the way to a lasting and worthy love?

"I have my own news to tell you," said Paulus, interrupting these thoughts. "I have been assigned a lawyer by the court. He came by today: a man named Laelius Disertus. He gave me advice on how to present my defense. We are scheduled for criminal court tomorrow in front of the Praetor Peregrinus, who handles cases involving foreigners. Apparently the government counsel has two witnesses against me; I don't know who they are. I think after that excellent meal we should get some sleep; it could be a long day tomorrow."

Aristarchus crafted a pillow from the clothes in his bag and stretched out on the dirt floor of the cell. He was used to sleeping without the comfort of a bed; the nearly six month trip on the boat taught him that. But he missed the motion of the sea underneath him, and the noises of the camp kept him awake long after Paulus had started to snore. "I'm not needed tomorrow anyway," he reasoned. "It is Paulus who needs the rest. He'll have to have his wits about him more than ever."

Chapter Three

It was late in the morning when the guards came looking for Paulus. "Are you the one with the trial in front of the criminal court?" Paulus nodded, and they proceeded to attach his chains to his hands and legs. These would be removed at the court, as defendants were allowed to walk around unhindered since they needed to question witnesses and examine any physical evidence. "Is this your witness?" they asked as well. Paulus agreed, even though Aristarchus was not technically a witness. Paulus wanted him at the trial nonetheless. He felt very alone in Rome on this particular morning.

The guards had some confusion as to which court he was supposed to attend: the Praetor Urbanus could sometimes hear criminal cases, but normally another praetor altogether handled such matters. The defendant himself had to straighten things out. "I was told this is an overseas dispute and therefore I am supposed to appear before the Praetor Peregrinus," contributed Paulus. "Oh!" said one of the guards, "Old Trebo, eh?" His tone was anything but encouraging, and both Paulus and Aristarchus wondered what was so alarming about the judge.

The soldiers took a path along the Tiber River rather than escort Paulus through the city precincts. Aristarchus realized he could have saved a lot of time in reaching the Forum if he had known of this route, but then he would have missed so much. He certainly would have missed Eumilia, who was on his mind this morning. He wondered if he would have an opportunity to visit her again.

Paulus' mind was on his coming trial and the defense he would present against inciting a riot and provoking urban disorder. He realized he should have been paying more attention to his surroundings, as he promised himself he would do yesterday, but a criminal trial was a very serious thing. Those who lost their case could sometimes be executed immediately thereafter. The matter resolved itself when the soldiers took a turn to the left and began marching prisoner and "witness" up a hill to the Capitol. Paulus could not help but stare in wonder at the multitude of temples and business buildings, the grandeur of the statuary, the bustle of innumerable people of all stations in life, and – when they reached the top of the hill and had a vista of the entire Forum – the sheer magnificence of this, the administrative center of the civilized world.

Aristarchus kept him occupied as well, describing all the sites he had seen yesterday, and pointing out the Senate as they passed by this structure. They were heading toward a giant building at the southwest of the Forum – the Basilica Julia – where judicial matters were handled. This building, erected by Julius Caesar, was already over 100 years old, and the columns with their acanthus-leave capitals were partially blackened with soot from a century of charcoal fires used to keep people warm in the winter. Several such fires were already going in a section of the building devoted to criminal trials.

There were two men in traditional Jewish robes seated on a bench on one side, and Paulus and Aristarchus were led to a bench on the opposite. There was a raised marble platform with an elaborate stool in the center for the judge, with chairs behind him. Three men in togas were already occupying these chairs.

Laelius Disertus came bustling in with a pile of scrolls and other official-looking documents in his hand. He immediately joined Paulus and introduced himself to Aristarchus. "Your trial is the only one on the docket today. It will be heard by Lucius Trebonius Cassianus, the Praetor Peregrinus. He can talk your ear off, but he is fair and has never been known to take a bribe. The three men in the back are your jurors – well, not exactly jurors. They are known as the Triumviris. The Praetor ultimately decides guilt or innocence, and punishment if necessary, but those men provide advice on matters of law and can influence the outcome. Make sure you address your remarks to the Praetor, but don't forget to look at them from time to time. In these courts you conduct your own defense. My job is to ensure that all points of law in your favor are brought up, and those against you are rebutted."

Paulus asked his counsel who the witnesses against him were. "I don't know much about them," said Laelius Disertus. "Their names are Enoch and Iram. They apparently were in the crowd at the time of the riot." An old man was seen shuffling up the aisle of the court, holding a cane in one hand. He had on a white toga with a broad purple stripe, which Aristarchus had learned signified a member of the Senate. "All rise for the Praetor Peregrinus, Lucius Trebonius Cassianus!" said one of the clerks.

Trebonius Cassianus had had several distinguished careers. He first gained attention as one of the adjutant military commanders to Tiberius Caesar's son, Drusus. Tiberius eventually appointed him as Chief Augur, a symbolically important post in Rome, which gave Cassianus direct access to Tiberius as Pontifex Maximus, in charge of the state religion. Cassianus filled this role with distinction, survived the reign of Caligula, and eventually was appointed as a judge by the Emperor Claudius. Cassianus was a bit of a scholar, having written several books on military affairs as well as religion. He liked to talk in his court, but his rulings had created several precedents, and Claudius began the habit of distributing them to the lower courts throughout the empire.

Cassianus spent a minute or two distributing the folds of his toga so that he could sit erectly and nobly on his curved chair. He was, after all, a member of a patrician family and a member of the Senate. "Where's my bowl?" he commanded. A clerk hustled about and placed a large bowl of pistachios on the praetor's lap. By the end of the trial, the shells would be sitting on a mound under the chair of the Praetor Peregrinus.

"The Defendant will rise!" said the clerk. "Paulus of Tarsus, you are charged with inciting a riot in the Temple courtyard at Jerusalem, causing physical harm to more than ten people, and damaging both private and public property. You have, moreover, a history of such behavior. A decision as to your guilt or innocence in this matter was to be rendered by the Procurator for Judea, Marcus Antonius Felix, but you asserted your right to a trial in Rome as a Roman citizen. You have previously claimed your innocence of these charges, and you plead innocent today as well. For the benefit of the court, the Defendant's citizenship has been properly verified and is not a matter of dispute here."

"The witnesses may state their case," said the Praetor. "Please identify yourself for the court."

The two Jewish gentlemen rose. "I am Enoch, son of Irad," said the older gentlemen. "This is my son, Iram. We are both staff members to the Chief Priest of the Temple in Jerusalem, Ananias. I also serve as head of the Temple police, responsible for maintaining order on the Temple grounds."

"This man Saul – he refers to himself as Paulus when speaking to Gentiles – has repeatedly incited violence on the Temple grounds. He has been warned many times to cease this behavior, but he deliberately ignores these warnings. His method is to mount the Temple steps, where he proceeds to shout at those who come to the Temple for worship. He chooses his moments carefully, always just before a service or sacrifice is about to begin. He makes insulting and provocative statements about the Jewish religion, all for the purpose of exciting someone in the crowd to shout back at him and challenge his statements. He lives for these moments, because that is when he can begin a 'debate,' as he calls it, about the teachings of our sacred fathers, such as Moses and the prophets. He encourages people to scream so he can scream back at them."

"I ask you, honored Praetor, how would a citizen of Rome respond to such taunts to your gods and your faith, especially if these slanders were made at a time when a crowd is assembling for worship? Such is not the atmosphere we have seen here in Rome when a sacrifice is taking place at a temple. We see reverence; we see obedience to the law and to the rules of the temple; we see civil authorities working in harmony with religious authorities to ensure that the faithful are allowed to worship in accordance with their beliefs and traditions."

"I speak to you candidly as the chief of the Temple police. We have neither the means nor the authority to put a stop to these transgressions. We can detain this man, but we cannot arrest him nor punish him. We must rely on the overall authority in Judea to put men such as Saul of Tarsus on trial and to punish them. The Roman procurator in Judea would have done exactly that in this case, if the Defendant hadn't appealed to Rome. And so here we are – seeking justice."

"One last point, your Excellency. The last outrage perpetrated by the Defendant was the most grievous of all and the most hurtful to our people. He deliberately brought Gentiles into the Temple, the holiest of our shrines, during services. He is an educated and experienced Pharisee. He knows the Law as well as any man and is aware of the shame he has brought to our Temple. Would you, honored Praetor, allow barbarians to invade your most sacred services?"

"For these and other deliberate acts of provocation, for the damage he has done to property, and for the personal harm he has caused many innocent people trapped in the riots he has instigated, we ask the court to find the Defendant guilty and to impose on him the maximum penalty allowed by law."

Enoch ben Irad sat down. The only noise in the court consisted of slight murmuring from the Triumviris seated behind the Praetor, and the click-click-click of pistachios being shelled and masticated by the Praetor himself. Trebonius Cassianus then motioned to Paulus. "The Defendant may now present his side of the case and question the accusers."

Paulus arose. "Your Excellency, Praetor Cassianus. Honored members of the court. I do not know what occurrence has just been described by my accuser. I was not at such an event. The occasion on which I was arrested involved no disruptions on my part; the provocations were entirely on the part of members of the Jewish community, who commenced throwing stones at me and physically attacking anyone who supported my views. Naturally, these people defended themselves. That is the extent of the 'riot'"

"Rather than merely assert my innocence of these charges, I will prove it by questioning the witnesses." Paulus walked over to Enoch and stared at him. "Enoch ben Irad, at what time did you arrive at this 'disturbance'?"

"I arrived with a contingent of Temple police at the point where people were fighting."

"And what was I doing when you arrived?" Enoch responded, "You were sitting or lying down on the Temple steps. That is when we arrested you."

"Was I injured in any way when you found me on the Temple steps?" asked Paulus. "You had a cut on your left hand that was bleeding," was the answer.

"I won't ask my accuser to say how I got that cut, since he wasn't there earlier, but I don't think he can deny there were rocks and stones around me on the steps when he arrested me." Paulus addressed this comment to the Praetor. He then added, "Your Excellency, I was hoping to have a witness attest to my behavior during this event, but he took ill on the ship and we were obliged to leave him at Crete. He has provided me, however, with a written testament."

Paulus grabbed a scroll from his bag next to Aristarchus and handed it to the Praetor, who ordered the attorney Laelius Disertus to read it aloud on behalf of the Defendant. Disertus was a trained rhetorician who knew the proper intonations required for such public reading, even of a simple document like a letter. Disertus read for the court the testimony of Lukas Kyrillos, who identified himself as a resident of Ephesus and a colleague of Paulus. He said he was at the Temple throughout the circumstances under investigation. He asserted that Paulus talked to the crowd in his usual tone of voice and in the manner he had used on previous occasions at the same location. Lukas stated that a group of men in the crowd began throwing stones at Paulus. He saw them take the stones out of their pockets, since there were no stones to be found in the Temple courtyard. Lukas said that this suggested to him that the attack was planned earlier. Several people in the crowd came to Paulus' defense, and some of them rushed at the attackers. That is when the fighting began in earnest and the Temple police arrived.

The Praetor then asked the accuser, Enoch ben Irad, whether the Temple police arrested any of the men said to have thrown stones. Enoch responded they had not. "And do you have any witnesses who can contradict the testimony of the Defendant and his colleague, Lukas, both of whom say the provocation began with Jews in the crowd and not with the Defendant?" asked Trebonius Cassianus. "I don't have a witness on that particular point, but my son here can testify that Saul deliberately provoked an uproar in the Temple when he brought Gentiles to our services," added Enoch.

"I understand that took place several days earlier, and that there was no arrest then" observed Trebonius Cassianus. "We don't need your son's testimony unless he was present and witnessed the circumstances leading up to the Defendant's arrest at the Temple." Trebonius Cassianus was beginning to fiddle with his toga as he made this statement, as if he was becoming slightly exasperated with Enoch ben Irad.

"Is there anything more the Defendant wishes to say?" asked Praetor Cassianus. Paulus rose and returned to the accuser's bench. "Enoch ben Irad, is it not the case that anyone who wishes to address the crowd at the Temple courtyard must receive a permit from your office?" Enoch agreed to this point. "And did I not have such a permit?" Enoch agreed to this point as well.

"So, I was permitted to speak at that time and at that place, in accordance with Temple regulations. Since I had spoken on earlier occasions with permits, and since there were no disturbances then, I conclude that the police had no reason to deny me a permit, nor to believe I represented a public danger."

"Your Excellency, I have nothing further to add, but my attorney has asked to present one additional piece of evidence." Disertus rose and addressed Cassianus. "Honored Praetor, I have been told by the clerk of the court that a letter regarding this case has been sent to the court by the previous Procurator for Judea, Marcus Antonius

Felix. I would like to read this letter, and I wish to defer introducing this evidence into the record until after I have read it."

Praetor Cassianus gave the court's opinion on this request. "You do have a right to read this letter since it does have some bearing on the case. In fact, I thought you had already received a copy. However, the accusers, who neither require nor have an attorney, also have the same right to read this letter, and in so doing they can require it be submitted as evidence even if you wish not to. These things cut both ways. I assume the accusers do not speak or read Latin, so we will get them a translator."

Laelius Disertus quickly translated the letter in Greek to Paulus, whose Latin was rudimentary.

> To the Noble L Trebonius Cassianus, Praetor Peregrinus,
> Basilica Julia, Rome
> From Marcus Antonius Felix, Procurator, Province of Judea
> Salutations Honored Praetor Peregrinus:
>
> I send to you for trial one Saul of Tarsus, also known as Paulus of Tarsus, a free Roman citizen who was arrested over a year ago in Jerusalem on the charge of inciting a riot on the steps of the Temple of Jerusalem.
>
> The Defendant was to be put on trial for these charges, but he invoked his right to a trial in Rome in consideration of his Roman citizenship. We have investigated his claim to citizenship, and it is in order, having been passed down to him through his father, who purchased citizenship through his military service to Rome.
>
> I have come to no firm conclusion regarding the Defendant's guilt or innocence, as we never reached the trial stage, and I do not have the benefit of testimony from witnesses. I enclose a short description of the facts we do have regarding this incident. Based on these facts, the case against the Defendant Paulus is weak, at best.
>
> I thought it important to inform you that we have kept the Defendant Paulus in safe custody for over a year while awaiting approval to transfer him to Rome for trial. We received undoubted evidence in Caesaria that certain Jewish interests were intent on assassinating Paulus whenever an opportunity afforded. We promptly transferred him from Jerusalem to our fortress in Caesaria, where he has been incarcerated for his own safety, until

we were able to arrange maritime passage to Rome for him and two guards.

The dispute between Paulus and his Jewish opponents centers around obscure religious differences of importance only to Jews. The Defendant worships a criminal who was crucified under orders of the Prefect Pontius Pilatus, some thirty years ago. The Defendant claims the criminal was able to raise himself from the dead following his execution, and the religious dispute seems to center on whether or not resurrection of the dead is possible. The opponents of the Defendant assert it is not.

For reasons that are unclear, the disputants have taken their argument to the streets, not merely in Jerusalem, but wherever worshippers to the criminal Jehoshua can be found. Whatever you determine regarding the incident for which the Defendant is on trial, it cannot be denied that the Jewish authorities, in Jerusalem and elsewhere, will not hesitate to use violence to enforce their doctrinal edicts. Therefore, when considering the guilt or innocence of the Defendant, it must be recognized that his accusers will use the Roman judicial system if necessary to achieve their ends.

Marcus Antonius Felix
Procurator

Both Laelius Disertus and his client agreed that the communication was favorable for their cause and should be introduced into the record. They made that recommendation to the Praetor, and since Paulus' accusers had nothing to say about the statement from Procurator Felix, Disertus was ordered to read the letter out loud for all the court to hear.

Paulus had nothing further to add to his defense, and his accusers had no further comments or questions, so Praetor Cassianus requested that his three counselors approach for a discussion of the verdict. Trebonius Cassianus was not about to stand up, much less disrupt his pistachio repast, so the three advisers were forced to lean in and listen to the Praetor's opinions.

The clerk walked over to the Praetor, interrupting the whispering and nodding and pistachio-nut-cracking that constituted a discussion of the verdict among the Praetor and his advisers. Laelius Disertus perked up at this interruption. The Praetor looked behind him to his left at a man standing at the corner of the court. He was wearing a toga that had seen considerable wear, and he had a look of impatience about him as he fidgeted with a set of scrolls in his hands. The men of the Triumviris returned to their seats.

"Before we pronounce the court's verdict," said Trebonius Cassianus, "another party has come forward with accusations against the Defendant. We will allow this party to step before the court and state his purpose."

Laelius Disertus arose and was ready to say something, but thought better of it and sat down again. The man who stepped forward, despite his less-than-resplendent robes, had a look of authority about him. He was middle aged, clean shaven, and with a distinctive hooked nose that only the most patrician Roman families seemed to sport. "I am Gaius Cornelius Plautis. I work in and am here representing the Office of the Pontifex Maximus. I appreciate the court's granting me the rights of an Accusator in this important trial. I accuse the Defendant of religious impiety towards the Roman gods and of perpetrating a fraud, inasmuch as he does not practice a religion of his own – he practices superstition and barbarism."

Once again Laelius Disertus stood up. "Honored Praetor, this is highly unorthodox." His mind was racing as he had to think quickly and carefully about how to frame his objection. He could not recall any previous instance where the Office of the Pontifex Maximus took part in a criminal trial. If they were involved in the legal system at all, it was over civil disputes regarding wills and benefices. This situation was tricky and possibly dangerous for himself and especially for his client. He went on to address the court: "While it is not unusual for an Accusator to come before the court at the last minute, it violates proper procedure for any Accusator to bring forth new accusations completely unrelated to those involved in the trial. We were on the verge of a verdict, and now the Defendant must face accusations about which we have received no advance notice, no opportunity to prepare testimony or procure witnesses for the defense, and no opportunity to inspect the evidence that the Accusator is now holding in his hands. Furthermore, this court has deliberately avoided making this case into a discussion of religious and theological matters, and this is not a proper place to deal with accusations of religious impiety."

Laelius Disertus did not sit down this time. His job was to use his skills at rhetoric in the service of his client, and rhetoric told him to remain standing and adamant and to stare down the Praetor if necessary to make his point. Trebonius Cassianus flicked a few empty shells off his toga so that they could join the mound of pistachio detritus sitting at his feet. "This court takes note of the objections of the defense attorney. We will not deliver a verdict if it appears to us that the defense needs more time to deal with these new accusations. We remind the defense attorney that the Praetor Peregrinus was at one time Chief Augur for Rome, and that I am very well versed in matters pertaining to the state religion. I am curious as to what the Accusator has to say, since there certainly is an undercurrent of religious dogma that flows through this case. Cornelius Plautis, you may proceed with your accusations."

Laelius Disertus sat down. He had no illusions that the Praetor was going to rule in favor of his objections, since no judge was likely to ignore accusations coming directly from an office so closely connected to the Emperor. Still, Laelius Disertus felt it was important that he lay down his objections in the record should his client need time to defend himself against these new accusations. Nor could he deny he was very curious about what Cornelius Plautis had to say. If the Emperor Nero was personally interested in Paulus of Tarsus and the Christians, Laelius Disertus, for the sake of his own career, had to know now. Like everyone else in the court, Laelius Disertus focused all his attention on the Accusator, who was about to speak.

Chapter Four

ornelius Plautis opened one of his scrolls which contained his notes. He was not a trained rhetorician and so had prepared carefully for this moment. "Several months ago I was ordered by my superiors to investigate the Jewish religious sect which calls itself Christians, or followers of the Christos, the Anointed One. I traveled to Jerusalem and to various towns in Galilee and Judea that were frequented by Jehoshua the Christos, including Nazareth, the town in which he was born. I have brought back with me the testimony of any number of people who knew the Christos and can attest to his alleged miracles."

"Let it first be said that our policy on religion has always been one of flexibility and liberality. For all tribes, communities, and cultures which have been brought into the Empire, it has consistently been the case that these people are allowed to continue to worship their own gods, as long as they recognize that we are allowed to foster the worship of our gods. Thus, in communities throughout the Empire, we have raised temples to Jupiter and Juno, to Venus, and – if a community so desires – to the Greek gods which are so closely related to our own. In turn, we allow local communities of emigrants to construct temples and arrange for worship of their own gods. Thus we have had for the past one hundred years, since Egypt was brought into the Empire, an expansion of the worship of Isis. Similarly, Jews have been allowed to construct their temples wherever they reside, including in Rome."

"This policy has worked admirably both in the modern era and under the Republic, as long as no one religion insists that its gods are superior to all others or in any way demands the elimination of any other religion. There is a third line which must be drawn, and it is that we must disallow superstition masquerading as religion. We are not talking here about whether any one religion is fostering mythology, as much as we are denying the right of any group which perpetrates outright fraud or engages in practices that are barbaric to call themselves religious. As an obvious example, we could never tolerate any group practicing human sacrifice under the guise of religion."

"With that important background, let me turn to the specifics of the Christos cult." Cornelius Plautis paused a minute to pull out a second sheet of notes.

"I interviewed any number of people who knew Jehoshua when he was alive and before he became known as the Anointed One. There were a number of elderly people in the town of Nazareth who remembered him from the time of his birth to the time he left the village as a young boy. He was sensitive and intelligent beyond his station in life, but there was no evidence he had exceptional powers or was somehow favored by the gods."

"More interesting, in some respects than Jehoshua, was his mother Miriam. She raised five children alone through her work as a hairdresser. There was considerable evidence that she lived a wanton life, associating with different men from time to time, to the point of cohabiting with them. While this has led to questions of paternity regarding several of her children, there seems to be no question regarding the father of Jehoshua. Wherever I went throughout Judea, Galilee, and neighboring communities, the Christos was known as Jehoshua ben Pantera. In Nazareth, the village was very clear that his father was a centurion assigned to the area, with a cognomen of Pantera. I checked the records and we did indeed have a centurion named Pantera assigned to the Third Legion Cyrenaica about sixty years ago, at the time of Jehoshua's birth. This man was later assigned to the legions in Germania and has of course long since died. I am not reflecting in any way on the character of this legionnaire, as it has always been common for officers assigned to long spells of duty in the provinces to take local woman as companions. The point to note is that Jehoshua was only half Jewish and perhaps considerably estranged from his Jewish roots. He carried a burden of illegitimacy throughout his life, which makes it doubly ludicrous that his followers now declare he is the son of a god."

"Turning now to his miracles, which garnered him fame soon after his death, I could find very few people who witnessed them directly. All other evidence to his miracles is entirely second-hand and based on hearsay. What seems evident is that Jehoshua's methodology for performing miracles was entirely that of any other magus practicing in the region. He used incantations in strange languages; he applied roots, herbs and other natural remedies; and he manipulated limbs, backs, and the neck to effect his cures. It was said that as a young man he fled Nazareth to go to Egypt in order to learn the magical arts, and his healing skills, such as they were, seem consistent with that allegation. A considerable amount of his success must have rested on the belief of the supplicants that he could cure them. In a number of places where people were hostile to his mission, he could affect no cures. I must add, however, that people who spoke about his miracles were most adamant that Jehoshua was no ordinary magus or healer. They believe he had unusual if not extraordinary powers of healing, and there were too many instances of exceptional healings – of the blind or the lame or those dying – to categorize him as a mere magus. I met one old man who claimed to have been born blind and who now had limited vision. He insisted his vision was restored by Jehoshua, and his descriptions of how it happened along with his fervent belief that his cure was indeed miraculous is the only confirmed incidence I could find of a possible miracle by Jehoshua.

"In regard to his teachings, most of the Jewish authorities I talked to said that what he preached was a perversion of traditional Jewish doctrines. He reviled a number of the prophets that are important in Judaism, instructed people to ignore all but two of the Laws laid down by Moses, and constantly ridiculed the leadership in Jerusalem. His words turned into aggressive actions against his own religious leaders once he began to travel to Jerusalem with crowds that were growing increasingly large and belligerent. The secular authorities also began to notice the threat he posed to both King Herod Antipas and to Roman authority."

"I heard it said by many people that his actions may have been motivated by a demon or demons which possessed him. Even as early as his boyhood years, he claimed to hear voices, he would talk out loud to these voices in his head, and he would fall down in faints on occasion. At least once, his mother and family members tried to have him arrested and restrained on the grounds that his mind was unstable. This was the man who was teaching the crowds about goodness, truth, justice, and love."

"It was only a matter of time before Jehoshua was going to come up before the Roman courts for incitement to riot or sedition. There are only a handful of military staff in Jerusalem old enough to remember anything about his trial, and they all say it was nothing out of the ordinary at the time, with the exception that some of the Jewish leaders were urging his conviction on the basis of crimes against their religion. The written annals from that period make little mention of his trial, but I should note that the prefect Pontius Pilatus took a very aggressive stance against anything that might have been considered insurrection or rebellion against Rome. There were a very large number of executions for rebellion during the six years Pontius Pilatus held imperium in Judea, so it does not surprise me that a man such as Jehoshua, who attracted large crowds with the potential to disturb social order, would be viewed as a danger by the prefect at the time."

"Following his death, stories began to circulate that Jehoshua appeared alive to various people. I was especially interested in these tales of his resurrection, as they feature prominently in the beliefs of the Christians. I inquired for anyone who saw Jehoshua alive after his execution to come forward, but I could only find people who claimed to have talked to other people who saw him alive. Sometimes these stories were three or four people removed from the original observer. I had no trouble talking to Jewish religious leaders who insisted that his followers deliberately spread lies about his resurrection, in order to show that his predictions about his death and subsequent resurrection three days later had come true. Some said that his followers stole his body in order to stir up these fantastic rumors. This seemed to me the least likely explanation for the stories of resurrection, because the military leaders in Jerusalem told me that execution details have always been scrupulously correct in their application of rules and regulations for crucifixion victims – no burials are allowed. Bodies are always disposed of by the elements as a lesson to others. I can only conclude that the stories that abound today about Jehoshua's resurrection from the dead are based on deceits that have no basis in fact. I must also conclude, as a direct corollary to that fact, that any cult which propagates the resurrection of someone like Jehoshua is a fraud, and unworthy of being classified as a religion under protection by the Empire."

"So much for the person Jehoshua. We can turn now to what has become the cult following of Jehoshua by people known as Christians."

"On my return to Rome I took a route that allowed me to visit several communities of Christians. I was generally unsuccessful in getting these people to talk to me, as they are very suspicious of Rome and very secretive. There was no problem in talking to Jewish communities or leaders about Jehoshua, because many of them feel the Christians represent a dangerous perversion of Jewish teaching, a physical threat to their own communities, and the source of a growing number of incidents involving street fighting among Jews."

"The court trial today is concerned with only one incidence among many where Christians provoke Jewish religious faithful to adopt street violence as a way of resolving religious doctrinal issues. There are instances of such violence now being reported throughout the Empire, from Egypt to Rome, and in the cases we have investigated, the instigation begins with Christians attempting to turn Jews against their own religion. This alone would be a matter of concern to civil authorities, but the Christians outside of our province of Judea are especially eager to proselytize what they call Gentiles, or non-Jewish peoples. While such efforts do not usually result in civil disorder, they cause ongoing social disruption. Those who elect to follow the teachings of Jehoshua are required to renounce their family and sever ties with non-believers. The young are especially vulnerable to these pressures, and we have received report after report from parents who are faced with the painful possibility of losing their children forever to this cult. In Roman families, this attitude has resulted in a challenge by children of the authority of their Pater Familias, which strikes at the very foundation of Roman culture."

"And what do these children face once they elect to follow Christian practices? Besides the renunciation of their families, they must turn over all their wealth to the leaders of this cult. They denounce our traditional gods, and they participate in barbaric practices involving eating human flesh and drinking human blood. We have some reports that the cult sacrifices infants in an offering to Jehoshua. Even one of these practices would disqualify the Christian movement as one worthy of protection within the Empire as a religion. All of them combined show that we are dealing with the most primitive and barbaric practices, occurring even here in Rome!"

"As our office is responsible for the state religion, we feel that the practices of the Christians certainly do not qualify as religion, are crude and inhuman to an extreme, and threaten the religions that are accepted within the Empire. And time and again, on my journeys from city after city, I heard about the defendant, Paulus of Tarsus, as a person instrumental more than any other in the establishment of this cult throughout the Empire."

"Honorable Praetor Peregrinus, I lay before you and this court the evidence we have obtained regarding the odious and impious practices of the Christians. I lay before you and this court the evidence we have obtained regarding the instrumental role the Defendant has played in fostering these practices. We beseech you, on behalf of the state religion and its principal defender, Imperator Nero Claudius Caesar Augustus Germanicus, to defend our religion, to outlaw the cult of Jehoshua, and to deal the defendant, Paulus of Tarsus, the maximum punishment allowed for promoting impiety!"

Cornelius Plautis had worked over and over on this peroration, and his effort was not in vain. The court had listened mesmerized by his summary of Christian crimes, and by-standers had found themselves drawn to the court, listening to these extraordinary accusations. Trebonius Cassianus had ceased eating his pistachios, mulling over the implications of this speech and the delicate decision that lay before him. He had realized early on that he could not risk exonerating the Defendant completely, not when there was the possibility that the Emperor himself was behind these charges. The last emperor to have any interest in the state religion was Augustus, who seemed genuinely devout in his observance of the rituals required of him as Pontifex Maximus. The successors to Augustus showed far less interest in religion, except for Caligula, who was mentally unbalanced, and who declared himself a god. The current Emperor, Nero Caesar Augustus, was showing incipient signs of Caligula's mental illness, which made the situation for Trebonius Cassianus notably perilous.

"Does the defendant have any response to these charges?" asked the praetor. He at least had to show good form and provide the defendant some opportunity of rebuttal.

Paulus consulted briefly with Laelius Disertus and then rose. "Your Excellency, Praetor Trebonius Cassianus: What was it the Accusator said? He could not get information from Christian communities because the people he talked to were secretive. Is it that Christians are secretive, or is it that the behavior of people he met in our communities was entirely normal when approached by a stranger with strange questions and accusations? Cornelius Plautis, who is no doubt an honorable man and was merely trying to fulfill the task he was assigned, could not possibly have expected cooperation if he showed up one day with no introduction and with a purpose that might be construed as inherently antagonistic if not dangerous for the community."

"Had I known of this visit, I would most happily have urged our communities to open up to Cornelius Plautis, to let him see the nature of our worship and the manner in which we comport ourselves, which is at all times in accordance with the laws of Rome and of our local authorities. He could have gone where he wished and questioned whomever he wished, and then he would have been able to make a better judgment regarding the validity of the testimony he was receiving. As it is, how does Cornelius Plautis know which of his witnesses had an interest in delivering malicious gossip rather than valuable and truthful testimony about the Christians?"

"And, Honored Praetor, what could be more malicious than the slander that Christians make human sacrifices, of infants no less? Unfortunately, Cornelius Plautis has chosen to believe this vile accusation rather than to see for himself what goes on in our communities. And because he believes in such tales, he misconstrues one of our practices, which is the entirely symbolic and ritualistic eating of the flesh and drinking of the blood of our Savior, Jehoshua the Christos?"

"I emphasize for the court that eating bread and drinking wine is only an act of symbolism. There is, of course, no consumption of human flesh, and no sacrifice of animals of any sort. Our rituals are entirely consistent with those of other religious groups which commemorate the death of their god through the symbolic eating of food and drinking of wine. Indeed, Honored Praetor, it is a fundamental contention of our faith that the death of Jehoshua was the ultimate and final sacrifice in the plan of our God – the Father in Heaven – to provide eternal salvation for all of us on earth. As this court will certainly learn upon a more careful examination, the dispute between the Jews and the Christians centers on our claim that animal sacrifices as practiced daily by the Jews are no longer necessary. You see, therefore, the contradiction at work here. We Christians abhor the concept of animal sacrifice, and we commemorate only symbolically the sacrifice of Jehoshua, which ended once and for all the need for Jews to continue with these practices. How then can we countenance something as barbarous as human sacrifice? And let me say to the court, that our sense of revulsion at the thought of human sacrifice is every bit as strong as that of any Roman, Greek, or other civilized person."

"I do not fault Cornelius Plautis for reaching the conclusions he did, given the limited information he had and his inability to distinguish malevolent testimony from truthful testimony. I only wish I could have helped him and introduced him to the proper people in our community, so that such errors could have been avoided. But it is not too late, Honored Praetor. Indeed, to avoid a failure of justice in this case, this court must rule that our communities be given time to defend themselves from these accusations. We would be honored to show Cornelius Plautis, or any other investigator, the true nature of our communities, our worship, and our beliefs. But you must allow us the opportunity to do so. Roman justice, which has been of such inestimable benefit to the entire civilized world, demands as much!"

Paulus had summoned up as many rhetorical flourishes as he thought possible. Even Laelius Disertus was impressed, especially with Paulus' refusal to be baited and goaded by the Accusator – indeed, to praise his accuser and offer a hand in friendship so that he could correct his "misguided" opinions. Laelius Disertus felt he could have done no better, and he understood the court system well enough to know that rhetoric by a defendant, if it was of high enough quality – if it was expressed nobly – and especially if it praised Roman jurisprudence - could even overshadow the evidence against the defendant.

Trebonius Cassianus reached for the cane next to his chair, brushed off the shell remnants from his toga, and joined the Triumviris in an animated discussion. Cornelius Plautis sidled up to the group and attempted to join in the discussion, but Laelius Disertus was pleased to see that the Praetor waved him off. Cassianus was not about to sully his reputation for fairness by allowing an Accusator, even one representing a powerful administrative constituency, to participate in a verdict.

At length Trebonius Cassianus returned to his chair but remained standing in front of it. Laelius Disertus motioned to both Paulus and Aristarchus to stand up for the verdict.

"This court," said the Praetor, "having weighed the testimony and facts regarding the Defendant's behavior at the Temple in Jerusalem, absolves the Defendant of the accusations against him. We find that the Defendant acted properly in obtaining a permit to speak publicly on religious matters. We have no direct evidence from his accusers that he physically incited violence, and we have testimony in his favor, which was not refuted by his accusers, that the Defendant said nothing incendiary or said anything different than he had previously presented to the public with no resulting violent incident. The evidence suggests that the Defendant acted only to protect himself from violence, and that the violence against him may have been premeditated. Indeed, we give great weight on this score, not simply to the written testimony from the Defendant's witness; we take into account the effort by the Procurator Marcus Antonius Felix to establish the basis for precisely this conclusion - that Jewish authorities sought to inflict the most grievous harm on the Defendant. Our vote of *absolvo* would in normal circumstances allow us to release the Defendant."

Paulus was visibly relieved at this verdict, even though he had been expecting it, but Laelius Disertus reached out and grabbed his hand. He didn't like the reference to "normal circumstances" and sensed something unfavorable was coming.

"This court," continued Trebonius Cassianus, "is also of the opinion that there are important religious matters that need resolution. We appreciate the work of the Accusator, Cornelius Plautis, in investigating and presenting his conclusions. For the most part, we would accept the testimony of this Accusator and rule accordingly. The word of a high official of the stature of Cornelius Plautis is, of course, to be taken seriously, but since matters of religious doctrine have now been introduced to the court, we feel obligated as a court to deal with them on religious grounds. I should add that there is no other praetor in the entire court system as well-qualified as I am to adjudicate such issues. Not only have I considerable background in religious matters as a former Chief Augur, but I have also written extensively on religious issues."

"The most heinous accusation made against the Defendant, and the Christians, is that of human sacrifice. While the Accusator says the witnesses to these acts are credible, we have no evidence other than hearsay. The Accusator does not present us with any document from someone who directly witnessed such a transgression against criminal and moral law."

"The Defendant, in the meantime, asserts that the eating of flesh and drinking of blood is entirely symbolic, involving the consumption of bread and drinking of red wine. In my studies of various religions, I find there are a number of examples of such behavior, and that the Christians would not be out of the norm of proper religious behavior if they too followed such examples. We note that the rites of Dionysos involve the ritualistic participation in his dismemberment and the drinking of wine in commemoration of this event. Indeed, at one time in the history of our Republic, attempts were made to outlaw this cult, though more on the grounds of sexual depravity rather than in the way they commemorated the death of Dionysos. More recently, the introduction of the rites of Osiris has brought to Rome a similar commemorative practice of drinking wine as symbolic blood. I could go on with other examples and show you the similarities and differences that exist, but I have a reputation for talking too much regarding such esoteric considerations."

"Let us merely say that we will need much more hard evidence that the Christians practice actual murder and human sacrifice, since it is likely they are practicing nothing more than a commemoration of a sacrifice through the use of bread and wine. For this reason, we urge the state to continue with its investigations, and if the Christian communities offer up the cooperation that has been promised to this court, both the state and the courts will learn the truth of this matter."

"As to the Defendant, the record shows he has been at the center of several disturbances between Jews and Christians, and not all of these can be assumed to be instigated entirely by the Jews. Also, the Defendant is a founder of many of the communities where Christians now flourish. He is a persuasive speaker and if released could begin to stir up turmoil here in Rome. Consequently, we cannot allow him to go free as long as the state and the courts have such doubts as to whether Christians are impious or not. We therefore order his house arrest in Rome, where he can be summoned as necessary by the authorities for questioning. If the practices of the Christians are exactly as he says they are, he will in due course be released."

"This is our verdict. The confinement of the Defendant is so ordered." Trebonius Cassianus had been shifting back and forth more vigorously as his summation progressed; clearly his knees or legs were hurting him. He hobbled out of the court soon after reviewing and signing legal documents given to him by the clerks. Meanwhile, the guards for Paulus returned to his side, assuming he was at least temporarily going to be led back to the barracks cell. The clerk of the court joined with Laelius Disertus to determine where Paulus could serve his house arrest. Did he know anyone in Rome, for example, who could commit to constraining him for as long as necessary?

"There is one man," said Paulus. "Simon Petros. A leader in our Christian community. I am sure he will vouch for me. Aristarchus will need to find him immediately and bring him to the courts."

Paulus counted out a substantial amount of money from his purse and handed it to Aristarchus. Virtually all the rest of his money he gave to Laelius Disertus in payment of his fee. "Aristarchus," said Paulus, "find the Jewish synagogue in Rome. They will surely know where to locate Simon Petros. Bring him here as soon as you can. He will also arrange for lodging and food for you while this is all sorted out."

The military guards had already trussed up Paulus in his chains. He was led out of the building back on the route they had taken in from the barracks. Aristarchus noticed that Paulus was shuffling a good deal more now than when he was brought to the Basilica. He wondered if this ruling wasn't more of a burden and disappointment than Paulus let on. He himself was both fascinated and dismayed at the turn of events. Why would the Romans go to such lengths to find out about Christians? And why would they believe such lies? As he saw Paulus disappear in the distance, he realized he would have to defer thinking about such questions. He had to find Simon Petros – and even more of a challenge – he had to convince him to come to the aid of Paulus. Everyone knew the two men did not get along, and suddenly the fate of so many Christian communities seemed to rest on the shoulders of Aristarchus. This was no longer a mere adventure for Aristarchus – it was a matter of importance that affected his family, his friends, and the other communities that worshipped Jehoshua. But where would he start? How would he find one man out of over a million people?

Aristarchus saw his only hope of help, Laelius Disertus, leaving the basilica, so he chased after him. "I'm sorry I can't help you," said Laelius Disertus. "I know nothing of these Jews or where they might reside. I was only assigned this case at the last minute. You might try the clerk of the court before he leaves."

Aristarchus approached the man who had been working at a table at the front of the court and who had been advising the Praetor from time to time. The clerk was pushing a pile of papers and scrolls into his satchel, preparing to leave. When he got closer, Aristarchus was surprised to see that this man was almost as young as he was. He was also the first Roman he had seen with a beard, albeit a short, neatly trimmed beard.

Aristarchus laid out his problem, reminding the clerk of the verdict that required that someone in Rome be found who would be willing to keep Paulus confined for some period of time. The clerk looked over Aristarchus more closely before responding. "I myself know little of the Jewish community, but there is someone back at the palace who knows them well enough. If you don't mind walking back with me, he should be able to help you."

Exactly what "palace" was being discussed was unclear to Aristarchus, and the young man wasn't volunteering that information, or even his name, but it was the best opportunity on offer, so Aristarchus readily agreed to follow him. Aristarchus made himself useful by offering to carry some of the papers for the court clerk. The two of them headed out of the Forum in an eastward direction, intended to circumvent the Subura. There were temples and gardens interspersed among street after street of apartment buildings. Clearly this was a wealthier part of Rome – quieter and no doubt safer. Aristarchus noticed they were climbing a hill, only to quickly descend. The second time this happened, however, Aristarchus began to recognize the hill he was climbing. Ahead beckoned an enormous garden at the summit; he would get glimpses of towering pine trees every so often as they rounded a street corner. Porcius had pointed out this very garden as the site of Nero's home.

"Are we heading to the Emperor's palace?" Aristarchus couldn't resist asking his guide. "Yes, indeed," replied the clerk, "but the Emperor will be dining in the city tonight. Otherwise, I would certainly not bring you there. Some of us at the courts work out of buildings near the palace." Aristarchus was immensely curious about what he would find at the Emperor's palace, but wary as well. Why was this clerk being so helpful, and what was it about the Christians that had piqued the interest of Emperor Nero?

Chapter Five

he road up the hill took a more gradual slope, and when Aristarchus and his guide reached the entrance to the Emperor's gardens, Aristarchus could see no building in sight. They were greeted at the garden gate by two Roman soldiers, dressed in what Aristarchus interpreted to be ceremonial uniforms. These men looked to him like centurions, with the elaborate crests on their helmets, but instead of breastplates they wore red tunics embroidered in gold. The effect was imposing, though a bit lacking in the restrained dignity that soldiers at the Forum displayed in their ordinary uniforms. After a brief consultation with the soldiers, the clerk motioned Aristarchus to enter with him.

There were still no buildings visible, but Aristarchus could see small temples in the distance, and to his right he could see a large pond with a waterfall and elegant white swans gliding on the water's surface. It was now mid-afternoon, and the day's heat was fading quickly. Aristarchus was glad he had brought his winter cloak with him. An occasional song bird would serenade them as they walked up a gravel path. Aristarchus marveled at the beauty of the scenery – it was unlike anything he had ever seen in Greece, and it reminded him that the climate in Rome was much different, allowing for a lushness in the landscape that was entirely new to him. The palm trees, for example, were taller and more luxuriant than those back home. And most surprising of all, there was no else in this garden. The two of them had been walking for almost ten minutes and hadn't passed a soul other than the guards at the gate. "How large was this place?" he wondered.

The question was answered when he reached the top of the hill. There was one large villa in front of him and several off to the side. The buildings seemed bigger than what he had visited at the Palatine, but not much bigger. The garden trailed off endlessly down all sides of the hill, and he concluded this was the only place that could possibly be described as a residence. Now he saw soldiers in uniform stationed at various locations around the building, as the two of them headed toward the main villa.

Once again the clerk had a conversation with the guards, and then both of them were admitted to a courtyard. Aristarchus was instructed to wait where he was, and he gravitated towards a charcoal burner where he could warm himself. Sometime later the clerk returned with a colleague, a man who appeared to be the same age as the clerk and wearing the same neat beard as the clerk. Aristarchus wondered if there was a fancy here at the Emperor's court for wearing beards.

"I am Hermogenes," said the colleague. "Welcome. You must be hungry." Hermogenes took Aristarchus by the elbow and led him to yet another courtyard, where sofas for reclining and dining had been arranged around a small fountain. Despite the cold winter weather, the fountain was operating and the room was comfortably warm from the charcoal burners located in each corner. Aristarchus wondered why he was receiving so much hospitality, but Hermogenes was such a congenial host – all smiles and conviviality – that Aristarchus found himself naturally at ease.

"You must try these field mice," said Hermogenes as he pointed to a tray of delicacies that had been brought in by a servant. Hermogenes poured out some wine for both of them. "This is the season for mice; they are plump and juicy in preparation for the winter. You'll also like this wine. It's from your part of the world, the valley of the Cedar mountains, just north of where Jehoshua lived. I've always wanted to see that part of the world." Hermogenes poured a bit of the wine into a glass of water and handed it to Aristarchus.

Aristarchus did indeed enjoy the wine – light, and smooth and fruity – so unlike the harsh and gritty red wines that were grown in Greece. "Now tell me how I can help you," said Hermogenes. They were seated next to each other on a sofa, and Hermogenes maneuvered himself slightly closer, staring directly at Aristarchus and giving him a look of the utmost curiosity and sincerity. Aristarchus explained the trial that morning and the need to contact the community of Christians in Rome.

"Yes, I've heard about your friend Paulus. I understand he is a significant figure in the Christian world. It must be quite an experience working for someone of his stature," said Hermogenes. Aristarchus recounted his impressions of Paulus – his selflessness, his belief in Jehoshua and the need to spread the message about salvation through Jehoshua's sacrifice, his establishment of

different communities of Christians, his skills at speaking and writing. Hermogenes was interested in Aristarchus's role as a secretary
and probed at his own ability to read and write Greek. How capable
was Aristarchus at learning new languages? Latin, for instance.

Aristarchus bragged a bit about his own talents, confident that he
could read, write, and speak Latin fluently in no time. Hermogenes
nodded and smiled, every so often asking another question about
Paulus or the Christians or Jehoshua, and the conversation was being conducted on such a friendly, and one might say intimate basis,
that it never occurred to Aristarchus he was being both interrogated
and interviewed.

"You really should consider coming to work for us here at the
Palace," said Hermogenes. "We could use someone of your flu-
ency in Greek and skills as a secretary, plus of course you are very
presentable. There is no hurry for you to return home to Greece, is
there?"

Aristarchus admitted he could spend more time in Rome if he
chose to do so. It had not yet dawned on him the enormity of the
proposition that was being made to him, so smoothly had the conversation gone. Slowly, though, it began to occur to him that he was
being asked to work for the Emperor, or at least near the Emperor.
What did he have that merited such a proposal, with so little experience and being completely unknown to Hermogenes or anyone else
in Rome? This question so nettled him when it first came to him,
that he blurted it out to Hermogenes.

Hermogenes replied, "You underestimate yourself, my dear
friend. I will tell you a little secret, but you must never, ever repeat
it to anyone. We Greeks run the Empire. It is too big a job for the
Romans, who have skills in administration but are sadly lacking in
diplomacy, tact, cultural sensitivity, imagination, and even the essential knowledge of Greek, which is spoken in more than half the
Empire. We are always looking for young men like you who have
the basic talents, and who can be trained and molded into a career of
service for the state."

"Of course, this is a very great honor we are offering you. I am
sure you would appreciate that fact and express your appreciation
now and then as necessary. You wouldn't mind, for example, letting
your beard grow. That is, after all, much more common among the
Greeks then the Romans, and the Emperor has always been fascinated with all things Greek." Here Hermogenes reached out and

stroked Aristarchus's cheek with the back of his hand. "Yes, you have the potential for a fine beard, blond and smooth to the touch. All of the staff here at the palace are growing beards, now that the Emperor has one of his own and has set the fashion."

"And then too, there is the matter of your devotion to Jehoshua. I trust you do not feel too strongly about that, as it would otherwise make it impossible to employ you in the government." Aristarchus had never given much thought about his devotion to Jehoshua. As a Christian, his belief in Jehoshua was just a natural thing to him, born out of the beliefs of his parents, especially his mother. Being such a natural part of his thinking and behavior, Aristarchus had never imagined a situation where he would not be a Christian, certainly not deliberately. Besides, there were other developments in this conversation and this very recent and surprising offer that were beginning to disturb him. He did not think it prudent to outright deny that he could ever denounce Jehoshua, so he only muttered something about having to think things over.

"Come with me," said Hermogenes. "I have something to show you." It was more of an order than a request, as Hermogenes grabbed Aristarchus by the arm and began guiding him out into the hallway and down a corridor. They reached an octagonal room that was unheated and in darkness. Hermogenes ordered a servant to light several lamps in the room. A series of excellently executed wall paintings of gods and goddesses were the first things Aristarchus noticed, but his eyes then settled on pillars holding statues arranged in a circle around the room. Aristarchus recognized a prominent place for Jove and Juno, and they were surrounded by other gods and goddesses, including Baal and Isis, whom he recognized from the various temples in Greece dedicated to these Asian and Egyptian gods.

"Nero worships all these gods and goddesses," informed Hermogenes. "He prays to them almost daily when he is at the palace. Do you see that empty pillar over there? Let me show you something." Hermogenes led Aristarchus over to a closet in one of the walls, covered by a curtain. When the curtain was pulled back, Aristarchus could see in the faint and sputtering light from the lamps a marble statue on the floor, broken into multiple pieces. It was the figure of a god with a beard and long hair.

"That is your god Jehoshua," said Hermogenes. Aristarchus had no choice but to believe him. Christians did not worship statues of Jehoshua, especially those Christians who had converted from Judaism, so Aristarchus wasn't exactly sure what he might look like. Hermogenes continued, "Nero had this statue made up when he began hearing about Jehoshua and the miracles he performed. He gave Jehoshua a place of honor in his pantheon. It was a trial run, so to speak, to see whether Jehoshua could work miracles for Nero."

"Unfortunately, your god failed him. Something to do with a request regarding his mother-in-law; I am not sure about the details. In any event, Nero was outraged and destroyed the statue, ordering us to keep it here in darkness as punishment. You can see now why it would be unhealthy for you to entertain any devotion to Jehoshua, though, of course, we would encourage you to continue your association with the Christians in Rome. We are always interested in their activities."

All during this conversation, Hermogenes had his hand placed on Aristarchus's back, rubbing his hand up and down the spine of his potential protégé. The entire situation was becoming more and more unsettling for Aristarchus. Just what was it Hermogenes wanted from him? Was Hermogenes really interested in recruiting promising Greek secretaries, did he want a spy situated among the Christians, or did he want something personal from Aristarchus in the way of "expressing his appreciation" for all Hermogenes was doing for him? Aristarchus now realized that the position he was in was more treacherous than he first thought. He had to be circumspect in his response.

"Sir," he said to Hermogenes, "I deeply appreciate the opportunity you are offering to me. It is almost beyond my comprehension, coming as I do from a small Greek city, to find myself in the center of Rome – in the center of the Empire in fact – being given a chance to work here. I must, of course, obtain my father's permission before accepting this opportunity, but first I have an obligation to the Praetor Peregrinus to find a person who will agree to confine my benefactor, Paulus. As you can appreciate, I must do this within a day, and as the afternoon is getting on, I should seek out the Christian community in Rome as soon as possible, before night falls. I was hoping you could help me locate them."

A slight look of disappointment crossed Hermogenes' face, as if he was fully expecting this young man to accept his offer immediately and move into the palace that night. Aristarchus, however, had said the right words – "Praetor Peregrinus" – which presented the indisputable fact that Aristarchus had taken on a task at the direction of the court, and Hermogenes certainly did not want to appear in any way to be interfering with court business. Consequently, he called for one of the guards, seeking out a certain soldier who spoke acceptable Greek. He called for a piece of parchment and drew out for the soldier a rough map that would allow him to locate the Christian community.

"I am sure this soldier will take you to the correct location. When you finish your business with the court, come back to the palace and ask the guards for me by name. They will be instructed to let you in."

Aristarchus gave the most fulsome thanks possible for all the hospitality he had received, but it was with a sharp intake of breath that he left the palace doors. He dared not discuss this conversation with the soldier, but the man was voluble enough that he gave Aristarchus a running account of the neighborhoods they would pass through on the way to their destination. It seemed the people he sought were outside of the walls of the city, to the south, near the Appian Way.

Chapter Six

s Aristarchus and the soldier passed through the southern gate, the soldier began asking people for directions to the Jewish synagogue. This was a polyglot area of Rome, where Latin was the rarity when compared to the Greek, Egyptian, Gaulish, Hebrew, and other languages used in the apartments and the shops that were clustered together outside of the protection of the city walls. "What was the name of the man you were seeking?" asked Aristarchus's escort. "His name is Simon Petros," replied Aristarchus, so the soldier began directing his inquiries accordingly. When they reached the building that the Jews in the area used for their worship, they were told that Simon Petros did not reside there. Fortunately, he lived but a few streets away, and with a few more questions Aristarchus and the soldier stood before a shabby, three story apartment building with a wooden door that was hanging half off its hinges. A girl about age ten peered out from behind the door in response to the rapping noise of the soldier's sword on the door. "We are seeking Simon Petros," he told her in Greek. "Does he reside here?" The girl nodded yes and disappeared.

Within a few minutes the door was opened fully, and an elderly man of medium height stood before them. He was slightly hunched over, and he wore a dark red tunic that was frayed along the bottom and at the arms. His face was blotchy, as if the sun had decided to tan only certain areas over time. There were no angles to his face, just a softness in the curves of his cheeks and his chin that suggested an overall gentleness in his character. His eyes blinked repeatedly – Aristarchus wasn't sure if that was due to sudden exposure to the sunlight or a sign of difficulty in seeing – but what struck him more were the dark circles under his eyes. There was an aura of intense weariness about him.

"I am Simon Petros. How may I help your Excellency?" Simon Petros did his best not to betray the alarm he was feeling at the presence of a member of the Praetorian Guard at his door step. He was wary of any official interest in his activities or those of his community.

Children were already beginning to mill around this soldier just to have a glimpse of his elaborate uniform.

"I am here at the behest of the court of the Praetor Peregrinus. A defendant named" - and here the soldier consulted his piece of parchment – "Paulus of Tarsus has been ordered confined to house imprisonment, and this defendant has given your name to the court as someone who could comply with the official order. If you accept this responsibility, I will accompany you to the prison holding area so that the prisoner can be released to your custody. This young man is acting in the capacity of an aide to the prisoner, and the confinement ruling may or may not apply to him. We still await word from the court." This was the first time Aristarchus had any cause to worry; he had thought he would have free run to explore the delights of Rome.

"I cannot say that I will provide confinement for Paulus, but I know someone who most certainly will," replied Simon Petros. "I will take responsibility for seeing that the defendant is properly confined before the night is over. You need not stay around; I know my way to the barracks outside of the city." He wanted to be rid of this soldier as quickly as possible.

"Well, my duty is not to see that the defendant is placed in proper custody, but only to deliver this young man to you. The court has appointed him to fulfill this requirement, and it is now on both of your shoulders to do so. We obviously know where to find you if you fail." With that the soldier fiddled a bit with his sword and scabbard and headed off with a pack of children trailing behind him.

Simon Petros motioned Aristarchus to follow him up the stairs. "What is your name?" he asked, as they entered his apartment. "I am Aristarchus of Athens. My family is a member of the Christian community there. I was chosen to accompany Paulus to Rome."

"I thought Lukas was to accompany Saul," responded Simon Petros. Aristarchus explained that Lukas took ill and had to be left in Crete. "Then we were shipwrecked, which added a further delay to our journey. And now just when we thought we would be free in Rome, the Pontifex Maximus has intervened with further accusations against Paulus, resulting in his house arrest."

"Shipwrecked!," exclaimed Simon Petros. "And what is this about the Pontifex Maximus? Wait a minute – Adriel must hear this." Simon Petros shuffled off to the back rooms and was accompanied on his return by a woman aged forty or somewhat more. She had sun-darkened skin, with wrinkles that creased her face and caused her arms to sag in folds. Aristarchus noticed an expensive-looking bracelet on one arm – it appeared to be gold – part of a dowry perhaps. Simon Petros introduced her. "This is my wife, Adriel. Tell us please what has happened on this trip."

Aristarchus related the whole sequence of events up to the court's decision. He left out the personal details of his trip and didn't mention the extraordinary offer he had received at the Emperor's palace, which he was beginning to think was too risky to accept. He realized with the telling of the tale the magnitude of the adventure he had been on – it was the first time he had been able to distance himself from the experience and view it objectively. Certainly, the open-eyed wonder and anxiety that his hosts displayed, helped make it apparent that Aristarchus already had a story that he would be retelling for the rest of his life. The questions both Simon Petros and Adriel directed at him showed they were acutely aware of the implications of the intervention by the office of the Pontifex Maximus.

Aristarchus could not answer the question Simon Petros raised about how long this house confinement would last. Adriel gave her own opinion. "It could last many months – even years – just as long as it takes this Accusator to return to Judea and Galilee and elsewhere to do a more thorough investigation. Simon, we cannot afford to let Saul stay in our house for that long a period of time. You know what he is like."

"But it is our obligation to help anyone from the community who is visiting Rome." Simon Petros was almost pleading with his wife. "How would it look to others if we turned our back on someone as prominent as Saul?"

"We have bigger problems than what others think of our hospitality," responded Adriel. "You know what has been happening on the streets of Rome – the attacks on our members, not only by Jews, but by those who follow Paulus. Diodorus has taken to calling us false prophets, and he has insisted that only he and others who obey the teachings of Saul have the right to be called true followers of Jehoshua. Saul belongs with those people, not with us, where he would otherwise preach to our members and confuse them. You know the power of his oration. At least if he is confined with Diodorus, he cannot add to our problems."

Simon Petros looked genuinely addled by the conundrum before them. "I see the wisdom of what you say, Wife, but consider that Diodorus will interpret the rules of house arrest very loosely. Saul will be on the streets within days, telling everyone about how Jehoshua was walking among the living immediately after his crucifixion. You know how that excites the crowds – even the Romans, who have heard every sort of strange tale. Yet you are right as usual, Adriel."

Simon Petros struggled to his feet. "At least when the officials from the Pontifex Maximus come to inquire about Saul, we can direct them somewhere else." Simon called out to the back for someone to bring his cloak, shoes, and his staff. With an afterthought, he asked for a cudgel to be found for Aristarchus. "This is Rome, young man. Do not venture out at night unarmed. The two of us should be reasonably safe, especially after Diodorus joins us."

Ariel added, "Do not forget you are an old man, Simon. Do not be afraid to call out for help, boy, should you need it, and use the loudest voice possible. People will respond more to you than an old man." She kissed Simon Petros on the cheek and accompanied them as he hobbled out the door.

"I am not used to hearing Paulus referred to as Saul. You must have known him a long time," observed Aristarchus, hoping to learn something about the rift between these two important men. "It is nearly thirty years now since we first met," replied Simon Petros. "He is a well-meaning individual, with a true devotion to the Christos, but his ideas are not always agreeable to those of us who knew Jehoshua."

Aristarchus looked up wonderingly at Simon Petros. In the darkness Simon Petros could not see well; his eyes were on the narrow pathways they needed to follow to reach the eastern gates of Rome, navigating by the occasional light from torches set near doorways, and always keeping an eye focused on the shadowy figures they passed now and then or who lingered in the darkness. He did sense, though, that Aristarchus was confused at the very least about why some people would not agree with Saul.

"You are a Greek, young man, and do not have the background to understand some of the disagreements we Jews have over matters of religion and Jehoshua. Let us say that some Jews believe there is no such thing as a resurrection; others say there is a resurrection of the body; and still others say there is a resurrection of the soul only. I accompanied Jehoshua for nearly three years on his journey of healing and teaching, until the very day of his execution, when I failed him by denying my involvement to others. I live every day with that failure, and if in my old age my back hurts or my lungs ache for a normal breath, that is but a small punishment for my sin."

"In all that time with Jehoshua, I heard him talk openly about the resurrection only three times, all towards the last few months of his life. Jehoshua always spoke in riddles or with stories as examples, so he never directly said he would be resurrected. He implied he would be, immediately in spirit and later in physical form, when he would return from his Father in heaven to judge all men, living and dead. This is what I was told; this is what I learned and understood."

"Several years later, a man known only to us as an agent of the Sanhedrin and determined to see us all executed, suddenly turned into a follower of Jehoshua, and he began preaching a different story about our Master – that he physically rose from the dead three days after his crucifixion. Saul also taught that Jehoshua was thereby ful-filling ancient Hebrew scripture that predicted a Meshiach, and that Jehoshua was crucified so that all of us would now have a means of entering heaven. Where he got these ideas no one could say, other than as a Pharisee, he was taught that the physical resurrection is what awaits all Jews who follow the Law. But I guess you wouldn't know about Pharisees and the Law and such things."

Aristarchus responded that he did not but would love to learn now that he was in Rome. He never had a particularly strong cu-riosity about Jehoshua – Jehoshua just was – someone his parents worshiped and whom he had accepted as a presence in his life from his earliest memories. Yet this old man had been there; he knew Jehoshua as intimately as perhaps anyone alive. Aristarchus real-ized he would be a fool to let slip an opportunity to learn from this man things no one back home in Greece would imagine.

"I don't know what I can tell you, young man," replied Simon Petros. "To be honest, I don't know what to believe anymore. I hear so many stories about Jehoshua these days that I wonder if my memory has betrayed me. Let me give you just one example of something I heard recently." They were turning a corner into a wider street where the going was easier.

"Several weeks after Jehoshua died, there was talk about his appearing in Jerusalem, showing his wounds, and obviously very much alive. All of us who were his closest followers had gone into hiding in different places, but gradually we began to lose our fear, and most of us found our way to the inn we had frequented just before he died. We assembled nightly in the very dining room where we last ate with Jehoshua and where he mysteriously told us to remember him. He had promised us to return one day; perhaps that day was already at hand, given all the stories circulating in Jerusalem about his appearances. So we waited for him every night, not knowing what to expect."

"Nearly all of us were there one night during a fearsome spring storm. The thunder was ceaseless, and the torches and lamps about the room provided very little light in comparison to the flashes of lightning which lit the room regularly. There was a sudden, prolonged silence outside, and then a gust of wind blew open all the windows and extinguished the torches. A strange blue light entered the room and traveled slowly across the ceiling until it struck Bartolomeo and Tomas and knocked them forcibly off the benches."

"We were all of us terrified and immobile in our seats. The blue light was not lightning; it traveled too slowly, and moved like a ball of flame. It evaporated like a wisp of steam after striking Bartolomeo and Tomas. I had promised myself I would never again cower in the face of anything sent to us by the Master, and this was clearly a visitation of the Spirit from Jehoshua or even the Father in heaven. Of that there could be no doubt. I was the first to recover and stand up."

"I remember saying something about this being a message from Jehoshua, but noticed that both Bartolomeo and Tomas were still lying in the floor. Were they dead? I rushed over to them and others began to stir from their fear. Both were still breathing, so I slowly fed them some water and massaged their chests. Tomas was the first to revive; his hands were red as if they had been burned, but he felt no pain, and for as long as I knew him afterwards he retained those red scars on both hands."

"It took the two men quite some time before they could breathe regularly and speak. Even then, Bartolomeo stuttered for months afterward. Tomas was the first to say something,"

"'I saw him, Simon! He was right in front of me. He was holding out his hands as if to show me his wounds from the crucifixion. He said nothing, but I could see the disappointment in his eyes. He was real, Simon. He could have been standing right where you are – perhaps he was – perhaps all of you were asleep like me. I know the truth now; I know he has risen and is among us. We must go find him!'"

"I restrained him as best I could. You have to understand, young man, that Tomas was the most skeptical of all of us regarding the stories of the resurrection. After that experience, he became the most vociferous in arguing for Jehoshua's resurrection in bodily form."

"I must admit that I no longer had confidence in my views, but I still could not, and never have, abided Saul's theory of the resurrection, redemption of sin, and so on. Now I hear people who visit our community in Rome talk about the famous night when Jehoshua visited all of us, and let Tomas feel the wounds in his hands in order to dispel his doubts, and then gave all of us the ability to speak in any language we wanted. Did that happen? Is my memory that bad? Sometimes I feel I am too old to provide answers to anyone about anything."

Aristarchus had taken to holding Simon Petros' right elbow as they slowly wended their way to the east gate. Diodorus lived outside the gates with his small community of Christians. Simon Petros had no difficulty in finding the door to the building, and several quick raps brought the man himself to the door.

"Simon Petros! What a surprise! Have you come to apologize for your attacks on our people?" Simon Petros pushed his way into the building and Aristarchus followed him. "I have come for no such purpose, Diodorus. Your friend Saul is in Rome and is now under house arrest. The Romans have given us one evening to find a place for him to stay for however long it takes for him to exonerate himself, if he can. He obviously cannot stay with us. You must accompany us to the barracks on the Campus Martius and bring him back to your residence. This young man is his assistant and will stay with you as well. We will have to find out if he will become your permanent guest. Get your things and come with us."

Diodorus stood with his mouth gaping, not knowing what to say. Paulus in Rome? Why hadn't he written to him? Was there a trial? Simon Petros was being so preemptory and insistent that Diodorus had no time to even ask his questions. He retreated to put on some sandals and a cloak. In the light Aristarchus had observed Diodorus to be a young man slightly older than himself, rather dark skinned for a Greek, and of medium height.

A baby was crying in the back rooms as Diodorus emerged from the curtains. Simon Petros hustled him out the door. Aristarchus noticed that Simon was in more pain than when they started out.

He grunted slightly, step by step, but he kept up a pace towards the Tiber River. He was in no mood to talk with Diodorus, but he did issue a serious warning to him.

"You need to understand fully the implications of house arrest, Diodorus. Saul is not to leave your residence at any time for any reason. He cannot preach or visit friends. Moreover, according to this young man, the office of the Pontifex Maximus has taken an interest, and not a favorable one, in Saul. You must impress upon him the seriousness of this problem, for all of us, not just for you or Saul. If the Emperor is involved, it could go very badly for us. Please keep Saul under control and do whatever the Romans want."

When they reached the barracks, Aristarchus took charge, informing the officer at the gate of their mission regarding a certain prisoner and the instructions that had been issued by the Praetor Peregrinus. Even Simon Petros was impressed with Aristarchus' ability to toss around the names of high officials. It was all wasted, however, because the officer spoke no Greek and had to find someone who did. They were told to wait while they reviewed the papers that Aristarchus had been given by the court, and after what appeared to be a very long time, Paulus was accompanied to the gate.

"Simon Petros! It is so good to see you again. Paulus rushed up to embrace Simon Petros, but he received a stiff, unresisting response. "We should waste no time," said Simon Petros. "This man is Diodorus, the head of your followers in Rome. You will be staying with him, as will your young friend here, who has served you well, I may add."

"Diodorus?" Paulus said with some confusion. "I have written to you from time to time, addressing your questions regarding the community, but we have never met before this, and I have no 'followers' in Rome. What is the meaning of all of this, Kefas?" Paulus was beginning to sound alarmed, more so than at any time during his trial, when his life was in the balance. Aristarchus realized that something serious had been happening with the Christians in Rome, and whatever the circumstance, it was of vastly more concern to Paulus than even his own life.

"Diodorus will tell you soon enough what has been happening to us here in Rome, but as you now know, this is not the time for Christians to be fighting," responded Simon Petros. "Not when the Emperor himself may be taking an interest in our affairs. And you know what I am talking about, Saul. I heard all about the intervention of the Pontifex Maximus in your trial."

They had come to the place where they would have to branch off, with Simon Petros continuing on a separate path to his home. He took Paulus by his hands and wished him well, admonishing him under no circumstance to break his curfew. He then led Aristarchus aside. "I am afraid I have forgotten your name, young man, but you have performed a great service this day and throughout this journey, accompanying Saul to Rome. Not even Lukas could have acted with greater responsibility. You may visit our community at any time, and who knows, perhaps I shall come visit Diodorus and Saul."

Simon Petros' eyes misted over. He looked off in the distance, as if a flood of memories had suddenly crossed his mind. "You would have been the sort of man our Master would have welcomed as a follower." Aristarchus began to sob quietly and was not sure why, other than to understand that he had just been given a very great compliment. Suddenly, he did not want to leave this man, who was a remarkable combination of strength and calmness.

Simon Petros embraced Aristarchus and kissed him gently on his cheek. He turned his back to him and began hobbling off into the darkness. Aristarchus had so many questions for him. He promised himself he would visit him at the earliest opportunity. Aristarchus walked quietly over to Paulus and Diodorus, but could not resist one last glance back at the stooped old man nearly invisible in the night gloom. It was the last time he would ever see Simon Petros.

PART TWO

We meet Chrysanthe and Crispus, two leaders of the vibrant community of Gentiles and Jews in Corinth who venerate the memory of Jehoshua the Christos. So absorbed have these two been in their leadership roles in the community, that they ignore warning signs of trouble with their son Alcaeus. The trouble erupts when Alcaeus is detected secretly engaging in the pagan rites associated with the Greek god Dionysos. This shocks Chrysanthe in particular, who eventually discovers the cause of Alcaeus's disaffection. Working with others within the Christian community, she is determined to deal with the problem and protect her two younger daughters from experiencing the same doubts and challenges as Alcaeus. The result is an innocent pantomime for the children of the community – a small play that is destined to have unexpected long term implications for the worshippers of Jehoshua.

Chrysanthe

Corinth
Year 60

Chapter Seven

hrysanthe and Crispus followed their son to the Acrocorinthos – the rocky outcropping that loomed over Corinth, and which served as the religious center of the city. Alcaeus had been sneaking away during the evenings, and his parents knew not where nor why. For six months he had been acting differently. His interest in family activities – which centered around the small Christian community in Corinth – had diminished to the point where he was hostile to the idea of even attending an Assembly, and he no longer paid any attention to his two younger sisters.

Crispus had the idea to follow Alcaeus this evening when he left the house, and Chrysanthe insisted on coming along. In early spring the days were warming up nicely, but the nights could still be cold, and Chrysanthe was thankful she had brought along a warm robe.

As Alcaeus reached the summit of the Acrocorinthos, Crispus and his wife saw him disappear into one of the many temples. Neither of them was that familiar with the different temples that were scattered about the summit. They were familiar with the very largest – the Temple of Aphrodite. Everyone knew this landmark, which could be seen from the sea or the mountains for miles around. But this smaller temple – the one with six columns framing its entrance – what was this place?

There were still people milling about the Acrocorinthos, and Crispus took the opportunity of finding out about this small temple from a stranger walking by. "It is devoted to the worship of Dionysos," Crispus reported to Chrysanthe. "Dionysos? Dionysos? What did he do?" wondered Chrysanthe. You could tell a lot about the people who worshipped at these temples by the nature of the god being worshipped. Unfortunately, Chrysanthe had long ago given up any interest in the Greek deities or figures like Herakles. They were all make believe, as far as she was concerned – at least this is what she had come to understand from the teachings of Christian leaders like Apollos or Paulus when they came to visit Corinth.

"He is a festivity god," said Crispus. "He is something like Bacchus. I see his processions through the marketplace from time to time. The priests are almost always women, and their processions are led by someone carrying a giant phallus. I don't know what goes on in their temple."

Crispus let this last sentence trail off to a whisper, as if he regretted saying it. He took a side glance at Chrysanthe. She was strikingly beautiful, even after nearly twenty years of marriage and three children. Many people saw a resemblance between her and the goddess Aphrodite as depicted in the giant ivory and bronze statue in her temple. There was the same straight yet elegant nose, the same curls in their tresses, the suggestion of a perpetual smile about their lips. Chrysanthe, if anything, had a more voluptuous figure.

Early on in their marriage Crispus had developed a jealousy regarding his wife, once he noticed men taking long glances at her. Over time he realized how foolish he was to be suspicious of Chrysanthe. She had but three passions in her life and felt very protective of them: Crispus, her children, and her devotion to Jehoshua the Christos. In the way that sometimes happens in a marriage, Crispus had been imbued with this same fervor. It was not a surprise that he came to love Chrysanthe and the children very deeply and worried incessantly about their safety and their comfort. What was surprising to him was his immersion into the world of the Christians, a group he knew little about when he married Chrysanthe (nor did she, for that matter), and a group he would have described as a perverse cult from what little he did know.

Together as the years went by they oriented their own lives, and those of their children, around the Christian community. Crispus had grown up with what might be described as the usual religious education of a modern Greek. His parents required him to join in the services of their own favored god, Poseidon. His father had been a fisherman before settling into urban life in Corinth, and Poseidon had been his protector. Crispus could appreciate this devotion; when he was allowed to accompany his father on the open sea, he understood, even though he was very young, what it was to be really afraid of the unexpected dangers that could overtake a man.

Once the family moved to Corinth, however, Crispus grew less and less convinced that religion had any real meaning. For one thing, there were so many gods and goddesses to worship, not to mention minor deities and half deities. The Romans had complicated things by letting new devotions into the city: to Isis and Osiris, to Baal, and to Ishtar. The Jews were allowed to organize their synagogues for the worship of their sole god, Yahweh.

The secrecy with which the Jews went about their religious duties set them apart; that and the fact that they were the only cult throughout Greece that did not encourage others to join their religion. Not that many requested; few people wanted to abide by the complex food restrictions that Jews observed, and no man wanted to undergo circumcision for any reason. These practices subjected the Jews to ridicule, and many Greeks considered them barbarians in their religious practices.

This is why it surprised Crispus when Chrysanthe one day asked him to accompany her to a religious meeting of the Jewish cult known as Christians. How she met these people he did not know. "Aren't the Jews unwilling to let others observe their worship?" asked Crispus. "These Christians aren't like the usual Jews, Husband," replied Chrysanthe. "They seem to worship two gods and not one. My friends say it is interesting because they worship their primary god but also the son of this god – a man who has lived during our own time. Whether he is just half a god like Herakles, or a full God, I don't know. They don't have a temple or a synagogue as is customary for Jews. They hold what they call Assemblies in a small hall or a home, and they allow strangers to observe and question them. Chloe told me they emphasize the proper upraising of children, and since we are starting a family, she thought we both would benefit from knowing them."

Crispus agreed to attend the meeting for Chrysanthe's sake, but he was surprised how much attention they paid to him rather than to Chrysanthe. He learned later that the Christians valued educated men. Crispus was a scribe in the marketplace and spoke and wrote both Greek and Latin. He was going to prove to be a very valuable man in a growing organization that was constantly sending written communications across land and water to distant Christian communities.

He remembered the first time he ever discussed this fully with Chrysanthe. It was several months after first meeting with the Christians. He and his wife were sitting in the shade of an olive grove on one of his days off, discussing the two prominent Christian leaders, Paulus and Apollos. "Do you know, Chrysanthe, they want me to start speaking in front of their Assemblies? I barely know what to say. All I know about them is that they are pestering me to make copies of the letters they receive from leaders like Paulus and Apollos. How can I possibly lecture anyone about their religion?"

"It's not hard, Husband, but you must believe first," responded Chrysanthe. "I too have been asked to speak up at the Assemblies. That shocked me at first; in most temples women are not allowed to participate as priests unless the worship is of a goddess. The Christians don't care who you are. Even slaves are encouraged to learn to read and write, just as they have taught me to do as well."

"You have made great progress in your letters," admitted Crispus. "You owe all that to the Christians. Even though I am a scribe, it never occurred to me you would have any interest in a formal education." Crispus added ruefully, "Of course, it is all a waste outside of the Assembly. Women are not allowed to be scribes."

"True," agreed Chrysanthe. "But Alcaeus is learning the trade quickly. He is fluent now at both Latin and Greek, and he has asked one of the Jewish elders in our community to teach him Hebrew. He can read their scriptures aloud tolerably well and translate them for us. They are very impressed with him in the Assembly, and one of the elders wants to introduce him to Paulus on his next visit. Paulus is always looking for someone with language and writing skills to accompany him on his travels."

"I'd rather have him stay at home and learn the business first," said Crispus. That is exactly what had happened. Crispus thought back to that conversation of nearly two years ago and realized that Alcaeus had finished his apprenticeship with him, much earlier than most young men would. The boy was fully capable of working on his own, given his predilection for languages. Perhaps that was what was irritating Alcaeus and keeping him so distant from the family. Maybe he was desirous of breaking free from his father and setting up his own business.

Crispus noticed the crowds on the summit were thinning out. He reached out for Chrysanthe's hand and felt the night chill that was beginning to affect her. He lowered his voice a bit as he thought of something to say that would pass the time. "Do you know what else he's done? One day he was talking to a customer in the market who wanted a document translated from the Phoenician. 'I can do that,' said Alcaeus, and he proceeded to write out in Greek a thorough interpretation of the document. Who has taught him Phoenician? It is a very difficult language. As much as I appreciate his initiative, it almost borders on the disrespectful the way he operates in secrecy, telling me nothing of what is going on in his life. What has happened to the boy?"

"It hurts me too," said Chrysanthe. "We used to be so close, the two of us. Now he has tightened up like a clam pulled out of water." Chrysanthe leaned forward to see if there was any movement at the small temple, but nothing had changed, other than the shadows were lengthening in the early evening.

The two fell again into silence. Something Chrysanthe had said earlier, when they arrived at the Acrocorinthos and saw Alcaeus enter the small temple, came back into Crispus' thoughts: "You must believe first." It was a reference to the invitation to become a leader in the Assembly, but after all this time, he was still uncertain of his beliefs. As a scribe, he certainly liked the fact that the Christians were nearly fanatical about education. It had benefited Chrysanthe and Alcaeus, and their two younger girls were no doubt going to be able to obtain some decent schooling if they wanted to. Crispus was modern in his thinking in that regard; young women should learn to read and write, if only to survive in the business world if they were ever widowed or remained unmarried.

But what else did he believe, now that he learned that men like Paulus, Apollos, and Simon Petros had different ideas about Jehoshua? Apollos believed the Christians should worship the Father as the only god in existence; Jehoshua was with the Father but only as any good man would be for having led a blameless life. Paulus, on the other hand, was always talking about "Lord Jehoshua Christos" and deliberately mixing him up with the Father when it came to the power of judging men worthy of eternal life. Simon Petros was interested mostly in the healing and miracles that could be performed in the name of Jehoshua. He rarely talked about the resurrection that was so important to Paulus.

As he first got to know these men, Crispus took the greatest liking to Simon Petros. The man was simple, quiet, direct, and in many respects innocent of the world. There was something dour about him; he only seemed to light up briefly when he was able to provide a healing benefit, even if it was only verbal solace, to some poor, sick soul. Simon Petros also had something that the other two lacked, and that was a real sympathy for those who were oppressed, especially when it came to the slaves who increasingly were asking to become Christians. This was yet another aspect of the Christian movement that intrigued Crispus – the welcome hand extended to both slaves and freemen, who were treated as equals within the community. Several slaves had risen to positions of leadership alongside Crispus.

Other religious cults encouraged the mingling of freemen and slaves, but the Christians were different. Paulus was always lecturing and writing about the fact that all members of the community, including women, were in the same position in relation to the Christos. They were all seeking salvation and eternal life through Jehoshua, and worldly considerations such as wealth and ownership of other humans mattered for nothing in the pursuit of salvation through the crucified Christos. Indeed, Jehoshua himself suggested it was harder for wealthy people to obtain salvation than it was for poor people to do so.

Crispus often noticed that the Greek attitude towards slaves was usually different than the Roman attitude. The Romans he met, especially the wealthy traders who bought and sold goods throughout the empire, or the men who ran the gladiatorial schools, displayed little of the guilt or sympathy towards slaves that Greek businessmen held. True, they recognized that maltreating slaves was an inefficient business practice that led to financial losses, but there was no moral impediment preventing them from beating or even executing slaves.

Perhaps that was because the Romans were conquerors and not slaves. Greeks, on the other hand, were themselves frequently enslaved to Romans if they fell behind on paying back their debts. The complicated relationship between conqueror and conquered was what caused Crispus to move away from supporting Simon Petros as much as he used to in front of the Christian community in Corinth. Simon Petros, of course, sympathized with the condition of the slaves, but Paulus – Paulus was the only elder who came now and then to Corinth and who offered a solution to those who were conquered and enslaved. Paulus understood the Greeks far better than Simon Petros, Apollos (who was Greek himself), or anybody else. Crispus couldn't at first quite put his finger on what it was about Paulus that drew him towards him, but it was Paulus whom he asked to baptize him formally as a Christian. Paulus was the one who pushed for Crispus to move into a leadership position in the community, which involved speaking publicly to the Assembly at the weekly meetings.

The strange thing about Paulus was that he said very little about Jehoshua the man or his life. Perhaps he simply didn't know much about him; he often admitted he was not an original follower of Paulus such as Simon Petros was. All Paulus talked about was the crucifixion and the resurrection of Jehoshua and what that meant not only to the Christians, but to the world. He would chide the Greeks for always seeking wisdom and a rational explanation for things, just as he would chide the Jews for always seeking miracles and signs from God. Was this a snide criticism of Simon Petros? – everyone knew the two men didn't get along well. Paulus would explain that God's message turned the world upside down; what was really important was what men deemed foolish, such as the possibility that anyone could rise from the dead. Christians would always be criticized by others for their insistence on something as irrational and foolish as belief in the resurrection of the Christos and his power to redeem humans from sin. But it was the Christians who were in possession of the secret to eternal life, however foolish this secret seemed to be.

Crispus read all of Paulus' letters over and over while preparing himself for a speaking position within the community. For many months he struggled in the Assemblies to make himself worthy of the role he was given. People would listen politely to what he had to say, but they seemed disconnected from his words. One hot July afternoon his listeners were notably inattentive, seemingly anxious for him to finish speaking so they could find someplace cooler to enjoy. Crispus decided to change topics and explore a phrase he remembered in a letter from Paulus - "Death is swallowed up in Victory."

When Crispus began talking about Victory, the men in particular began to listen to him. As he pursued this idea, he found his voice rising and the interest in the room waxing. What did Victory over death mean to a modern Greek? Crispus had to be careful how he expressed things, so he alluded only to the fact that Greeks had often been deprived of meaningful victories in their daily life. What Jehoshua the Christos offered them was a victory that transcended all others, one that made enemies foolish and everyday concerns inconsequential.

The men certainly knew what he was talking about. Two centuries earlier the Romans had utterly defeated the Greeks at a battle near Corinth, which marked the end of any active resistance the Greeks might offer to Roman rule. The Corinthians suffered more dearly than any other Greeks from this defeat; they lost soldiers and many thousands of elderly and children, whom the Romans slaughtered randomly. Their entire city was burned to the ground, all their wealth carted off to Rome, and the survivors enslaved. The world might remember what befell the Corinthians if it weren't for the fact that the Romans inflicted the same destruction on Carthage that very year. Carthage was a much more bitter enemy of Rome, and the Romans had commemorated that victory ever since. The battle of Corinth was eventually forgotten even by the Romans. No one remembered it but the Greeks themselves, and especially the descendants who lived their lives in a Corinth rebuilt along Roman lines, with Roman architecture, a Roman forum to replace the agora, and Roman slaves - most of them Greek - constituting over half of the population.

Everything about Corinth was perpetually and subtly unfamiliar to the Corinthians themselves. Men didn't talk much among themselves about what it was like living under Roman rule. The possibility of a further revolt against the Romans died out a long time ago. All that was left was the sense of inferiority, the ongoing feeling of failure, and the subdued animosity towards the Romans that every Greek felt.

Was it any wonder that such men would snatch at any prospect of Victory, even if it was a victory in the next world? Crispus realized that Jehoshua – or was it really Paulus? – had discovered a way to penetrate into the very soul of the modern Greek man, to excite him, and to provide him with a sense of worth and purpose. A Christian could walk along the streets of Corinth knowing to himself that he held a secret no Roman could take away from him – a secret so profound and so powerful that it turned the relationship of conquered to conqueror upside down.

Crispus had come to appreciate something deeply insurrectionary within the philosophy that Paulus taught with such subtlety. The Roman authorities seemed only dimly aware of what type of threat to their rule existed within the Christian communities. Yet look how many such communities had sprouted up throughout the cities of Greece, in Anatolia, in Syria, and of course in Judea and Galilee! Crispus thought frequently of the many other men who existed within the Empire and who would be susceptible to hearing this message. Egyptians, Gauls, Goths, and now these Brits whom Claudius had brought into the Empire -- all of them waiting for someone or something to take away the sting of living as servants in their own home.

Yes – the men understood Crispus very well when he talked about Victory. As for the women? They understood it too, but they didn't feel it in the same way as the men. For the women, the appeal of the Christos lay in the words of love and the deeds of compassion that marked his life. This too Paulus understood implicitly and talked or wrote about constantly. It was one discussion in which Crispus played a helpful role, because he noticed that Paulus was using a Greek term for love – *philia* – that did not fully correspond to the human relationships and behavior Paulus went on to discuss. To Crispus, *philia* was a word that referred to the love that exists within a family – of parents for their children and children for their parents, brothers, and sisters. Crispus felt that the word *philia* was a rather restrictive term.

The Greeks had other terms for love; the one word most frequently used was *eros*. Clearly this was not what Paulus was talking about. *Eros* connoted sexual as well as emotional attraction, and Paulus was if anything too anti-sexual. He felt very uncomfortable traveling around Greece and watching the sexual displays that accompanied religious processions, especially in Corinth, where its multitude of temples offered prostitution as part of their religious practices. Corinth was celebrated in Greece as the one city where any sexual desire could easily be satisfied. The Greeks were, in contrast to Paulus, very proud of their advanced views about human sexuality; they encouraged their young to consider sexual relationships as a completely normal and shameless aspect of their lives. These relationships were not limited to those between men and women; they could include men with men and women with women. Greek legends even included many instances of Zeus assuming the form of a beast and having carnal relationships with humans.

Yes, all of this openness about sexuality and different forms of human sexuality made Paulus very uncomfortable. Perhaps it was his upbringing as a Hebrew scholar – the ancient texts that the

Jews referred to as their scripture were apparently condemnatory towards any expression of human sexuality beyond that between a husband and wife. Crispus was by no means the only person to advise Paulus to refrain from denouncing sexuality when he visited the Christian communities in Greece. Of course, this advice was ignored. Paulus was his own man and said what was on his mind. It was not that he was stubborn. It was more that he was completely convinced that this philosophy he was creating around the life and resurrection of the Christos was divinely inspired and could not therefore possibly be in error. It was the job of his Greek listeners to come around to his style of thinking, not for him to soften or weaken the requirements of those who followed The Way.

Realizing that Paulus wasn't going to change his views about sexuality, Crispus wrote to him and suggested he consider discussing love in terms of *agapé*. Crispus knew that this was a Greek term used more by scholars, but it encompassed a very broad concept of love – of father for his children, of leader for his flock, of siblings for each other, and of any individual toward his communities or fellow man. It even contained an element of self-sacrifice, which fit in perfectly with the philosophy Paulus had developed around the crucifixion of Jehoshua.

Crispus noticed that Paulus began mixing the term *agapé* into his letters. He still used *philia* when talking about the family, but he seemed to appreciate the scope the new word afforded. Crispus was to realize only much latter what he had accomplished. For the most part, Paulus took advice from no one and relished a debate or intellectual fight seemingly for the fun of fighting, since Paulus never conceded a point of debate. In this he truly was obstinate, and Crispus watched with sadness as Paulus would over time estrange himself from others in the Christian community. Still, it was with a sense of pride if not embarrassment that Crispus one day heard Paulus stand up before the Assembly in Corinth and announce that the Father had sent Crispus to them to help the community grow and flourish.

Crispus and Chrysanthe even found themselves discussing whether it wouldn't be better if their children avoided the openly sexual aspects of modern Greek society. This is how they began raising Alcaeus and the two girls. Alcaeus! Crispus jolted his head slightly as he came out of his reverie over the early days of their experience with the Christians and Paulus. He realized he hadn't been paying any attention to what was happening at the Temple of Dionysos. Night had now fallen completely; Venus could be seen and the moon was promising to be nearly full and very bright tonight. Was Alcaeus still in the temple?

Chapter Eight

What has been happening, Chrysanthe? I nearly fell asleep." His wife told him some other young men had entered the temple, but there was as yet no sign of them or Alcaeus. "What could they be doing in there?" she asked Crispus in a whisper. "I'm worried for him, Crispus. You know how impressionable he is. And lately he has been talking about how he is now a full adult and deserves to be on his own. Maybe we have treated him like a child for too long."

Crispus patted his wife's arm and told her he didn't think that was a problem, but he spoke only to reduce her concerns. He tried to assure her that Alcaeus was a responsible young man and would not make foolish decisions. He did not confide in her his fear that there was something fundamentally sexual about the cult of Dionysos that attracted Alcaeus, and that no young man however properly raised could easily ignore the sexual impulses that accompanied them into adulthood.

They waited quietly for what seemed another very long time. The grounds of the Acrocorinthos were now deserted of people except for the occasional passing of a priest or priestess. At long last a shaft of life erupted from the temple, as the great bronze door of the temple opened. Chrysanthe and Crispus shrank back into the shadows as they watched a procession emerge from the temple. An elderly woman led the procession – presumably she was the chief priestess of Dionysos, since this was a cult led by women. She was followed by a younger woman carrying what seemed like a large statue covered in a cloth. Behind her were other priestesses with torches, and then at last four young men in white robes and wearing victory wreaths of laurel on their heads. They looked as if they were figures from a vase come to life. Even in the limited light from the torches, Chrysanthe remarked to herself how brilliantly white their gowns appeared to be.

Crispus pointed out to Chrysanthe the third youth in the group, their son Alcaeus, walking proudly in his white linen robe and sporting a laurel crown as if he were an athlete at Olympus. The procession moved silently towards the edge of the summit and followed a small path down the rocky promontory. Crispus remembered that this path did not lead down to the city but lead instead to the forests that ranged up the mountainside that served as a backdrop to the city of Corinth. He rose to his feet and helped Chrysanthe up, both of them rearranging their tunics and pulling their robes around their shoulders for warmth. Chrysanthe used her robe to cover her head as well. Silently they began to follow the procession from a distance. Without the benefit of torches for themselves, they had to tread warily along the rocky path, and Chrysanthe regretted she had only worn sandals rather than boots. Who would have thought her son would be participating in such a procession?

An intonation had begun emanating from the procession ahead of them. The young women were humming or whispering some phrases in praise of Dionysos. The torches rocked rhythmically from side to side as the priestesses and their acolytes moved steadily along the path. They were neither ascending nor descending the mountain, so the going was not terribly difficult for the procession, but Crispus and Chrysanthe had to keep a careful distance so as not to be heard by the group. More than once Chrysanthe tripped on the rocks along the pathway.

The group was now far away from the Acrocorinthos and the city in general, and as no one could hear them, someone in the procession began pounding out a steady beat on the tabor, to accompany the chanting, which was becoming louder. "Dionysos! Dionysos! Come to us from the afterlife!" Chrysanthe could hear clearly what they were singing; she was more musical than Crispus and had a better ear for chants and hymns, since she often organized them at the Christian Assemblies.

"Come to us from the afterlife!" The sonorous tones of the four male voices could now be heard mingling with those of the priestesses. The trees were more spread out, and Crispus and Chrysanthe could glimpse the light from street torches in the city below them. The chanting had picked up tempo; the young girls in the procession had begun to sway their bodies back and forth, their hands raised above their heads. The procession had arrived

in a clearing among the trees, with one side of the space dominated by a sheer wall of rock.

The wind soughed, rustling the leaves of the laurel trees. The
young girls were now moving about in a circle, surrounding the
four men, and in the center of it all the covered object had been laid
bare, revealing a large, carved phallus of the sort Crispus had seen in
processions about the city. Crispus could make out something that
he hoped was unnoticed by his wife; the young girls wore only their
tunics, and their breasts undulated gently as they moved slowly
around the men. This ceremony was not simply a celebration of the
erotic – it was an evocation of the erotic. No man of Alcaeus's age
could be insensitive to the invitation that was being offered him.

"Dionysos! Dionysos! Son of God and Lord of Rebirth. Hear
our Plea and Join Us Now!" The tempo had picked up pace just
a bit more. The group was not in a frenzy, but the chanting and
the sound of the tabor had now been joined by the notes of a flute.
Imperceptibly, the girls had approached the men and disrobed them
of their tunics. The men were dancing now only in their loincloths
and crowned with laurel wreath, their bodies moistened by their
sweat as they circled the phallus and jostled every so often with the
women around them.

Crispus was both fascinated and embarrassed by the spectacle,
fully expecting that all of the participants would be completely naked in short order. Chrysanthe, on the other hand, was absolutely
horrified. It had been years since she had given any thought to the
activities of the pagans all around her, so isolated had she been
within her Christian community. And to witness her own son in
such debauchery! What had happened to his morals? Had all their
years of teaching been for nothing? Alcaeus was still in her mind a
young boy – an innocent – someone she couldn't possibly think of in
a sexual way. Yet here he was participating in the very type of idol
worship that made Christians ashamed of their fellow Greeks.

"Husband! We must do something!" Chrysanthe whispered to
Crispus. "There is nothing we can do," responded Crispus. "It is not
permitted to interrupt." Crispus hoped she would understand, since
there was no time to go into detailed explanations. As a scribe he
was very familiar with the law, and he knew that religious organiza-
tions were protected in their ritualistic practices. There were severe
penalties for interfering with religious ceremonies, especially those
conducted in the precincts of a temple or in a private setting away

from the public eye. Besides, Alcaeus was of legal age to make his own decisions to join any cult he wished. However embarrassing it was for him and his wife to observe this ritual, it would be doubly embarrassing for Alcaeus to have his parents suddenly burst forth and interrupt the proceedings. They might lose him as a son altogether. Crispus thought their only option was to steal away quietly rather than witness something even more shameful than what they had seen.

At that moment the music stopped. The high priestess, whom they had not observed for some time, emerged from the darkness of the mountainside. "Acolytes! Come join us in the Mysteries of Dionysos!" She took a torch and led the men plus four of the women to the mountain wall. For a minute the torch disappeared and Crispus could not understand what the group was doing. "They are going below – into a cave," said Chrysanthe. Crispus then made out a sliver of light running along the ground. Indeed, he thought to himself, this was a well-chosen spot – their most secret of ceremonies could be conducted in complete privacy.

"What can we do?" pleaded Chrysanthe. The desperate tone in her voice sickened Crispus. He felt powerless and ashamed at the same time. "There is nothing we can do, Wife," he said. "We are in the wrong here if we take any action to interrupt a legal religious practice." With not a further word, he took her by her arm and led her quietly back along the path, looking for the route that led back down to the city. With only the moonlight to guide them, they had to find their way with great care. Crispus could feel the tension in Chrysanthe's body as they steadily made their way back to Corinth.

They said nothing to each other until they reached home. "I must see to the girls," said Chrysanthe when they entered the house. Their eldest daughter, Olympias, was eleven and was accustomed to watching her little sister on her own, but Chrysanthe and Crispus had been absent for an unexpectedly long time. Once assured that they were sleeping well, Chrysanthe returned to the outer room and sat in a chair, her faced cupped in her hands. Crispus implored her to get some sleep, but she obviously intended to wait there until Alcaeus returned home. That could be a very long time, thought Crispus.

Chapter Nine

rispus found Chrysanthe asleep in the chair the next morning, slumped over, her long black tresses draped down over her head and hiding her face. "You must come to bed, my love, for some proper sleep," said Crispus, as he shook her shoulder. "I will let you know the minute Alcaeus returns." Chrysanthe rose and silently walked to their bedroom. She fell into the bed and pulled the covers over her, with her face to the wall. Their two daughters shared the bedroom with them and were not awake yet. Crispus would have to alert them to remain quiet when they did get up. They would think it very odd to find their father at home in the morning on a work day, but Crispus had nothing to say to them. Much would depend on what Alcaeus intended to do.

It was mid-morning when Chrysanthe bestirred herself from the bedroom. Her face had a wearied look that alarmed her two daughters. Crispus had never seen her like this. No, that was not true. He had seen her like this, much worse in fact, when their second son died at birth. That was the only time Crispus had ever seen his wife weep. He had seen her cry now and then, but only at that moment had she laid open her soul to inconsolable grief. That was a long time ago and he had grown used to his wife and her businesslike manner, her steady moods, and the feeling of quiet cheer one sensed in her presence.

"You must find him, Crispus. Bring him home." It was all she said. He knew she was right. She was in her clothes from the night before, wrinkled and damp from sleeping in them. "Has something happened to Alcaeus?" asked Olympias. "He is fine, Olympias," muttered Chrysanthe with a great weariness. "He was out late last night. Your father knows where he is." Chrysanthe did not wish to discuss Alcaeus with his sisters. Olympias might have understood – she was developing into a young woman now, faster than Chrysanthe would have liked. Olympias understood something of the world. Theodosia, however, did not. She was entirely too young for such a conversation, thought Chrysanthe.

"We need some water, Olympias," instructed her mother. Theodosia immediately reached for the water bucket. "I'll help," she volunteered. Theodosia went everywhere Olympias went. She idolized her sister, and Olympias had become fond of this sisterly heroine-worship. As Chrysanthe busied herself with inspecting the bread to see if it was still edible, Crispus put on his sandals and stepped out to check the weather. The day was cloudless and was already uncomfortably warm. Crispus went back inside to fetch his purse and made sure it had a few coins inside. He kissed Chrysanthe on the cheek. "Everything will be fine, Chrysanthe," he whispered to her. She managed a brief smile, but Crispus could feel the worry emanating from her body.

Crispus set out for the Acrocorinthos. The marketplace down by the harbor would be busy already this morning, but the temples atop upper Corinth would likely be empty this early. Crispus found the walk up the peak more tiring than usual. It reminded him that he hadn't slept well last night, but if he were being truthful to himself, he would have admitted that he was no longer young enough to trudge up mountaintops without feeling the exertion. He rested for a minute when he reached the peak. The great temple of Aphrodite was already "open for business," as Crispus liked to put it. He understood that these temples were as much commercial enterprises as they were religious institutions. Pilgrims were already beginning to file into the temple to make their pleas to Aphrodite and leave a tidy deposit behind for the priests.

The temple to Dionysos was off to the side. It looked smaller in the slanting rays of the morning sun. The temple was not open, and Crispus did not bother to approach the elaborate bronze door at the front. He went to the back, where there was always a small entrance, and hoped a caretaker would be there. No one lived in these temples; the priests and priestesses would have their shelter in a nearby apartment, but Crispus had no idea where that might be.

He knocked on the wooden door at the rear of the temple, and waited a minute or two. There was no response. He had no walking stick or any other hard object with him, so he looked about for a small rock and used that to knock more forcefully on the door. He could hear the sound of his rapping echo through the temple halls.

The response came sooner than he expected. The door opened slowly, and Crispus was greeted by a shrunken elderly man with a cane. Crispus had seen his sort before in the countryside, bent over from toiling in the fields, with a face browned and etched in wrinkles from daily exposure to the sun. "Wa u wa?," inquired the caretaker. Crispus did not understand him at first and noticed that the man had at most three serviceable teeth in his mouth; his gums were an ugly mixture of blackness interspersed with white pockets of pus. Crispus could not fathom how the temple owners had not done something for this man.

"Wa u wan?," asked the caretaker once more. Crispus understood him this time. "I am seeking my son. His name is Alcaeus." The old man muttered something that sounded like "other building" and hitched up his tunic in the process. He closed the temple door behind him and, saying nothing to Crispus, headed off down the dark lane that ran behind the Temple of Dionysos. A few buildings down this lane he approached what appeared to be an apartment building, fumbled for some keys attached to his tunic belt, and led Crispus inside.

Crispus was astounded at the interior of this building. It was anything but an apartment building. It was a full country villa located in the center of the Acrocorinthos and much larger in size than one would expect from the outside. The courtyard was graced with a fountain that splashed water happily on a bronze statue of Dionysos. Lemon trees surrounded the atrium, and the walls were painted with expensive murals that featured scenes from the life of Dionysos. Given the phallic worship that characterized this cult, Crispus was expecting these scenes to be vulgar and erotic, but they were instead pleasingly bucolic. One had the impression Dionysos spent his time tilling the soil rather than entering dank caves in order to be reborn. Though he was used to the worldly preoccupations of these religious orders, Crispus was unprepared for the amount of wealth even a small temple like this one managed to procure.

He waited on a bench in the atrium, sitting in the cool shade with the smell of lemons gracing the courtyard. The old man had left him, and Crispus could hear people stirring about in the back rooms. The clip-clop of sandals on the marble floor alerted Crispus to the arrival of someone to deal with him, and he saw rounding a corner and heading into the atrium the elderly, gray-haired woman who had led the procession the previous evening. She was wearing a blue linen cloak that was pulled up over her head, giving her a distinguished, matronly mien, and her body seemed to shimmer as she walked. When she came closer Crispus was able to see her cloak was embroidered with gold thread, a luxury only the very wealthy could afford. Once again he was surprised by the tasteful but purposeful display of riches that this cult presented.

"You must be Alcaeus's father," she said to him, bowing her head slightly to Crispus but not offering him her hand, since that would have been an improper thing to do for a woman in her station, meeting a strange man for the first time. "He looks so much like you. I am Mother Sophia, the head of our small order here in Corinth. We are very honored to have someone of Alcaeus's intelligence express an interest in our devotion to Dionysos. He is such a presentable young man. You must be very proud of him. I would like to meet his mother someday if she would deign to honor us with a visit. I am sure she...."

"I have come to talk with him, if I may," replied Crispus. He rushed these words out as quickly as he could. He could see that Mother Sophia's prolixity was not going to allow him much opportunity to say anything. For all that, she was an inviting rather than intimidating presence. There were none of the wrinkles in her face that betrayed an elderly woman, and Crispus would have been astounded to learn she was nearly seventy years old. She smiled frequently as she talked, and her eyes closed ever so slightly when she smiled. Crispus took an instant liking to her, despite his perception that they were on completely opposite sides of the fence when it came to his son.

"Of course, you may see him." Mother Sophia pushed her hair back neatly under her scarf and appeared as if she were about to get up, but then she settled in for more conversation. "None of our acolytes is required to stay here or spend much time here. In fact, we have no boarding facilities here, so it is quite impossible for any of the young men or women who wish to join our worship of the divine Dionysos to live here permanently. I am sure Alcaeus explained all that to you."

"Alcaeus told us nothing about your temple or his interest in Dionysos," responded Crispus.

"Oh dear," said Mother Sophia. "Oh dear," she said again. "Alcaeus said that...." She broke off her statement as if she was about to say something indiscreet. "It is best if Alcaeus explains his intentions to you. We encourage our acolytes to share their desires and experiences with their family so that everyone can understand the nature of our Dionysian worship. We are, after all, interested ultimately in allowing each person to open their hearts, their minds, and their bodies to new and ennobling experiences."

She rose and once again settled her robe neatly about her. Crispus was expecting her to carry on with more details about the Dionysian cult, but instead she merely informed him she would fetch Alcaeus. The wait for his son was longer than he expected; Crispus fidgeted with the coins in his purse, rehearsing what he would say to Alcaeus. What if his son refused to come home? What if he wanted to leave his apprenticeship in the market place? Where would he live? How would he live?

Crispus was so intent on these questions that he did not hear his son approach from behind him. "Father," said Alcaeus. "You have asked for me?" Crispus stood up quickly and faced his son. Alcaeus's black, curly hair was glistening in the morning light, and he looked taller for some reason, even though Crispus noticed Alcaeus was in his bare feet. He was also no longer wearing the white robe from the night before but had changed back to his normal tunic.

"We want you to come home, Alcaeus," was all that Crispus could think of saying. All of his rehearsed speeches had fallen by the wayside. He could have demanded that his son return home – he was still within his rights to do so – but he felt intimidated by his surroundings in this palace of sorts, and he realized for the first time that he felt intimidated by his son.

"I have some things to do here still, Father. I will be returning home soon," responded Alcaeus.

The anger that accompanied Crispus as he walked up the Acrocorinthos returned; he felt it churning in his stomach. "You will return home now," said Crispus, putting as much paternal insistence in his voice as he could muster. Crispus grabbed hold of Alcaeus's arm, as if to drag him along, but Alcaeus stiffened and pulled himself away. His eyes were flashing with distrust.

"Do not make me raise my voice, Alcaeus, and cause you embarrassment. I have come here with the intention of treating you with respect, like an adult, and have spoken to you as a man would to another man. Do not make me treat you like a child, because I will if I have to. Go get your shoes and your other things – we are returning home now!"

Alcaeus retreated a few steps, his body simmering with resentment, and then turned his back on his father and walked off to the courtyard rooms. Crispus paced a little around the fountain, and was soon joined by the temple caretaker. The old man attempted a conversation regarding the warm weather, but Crispus was in no position to talk pleasantries nor put in the concentration necessary to understand what this man was saying. He was saved from any further talk by the reappearance of Alcaeus wearing his sandals and carrying a cloth that wrapped around something soft.

Without a word the two of them headed out to the entrance door, the old man positioning himself ahead of them in order to release the latch. They left him in the street locking the door again, while they headed to the path that led down to the city. "Your mother is very distraught about this, Alcaeus. Do not raise your voice to her." Crispus thought it best to say nothing more than this, and as they worked their way down the slope of the mountain, neither said anything further.

Chapter Ten

"Alcaeus! Alcaeus!" Theodosia was delighted to see her brother. In her eyes he was not as deserving of worship as Olympias, who knew about all the things that might interest a young girl. Yet now and then he still took the time to play games with her. "Where have you been, Alcaeus?" she asked. "We had bread for our morning meal but it didn't taste very good. Did you know Father didn't go to work today?"

"That's enough, Theodosia," said Crispus. "Why don't you and your sister play in the bedroom." Olympias, who had been listening to this conversation with intense curiosity, recognized a command when she heard one. She reached for Theodosia's hand. "Come, Theodosia," she said. "There is a new type of sewing stitch I've been meaning to teach you."

Crispus bade his son to sit down with him at the dining table. By this time Chrysanthe had appeared from out of the bedroom. Alcaeus was surprised at the sad look in her eyes and the disordered condition of her hair and clothes. She always took pride in her appearance, whether in the home or outside in public. Maybe she was sick, he thought. Surely this could not be related to his one night at the temple of Dionysos? Why would anybody be upset at that? None of the other young men had problems with their families.

Chrysanthe came up to Alcaeus and kissed him lightly on the forehead. "Talk to your Father. We need to know what has happened to you." Chrysanthe returned to the bedroom to join the girls.

"Alcaeus, we have a right to know where you were. What were you doing at that temple?"

"You didn't need to know where I was. Someone obviously told you." There was a look of smoldering anger in Alcaeus's eyes.

"Yes, somebody told me," responded his father. "That does not mean it was right for you to leave the house for an entire evening without telling me or your mother where you would be. That was disrespectful of you, Alcaeus. We have taught you better behavior than that. What happened to the things you learned from our community?"

"And what did I learn from our community?" Alcaeus hissed out the word "community." "That I am supposed to worship an executed Hebrew? What am I supposed to learn from the men who come up here from Jerusalem when they don't even speak Greek? And the one who does speak Greek – Paulus – what is he teaching us? He never visits us without having his hand out asking for money. What does he offer us? The promise that Jehoshua will return any time now to take us all into heaven because we are the new Chosen People? How does that help me today – at this moment?"

It was Crispus' turn to feel the anger rolling inside of him. He had never heard his son speak this way. Alcaeus had always been respectful at the Assemblies, though a bit aloof and detached from the services. Where was he getting these ideas? Who taught him to talk this way to his own father?

"Alcaeus, you know better than that. You know that The Way is open to all men and that Jehoshua's message is not limited to the Jews or even to the Greeks. If it were, we would not have communities in Corinth, Athens, Ephesus, Alexandria, and even Rome. You know that we do not worship Jehoshua as a god – only his Father is the one true god. What we teach in our Assemblies is a new message – a way for all of us to preserve our spirit after death. This is not something you can learn from the Greek gods!"

"What do you know about the Greek gods?" Alcaeus's insolence was now alarming his father. Alcaeus' voiced was raised and Chrysanthe as well as the two girls could not but stop what they were doing and listen to what he was saying. "At least the Greek gods are our own gods, not some foreign god that people in the desert invented. The Greek gods understand us and how we live. They don't set rules down for us to follow and then condemn us to Tartarus if we break even one of them. They let us live our lives in our own way and not spend all of our time worrying about our life after death."

"Did you learn nothing from years of attending our Assemblies?" sputtered Crispus. "Even my own preaching seems to have entered your head and left it immediately. There is only one road to the afterlife and that is through Jehoshua. His sacrifice has made it possible for us to spend the afterlife with the Father, rather than in eternal darkness and sorrow. You cannot obtain happiness other than through The Way"

Crispus was now shouting as well. Alcaeus had risen from the table, his two hands placed firmly on the table top, forcing his father to look up to him.

"That is where you are wrong, Father. There are many paths to the afterlife. Jehoshua is not the only one to have come back from the dead. Dionysos accomplished this before he did, and Osiris before Dionysos. At least Dionysos is Greek. He allows us to breathe the air of our native land. He allows us to enjoy life, to use our minds and our bodies to the fullest extent!" Alcaeus found himself parroting the teachings of Mother Sophia and the other priestesses at the temple. He had no other arguments he could use that would make sense to his father.

Crispus was now standing as well. "Oh yes, I know all about using your minds and your bodies. I've seen the way these temples parade around Corinth with their phalluses. What a thing to worship! They don't teach you how to use your bodies. They allow you to abuse your bodies, to give in to lust. I've seen how they take you up to the mountain, singing and dancing, and then they allow young girls to disrobe you, to excite you, and to 'initiate' you, as they call it. It's an excuse for a religion; a shameful pandering to a man's greatest weakness. It has all the nobility of animals mounting each other in a farmyard!"

Crispus took a second to catch his breath. He realized he had just made a mistake, falling into the trap he had most wanted to avoid, but now this made him angry at himself as well as his son.

Alcaeus's face turned ashen white; his body trembled under the suspicion that his father had witnessed what had happened the night before. He was ashamed, but at the same time now his anger knew no restraint. "How could you watch us? It is a forbidden ceremony! Were you hiding? In the bushes? Is this what you do at night, skulking about Corinth in the hope you can spy on secret religious rites?!"

Alcaeus had been pacing back and forth as he delivered these accusations. Now he stood still, his arms folded across his chest, his eyes locked in combat with his father. Crispus was if anything even more furious than his son, and the urge came to him to deliver a firm beating to Alcaeus, something he had never done before. Before he could even raise a hand, Alcaeus strode to the door, walked out into the street, and slammed the door behind him.

Chrysanthe came running out from the bedroom. "We can't let him go like that! We might never see him again." She felt rather than saw the violent impulse that had surged within Crispus and decided she must take matters into her own hands. She opened the door to the street, and looking out she saw Alcaeus walking quickly down the street to the path that led back to the mountain top.

She ran after him. "Alcaeus! Alcaeus!" He did not hear her voice at first; instead he heard the sound of sandals running along the stones behind him. He turned briefly to look. "Alcaeus – you cannot leave like this. We are your family!" He instinctively froze when he realized it was his mother. Chrysanthe ran up to him and folded her arms around him. "Oh, Alcaeus! It is me – Mother. We have always talked to each other openly. Tell me what has happened to you!"

The pleading in her voice – the sight of her tangled hair – her sense of desperation – the comfort that immediately came to him with her arms around him; it was all too much for Alcaeus. His anger drained away from his body in a second, and in its place came tears and sobbing.

"I am sorry, Mother. I am sorry. I am sorry." She could feel his body pulsating as much from the loss of anger as from his crying. They were close to the neighborhood water well, and she led him to the bench that stood next to it. No one else was there at the moment as they sat down.

She held an arm around him, letting him cry his emotions out. Her own emotions were muddled and confused. For years now she had forced herself to allow Alcaeus to grow into a man. The hugs, the running of her fingers through the curls of his hair, the kisses on the cheek – all these were deliberately held back. She knew at some point some other woman would have that privilege, and not her. But for now, at this moment, she gave in to her own needs. At this moment, he was her Alcaeus again, a boy and not yet a man, someone she must protect from harm and pain. She used her cloak to dry his eyes.

"Maybe we did wrong to witness your ceremony." He looked up at her with surprise as she continued to dab at his tears. "Yes, I was there too, Alcaeus. I am sorry for that, but please understand we were terrified we were losing you to this cult. What if I never saw you again! I could not bear that pain. And Olympia and Theodosia – they adore you, Alcaeus. How could we allow our family to be broken up that way?"

"I was never going to leave you Mother; you must know that."

"We didn't know that, Alcaeus. It has happened before. Young men or women enter these temples and are never seen again. Parents whisper these things among ourselves, because it is not the sort of thing you can talk about out loud. Some of these temples are very powerful."

Alcaeus had not looked at it in this light. Everyone at the Temple of Dionysos had been so welcoming, so overtly eager to assure him he could come and go as he pleased. No one had pressured him to do anything he didn't want to do. "It is not like that at the Temple of Dionysos, Mother. They want us to stay with our families. Mother Sophia asked many questions about you and Father and about Olympias and Theodosia. She said she hoped someday my sisters would consider joining the temple as well."

He realized the minute he mentioned his sisters that something didn't sound right about this. He saw it in the look of worry that crossed his mother's face. He also saw that he might have been too trusting after all. Perhaps Mother Sophia's intentions were not completely innocent. The temple had to get young girls as novices from somewhere.

"But why would you want to go there in the first place, Alcaeus? Is there a girl that has tempted you to do this?

"No, Mother, there is no girl." Alcaeus by now had calmed down enough that he could think more clearly. His mother must have assumed something happened last night in the cave that would bind him forever to the temple or to one of the priestesses. He needed to assure her convincingly on this point. "No girl tempted me to join the ceremony last night. And there was no physical activity in the cave" – Alcaeus didn't feel comfortable using any more graphic term with his mother. "Relations between the acolytes and the women of the temple are not allowed without Mother Sophia's permission, and then only after there is evidence they are suited for each other. What occurred in the cave, Mother, was a reenactment of the resurrection of Dionysos; this is a ceremony the temple performs once a year before Spring arrives. There are prayers, songs, anointing with oil – but nothing else."

Chrysanthe had so thoroughly convinced herself that Alcaeus had been enticed by the possibility of frequent sexual opportunities that she was now honestly puzzled as to why he would want to join such a group. "Well if there is no girl, why would this group interest you?" she asked. "We have prayers, songs, and anointing in our Assembly. Isn't that enough for you?"

"It is not the same, Mother." Alcaeus looked a bit exasperated. He shifted his position so he could face his mother directly. She still held his hand in her own. "Pardon me for saying this, Mother, but you don't know what it is like being a Christian and facing the outer world. You spend your time at home or with the community. I have to go to the marketplace six days a week as an apprentice to Father. The boys my age laugh at me. They think I have become both a Jew and a Christian. They want to know if it is true we eat human flesh and drink human blood. One day one of the beggars who frequents the marketplace hobbled over to me on his crutch and pointed to his twisted foot. 'Here Christian,' he said, 'touch my foot and heal me. Give me a miracle in the name of Jehoshua the Magus.'"

"The Jews in the marketplace are even worse. They hate us – ask Father. They say no respectable Jew would ever worship an executed criminal such as Jehoshua. His miracles they describe as tricks that any well-trained magus could perform. That is why he went to Egypt when he was my age – to learn how to perform magic. Even Master ben Adam – he is a good man, the one who is teaching me to read and write Hebrew – he says Jehoshua was a fraud. He could not be the Anointed One he claimed to be, because he is not of the Jewish tribe of David. He is from some other tribe in Galilee. Their scriptures are very clear on this point."

"I have nothing to say to any of these people. I didn't ask to be a Christian – you and Father decided that. When people ask me where Jehoshua was born, or who his mother was, or where he learned to read, I just remain silent rather than make a bigger fool of myself than I already am. I cannot quote from the Hebrew scriptures to prove that Jehoshua fulfilled some prophecy or another. No one has any proof he was resurrected. Even Paulus tells us we just have to believe this without proof – with him it is always about having faith, faith, and then more faith, because nothing about Jehoshua is proven and most of it makes little sense."

"You asked me about girls. I cannot even meet girls or talk to them. Do you know Jael, the girl who lives two streets down from us? She is telling all her friends that now that I am a Christian I have been circumcised. No girl in Corinth will have anything to do with me now that they think that of me. They all view me as no better than a barbarian to have allowed myself to be cut up that way. What am I supposed to do? Unclothe myself so that they will all know the truth?"

Alcaeus had adopted a more and more doleful look with the telling of each of these stories. Chrysanthe had matched him look for look; she had no idea he had been suffering so because of their small community of Christians. Alcaeus was right. She had isolated herself for too long from Corinth and the outer world.

Chrysanthe had taken to running her fingers through Alcaeus's hair, out of old habit. It seemed to keep him calm. "You are right, Alcaeus. I have been too much involved in our little community. I had no idea such things were being said about you or said to you." She stopped and looked down at her feet, her mind racing with ideas. We must fix this, Crispus and I, she said to herself. The question was – how?

"Aren't there any girls in our own community who interest you? What about Chloe's daughter? Or that other girl – Rebekah – she is younger still, but I've noticed the way she looks at you."

"The girls at the Assembly are all the same, Mother," he responded. "They all act like mice; too shy to approach me without permission from their family. If you do try to talk to them, they have nothing to say. They know nothing of the marketplace, of the affairs of men, of what happens in Corinth – much less anything of the outside world. Olympias knows vastly more than they do. How could I make a life with these sort of women? You and Father educated all of us, even though some people I know criticize our family because Olympias and Theodosia are being taught to read and write just as if they had been young boys. They say it is not right what you are doing, but I say it is. I know it is. If you took away learning now from Olympias she would just shrivel up and die."

"I'm sorry, Mother, but the girls in our community would make miserable wives. As for Rebekah – she is expecting her parents to arrange her marriage for her, and that will be to a Jew without doubt. Though who knows? Now that everyone thinks I am circumcised, maybe I am now eligible!"

Chrysanthe laughed a little at his joke. It was good to see he was returning to his normal ways. It had been many months since she had seen him in such a mood. Now, though, the thoughts were coming into her mind so fast that she had no time to analyze them. Maybe Crispus could say something among his friends about the terrible rumor that Jael was deliberately passing along to other girls. Crispus would know how to handle something this delicate. How exactly was Chrysanthe going to extricate herself from her isolation? She knew no one else in Corinth outside of her community. Maybe Crispus could introduce her to the wives of some of his business associates.

And what about Olympias and Theodosia? It was true what Alcaeus said about their learning to read and write. Chrysanthe knew the gossip that others said about her for allowing her daughters to be educated. She had never cared. Her own parents had brought her up in the same way, and she could not imagine living in a world of darkness, not knowing how to read, dependent on others to guide her through the world. She could never take that gift away from her daughters, but Alcaeus had opened her eyes to the cost such privileges carried. Wouldn't both Olympias and Theodosia go through the same doubts and struggles that were now troubling Alcaeus? It might be worse, in fact. They will definitely have trouble finding husbands who are open enough in their thinking to want a wife who is educated.

"Alcaeus," she said, "it has been too long since we've talked like this. I've spent so much time worrying about you becoming an adult that I did not realize you already are one. I've been thinking ever since last night that you might be breaking up our family, but I realize now from what you have said that you might be saving it instead. You've alerted me to what could very well happen to your two sisters a few years from now. Your father and I need to be prepared, just as I need to think about our community and our Assemblies. I always assumed that what your father and I enjoyed within the community of Christians would be something our children would naturally want to follow. I see now it is going to be more difficult than that."

"But tell me, Alcaeus," – and here it was Chrysanthe's turn to position herself so she was facing him directly – "do you really want to pursue these activities with the Temple of Dionysos? I won't stand in your way, and I'll see to it that your father will not either. Still, is there nothing in what you have learned about Jehoshua and The Way that appeals to you?"

"I don't know enough, Mother – I need time to find out. I can tell you that I felt very much alive last night during the ceremonies in a way I've never felt at an Assembly. It felt natural to me to use my mind and my body in worship. Of course father was right – it was exciting to be around all those young women – to feel their hands on my arms and chest; who wouldn't be excited by that? But it is not all physical – you have to open up your mind to new ways of thinking."

"Mother Sophia talks about new and old ways of thinking. I felt for the first time like a Greek, connected to our ancient past and our sacred ways. I don't feel this way during our Assemblies. I feel out of place, as if I am supposed to be a Jew following rules in their ancient scriptures, which I can barely read. As I also said, there is so much about Jehoshua's life I cannot explain and questions I cannot answer. It is not like us Greeks to let questions like that go unanswered."

"Then Alcaeus," said his mother, "take your time to find things out. Perhaps you will look at our community of Christians in a new light. Perhaps you will find some answers that will help us. I do know one thing – I have missed these conversations, but now it has gone beyond that. I need these conversations. You are a young man now. You have things to teach me. I understand now that I too am out of place in my life, having cocooned myself in our little community with no awareness of what was happening with my own son. I hope you will continue to open up to me."

"Of course I will, Mother." Alcaeus took the opportunity to run his hands through her hair, as he used to when he was a young boy. Her hair was unkempt at the moment, but the sensation of softness that he remembered was still there, and there was not a gray hair to be seen. "But let us not move too fast on this idea that I am a complete adult now. I like the idea of sometimes being a boy and not a man. Do you know what I miss? Do you remember in late summer you would squeeze apples and make this juice with mint leaves and other spices? It was my favorite thing of all, and I would sip it slowly as if it was nectar from Mount Olympus, and you would read to me. Do you remember that?"

Chrysanthe had completely forgotten about those little rituals; it had been such a long time ago. Why had they stopped? She did not know. She was about to answer that she would be delighted to do that again, when Alcaeus went into another topic.

"I've been very bad to Father, haven't I?" Alcaeus was caressing his knees and rocking forward and backward a bit – a habit he had when he was nervous. "Here I am talking about our Greek traditions and wanting to honor them, when I have violated one of the most sacred of them all."

Chrysanthe felt now was not the moment for her to give advice. She had to trust her instincts that Alcaeus would do the right thing given his upbringing, and she had to stand by her statement to him that he was a young man now, entitled to make his own decisions.

Alcaeus stood up. "Let us go home Mother." He led her quietly back to the house and stood for a minute at the doorway upon opening it. Crispus had poured himself a cup of wine and water, something he rarely had except on special occasions or at the ceremonies during an Assembly. He seemed to need it now to calm himself.

"Father, I need to apologize to you. I did not behave as a son should." Alcaeus spoke softly and remained standing at the threshold. Crispus turned his cup about in his hands. He appreciated the apology from Alcaeus, but it was after all no more than his due. A son should never criticize his father or raise his voice to him. All this time Crispus had been thinking of an old Greek saying – "As you are to your father, so your son will be to you." Crispus had never spoken to his own father in a disrespectful way – not that there weren't times when he wanted to. It was just something young men never did, or if they did, they received a physical beating to remind them of their manners. He had never done anything to warrant this sort of treatment from his own son. Well, if this was the way Alcaeus was going to treat him, then the gods – no, no, the Father in heaven – would punish him. He would wind up with a disrespectful son or two of his own.

Olympias and Theodosia had heard Alcaeus come in and they peeked quietly from the curtain that covered the bedroom door. They saw their mother move over to their father, but then Alcaeus saw the two of them spying on the conversation. "Olympias – Theodosia – could you come in for a minute please," instructed Alcaeus. "I have something to say." The two girls edged into the room, but Theodosia eventually couldn't resist running over to her brother and holding his hand.

Alcaeus stood up a bit taller and elevated his voice as if he were speaking to someone in the marketplace. "Father, I owe you an apology. I was disrespectful to you. A son should never speak that way to his parents. And I should not have left the house without telling you where I was going. I see that now. This is not the Greek way, and it is not the way you have raised us."

Alcaeus looked over at his mother and added, "nor is this how Jehoshua taught us to behave. You are perfectly within your rights to punish me."

Crispus was now mollified. This was a worthy apology – one that a grown man would make to another. He could almost be proud of Alcaeus, but he was still troubled and disappointed in his actions of the past two days. Nevertheless, a worthy apology was deserving of a worthy response.

Crispus stood up from the table. "I accept your apology, Alcaeus. You are right – you should be punished. And your punishment will start with explaining to me what has been going on in your life that has caused you to abandon our community and fracture our family. But we will not do that here. You and I should head down to the marketplace. It is almost time for our mid-day meal. I think we should go to that one tavern you like – the one that serves mussels in a red sauce with the fried squid that you enjoy. I will buy you some wine too."

Chrysanthe could see that her husband was going to need some quick explanation of what she had learned about Alcaeus from her talk with him – particularly of the vile stories that Jael was spreading about him. "You could use a fresh tunic, Husband, if you are going down to the marketplace," said Chrysanthe, as she ushered Crispus into the bedroom. It would give her an opportunity to have a short conversation with him.

Olympias came up to Alcaeus and joined her younger sister. "What has been going on, Alcaeus?," she queried. "What is all this about you and a temple and secret initiation ceremonies. I want to know everything. I want every detail."

Alcaeus laughed. He lifted Theodosia up in his arms. "I will tell you everything you need to know. And you will not need to know everything. But it can wait for later." With that he kissed Theodosia and set her down. He repaired to his little bedroom off from the kitchen – an alcove that had been assigned to him when he grew too old to share a room with his parents.

His spirits were much higher now. The conversation with his mother had cleared the air of many things that were bedeviling him. His impulse to apologize to his father had been correct; he could see that in the way his father treated him like an adult in return. He had thought it would cost him nothing to say those words, but he was wrong. It was much harder to speak them out loud than to practice them in his mind as he was walking back to the house. Alcaeus had already met some men in the marketplace who could speak fancy words and act as if they believed everything they were saying.

Alcaeus was not like that. He had to speak not only what was on his mind but what was in his heart. In his heart he knew what he had said to his father was hurtful and that he had broken a fundamental rule of the family. That is why he invited his sisters into the room; this was a family matter that deserved a hearing before the whole family.

In due course, over a dish of mussels and squid that was one of his favorite pleasures at the marketplace, he would learn that it was the act of bringing Olympias and Theodosia into the room to hear his apology that truly impressed his father. Yes, what Alcaeus said was proper and noble – the words of a man whom others would come to respect. But the fact that Alcaeus chose to bind the family closer lifted a burden from Crispus that he had not known how to solve. That was the moment Crispus realized his son was not lost to him after all. That was the conversation that marked for Alcaeus the moment when he knew his father considered him an adult – someone who could help with the family and not merely be a part of it.

Chapter Eleven

hrysanthe thought she would first consult with Chloe. Chloe was her oldest friend – the person who had introduced her to the community of Christians. They were the same age and had found themselves growing middle-aged on the same path in life, watching their children mature, hoping they would find a suitable match in marriage, and eventually bringing grandchildren into the family.

Chloe had aged far less gracefully than Chrysanthe. Her hair was a mottled and often uncombed mass of gray and white strands, and her skin had not held up well over the years. She looked considerably older than Chrysanthe, even though in truth she was a year younger. She owned only two dresses, as far as Chrysanthe could tell, and her robe was an interesting collection of patches and repairs in whatever loose bit of fabric she could muster. They were sewn on with relative indifference by Chloe – she was in fact so unmindful of her harlequin appearance that some of the children in the community would make rude comments that she belonged on the stage of the theatre as one of the clowns.

Those children would be promptly scolded by their parents, and for good reason. Chloe may have been neglectful of her own appearance and even her own physical problems, but she was completely dependable when it came to taking care of the community's sick and elderly members. She had volunteered years ago to take command of the Christian community's efforts on behalf of the dying, her way to repay what she saw was an enormous debt she owed to the community. She had sought out the Christians in the first place because she was searching for an answer about what to do with her aging mother, who had lost her memory nearly completely and required constant monitoring, feeding, and bathing. Chloe had just had her first child, and her husband, although he was a municipal official, did not make enough money to afford more than a small three room apartment.

The Christians offered to watch her mother for her during the daytime, as long as Chloe paid a small fee for the cost of food.

Eventually, once Chloe was more trusted by the community, she agreed to be baptized as a member, and one of the members who had the space and time took her mother in to their own home. At this point Chloe's mother no longer recognized her own daughter or anyone else, and while Chloe missed her deeply, it was the first time she could concentrate fully on her baby and her husband. It was, she said, a blessing from the Father – something that no temple on heights of upper Corinth would do for her.

This was the beginning of Chloe's debt to the community, one that she felt was life-long, and one she cheerfully met by volunteering to help other Christians with similar problems. She had arranged permanent space in the community center for the sick and the dying, and she kept a list in her mind of Christians willing to provide assistance. Most members were on that list, cajoled or either shamed, by Chloe's constant reminders that one day they too would need such help. It was a potent argument.

Chloe's husband had little if anything to do with the Christian community. He was responsible for the slaves who collected and carted off all the garbage that accumulated daily in a city the size of Corinth. This was important and in many respects a distinguished job, because for one thing his department never touched human waste – that was the work for criminals and barbarian slaves who had no hope of ever purchasing their freedom. In addition, her husband had to work regularly with the Roman administration, which took an obsessive interest in all things having to do with municipal services, such as water supply, maintenance of the baths, road repairs, sewage and garbage disposal, and the lighting of torches and lamps at night.

With her husband preoccupied until late in the evening on most days, Chloe found herself orienting her time and that of her children around the Christian community. She had come to rely on Chrysanthe for friendship, for her steady emotional character, and for her common sense ideas. It was a surprise, therefore, to have Chrysanthe visit her one morning distraught and as poorly groomed as she herself always was.

"It's Alcaeus, Chloe. We don't know what to do with him. At first we thought he was going to leave our house forever and we would never see him again. Now it appears he will stay but have nothing to do with our community of Christians and will not be attending our Assemblies. He says there is no girl involved, but I don't trust those women in the temple. A young man doesn't always know his own heart and can become infatuated with a girl overnight. These women, on the other hand, know exactly what they are doing and may be slowly luring him into their cult."

Chloe had risen and poured a glass of water into a mug for Chrysanthe. She also handed her a linen handkerchief – in her line of work with the elderly and their families she learned that having a supply of these handkerchiefs available at all times was important. "Chrysanthe," she said, "you have to remember I know nothing of what you are talking about. Take some water and rest a minute, and then let us start over from the beginning."

It took more than one handkerchief for Chrysanthe to gain control of her emotions. She had been sensible and calm when dealing with her son and even more so when handling Crispus, whose anger could easily have spiraled out of control. Now she could no longer suppress her own emotions. Chloe was very skilled at letting people in acute personal distress take their time to master their emotions, and for Chrysanthe, she had all the time in the world.

As the tale unfolded of Alcaeus's changing behavior and of the nocturnal ritual involving the worship of Dionysos, Chloe found herself increasingly sympathetic to Chrysanthe's plight. She thought to herself, "What parent wouldn't want to do anything possible to save their child from falling into the control of these temple parasites, who do nothing but feed off people's ignorance and superstition? And this girl – Jael – what a streak of cruelty she must have inside her. Young men like Alcaeus are both proud and insecure at the same time, and this girl has put him in an impossible position."

Chloe asked what it was Chrysanthe had decided to do. "I cannot interfere with Alcaeus's decisions," responded her friend. "I gave him my word, and I must trust to his good sense and his upbringing. Crispus said he would give some thought about ways to deal with the accusations of that young girl, Jael. But I don't know what to do about Olympias and Theodosia. They are even more vulnerable than Alcaeus to the slanders that will be said about them as they grow older. We haven't done enough to prepare them as adults, and the result will be they will abandon what we have taught them about Jehoshua."

Chloe, in working with the elderly and the sick within the community of Christians, had come to hear more about the outside world than Chrysanthe ever did. "Let me guess what is being said," replied Chloe. "Jehoshua cannot really be the Jewish Meshiach. He does not fulfill the prophecies contained in Jewish scriptures. None of the usual omens existed at his birth that would provide proof of his royal lineage. His miracles were tricks meant to fool the ignorant – the work of an ordinary magus. He was condemned as a criminal by the Romans and died shamefully. There is no proof he rose from the dead. We Christians here in Corinth are credulous simpletons for believing such things, and we are not true Greeks because we follow barbarian practices such as circumcision. I have heard all these things about us, and worse, Chrysanthe, from Jews, from Greeks, and even from Romans."

Chloe poured more water out for both of them and continued. "I think the problem does indeed start with providing answers to questions about Jehoshua's birth, his miracles, and his death. You and I cannot answer many of these questions, which is why you are so frustrated, as is Alcaeus. I think the person to help us is Hannah. We need to discuss this situation with her and develop some solutions."

Hannah was at least fifteen years older than either Chrysanthe or Chloe; she was considered one of the most distinguished women in the Christian community. Her husband Moses was an enormously wealthy man who had made his fortune developing and operating a shipping fleet that brought goods back and forth between Greece and Egypt. He was the largest provider of Greek olive oil to Egypt, and the largest provider of Egyptian wheat to Greece. He was respected in the marketplace for his fair dealing and was the only Jew admitted to the council of magistrates which controlled the political life of Corinth. Anyone who had extensive dealings with Moses ben Hezekiah knew that his wife Hannah was an equal but behind-the-scenes partner in his business successes.

She was at the moment in Thessaloniki negotiating the purchase of several hundred amphorae for use in shipping olive oil and wine. When she returned in several days, Chrysanthe and Chloe met with her after the Assembly service. "Certainly I can review what the prophets say about the Meshiach in our scriptures," said Hannah in response to Chloe's question about the birth of Jehoshua. "There are many references in Isaiah to the coming of a Meshiach, but the prophecy that is most problematic comes from the writings of Daniel. I remember discussing this with our local teacher, Master Zibia. He said Daniel was very specific – the Meshiach will be from the house of David. Jehoshua was born in Nazareth and could not have been of the house of David."

"Excuse me, Sister Hannah," said Chrysanthe – she preferred to use a respectful term for a woman who was much older than her and also very distinguished in the community. "How do you know Jehoshua is not from the house of David? Just because his family settled in Galilee does not mean he was born there. After all, there are stories of his spending time as a youth in Egypt. Why could he not have been born somewhere else – wherever the city is that those from the house of David usually reside?"

Hannah rubbed her chin with her hand. "I suppose it is possible. We have no firm information. I remember Simon Petros, once when visiting us and talking about Jehoshua to our Assembly, said that he referred to himself occasionally as the Son of Man. That is exactly how Daniel described the Meshiach. Jehoshua must surely have known Daniel's descriptions of the Son of Man. I shall talk again to Master Zibia about this; maybe he can use his imagination and find a way to connect Jehoshua to the house of David. Still, I don't know how this helps your problem, Chrysanthe."

"I know exactly," interposed Chloe. "I have been thinking about Chrysanthe's problem with Alcaeus and the way he felt alive and excited during the ritual in the forest with the Dionysians. Why can we not do the same thing? I don't mean of course with the pagan use of sinful acts. I mean in a respectable way, for the children, so that they have the same feeling of reverence for Jehoshua that any Greek child would have for a Greek god."

"What do you mean exactly," asked Chrysanthe. "Are you expecting us to take the children out to the mountainside in the dark of night?"

"Of course not," said Chloe. "But there is no reason we cannot create something of that atmosphere at night, here in our own Assembly hall. It would take but a few oil lamps. We could create a story describing the birth of Jehoshua and provide the children an answer to the questions they inevitably are going to face. Some of the children could act out the parts of the story. Chrysanthe – you are an excellent writer – perhaps you would be willing to write out the story for the children."

Chrysanthe did not hesitate to agree. The idea had appealed to her the minute Chloe mentioned staging a theater of sorts for the children. Olympias and Theodosia would not only be receptive to something like this – Olympias might be eager to participate. "Sister Hannah, I could certainly use any help you can provide. I do not know the Jewish scriptures to answer some of these questions. I could then write out the parts for each child. In thinking about this, I believe my Olympias would be a good choice to enact the part of Miriam, the mother of Jehoshua. She is almost the right age for the mother of a first born child, and she reads Greek as well."

"I think she is an excellent choice, Chrysanthe," agreed Hannah. "I have watched her mature admirably these past few years. I wonder, though, whether in doing this we are forcing ourselves to 'pad the truth,' as they say. In answering the lies that are said about us as Christians, we do not want to create our own lies about Jehoshua."

"There are no lies to be created," said Chloe. "We know so little about Jehoshua in the first place. We are only asking to describe what has possibly occurred in his life, and we will tell this story only to the children. If there is anything exaggerated, we can always tell the children what it was when they are older and can understand better."

The three of them agreed this was an excellent plan. They set early spring as the time they should mount this play. That gave them a little more than a month to prepare. It gave them much to do, but they were all excited about the idea and eager for their efforts to succeed.

Crispus and other senior leaders of the community agreed to move the first Assembly in the spring to a later hour in order to take advantage of the darkness. Hannah had finished her work with Master Zibia and passed along to Chrysanthe some ideas regarding the birth of Jehoshua. She in turn felt these ideas to be useful but incomplete, and she realized that what the children would respond to best was a story, a narrative with a start, a middle section, and a satisfying conclusion. She worked hard to write out such a story, consistent with the facts given her, and elaborating only as she felt necessary. Olympias was enthusiastic about the idea of performing as Miriam. A boy slightly younger than she was chosen to play her husband, Yosef.

"We have no information about Jehoshua's real father," Chrysanthe had asked Hannah. "What should we do about this?" Hannah had already thought about this problem. "Provide him with a father nonetheless. Make him a tradesman or a farmer – something respectable. I would call him Yosef. It is a common-enough name in both Galilee and Judea. Besides, it was my father's name."

Yosef it was then.   Once she was finished with the script, Chrysanthe began schooling the children who were to perform before the Assembly. The children had to learn entirely by memorization, since none of them could read yet.   Only Olympias and the boy playing Yosef (whose father was also a scribe like Crispus and who wanted his son educated in this skill) were proficient at reading. Chrysanthe reserved the complicated dialogue for these two children.

Chloe was responsible for the costumes and was given substantial amounts of fabric by Hannah. Some of the fabric, intended for King Herod and members of the court, was quite sumptuous, but Hannah was a woman of means. What surprised everybody was Chloe's facility at designing and sewing the costumes, since her tatterdemalion appearance suggested she had no fashion sense whatsoever, much less any skill at sewing. Hannah began to think Chloe's problem was one of want, not of desire. She was determined to discreetly give her some fabrics for her own use once this production was over.

On the night of the performance Chloe lit several oil lamps positioned strategically throughout the room. The Assembly hall had a warm glow and more than enough light for everyone to see what was happening. The stage was set on the ground floor, and Chloe retreated outside of the building to manage the actors on their entrances. Chrysanthe acted as narrator, and when all the children were seated on the front benches, she began the performance.

Narrator: This is the story of the birth of a young baby boy. He would grow up to be very important, work many miracles, and then suffer a terrible death. He would triumph in the end by overcoming death through his resurrection. But that is in the future. Tonight we learn how he came into this world.

The ancient Jewish scriptures predicted the birth of this boy. It was written, "Behold! A young maiden shall conceive, and give birth to a son. His name shall be Jehoshua, and he will be the Christos – the Anointed One!" (Chrysanthe decided to use the Greek word Christos rather than Meshiach as it was easier for the children to understand – it meant the same thing.)

[Enter Miriam and Yosef, wearing ordinary robes of common folk. Miriam is obviously pregnant with child.]

Yosef: Miriam, my wife. I have received news that Quirinius, the Roman prefect, requires that everyone in Galilee and Judea register for the census. We must all return to the village where our tribe was established and record our names for the census.

Miriam: Yosef, my husband. I am very close to my time of birth. My tribe is that of David. I would have to return to the city where David was crowned king – to Bet-Lehem, which is a journey even farther than Jerusalem. How could I make such a journey safely?

Yosef: Do not worry, my wife. I will find a way for you to make the journey comfortably, even though we are poor. I will find a way for you to journey to Bet-Lehem without taking one step.

[Exit Yosef and Miriam.]

Narrator: As it was written in the Jewish scriptures, the Christos shall come from the House of David. So it shall come to pass!

[Enter Yosef and Miriam. Miriam is riding a donkey. Enter inn-keeper.]

(At this point laughter erupted throughout the Assembly hall. Everybody recognized Beulah, a neighboring donkey who could be heard at all hours night and day throughout this part of Corinth. The children especially squealed with delight as Miriam rode atop Beulah, making three rotations around the hall on her journey to Bet-Lehem.)

Yosef: Wife, we are now in Bet-Lehem. I have kept my promise to you and made you comfortable. Tonight we will find lodging and tomorrow we will register for the census.

Inn-keeper: [In response to Yosef knocking on an imaginary door.] If you are looking for lodging I cannot help you. All rooms in Bet-Lehem are taken as everyone is traveling here for the census.

Yosef: But I must find lodging. My wife is late with child and could give birth at any time. Please help us!

Inn-keeper: I can only offer you a place to sleep in the stable. It will not be very warm and you will have to sleep with all the barn animals. I am sorry it is all I have.

Narrator: And so Yosef and Miriam went to sleep in the stable. That night Miriam gave birth to a boy and named him Jehoshua. She wrapped him in a cloth and lay him to sleep in the manger used by the animals for feeding. This fulfilled the Jewish prophecy: the Christos shall be born in poverty, though he will one day be a king.

(Miriam and Yosef arranged themselves around the baby Jehoshua. The smaller children were invited up to see the baby, which Chloe had cleverly arranged as a doll with sleeping eyes and short black hair. Once the children were back in their seats, a boy entered the hall with a lighted torch, which illuminated the room enormously. He stood close to the manger.)

(Beulah unfortunately was terrified by the lighted torch and brayed anxiously. She had otherwise been very well behaved up to this point, not even soiling the floor in any way, but Chloe sent someone in to escort her out of the hall.]

[Exit Yosef, Miriam, and the Inn-keeper. Enter King Herod, arrayed in a robe of golden silk, with a splendid gold crown. Herod is followed by his three advisers.]

(Hannah outdid herself by buying expensive silk for the gown and commissioning the local tinsmith to make a shiny gold crown. None of the children had ever seen anyone wearing robes and a crown so resplendent and so realistic.)

King Herod: My advisers – what is that bright star shining in the sky? [King Herod points to the torch.] I have never seen anything like it. It must foretell the future in some way.

Advisers: O King! We are your magi – famous for our ability to perform miracles and see the future. We have consulted among ourselves and agree that such a sign in the heavens only occurs when a new king is born.

King Herod: But what new king is this? I am the only king, and my son is to be the king after me. There can be no other king. I command you to find this newborn king and bring news of him to me!

[Exit King Herod. The advisers walk slowly about the hall, as Yosef and Miriam reenter and position themselves over the manger with the baby Jehoshua. The magi approach Yosef and Miriam.]

Advisers: Hail! We are magi for King Herod, who has commanded us to find the newborn king foretold by this star. The star has led us to this stable, where we find you and your son.

Miriam: We know nothing of the future and do not understand how our son could be destined to be king. As you can see, we are poor people, come to Bet-Lehem to enroll for the census.

Advisers: The portents cannot lie. Your son shall be a great king one day, and as a magus greater even than any of us, he will perform miracles that will astound all who see or hear of them. Allow us to anoint him as a king.

Miriam: If you believe him to be a king, you may anoint him as a king. [One of the magi places sacred oil on the head of the baby.]

Advisers: King Herod has asked us to report to him about the baby. He professes to desire to honor the baby, but we suspect what he really wants to do is send his soldiers to kill your son. Your whole family is in terrible danger. You must flee tonight.

Miriam: What is to stop King Herod from finding us in Nazareth? If he is truly intent on killing our son, there is no safe place for us in either Judea or Galilee.

Advisers: You must flee to Egypt. There your son can learn from the great magi of Egypt. We see that you are too poor to travel such a long distance. Therefore accept these gold coins from us to help you on your journey and in your new home. We will prevent King Herod from learning where you have gone.

[The boy with the torch leaves the hall, followed by Yosef, Miriam, and the Advisers.]

Narrator: This ends our story about the birth of Jehoshua. He was born into a poor family from the house of David, thus fulfilling scripture and prophecy. He was anointed king but not a king of this world. Instead he is a king of all creation, living in heaven now with his Father.

The actors were invited back to the front of the hall to receive the applause of the entire Assembly. Many members of the community came up to Chrysanthe, Chloe , and Hannah to congratulate them on their work. One woman who was visiting from Ephesus was so enthusiastic about the performance that she insisted Chrysanthe send her a written version of the play. The parents of the young children in the front rows were especially grateful for the clever way complicated ideas were simplified for the children. Olympias was standing at the center of a circle of her own admirers.

"I certainly hope this helps her in the future, growing up in a world that can be hostile to Christians," said Chrysanthe to her two colleagues. "I am sure it will," replied Chloe. Hannah nodded in agreement, but she thought to herself that sometimes more direct measures are needed to help children cope with the pressures of life. She just might need to quietly intervene with some direct measures of her own.

Alcaeus was standing in a corner talking to Rebekah, the very girl he thought would have no interest in him. They were laughing about something that occurred during the drama. Chloe asked Chrysanthe whether his problem with Jael had been solved. "He solved it with the help of a friend. These young men occasionally go to the Roman baths, and he asked one of them who certainly knew the truth about his personal situation to spread the story among Jael's friends that Alcaeus was every bit a man as any unmarried Greek girl could desire. Jael was made to look very foolish as a consequence."

Hannah took Chrysanthe aside for a private comment. "I am very proud of you, young lady (Hannah was not averse to calling even middle-aged women 'young ladies'.) But heed carefully what our guest from Ephesus requested. A written version of this drama could prove dangerous – it might mislead people. Even adults cannot sometimes distinguish between fancy and fact."

"I shall certainly consider your concerns, Sister Hannah," she said. But in her mind, Chrysanthe had already decided that as many parents as possible in other communities needed to understand the problems their children were having as Christians. Besides, in the Roman and the Greek world, women were not allowed to be writers or scribes or even scholars, except perhaps as poets. Christian women needed to show that in their world, women were allowed to be the equal of men in many things. Chrysanthe had not gone to all this trouble to educate Olympias and Theodosia to step back now into the shadows. She would write out this drama and send it to the communities in Ephesus, Thessaloniki, Athens, Antioch, Alexandria – why, even Rome itself.

Chapter Twelve

annah's silver-tipped cane was almost useless on her climb up the Acrocorinthos to the summit. She rarely ventured anymore to the temple district of Corinth – not at her age, and with the soreness in her knees and ankles that made walking so difficult. She could easily afford to hire bearers to carry her up her in a palanquin, but then Moses might find out, and she wanted to accomplish this task on her own. Here she was, in any event, at the door of the house of the Dionysian order. She gave a small coin to the young boy who helped her find this place and then rapped twice on the door with her cane. She announced herself to the attendant as Hannah, wife of Moses ben Hezekiah, and stated that she desired a meeting with Mother Sophia. She was led to the inner courtyard with its fountain and lemon trees and sat in the same chair that Crispus had used months earlier. Like Crispus, Hannah was surprised at the largeness of the space and the luxuriousness of the surroundings. The Dionysians must have purchased several apartments and reconfigured the space into this country villa in the center of ancient Corinth, thought Hannah.

She detected curtains fluttering in the rooms off to her left; clearly someone was spying on her, trying to figure out why she was there. "May I help you?" asked a voice to her right, startling Hannah for a moment since she had heard no one approach. "I am Mother Sophia. Welcome to our home." Hannah stood up and gazed fixedly at her adversary. Mother Sophia was adorned in a cream colored linen robe with subtle pink and green flowers embroidered in the fabric. She had matching slippers on, allowing her to glide quietly along the floor, and explaining her sudden appearance.

"May I?" asked Mother Sophia, and almost instinctively she reached out to Hannah's necklace, fondling several of the large blue stones, mottled with white. "Lovely – lapis it must be," she said almost to herself, before letting go of the necklace. Hannah had not misjudged this woman. She herself rarely wore her lapis necklace and her matching robe of rough blue silk, but she deliberately chose this ensemble for this interview with Mother Sophia, and she was delighted with the result. Very few women gave more than passing attention to this necklace, which Moses had bought for her on a business trip to Rome. A member of the imperial family was in need of money and had been discreetly shopping these gems to potential buyers. Moses had the means to purchase the necklace, which he felt was very attractively priced by a desperate seller, and time had proven him correct. Tiberius was said to have been furious when the necklace left the imperial family, and among those with a knowledge of fine jewelry, it had become legendary as the property of a wealthy Greek businessman.

"It was supposedly brought back by Alexander himself," informed Hannah to Mother Sophia. "The stones are large and rare, coming only from a mine in the high mountains east of the great Arabian desert – the very point where Alexander chose to end his journey and return to civilization. But I am not here to talk about trifles." Hannah used the word "trifles" deliberately; she could have gone on longer about the necklace, how ancient pharaohs would pay a fortune for but one of these stones, and how it was likely this single necklace could purchase the entire villa she was sitting in several times over, but she wanted Mother Sophia to know a necklace of this rarity, reserved only for royalty, was but a small thing to herself.

"I am here to discuss a matter of some personal interest to both of us. If you do what I tell you, it may allow you to continue in your role here as head of this religious order. If you do otherwise....." Hannah left the uncertain ending to that sentence up to the imagination of Mother Sophia, whose smile had quickly transformed itself into a momentary sneer – a slight turning down of the mouth that Hannah detected immediately. Mother Sophia was clearly not used to being told to do anything by anybody. She had quickly divined that Hannah was here on an antagonistic mission. She took a seat opposite her and waited to hear what she meant by her threat.

"While this is our first meeting, I have known you for a long, long time," continued Hannah. "You may have heard of my husband, who has been in the shipping business for many years. We came across you when we bought our first vessel and hired our first crew. Men on long sea voyages have only one thought on their mind when arriving at port, and that is to find the nearest brothel. In those days in Corinth, the nearest brothel was an establishment run by a woman named Eunike. I would watch this woman stand at the door and invite sailors into her business. I have an excellent memory, and I am not mistaken in stating that you are that woman. Of course we have both aged since then, but after all these years, I gather you have remained in the same business."

Mother Sophia ignored the deliberate insult. Her smile had long since deserted her. She pulled her shawl tightly over her head, as if she were hoping to appear demur and shy. "I make no secret of my background. My close friends here – and in the municipal government (these were words she emphasized) – know my history and they know how I have changed over the years. This conversation seems completely pointless if you have come here to insult me and then tell me things everyone already knows."

"Oh, I have come to tell you things hardly anyone knows," asserted Hannah. This certainly attracted Mother Sophia's interest – she yanked once again at her shawl over her hair. Hannah continued. "While my husband and I are Jewish, several years ago we entered into the worship of a Jewish prophet named Jehoshua and are now members of a group named Christians."

"I have noticed that sailors inevitably turn to questions regarding their immortal soul if they are at sea long enough – perhaps the daily risk of being overwhelmed by fate and swept down to the bottom of the sea forces their mind to focus on their own mortality. Now and then one of them – it is always one of the older men – asks to join our small group of Christians. We offer solace to those who fear for their soul after death – Jehoshua has shown us the way to eternal life and has conquered death. I see your slight smirk at this idea; I am not here to convince you one way or the other about us Christians."

"About a year ago one of these men named Neophytos, prior to his being baptized as a Christian, asked to confess to me a terrible sin of his youth. He said he was once in the employ of a woman named Eunike when she headed a brothel – that is to say, he was in your employ. His job was to lure other sailors to the business. One day you came to him and told him in confidence that a particular customer was giving you trouble. You later learned that this young man – Idaeus – had discovered that the brothel was also a location for smuggling stolen goods into Corinth, and he was seeking a portion of the profits as a price for his silence. You inveigled Neophytos into a plan to 'teach the young man a lesson.' Neophytos was shocked when he discovered the lesson was a permanent one. It was you who thrust the dagger into the back of Idaeus, delivering a fatal wound. Neophytos was given the task of disposing of the body to the bottom of the bay. He has kept his silence all these years, until he felt compelled to confess this crime to me."

Mother Sophia had maintained her composure throughout this recitation, but her nervousness was betrayed by the slight jiggling of her right foot. "This is a very fanciful story you are telling me, but it is only that. I have never known anyone named Neophytos. I have known many a sailor unhappy with my services for whatever reason and willing to tell any number of preposterous lies to damage my reputation. I assure you there is no one with any sense who would believe a word your friend is saying."

"Of course Neophytos knows that," replied Hannah. "That is why he saved the blood-stained clothes of the victim, along with your robe covered in blood – the very items he assured you had been burned. Your robe back then was very distinctive; I am sure any number of girls who were formerly working for you would recognize it. He has entrusted these appalling items to my care, where they are in a most secure place. Further, Neophytos has had a scribe take his testimony and put it to paper, registering it with the municipal officials responsible for last testaments. Finally, this man will offer to submit himself to torture by the Romans in order to provide convincing proof as to the truth of his statements. He has, you see, nothing to lose. He is old, and should he die under torture, he believes that will only serve as expiation for his participation in this crime."

Mother Sophia had blanched during these revelations. Her fidgeting extended now to her hands and her feet, both moving rhythmically under tension, as Mother Sophia thought through what she needed to do.

Everything Hannah had said was true up to the point of Neophytos keeping the blood-stained garb of Mother Sophia, writing out a final testament, and agreeing to submit to torture. Hannah had invented all of this, preparing to use it if he she felt Mother Sophia – Eunike in her previous life – was refusing to admit to her guilt. Mother Sophia's nervousness was, in Hannah's eyes, very close to a confession; any other woman of her position and stature would have objected heartily to these accusations and shown Hannah to the door.

"Your Christian community must be chronically short of funds considering how small you are. Perhaps our religious community can help yours," volunteered Mother Sophia. It was now Hannah's turn to smile; that statement was tantamount to a confession if ever there was one. "No, no! You misunderstand me. Our community is quite comfortable," Hannah informed her.

"What then is this sailor expecting? It is not that I am confirming anything of his wild tale, but I recognize an attempt at extortion when I hear one. What is he looking for?"

"He is looking for nothing," said Hannah. "It is I who am expecting something from you." Mother Sophia looked more perplexed than ever. "You recall recent visits from a young man named Alcaeus?" Mother Sophia nodded her agreement. Hannah continued. "Alcaeus and his family are members of our Christian community. His mother has promised him that as an adult he can become a member of the Dionysian temple if he wishes. However, he has two younger sisters. You and I here and now will come into an understanding, and I must put trust in your word. The Temple of Dionysos is to leave these two girls alone. Olympias and Theodosia will not be invited to any of your functions, even if Alcaeus extends the invitation. And I hope by the heavenly Father that Alcaeus will himself quit any association with your organization."

Mother Sophia began to giggle, and eventually laugh. Her body let out a long sigh of relief. She stood up and walked about the courtyard, laughing quietly to herself so that her fellow sisters in the private quarters would not hear her. "Oh you Christians!" she said to Hannah, standing in front of her and staring down from above. "I have heard stories about you, but I never imagined you would be so pious as to go to all this trouble to protect the 'innocence' of two young girls. Who would have guessed you would concoct such a fantastic tale to keep these two children from growing up and learning about the world outside of their sheltered existence?"

Hannah reached for her cane and struggled to get to her feet. Mother Sophia was prattling on and on about Christian credulity and naiveté; Hannah was content to let her play her game anyway she cared, as long as she agreed to Hannah's terms.

Mother Sophia walked over to Hannah and stood in front of her, another look of worry having crossed her face. She was still several inches taller than Hannah now that both were standing up, and she attempted to use this to her advantage, pushing her face as close to her accuser's as possible. "What is to prevent your so-called criminal Neophytos from making these baseless claims even if I agree to what you demand?" asked Mother Sophia. "And why should I agree to any of this if his testament resides with the municipal records? The testament will surely be opened upon his death, and I will still be subject to false testimony."

"The testament will be withdrawn from the public records tomorrow," replied Hannah. "You can have your agents check later in the day that this is done, since you have such excellent relations with our municipal leaders. I will hold on to the testament should there be any approach made by the Temple of Dionysos to Olympias or Theodosia. As to Neophytos' silence, you will have to accept my word that he will maintain his silence unless I release him from the vows he made to me when he made his confession." Hannah began fingering the stones of her necklace as she said these words, intending to show that her promises had the full backing of her wealth behind them. She counted on Mother Sophia's venality to understand this point.

"Very well, Hannah, wife of Moses ben Hezekiah. You have my assurances that your two virgin girls are safe from me or anyone associated with our Temple. I consider them entirely unworthy of the wisdom, beauty, and grace that comes to those who worship Dionysos. I expect in return to never again hear of you, of your friend Neophytos, or of these absurd accusations you have brought to me this morning. Allow me to help you to the door."

Hannah pulled herself away from the cloying grasp of Mother Sophia. "I can make my own way out – just open the door for me, please." Hannah did not bother to look back as she began walking away from the private home of the Dionysian order. She thought of the long and painful walk down the Acrocorinthos – a journey even more difficult than the climb up, considering the strain it would put on her knees. She thought a small prayer might be in order.

"Lord Christos. I beseech you, and through you the Father in heaven, to ease my journey home. I have not been entirely truthful today – I confess it. It was for the future of our small community here in Corinth, that it may prosper and that the fate of two young girls may be fortunate rather than desperate. I consider I have done very good work for you today. Very good work indeed."

Hannah reached the path leading down to the city. She looked out over Corinth, glistening white in the morning sun, and beyond it the limitless stretch of the azure sea. She once again fingered the stones of her necklace – the blue color was similar to that of the sea itself, as if somehow the stones had captured the vast ocean's essence within them. How peculiar, she thought, that something brought up from deep in the earth could match so easily another element altogether.

She realized that Moses might be worried about her absence, so she took the first faltering steps down the path to the city below. Quite to her surprise, her knees ached far less than when she was walking up the hill. This was entirely unexpected – it was always much more painful walking downhill. "Thank you, Lord Christos," she said to herself. This was a greater beneficence than she had ever anticipated before setting out on this mission. As a Jew, she knew well that the Lord God Yahweh had worked many marvels, but he had also demanded innumerable sacrifices and had never done anything like this for her. It reminded her of what attracted her to Jehoshua in the first place. Unlike Yahweh, Jehoshua had made an eternal sacrifice for her and all mankind – and he would grant personal favors if your intentions were honest and your faith was strong.

Too bad he wasn't a god, thought Hannah. He would tower over all those other gods and goddesses that the Greeks worship – even almighty Zeus himself. On the other hand, Paulus on his visits always mentioned to the Assembly that Lord Jehoshua Christos was up in heaven with his Father. Was not that the very definition of a god? It was all rather confusing to Hannah.

The walk down to the city was turning out to be positively enjoyable. The pain she had dreaded hardly existed, and she could turn her attention to the springtime flowers that edged the path and to the occasional vistas of the city below, the port, and the sea beyond. It had been many years since she had feasted on nature to such a degree.

"This little visit to the Dionysians will be our secret," she said in her mind, as if conversing with Lord Christos himself. "Chrysanthe need never know, but I will keep an eye on this Eunike just in case. There is a vileness in her that cannot be erased by the splendors of her home or the respectability of her position. I do not doubt that she will now pay more attention to our small community of Christians, and these pagan temples have substantial power. It doesn't take any gift of prescience to see that someday, perhaps soon, we Christians are going to come into conflict with the pagan religions and maybe even with Rome itself."

That day could wait for the future. Perhaps she and Moses would no longer be around to see such terrible times. She stopped and stooped down to pick a bluish flower, and then placed it in her hair. It complemented her necklace, she thought. Moses would be pleased, but not so pleased when he heard the details of her "adventure." He would, nonetheless, come around to her own point of view – Hannah was sure of that.

In fact, when all was said and done, she fully anticipated he would say to her: "You have done a very good thing, Hannah, my love!" That would be such a wonderful affirmation. Almost as rewarding, she thought, as she inhaled deeply the sweet odors of the forest, as this gift of natural incense that Lord Christos was offering to her now.

PART THREE

Ananus ben Ananias, following the death of his father Caiphas, now succeeds to the position of High Priest at the Temple. Two other events occur at the same time which conspire to hand unchecked power into the hands of Ananus. The first is the death of Gamaliel, the Nasi of the Sanhedrin and a protector of the small group of Jews now called the Christians, who worship Jehoshua of Nazareth as the Christos. The second is the death of the Roman procurator Festus. His successor, Albinus, must unexpectedly remain in Alexandria for several months before taking on his new role in Jerusalem. With no one to stop him, Ananus decides to continue with his father's policy of persecuting the Christians. He organizes a rump session of the Sanhedrin, orders the arrest of the Christian leader Yakov of Nazareth, and brings him to trial on capital charges. Protests from the Jews to Albinus at this arbitrary and illegal action by Ananus will eventually cost him his job as High Priest several months later, but not until he has done terrible damage to the group of Christos worshippers in Jerusalem.

Yakov

Jerusalem
Year 62

Chapter Thirteen

here was no comfortable way for Yakov to position himself on the prison cell floor. The cell housed two men at the most, but the Temple police had imprisoned four. Somehow, the three other men managed to sleep, but Yakov was restless over the uncertainty of their situation. Perhaps if he closed his eyes and thought of something more pleasant, something from his childhood. He slowly began to drift asleep and his dreams about Jehoshua returned. He remembered the time he and Jehoshua were caught in a fight with those neighborhood boys. They won that fight, but what were they fighting about? It was about their mother, wasn't it? ....

"Your mother is a whore!" Yakov looked back up the hill and saw Ehud shouting down at them. Ehud had taken to tormenting Yakov and his little brother, and he had attracted several other bullies to his sadistic pleasures. Ehud wasn't that much older than Yakov – maybe twelve or thirteen – but he strode about the town of Nazareth with a bravado that came from an innate sense of superiority. Maybe it was the fact that his father was a priest at the synagogue, and a Sadducee as well.

Yakov saw one of the boys reach for a stone. "Yesh! Get down!" he yelled to his brother. The first stone whistled past them as they both sought cover among the scraggly bushes on the hillside. Then a fusillade of stones followed, and Jehoshua was hit squarely on the back of his head. He began to cry, and then he cried even louder once he put his hand to his head and discovered he was bleeding. "Run on home!" Yakov instructed his younger brother; Jehoshua may have been eight years old, but he knew his way home. From where they were on the hillside they could even see their small mud dwelling on the outskirts of the town.

Jehoshua tumbled his way down the hill, crying at every turn. The two brothers had been through this routine several times now, and Yakov had learned he had to act quickly. The few goats that the family owned were beginning to panic, and Yakov didn't want to spend all afternoon rounding them up. Yakov looked about for a few choice rocks, dodging the stones that continued to rain down from Ehud and his friends. There was one of him and four of them, but he knew that didn't matter. He only had to hit one of them, preferably one of the younger boys, and they would all flee. He took careful aim, and on the third try he hit his mark: a gaunt little boy named Avram. He was more successful than he expected. The stone struck Avram directly on his mouth, and dislodged a few of his teeth. As Yakov anticipated, this sapped the courage of Ehud and his band, who began retreating back over the crest of the hill, but not before Ehud issued a final threat: "Wait until I tell what you and your bastard brother did to Avram! You and that whore you call your mother won't be staying around here any longer!"

Yakov looked about and began rounding up his goats. They hadn't gotten far, and he could see Jehoshua entering the stockade that was behind their house. It was too early to bring the goats in, but Yakov felt he had no choice: his mother was going to demand an explanation. He located his herding stick and began chasing down each goat, nudging it closer to the others, until they were all heading in a line to their pen. Yakov would have to set out some water and food to make up for the forage they weren't able to eat today, but that would have to wait until he tended to his mother.

He found Jehoshua sitting on her lap. She was daubing some liquid on his scalp; she had a professional understanding of lotions and salves and knew how to make them, though where she got her unusual plants was always a puzzle to Yakov. He assumed it was through her Roman friends, who Yakov felt were much more worldly than the people living in a backwater like Nazareth. "You should have seen Yesh, mother! He was like a real man out there." Jehoshua looked up at his older brother with a glint of satisfaction in his eyes. He had controlled himself enough to stop crying by the time he got back home, and as young as he was, the last thing he wanted was for his older brother to accuse him of being a baby.

"Yakov, he's only eight. He shouldn't be involved in fights or having to prove what sort of man he is. It was that Ehud ben Eliazar again, wasn't it?" Yakov nodded. "I think it's time I have a talk with his father," said Miriam. "I don't care how important he is in the synagogue. We have just as much right as anyone else to feed our goats on the hillside. I don't know what he is teaching his son, but we've done nothing to hurt them."

"They called you a 'or', Momma," said Jehoshua. "Then they started throwing stones at us." The pain that traveled over Miriam's face was instantaneous on hearing this. Yakov realized as well the sense of shame that his mother felt. He reached for Jehoshua's hand and pulled him off his mother's lap. "Go find your brother Simon, Yesh, and put out some food and water for the goats," Yakov watched Jehoshua head to the back rooms, seeking out Simon.

Yakov sat next to his mother on a small set of cushions in the outer room and held her hand. "These are things boys say to each other, Momma. They don't mean anything." Yakov knew he was lying, but it was the best lie he could think of at the moment. He was thirteen, and in a few years he would be an adult capable of moving out and starting a family of his own. He was already noticing young girls, and he had his eye on one in particular – Kediah – a raven-haired Jewish girl his age who lived a few houses away. But would her father consider him a suitable match, and how could he leave his mother and family in the first place? Ever since he could remember, he was the man of the household. There was never someone around he could call "Father," and he didn't know properly who his father was. For that matter, none of his brothers or sisters had any better idea of their father.

Yakov was also old enough to know exactly what "whore" meant. He didn't have an answer for the insults thrown at his mother and her family. He didn't know why men would be around their house for a while and then disappear. Nor did he know why he was the only one in the family with red hair, while his sister Judith had darker skin than all her other brothers and sisters. As if knowing what he was thinking, Miriam said, "I have had to raise all of you by myself. Of course, I would have preferred to have a man around, but your father died when you were very young, and it is not easy for a widow with children to find a new husband. I am sorry that the burden of being the father of the family has fallen on you, Yakov, as the oldest, but your strength has proven to be a blessing for the entire family. I am thankful for that every day."

A sense of warmth spread over Yakov's heart at hearing these words. He no longer felt like a child; he was an adult, with an understanding of the adult world, its possibilities, and responsibilities, and the secrets that adults seemed to carry with them. He had given up pressing his mother for any information about his father; for all he knew he was the son of a Roman named Pantera, just like one of the neighbor boys said, hearing it from his own father. He promised himself that one day soon he would ask his neighbors if this man Pantera had red hair like his own. Then he would know for sure.

His mother rose and began tidying up her lotions and scissors. The large public room of the house also served as his mother's work room, where she conducted her business as a hairdresser, and a client was due to arrive. Miriam was good at what she did, and she earned enough to support herself and five children. She had a special talent for arranging the complex hairstyles that were fashionable among the Roman nobility, not that there were very many such woman out in the far provinces. Many of the Roman officials who arrived in Syria or Cilicia or Judea came without wives, and it was common for military officers and mid-level administrators to find themselves a Jewish companion or wife. Still, it was surprising how many of these women eventually took on airs, taking their cue from the wives and daughters in the court of Herod Antipas. Herod had a preference for educating his children in Rome – which did nothing to ameliorate his reputation among the Jews as a Roman puppet – and many a time messengers would arrive at Miriam's lowly abode, requiring her presence in Caesarea to attend on one of the women at Herod's court.

This alone would have risked Miriam's being viewed by her neighbors as an outcast. Doing business with the Romans wasn't deemed simply as poor taste, considering that the Romans were conquerors whom many Jews detested. The problem was religious: the Torah had explicit prohibitions against association with

*outsiders, and what Miriam was doing fell into the sacrilegious
category. To make matters much worse, she did not confine her
business to women. Jewish and Roman men frequented her salon,
which instantly branded her as a "loose woman."*

No, Yakov did not have an answer to the jibes and taunts he
received from young men his age. "I need the money, Yakov,"
his mother would often tell him, and he certainly conceded in
his own mind that his mother was doing what was best for him
and the four other children. But her other explanation, that their
father had died, he knew to be a lie. She had given birth to his
two youngest siblings when Yakov was old enough to understand
that none of the men who were always around the house was
there long enough to be described as a father. The only "father"
in the household was Yakov himself, taking care of his brothers
and sisters when his mother was working, educating them in the
practice of goat-herding, and crafting simple toys to keep them
entertained.

And of the four other children, Jehoshua was by far the most
sensitive to the slurs that were beginning to meet him as he engaged
with the larger world outside his house. "Yesh is a deep thinker,"
Miriam would say, but that covered over the fact that Jehoshua
was a brooder, often lost in his own thoughts and uncomfortable
associating with people outside the family. Jehoshua would prefer
to sit silently in a corner, observing people as they went about
their daily business. When he was younger, his favorite moments
were spent in his mother's salon, unobtrusively listening to the
women gossip or the men talk about politics or the trouble they
were having with the women in their own lives. He was too old
for that now – people wouldn't talk to Miriam or ask her advice if
they realized someone was listening in and understanding it all.

He then began to frequent the synagogue in the center of Nazareth.
It was really only a synagogue such as existed in any small
Jewish town, but there were learned men there, and Jehoshua had
a propensity for learning. When Miriam realized what he was
up to, she entered into an agreement with one of the scribes to
teach Jehoshua to read Hebrew for a few coins a week. He took
to it rapidly, and began to explore the mysteries embedded in the
Torah, with its history of the Jews, its poetry, its tales of morality,
and its vengeful God. There was something not right about

this God – Jehoshua sensed it immediately. What God could possibly expect love and respect from his people if he was willing to treat them with cruelty imposed unexpectedly and arbitrarily? Jehoshua would get into arguments with his teachers and then with some of the priests at the synagogue, over the nature of God – someone so awesome that Jews were forbidden ever to say or write his complete name.

At least Jehoshua was developing the skills for a trade, thought Miriam. Scribes were well-paid and could rise up in society if they combined their language skills with a proper study of the law. Some of the scribes at the synagogue were considered the equal of any of the priests, and most of them married well. Jehoshua would be able to advance in such a profession, and he certainly had the love of knowledge to go far. Besides, it helped any family to have at least one member able to read and write – that way you couldn't get cheated on legal contracts.

Yakov agreed with this assessment except for one thing: he knew Jehoshua didn't have the temperament for such work. In his studies of the Torah Jehoshua was becoming entirely too moralistic, questioning why some of the laws laid down by Moses weren't being followed strictly by even the high priest of the synagogue, and questioning why many others had to be followed at all. Why didn't the synagogue police monitor what was being sold in the marketplace, to make sure customers weren't victimized by unscrupulous traders? For that matter, why was the marketplace allowed to function once a week in the outer courtyard of the synagogue? Wasn't the synagogue supposed to be reserved entirely to the worship of God? It irritated him as well that the priests focused most of their time on petty aspects of the law, such as what clothing to wear or food to eat, rather than teaching the people about proper moral attitudes and behaviors.

Then there was another problem. One day Jehoshua came back from the synagogue flushed, sweaty, and bruised from a fight he had gotten into with a merchant or a worshipper – it wasn't clear with whom he fought or what the fight was about. Yakov began to spend more time when he could watching Jehoshua at the synagogue, and he discovered his younger brother was not just a brooder. He was a smoldering mass of anger as well. He was very slow to anger, but when it happened, his fury erupted almost always with violence. Seeing several of these episodes, Yakov decided to take his brother aside for some advice. "Yesh, you cannot carry on this way as an adult. People are tolerating it less and less now that you are older, but once you are an adult no one will want to do business with you, and fathers will keep their daughters well-clear of your path. You have to keep your anger under control if you expect to succeed in life."

"I cannot control it," responded Jehoshua. "It controls me. It isn't even a part of me. It is like something separate or some separate person who does whatever he wants. Besides, the real problem is that he is always right. People need to be told if they are violating the law or disrespecting God, and sometimes the voice in my head tells me when others need to be taught a lesson."

Yakov sat silently, his mind off on another thought altogether, which was that when he was talking to his younger brother, he had the impression he was talking to a fully-formed adult. Jehoshua was mature to such a degree that people were surprised at first at what came out of the mouth of such a small boy, and then they quickly settled in to treating him like any other adult. More than one priest at the synagogue had remarked on this.

There was nothing more to be said on the topic. Jehoshua seemed either incapable of dealing with his anger or unwilling to eliminate this "person" from his real self. He did admit to Yakov that the best thing he could do about his anger was to avoid situations where he might be provoked into violence. This also meant he had to surround himself with people of "love" – whatever that meant. Yakov thought it might mean associating with meek or timid people, but over time Yakov understood it was altogether different. Jehoshua wanted people around him who loved him – and whose love he could trust. He began to develop a small following of young men, and occasionally a young woman daring enough to disgrace her father and mother by spending time with boys in public. They followed Jehoshua around wherever he went in Nazareth and increasingly on trips to the countryside. They doted on his every word – he was eleven by now – and as he was mature for his age, his followers felt like the adults they desperately wanted to be.

Miriam watched these developments with grave concern. She sensed that this was more than a young boy distancing himself from his family and growing into his own adulthood. Jehoshua was spurning his own family – rejecting them by spending little time at home and treating his new friends as a surrogate family. He was play-acting at being a father to these young people – a kind and loving father – the sort of father he never had. There was danger in this. Nazareth, and all of Galilee for that matter, was a conservative society. Jews valued family more than anything else, and a young boy who took other young people away from their family was a definite threat. "You have to promise me, Yakov, that you will watch over Jehoshua," pleaded Miriam. "He is young and he is naïve. He thinks he understands the world, but he has no real experience of the world. Promise me you will keep him out of trouble."

"Yes, Momma, I promise. I will watch over him. I will keep him out of trouble."

I will watch over him.

I will watch over him.

I will keep him out of trouble......

Chapter Fourteen

Yakov was jostled out of his slumber by one of his fellow prisoners, who had kicked him in the stomach while the both of them were trying to sleep. Yakov sat up. Everything ached – his legs, his knees, his back, his shoulders. His head was sore from sleeping on the stone floor without any pillow. How many days had they been in here? Two at least, maybe more. There was no window in this cell, and for a few minutes he was unsure if it was morning or nighttime. It must be morning; he remembered someone saying it was nighttime before he fell asleep, but of course, how long he was asleep he couldn't say.

He got up and looked out the slat in the door. There was a torch lit down the hall from their cell, but he otherwise couldn't see anyone or any hint of daylight. In the deep gloom of the cell he could barely see the three other prisoners, but he could certainly hear the snoring and their occasional grunts. They had one chamber pot to share among them, but the urge to use it was fading away, as the guards had not given them one morsel of food or one bowl of water since they were thrown into the Fortress Antonia. He was definitely thirsty, though not hungry. Surely Ananus couldn't begrudge them water?

Ananus could not possibly expect to get away with this – this incarceration of four of his "enemies," as he perceived them. One of the prisoners was the most prominent merchant at the Temple, another was a priest, and then there was Yonathan ben Ananus, a relative and also a member of the Sanhedrin, but he had somehow run afoul of his cousin's temper. As for Yakov – well, he was the leader of the Christian community, and that was all that needed to be said. Ananus had wanted to strike down the Christians for a very long time, and now that he was appointed High Priest, he had his opportunity. It didn't help that the Nasi Gamaliel had died the previous year, removing the last impediment in the Jewish establishment to Ananus' ambitions.

Still, none of that explained how he managed to take command of the Fortress Antonia. Yes, all of Jerusalem was waiting for the arrival of the new Roman Procurator, but he had been delayed several months, leaving Jerusalem leaderless. Ananus had increasingly been acting as a dictator, canceling meetings of the Sanhedrin, unilaterally raising fees for the merchants who paid for their stalls on Temple grounds, and now this. He had to have bribed someone – that is all that Yakov could determine. One of the centurions had to have accepted a bribe to allow the Temple police to take control of the jail cells in the Fortress. Ananus certainly had the money to make it worth someone's while to take such a risk, a flagrant breach of military discipline.

Now that he had jailed the four of them, what could he possibly do with them? Put them on trial? The Sanhedrin was still populated with Pharisees who loathed Ananus and had a clear majority of votes. Yakov knew they would not be bribed to permit a show trial that would endorse Ananus as a dictator for life – or at least until the Procurator arrived. Was he going to starve them to death, hoping that no one noticed or word didn't get out as to what he was doing? Yakov assumed most everyone in Jerusalem must know about them now. He had this terrible image of Kediah screaming when the Temple police rushed into the community center and dragged him away. It wasn't the image so much – it was the sound of her screaming that was in his head and wouldn't go away. Everyone up and down the street must have heard it. Surely Kediah was working with someone who could reason with Ananus or threaten him somehow, so that they could all be released.

Maybe it was still evening and not morning. He sat down again and rested his head on his chest. He had nothing else to do. Perhaps he should pray to the Father for deliverance from this place. Some people prayed to Jehoshua for favors, but Yakov couldn't imagine doing such a thing. Who prayed to their brother? His head bobbed up and down a little as he lost focus on what he was thinking about. Someone was speaking to him, but his voice was low. Or was he shouting? Yes, he was shouting! …..

"Yakov! Yakov, wake up." It was Lysander, in one of his angry moods again. *"You have to read this, Yakov. He has it wrong. I knew this would happen if someone who wasn't there started writing about Jehoshua. He's just like Saul."*

Yakov stretched his arms out and dangled his feet over the side of his cot. Now what was Lysander shouting about? He was waving a scroll in the air so it had to be something someone had written.

"Lysander, you have to start at the beginning. I don't know what you are talking about," said Yakov. Lysander poked a parchment scroll into Yakov's chest. "It's this scroll Marcus gave me to read. It's filled with errors. We have to put a stop to this sort of thing. Here – read the very ending and see for yourself."

Lysander nearly shoved the scroll into Yakov's hand and then grabbed it back from him and unrolled it from the ending. "Here – read this!" Yakov peered at the words, and then he gave out his usual excuse when it came to reading, which in truth was something he never learned to do well or with even modest competency. "Read it for me, Lysander. You know my eyes aren't as strong as they used to be."

After the Sabbath was over, Miriam of Magdala, Miriam who was the mother of Yakov, and Salome bought spices to anoint the body of Jehoshua. Very early that morning, at sunrise, they went to the tomb.

On the way they said to one another, "Who will roll away the stone for us from the entrance to the tomb?" for it was a very large stone. Then they looked up and saw that the stone had already been rolled back. So they entered the tomb, where they saw a young man sitting, wearing a white robe of much brightness —and they were afraid.

"Don't be alarmed," he said. "I know you are looking for Jehoshua the Nazarene, who was crucified. He is not here – he has been raised! Look, here is the place where he was laid to rest." And he pointed to the stone shelf on which Jehoshua had been placed. He then said, "Now go and give this message to his disciples, including Simon Petros. Jehoshua is going to Galilee ahead of you; there you will see him, just as he told you."

So they went out and ran from the tomb, distressed and terrified. They said nothing to anyone, because they were afraid.

'I assume, Lysander, that you are talking about this young man and his story that Jehoshua was now raised and was preparing to meet us all in Galilee?" asked Yakov. "That is only part of it,"

responded Lysander. "There are other exaggerations throughout his manuscript. They mount up and accumulate into real distortions. You have to do something about this."

Yakov thought a minute before replying. "Marcus does not live here, and our authority – or at least whatever authority I have – does not reach to Alexandria. We can try and persuade him to change some things and hope that he does, but you know I can't promise you he will do that."

"I know you can't force him to do anything," said Lysander, "but you would be a lot more persuasive if you had both Miriam and Simon Petros to back you up. Marcus is staying for a few more weeks in Jerusalem, but Simon Petros is leaving soon on his trip, so you have to act now if you are going to put a stop to this."

Yakov tried to hold back a yawn and hoped Lysander would not think he was disinterested in the problem. At the very least, he should have the rest of the manuscript read to him, and Miriam of Magdala and Simon Petros would benefit by joining him. He had no idea how many months Simon Petros would be gone, so Lysander was right in that respect – they should do something soon – today if possible.

"All right, Lysander. You find Marcus and see if he can be here at the community center this afternoon. I will go visit Miriam and Simon Petros and try to get them to join us." Yakov went off to find Kediah and explain the situation and the need for him to leave for an hour or so.

He was successful in freeing up Miriam, but only after she brought the two children over to her husband Javan's workshop where someone could watch them for the afternoon. She and Yakov went next to visit Simon Petros, who they found sleeping soundly. He was much older than both of them and did not bother to make any excuse for his sleeping habits. "I suppose I should read this manuscript, but I hope this doesn't turn into one of his arguments that Lysander likes to provoke over each word," said Simon Petros. Yakov thought the discussion was probably going to be more substantial than that.

The three of them found both Lysander and Marcus waiting for them, Marcus with a look on his face of confusion mingled with apprehension, as if he was being dragged before a tribunal. Yakov *tried to calm him down, and went over to him so that he could place a hand on his shoulder. "Marcus, we all appreciate what you are doing in creating a history of Jehoshua's work. No one is here to judge you. Lysander thought that you might benefit from our comments regarding some of the events you cover. That is all that we are offering to do here. Since this is your manuscript, perhaps you should read it out loud to us."*

They decided to go upstairs to the Assembly hall where they might find some quiet and privacy. Simon Petros put two benches together and lay down flat on them with his eyes closed; Miriam, Lysander and Yakov all decided to sit on the floor, while Marcus paraded back and forth in front of them, reading from his literary creation. It took well over an hour for him to complete his story, after which the group was silent for a minute or so. Lysander was about to say something, but Yakov motioned him to remain silent. It would be better if one of the others started the conversation.

Simon Petros sat up from his bench. "I was told we were to point out things that were not accurate. What I heard from your reading, Marcus, was not so much inaccuracies, but elaborations or exaggerations. For example, the story of the man with the withered hand. You make it sound as if Jehoshua touched him and his hand grew into a normal hand. That is not the way he worked his healings, and now that I have been granted some small capacity to help others in this way, I think it is important to describe what is really done. In this case, Jehoshua inspected the hand, and moved it about, and helped the man move his whole arm and shoulders in addition to his hand. He showed him how it could be more flexible if he moved his entire arm, and he asked him about pain. And he always ended with a prayer to the Father to help the person. That is how it worked."

"And then your story about our boat on the Galilee Sea. It was true that some of us were afraid to go on the boat because of the wind and the waves and the rain. But Jehoshua thought it would be safe, and he also looked up into the sky, as he often did when praying, and asked Aba for protection. He was right. Soon after casting ashore, the weather improved. We did marvel at that; I wondered if he had some special power granted him by the Lord God, and I may have said something like that to the others. It is

just that the way you put things, Marcus, makes the event sound much bigger than it was."

"And what about his comments that Jehoshua told you he was to rise up in three days after being crucified?" interposed Lysander, as a question to Simon Petros. "And Miriam," he added, "you have to tell Marcus that what happened at the caves was not the way he is describing things, with a young man there who told you Jehoshua would meet his followers in Galilee."

"Lysander is right, Marcus," said Miriam. "I don't think you and I talked about this on your last trip here, but we had gone to the caves because we thought the bodies might be there. At least someone said that. No one knew anything for certain, and to be honest we were afraid of being captured and killed. Everyone was afraid. But Salome said Jehoshua deserved at least to be properly cleansed and perfumed, so the three of us went to the caves at dawn. All we found was a caretaker, and he certainly wasn't young. He had heard about Jehoshua but had no idea if his body was there or not, and frankly, searching among the caves for dead bodies wrapped in burial cloths seemed pointless to me. We would never find him that way. The caretaker said something about maybe he had resurrected himself, and I thought he was making a joke – that was the sort of thing people were saying to Jehoshua on the way to Golgotha. I thought too that the man's mind was not right, that maybe he had a demon inside of him, and I wanted to get out of there. So did Salome and Miriam - the other Miriam besides me. She is no longer with us, but Salome is still here. You and I should meet with her, Marcus. She may have a better memory than I have."

"You see, Marcus! That is exactly the sort of thing I've been talking about. You've turned things around into a fantasy tale," said Lysander.

"If I told things your way, Lysander, no one would read my story. We writers don't work that way." Marcus thought briefly that he was puffing himself up too much by putting himself into the category of other writers, but Lysander was starting to anger him. "When you are telling the story of a man's life, then he is at the center of things. The story has to build up over time, to a satisfactory conclusion, and it has to tell a moral as well. There *has to be something in the story that improves the reader and forces him to want to read all the way to the end. This is very, very important. Jehoshua is the center of the story, and he is therefore the hero who has to triumph at the end. If you end the story with a few women meeting a deranged caretaker, you don't have a story at all."*

Marcus realized he was starting to sound like Philo, but that is perhaps because he followed Philo's advice and he had worked hard to build a story about Jehoshua that would excite people. In fact it took him years to write what he did – well at least years working on and off. And that was because he wasn't really a writer. He only started this project to impress Philo, and because he was honestly interested in Jehoshua as a miracle worker. Writing, however, took much more work than he was expecting. It wasn't that the words were difficult to conjure. What was difficult was to put the sentences in the proper order and to make things flow. When he finally got something he was happy with, Philo read it and praised it, though he asked for more emphasis on the hidden meanings behind Jehoshua's sayings. So Marcus obliged him and added instances where Jehoshua would instruct a follower or someone he healed to keep things secret.

He had honestly thought he had created something that would interest the reader and compel him to keep on reading. Why didn't these people see that? Didn't they want to have something that those who did not know Jehoshua would enjoy reading? Surely the miracles alone would be unusual material. How could Simon Petros criticize him for the way he presented the miracle of the man with the withered hand? Didn't he understand any Egyptian magus could manipulate a man's hand and make him feel better? Jehoshua had to be greater than those men in Egypt, or the story wasn't worth writing.

"I suppose then," said Simon Petros, "that you have Jehoshua tell me that he will rise in three days after he was crucified so that your ending will make more sense?"

"Precisely!" said Marcus. He was nearly shouting now, but at least he was reaching somebody in this room. "Those scenes set the stage, just as in a theater. The reader is expecting that the hero will at the end of the story rise up from the grave in triumph.

And to be honest, Simon Petros, you must admit when we talked last, which was several years ago, you said something like this happened. I am not fabricating events out of thin air."

"What happened, Marcus, is that Jehoshua would make hints to us, sometimes allusions to a resurrection. Things were never precise, and one thing you did get quite correct – he would tell us to keep secret these messages that were meant for us only. For example, he wouldn't say, 'In three days I will be with you again.' He would instead talk about Jonah in the whale, which we all know meant three days. And I don't think he was always clear in his own mind about the future. Sometimes he would say the End of Time was very near; other times he would say no one knows when the End of Time was to arrive, except for the Father."

"I guess the big difference is that I never had the clear impression he was going to be walking among us within three days after his death. I thought his spirit might return in some form, and that is exactly what happened – at least for me, and apparently later for Tomas and possibly even Saul. We all had clear visions of Jehoshua after his death. What you have written is something different – that he was literally going to walk in physical form with us in Galilee. If you need that to tell a story I don't know what to say – I'm not a writer. All I can tell you is my interpretation of things."

Miriam could see the look of hurt in Marcus's face as it was building up, and she thought he might be about to cry. That would not be an unmanly thing; Javan often cried, especially if something went wrong for him at his work. But she wasn't sure how the other men in the room would respond, and she thought people might be underestimating how much effort Marcus put into this story.

"It moves very well, Marcus," she said. "I don't know if I am using the right word, but it has motion. I truly did not want you to stop once you started reading your scroll."

Yakov decided to elaborate on this. "What I liked, Marcus, were the scenes before the Sanhedrin and Pilatus. I thought you did that very well. I doubt if we can confirm the sequence of events as you described them – you have to already be an old man even to become a member of the Sanhedrin, so I don't think many of those *men back then are still alive today. But what you wrote sounds exactly like a meeting of the Sanhedrin."*

"That still doesn't resolve the bigger issues, such as the ending," insisted Lysander. "We can't have it stay the way it is."

"We still have some time, Lysander," said Yakov. "Can you think of some way, Marcus, that you can change the ending to be consistent with Miriam's view of what happened and still have the satisfactory conclusion for your hero that you say is essential to the story?"

"I'll think about it," was all Marcus could promise. "I may put the scroll down for quite some time and come back to it later. Maybe some new idea will come up after meeting with Salome and Miriam. I just don't know. It's so hard getting these things right."

Marcus's exasperation was starting to show through, and it was Simon Petros who first got up. "I'm afraid I have much to do in preparation for my journey. I'm around a few more days if you want to meet again, Marcus, and I certainly want to say a proper farewell to you before I go. Perhaps I can induce you to come to Rome once I am out there. I think I've said everything I want to about what you have written. As I said, I am not a writer, and I leave these things to those who have that talent. But by all means, let us talk some more if you wish, unless it is one of those endless conversations about the physical or the spiritual resurrection. I've had enough of those."

Simon Petros started ambling towards the staircase. Miriam and Yakov came up to Marcus and tried to encourage him to continue with his work and to see if he could make the changes that were recommended. Lysander lurked in the background listening to this, but was very uncertain whether Marcus would do anything. Maybe the best anybody could hope for would be if Marcus would set the manuscript aside and then forget about it altogether. More than anyone in the community in Jerusalem, Lysander was in favor of creating a written record of Jehoshua's life and his teachings. But having nothing would be better than having a flawed and misleading document, in his opinion.

Yakov saw the group to the door and again tried to be encouraging for Marcus. It was not simply that Marcus was trying to help by writing things down. He was taking on a role of leadership in the small community of Christians that had formed in Alexandria, and if Christians were to make any progress at all, Alexandria had to be part of the effort. It was the second biggest city in the Empire.

Once everyone left, Yakov once again found himself yawning. He had not finished his nap, now that he thought of it. He was certainly entitled to get some sleep. .....

Chapter Fifteen

he door to the cell was pulled open. Guards came in one at time, yanking out the prisoners, and trussing up their arms behind their back with rope. "Where are you taking us! We have a right to know why we are being held here!" Yonathan ben Ananus was screaming at the top of his voice. "I demand to see my cousin!" The guards responded by slamming his face into the stone wall, which effectively shut him up. "You'll meet him soon enough," was all one of the guards could say.

When the guards came in, Yakov had found himself slumped in the corner, dreaming of Miriam of Magdala and Simon Petros and Marcus and Lysander and a time several years ago that now seemed not even remotely connected to this disorienting and increasingly frightening experience he was undergoing. He knew this had something to do with being head of the Christian community, and he suspected Ananus was behind it, but he was still puzzled as to what Ananus could possibly hope to accomplish.

There wasn't the slightest aspect of legality to what was going on, and it seemed to have nothing to do with the Temple. He saw that his fellow prisoners were being tied up with their hands behind their back, and he quickly reached in the right pocket of his tunic and grabbed hold of a small glass vial he had taken to carrying with him at all times for the past year or so. It was the same glass vial a centurion had given him over thirty years ago on Golgotha, at a defining moment in his life. He would turn it about with his hand in his pocket at times of nervousness, but never show it to anyone. Now he grasped it tightly, concealing it as the guards bound his wrists together. The four of them were marched down the corridor and up one of the flights of stairs in one of the towers that were positioned periodically along the Temple walls. At last Yakov could see through the window slits that it was daylight out, and possibly morning or mid-morning; he tried to determine the time of day by looking carefully at the shadows on the courtyard below. He judged he was in the inner courtyard of the Temple.

Eventually the group was marched out of the tower and down a walkway that led them to a large room used for Temple administrative proceedings. They were met by a semi-circle of men sitting on benches, positioned on risers so that they could see over the heads of the prisoners. In the middle of the first riser, with a table before him, sat the High Priest Ananus, in full religious regalia, as if he was about to make a sacrifice – which in fact he was.

Yakov recognized a few of these men – they were religious or judicial eminences. Yonathan ben Ananus recognized them all; they were his colleagues on the Sanhedrin. Except they weren't all the membership of the Sanhedrin....they were mostly Sadducees, with a few others who constituted a block of supporters of the High Priest. Yonathan recognized an illegal court when he saw one. "What is the meaning of this, Ananus?," he said in his most rational and unemotional voice, hoping that reason would at least appeal to someone in the room. "This cannot be considered a legal session of the Sanhedrin. You are missing over half of the membership."

"Constrain yourself, prisoner, or we will do so for you," was the response he received from his cousin, the High Priest. "I decide here what is legal and what is not." Ananus went back to rifling through parchments on his desk, consulting with a clerk on occasion. A group of men was brought through the door of the room and obliged to stand along one side of the chamber. They looked to Yakov like they were the type of men who frequented the outer courtyard on market day – vendors or suppliers, businessmen of sorts, in worn tunics and faded robes. They appeared to Yakov to be as nervous as he was.

He desperately wanted to rotate his glass vial in his hand, but he dared not. He had no idea who was watching him from behind, and he had no intention of revealing what he was concealing. Instead, he squeezed the vial tightly, relaxing his grip every so often, and developing the idea that this would bring him luck somehow. He wanted to invoke the presence of Jehoshua if he could, in his mind only, to keep from thinking about anything else or anyone else like Kediah, who would be more frightened than he was if she knew what was happening to him.

"The clerk will read the charges!" Ananus put the trial in motion with this order. "Yonathan ben Ananus," said the clerk in a stentorian voice, "You are accused of a betrayal of trust as a member of the Sanhedrin, through your secret association with the terrorists who call themselves Zealots. Abram ben Hosah, you are accused of embezzlement of Temple funds in your capacity as treasurer of the merchants league. Yakov the Nazarene, you are accused of fostering heresy through promotion of the pernicious doctrines of Jehoshua, the so-called Christos......"

Yakov didn't hear the name or the charges of the fourth person. He blanked out, concentrating only on the word "heresy." This could mean anything Ananus wanted it to mean – blasphemy, insolence, violation of the Law in some way, insurrection. He was coming to the same conclusion Yonathan had reached; this was a mock trial, meant to arrive at some foregone conclusion. The only question was what punishment was to be imposed.

It was now that Yakov understood the gravity of his situation. He began to sweat even more than he would on a hot summer day, and he could feel his hair grow damp and a bead or two of sweat drip down into his eyes every so often. He wasn't in any real danger, was he? The Sanhedrin didn't execute people – it didn't have that power. Executions were the province of the Romans. But where were the Romans? There were no Roman soldiers to be seen – not that they would be seen in the inner courtyard of the Temple, but he saw no hint of them through the tower window slits. Where was the Procurator? Oh yes – that's right – he was delayed in getting to Jerusalem. But his absence would explain a lot of things. That would explain this court, with Ananus deciding whatever he wanted to decide and calling it legal.

But surely he wouldn't execute any of them. Jews did not execute Jews anymore. Yakov was in no real danger, or was he? His mind was beginning to race a little bit faster. What was that they were saying? Those men along the wall. Something about Yonathan, the prisoner on his far left. It was testimony they were giving, saying he was witnessed at several meetings of the terrorists – those Zealots – some of whom had already infiltrated the city.

"This is entirely false! This is perjured testimony, or you extracted it from these men through torture! How can you believe any of this!" Yonathan was shouting again. "Prevent the prisoner from speaking." It was another order from the High Priest, and a cloth muzzle was tied across Yonathan ben Ananus' mouth. He continued to mumble something through the cloth and began twisting his hands, as if it were possible to free them from the ropes. Two of the Temple guards grabbed him by the shoulders and held him in place.

"We presume the prisoner has pled not guilty to these charges. I call for a vote of the Sanhedrin. All those who find the prisoner guilty, please rise!" The entire two rows of judges, including Ananus, rose to their feet. "Seeing no votes for acquittal, the prisoner is judged guilty. Members of the Sanhedrin, you may sit down. Bring forth the witnesses against Abram ben Hosah!"

Guilty? Guilty of what? Yakov didn't know this man Yonathan ben Ananus, but he had said something about being a cousin to the High Priest. Surely that would protect him from a false judgment, or worse still, any sort of punishment. But the man was given no opportunity to speak in his defense! This was more than a mock court; it was a criminal proceeding, only the criminals were on those benches in front of Yakov. He squeezed his glass vial tighter still, and then let go, and then squeezed again. He kept repeating this motion, hoping it would stop the sweat that by now must be embarrassing him, but it didn't work. Maybe this is what Jehoshua felt like when he was on trial in this very Temple in front of Caiaphas, so long ago. Could he possibly have been as scared as Yakov felt at this moment? ...

"Don't be scared, Yakov," said Yesh. He was holding a small scorpion in his hand, as it attempted to curl up its stinger and strike out at him. "Watch this, Yakov," said his younger brother. He then deftly grabbed the scorpion by its head and torso, and gave a quick twist, breaking its head off while at the same time tossing the body aside, before the stinger, which was wildly thrashing about, could dig into his hand. The body was still pulsating along the ground. "They do that for a while," said Yesh. "Then it stops. Then you can eat them." Yakov watched as Yesh grabbed a rock and smashed the stinger, separating it from the rest of the body. He then took the meaty part and held it up so that the remaining blood or other fluids would drain out, and when he was satisfied, he plopped it into his mouth, giving Yakov a slight smile at the same time.

"Come on, let's find one for you!" Yesh was off running across the desert, moving rocks about, and investigating shady areas, not that there were many. "I don't want to eat a scorpion, Yesh," said Yakov. "I want to go home. Let's go home." He had to say the last words louder, to make sure his brother heard him. Yesh turned around and started walking back.

"Why should we go home? There's nothing back there for me."
"Mother has been asking for you," replied Yakov." We are all worried about you. If someone hadn't spotted you out here in the desert, we might never have found you, and then never have seen you again. Don't you want to come home to the family?"

"I don't have a family, Yakov." Yesh said this matter-of-factly, without any indication that he realized such words might hurt his brother. "People like me don't have families, so that we don't hurt our families. Besides, Mother doesn't want me in the family or she wouldn't have tried to lock me up."

"Mother wasn't trying to lock you up, Yesh," said Yakov. "She was just trying to get you home so you would be safe." "But I am safe out here," protested Yesh. "Aba protects me; he always will, even from Him." Yesh lowered his voiced when he said that, and looked around suspiciously and then off to the horizon.

"Who are you talking about, Yesh? You're all alone out here. Look at you! You are almost all bones with no skin. You smell, your feet are all cut open, your hair is so tangled up it will have to be cut off. The only person who is a danger to you is yourself!"

"Oh no," insisted Yesh. "There is great danger here. He is out here. Satan. I have seen him. Sometimes he is normal looking, and sometimes he can be a beautiful woman. He wants me to hurt myself. He touches my head and causes it such pain that I want to hurt myself. But I defeat him! Aba has taught me how. I know the words to say, and I know how to turn my back on him until he goes away. Aba protects me. He shows me where the water is, and where the animals and insects are hiding. I am safe out here now that I know the secrets."

Yakov was running out of arguments. "They have missed you at the synagogue. There is a new teacher who has arrived. A Pharisee from Jerusalem who was looking for you. He wants to discuss something with you about Jeremiah and his prophecies. He may have to leave soon. I would hate to disappoint him."

"Jeremiah?" said Yesh. "What about Jeremiah? Does he want to talk about his treatment from his family? I'm sure that's it! Jeremiah and I have much in common. Did you know he was beaten by his brothers, and when he was very young, the Lord God instructed him to preach and prophesy, but he did not know

how. Or he thought he didn't know, but the Lord God told him to have faith, and so he began to prophesy. Maybe this Pharisee from Jerusalem will tell me how to deal with the false prophet."

"I'm sure he will want to talk about those things," replied Yakov. "But you can't see him the way you are. I have a little money saved up from my business. Do you remember I do some carpentry work now? There is an inn at the village nearby. We can stay there for a few days while you get cleaned and shaven and eat some real food. Do you know pomegranates are coming in season now? We should get going, though, before it is too late."

Yesh began heading out in a different direction, the way out of the desert, and Yakov had to hurry to catch up with him. Once he decided something, Yesh did not hesitate to act. Yakov was relieved, but now he had a different problem. He was going to have to conjure up a visiting Pharisee, or maybe even Jeremiah himself, to commune with Jehoshua. He would solve that problem later. For now, the important thing was to get Jehoshua home, and if it took a little deception to accomplish this, Yakov didn't feel guilty at all......

"Do you plead guilty or not guilty!" The clerk was looking at him, shouting at him. Everybody was looking at him. Yakov snapped out of his reverie but his words came stammering out of his mouth, unintelligible. "Put him down as not guilty," instructed Ananus. "Call the witnesses!"

Some of the men along the side of the room stepped forward and began speaking. Yakov didn't know any of these men, but they said they had seen him bringing Gentiles into the inner courtyard, and pretending that he could heal people, giving them false hope that miracles could be done in the name of the criminal, Jehoshua. When had he last been at the Temple? Years ago, at least? Yakov began to get even more worried and thought he ought to say something, but nothing would come out of his mouth. He realized that the sweating had stopped, but now he felt chills come over his body. He was shivering and nearly shaking. Everyone could see that, couldn't they? He looked sideways to the prisoner on his right. The man held his head down, his chin on his neck, his face deadly pale. We are all afraid, thought Yakov. We all think we are going to die. How could we die? None of us has done anything!

Why are all those men up front standing? "Seeing no votes for acquittal, the prisoner is judged guilty. Members of the Sanhedrin, you may sit down."

The High Priest called for the next witnesses. Yakov's shivering and shaking accelerated. His feet felt leaden – almost numb. He was guilty! Guilty of nothing! Yet these people were going to kill him. Execute him! He felt his face go pale, like the man to his right. He could sense his mind moving faster and faster, as if it were spinning around, the thoughts coming unbidden. He couldn't control them. He couldn't control his thoughts – that never happened to him before. How were they going to execute him? When was this going to happen?

His heart was beating so quickly he was certain others could hear it. The rush of blood into his head at each pulse was beginning to close off his ears. He felt isolated in his fear and terror. He wasn't going to die? There must be some way out of this. He squeezed his glass vial and this time did not let go.

"Father – Jehoshua – help me! I will do anything. I must see Kediah again. I must tell her how much I love her. You can't let me die. Think of the pain it will cause her. We've been together almost all our lives. This is not right. What do you want me to do? Should I pray more? Pray every day? Bring more people to our Assemblies? What must I do?"…..

"You must get the stewards to bring out some empty wine skins, and then fill them two-thirds with water." How much do you need, Yesh? asked Yakov. "Let's start with eight first." His brother was in his authoritative mode, giving orders to people, even adults. It was amazing to Yakov how people responded immediately when Jehoshua began to instruct them to do something. What was it about him? It was more than just his self-confidence or his assuring attitude. There was something else that happened to him at times like this. Perhaps it was the inner voice speaking to him again – his Father, Aba.

"Now how many skins of wine do we have left?" asked Jehoshua. The steward counted three. Jehoshua went over to inspect them and then carefully lifted one of the wine skins. He brought it over to the first of the newly-filled water skins. He motioned for his brother to join him. "Now we have to hold it exactly in the position we found it on the floor. Aba says the heavy part of the

wine and the sediment will have settled on the bottom. I need a knife."

He looked at the steward, who heard him and fetched a carving knife. "Hold open the water skin," instructed Jehoshua. He then slowly slit open the wine skin, holding it right above the water, and a dark, viscous purple liquid oozed out into the water. Jehoshua held back the wine skin for a moment and asked for a cup and something to stir the water. He swirled the water around, took a sip, but was not satisfied. He allowed more of the wine to drip into the water skin, and when he had tasted it again and was happy, he went on to the next water skin. He was able to fill all eight of them to the brim, with about half a skin of wine left over. "Let's hope this is enough," said Jehoshua.

He offered a sip of the new wine to Yakov. It tasted fine to him, not that he was a connoisseur of such things. "They've been drinking all night at this wedding, Yesh," said Yakov. "I don't think anybody is going to notice any difference."

Jehoshua motioned for the steward to come over and test the wine. "Is it suitable for serving?" he asked the steward. "It's exceptionally fine," was the reply. "What did you do? How did you know what to do? How old are you again?" Jehoshua just smiled and said nothing. He liked keeping secrets.

"Let's get back to Mother and the others, Yakov," instructed Jehoshua. "I want to be there before they carry out the new wine skins."…..

Chapter Sixteen

"We shall carry out the executions immediately," commanded Ananus. As if the rump Sanhedrin that Ananus had convened needed yet another reminder, Ananus assured them everything being done was perfectly legal. "In the absence of the Roman Procurator, the defense of the city falls to us as priests at the Temple and members of the Sanhedrin. We must protect Jerusalem. We are perfectly within our rights to take the actions we have today."

Yakov heard little of this. The pounding in his ears and chest was now overwhelming. The guards had turned the group of prisoners to the rear and began forcing them back out of the chamber. Yonathan ben Ananus continued to struggle and grunt through the cloth stuffed in his mouth. The man in front of Yakov seemed to have lost control of his legs. The guards had to drag him forward. Yakov felt like he was moving in a separate world of his own. He body was performing the motions – he could walk and propel himself forward – but he could hear virtually nothing. He was going to die. He was going to die! The realization was upon him and he had to come to grips with it. Fear would mount in his throat and he felt like he would choke or vomit, but he forced it back. They were being led down a long hall to the front of the building. Maybe it was the outer courtyard, thought Yakov. Was that where he was going to be killed? In the outer courtyard, for people to see?

He could see Yonathan ben Ananus being forced to crawl up another flight of stairs. He was still resisting as much as he could. The second man had to be carried up the stairs. It took four guards to do it, he was so heavy. Yakov made it on his own, but it was almost as if he had no cognizance of what he was doing. His mind was outracing his ability to comprehend his own thinking. Images would come and go. They had no order to them. Who were these people? Oh yes, I remember her, that young girl who lived down the street from us. And who was that other girl with her – the one with the dark black hair? Kediah? What a pretty name! Maybe she will be at the top of the stairs once I reach there. They seem so high up. What is taking so long?"

At last they made it to the top, to the top of the wall overlooking the outer courtyard. An intense sadness came over Yakov. He was afraid, but he was morose at the same time. He wanted to say good-bye, but no one would let him. Even his own mouth betrayed him when he tried to shout something. There were people below, many people that he could see. Was his Kediah there? Please don't let her be there, Lord God! Father! Jehoshua! Spare her please!!

Somehow the High Priest materialized atop the wall as well. He was shouting things to the crowd. Great noises were welling up. The people were shouting something back, but Yakov could not hear them very well. He was cocooned in a shroud of desperation – desperate to escape, desperate to say farewell if that is all he was allowed, desperate to escape the shame he was feeling. He kept holding on to his glass vial behind his back, determined to keep it hidden, but he felt something ooze down his leg. Was he embarrassing himself?

He saw the back of Yonathan ben Ananus. He was somehow standing no longer on the wall, but higher up, on the tips of the crenellation that ran along the wall. Two men were holding him up there. Then he disappeared. Another great noise came up from the crowd below.

Yakov looked around him. The deep blue sky. The bright sun. The roofs of Jerusalem. Was his home out there to the south? Could he see it? He tried to squint his eyes. Was Kediah there? What would she be doing now? Please let her be there. Maybe she is cooking. How she loves to cook! The sadness was eating into Yakov's skin, permeating every pore. So much sadness. So much sadness, not even to say good-bye, not even to tell her just once more how much he....

Some people were lifting him up. Was this it? Was this it!? He trembled all over. His feet were barely touching the stones atop the wall. He had never been up this high in all the time he had lived in Jerusalem. He could see all the way to the second wall of Jerusalem. There was the Damascus Gate! He recognized it. And just beyond there, he could see Golgotha. Golgotha! It almost seemed to be beckoning to him. He squeezed his glass vial ever so tightly. Somebody bumped into him, and then he saw many colors, swirling, mixing together.

And then, blackness.

No one noticed a small glass vial roll gently away from the hand of the man who hit the stones of the Gentile Courtyard. It rolled quietly along the pavement until it lodged in a crevice next to a stone column.

Kediah saw a flash of red hair as a body came hurtling down from the top. Her scream was entirely involuntary. She knew at that minute it was her Yakov. In that sense, her torture was over – the uncertainty that he was one of the men being executed, the horrifying thought that maybe that was one of the names shouted out by Ananus, and then hope that he was still in prison, and then doubt all over again. The uncertainty, the fear, the hope, the renewed uncertainty – it was eating at her internally. Now that it was over, a whole new torture was setting in, signified by a scream that Miriam and some of the other women who were standing in the courtyard could hear, but few else, over the roar of the crowd.

Kediah ran out to the courtyard, and Javan had to rush to pull her back, using all his strength. "No, Kediah, you cannot go out there. There is nothing you can do for him." Javan handed her to Miriam and Salome, who held to her tightly. She was alternately crying and screaming. "You must take her home, Miriam," said her husband. It was then that he saw a giant of a man come out from the crowd on the opposite side of the courtyard. He was easily a foot taller than anyone else, the sort of man who could be found in the mountains of Anatolia. He dragged behind him a club, carved from the trunk of a large tree.

Javan did not like the looks of this. "You must take her home now, Miriam!" His voice was preemptory, and looking out into the courtyard, Miriam comprehended why. She eased Kediah and her friends out through the crowd and away from the Temple. They did not need to see what was to follow, and neither did she.

The giant pulled his club to the center of the Gentile Courtyard. He waved to the crowd with one hand, which let out an enthusiastic cheer. There were four bodies sprawled over the courtyard, all twitching still. The giant pulled his club over to the first of the victims, and grabbing his club by the middle of its neck, he bent over and began rotating it back and forth like a pendulum, arcing in ever-wider distances. He didn't need to bring the club down with his own strength; the club would do its work on its own. All he needed to do was give it the right momentum, and when it reached the top of its arc, take one step forward over the body of Yonathan ben Ananus, and let the club impact his skull with a thud that all could hear.

The giant proceeded with his motion, and after several swings the club swooped down from its highest point and virtually obliterated the head of Yonathan ben Ananus. The crowd gave a cheer, but there were some boos as well. A few people threw out some coins.

The giant approached another body, that of the red-haired man. He went through the same motions, and then came a sound that seemed to combine a whack and the noise of bones cracking. His club was covered with bits of red hair, and the brains and skull of Yakov the Nazarene. Now there were more boos and fewer coins.

It was a game that was being played here, and the giant attained success at last with his fourth victim, the unfortunate Abram ben Hosah. This time the club hit in exactly the right way, and with the right force, so that the entire skull disconnected from the body and went rolling out to the feet of the crowd. There were no boos this time. A great cheer went up that could be heard well outside of the Temple. Coins of all sorts rained down on the giant, who eagerly went scrambling about the courtyard, grabbing them up, mottled though many of them were with blood and gore. Ananus the High Priest made a particularly ostentatious display from atop the wall overlooking the courtyard. He held out a whole bag of silver denarii and poured them out to the delight of the crowd, but to the delight of the giant in particular.

Some people scrounged on their own for coins, but it was considered bad form depriving the giant of a decent reward for his day's work.

Chapter Seventeen

iriam of Magdala managed to bring Kediah safely home, despite her increasingly frantic behavior on the way there. At moments she would cry or wail, and then she would fall deadly silent. "I am fine, Miriam," she would say. "Just let me think." Then her grief would overwhelm her again.

Once back at the community center, Kediah took on a purposeful demeanor that was, if anything, more worrisome than her previous behavior. She immediately went to her room and began rooting through her clothes chest and that of Yakov. She picked out clothes selectively, according to some pattern apparent to her only. She made several trips outside to the back of the building, where she amassed them into a pile.

Miriam kept following her. "What are you doing?", but she would say nothing. Finally, when she was content with her collection, Kediah searched around for kindling and a flint and lit fire to the pile.

"But that was your wedding dress, Kediah," lamented Miriam. Kediah kept on stoking the flames higher. "Yes it was, Miriam," she said. "Those were all my clothes from my wedding and from when we were younger and would wear them to the Temple. They were all my clothes, and Yakov's too, that reminded me in any way that I was once Jewish, because as of now, I am no longer a Jew. And as long as I have anything to do with this community center, no Jew will be allowed to walk through the door of this building. If you don't agree, Miriam, you can force me to live elsewhere, but I will not have any Jew disgrace us with his presence. Those in our community will have to decide: Christian or Jew. They can no longer have it both ways."

"And if I could, Miriam, I would have Ananus ben Ananias placed on this fire, and I would roast him alive, as slowly as possible, until every ounce of fat and blood was boiled away and he was nothing but bones that could be thrown to the dogs. Until I die, I will hold in my heart the blackest form of hatred for him and all of his jackals on the Sanhedrin or at the Temple who do his bidding. I will keep that hatred alive, and I will stoke it into greater blackness day by day, just as I am stoking this fire now."

Miriam kept silent. She had never seen Kediah like this before. She hoped someday that the person she knew – the woman with the quick smile and cheerful welcome – would return, but she couldn't be sure if that would ever happen. She thought back to the scenes at the Gentile Courtyard, and she let the emotion of those moments return to her. Then she searched around in the yard, and finding a stick of her own, she joined Kediah in forcing the flames higher still.

Chapter Eighteen

The bodies in the Gentile Courtyard had long since been carted away, and slaves had been put to work with buckets of water and brushes, washing away the blood and other human remains which stained the pavement. A lone mendicant was walking slowly over the stones and searching along the colonnade for any coins that might have fallen into cracks during the day's festivities. He had had some luck – a few bronze coins and one silver denarius – enough for some decent food this week.

The Temple police did not bother him. He was Greek and as such was allowed into the Gentile Courtyard, as long as he wasn't bothering anybody. He continued his search, hoping to cover the whole area before the sun set. The work for him wasn't easy. As a youth he had fallen into an olive oil press and his right hand had been crushed. That pain was the most distinct memory of his childhood, followed by his second-worst memory – the years of pain he suffered as his arm settled into its useless and ugly condition.

But then the gods took pity on him. The pain began to disappear until one day he noticed nothing whatever. His hand and half of his arm were completely numb, as well as being unresponsive to any suggestions from his mind that it move in any way. He thought on occasion of having it cut off, but he was really in no mood for more pain. Then he noticed that his misshapen arm had its uses. It excited pity in some people and brought in a few coins. What started as a curious pastime for him eventually turned into his occupation.

Something glinted nearby, a spark of light set off by the setting sun. He walked over to a column and saw something shiny wedged next to it. He fingered it gently and removed a small glass vial filled with a dark substance. Liquid, solid? He couldn't tell. He sat down next to the column to inspect his find. It couldn't possibly be worth anything, except the glass maybe.

He wedged the vial between his knees and began working on the stopper, twisting the cork back and forth. Little bits fell off, and he feared he was going to have to find a knife to get the cork entirely out, but then it all began to move at once, and he was able to extract it as one piece.

What was this stuff? He held the vial to his nose, and it hurt to breathe it in. It smelled like dead animal, only stronger, or maybe vinegar that had gone bad. It was very likely poisonous. He found a thin stick and poked around inside. It clearly wasn't solid; it was like some sort of paste. He pulled the stick out and twirled it around a bit, holding it up to the light. As he set it down he accidentally brushed it up against the palm of his right hand, but he didn't notice, because he felt nothing there.

He looked around for the cork and proceeded to push it back into the vial. Well, he thought, "when I get a chance I will empty it out and keep the bottle; it will be good for some purpose." Then a very strange thing happened. He felt a tingling in the palm of his right hand. He looked and observed a reddish brown splotch spreading out from the center of his hand, and with it came more sensations. He hadn't felt anything in this hand for years. Then something odder still happened. His thumb began to twitch up and down, and if he thought very hard, he could make it stop and then allow it to start up on its own naturally.

This positively frightened him. In a panic he grabbed the hem of his robe and wiped off as much of the paste from his hand as he could. He looked at his glass vial and decided he would not empty it out. He would experiment first; slowly, of course, and carefully, to see what happened. What if he could use his right hand again? The thought was beyond his comprehension and certainly he did not want to raise his hopes.

From his experience he found the Jews to be a very strange people, and they were said to be in possession of ancient secrets of magic. Perhaps he had stumbled onto something that was supposed to be of benefit only to Jews, and by accident, he – a poor traveling beggar and a Gentile as well – could now avail himself of its magical powers.

He stood up and gathered his things. He decided to quit his work for the day, as it was getting dark anyway. He had done well with his coins, but this glass bottle, this paste – that was something altogether different. It would be something unique if it performed on others what he believed it could do for him. He would have to leave Jerusalem, however, and all of Israel for that matter. The Jews already knew about such things. But the Gentiles? They would be astounded. He couldn't wait to tell them the good news.

PART FOUR

In the Year 66, Jewish resentment at Rome finally boils out of control. The spark is an incident involving a perceived sacrilege by Gentiles who sacrifice birds on the sacred grounds of a synagogue, in contravention of Jewish religious doctrine. Rome does nothing in response to Jewish complaints, and as a result riots erupt throughout the Jewish provinces. The riots are a ready-made opportunity for those who have long been resisting Roman rule, chiefly the insurgents known as The Zealots. They create an organized military resistance, and when the governor of Syria brings his legion down to restore order, The Zealots ambush the Roman troops, putting to death 6,000 soldiers, capturing the legion's aquila, or ceremonial eagle, and forcing the Romans to abandon Jerusalem and all of the provinces. This is the greatest loss of Roman troops and territory in at least fifty years, leaving the Emperor Nero in shock. He commissions the most experienced general he can find – Flavius Vespasianus – to retake Jerusalem. Vespasianus will invade a year later from the north, through Galilee, and meet his first serious opponent at Jotapata, under the unlikely command of a Jewish religious scholar, Josephus.

Josephus

Jotapata in Galilee
Year 67

Chapter Nineteen

his will lead to the destruction of all of us!" said Josephus. Everyone looked at him with fear; he was of priestly descent and had a reputation for foretelling the future.

"But we must defend ourselves," rejoined Yohan the Essene. "If you do not feel confident in accepting a military commission, Josephus, then why are you here?"

Josephus looked intently at the other members of the Sanhedrin who had managed to attend the meeting. Ananus ben Ananias, Yosef ben Gorim, Mannaseh the merchant, Philip ben Josimus, and the others were all putting on a brave front, but they were just as terrified of the situation as he was, thought Josephus.

"It is not the Romans who are our bitterest enemy," replied Josephus. "With them we can make peace. It is the war among ourselves that will be our destruction. How can we possibly stand up to the Romans if we do not deal first with the Zealots? Everywhere they go – Judea, Idumea, Samaria, Galilee – they stir up hatred against the Romans. We have tolerated them to the point where even the streets of Jerusalem are not safe. People are afraid here of speaking out against them for fear of being knifed as they walk to the Temple."

"They say they want to expel the Romans, but look at their most recent actions," continued Josephus. "They attacked the garrison at Masada, killing dozens of Roman soldiers. That only served to draw the Twelfth Legion from Antioch onto our doorstep, leaving us – the Sanhedrin – to organize a defense of Jerusalem. I'll admit the Zealots fought like wild animals when the time came to repulse the Roman siege, but where was their discipline, their willingness to follow orders? Then, when Cestius Gallus retreated, rather than let him alone, the Zealots pursued him through Samaria and Galilee, ambushing his troops at Bet-Horon, killing thousands of Romans this time, and walking away with the Roman aquila."

"Do you know what the Romans do when they lose one of their eagles? They do not rest until they get it back. It is the standard which represents the honor and dignity of the entire legion. You may be certain Nero is plotting at this moment to put together at least three legions to avenge the loss of this one legion." Josephus whacked a scroll on the table in front of him to give emphasis to what he was saying. His startled audience squirmed in their chairs.

"How do we stand up to them?" asked Philip. "You saw how the people of Jerusalem reacted to the defeat of the Romans at Bet-Horon – the dancing in the streets, the celebrations that lasted over a week. This was one of the greatest victories in the recent history of the Jews! And now thousands of Jews are rushing to join the Zealots in Galilee and Samaria, since no one is afraid of Roman might any longer. You say, Josephus, that the Zealots are undisciplined and unorganized, but leaders are sprouting up every day. In Galilee we now have this man Yohan, from Gischala, organizing an army to defend the cities. I've heard at least 1,000 men have joined his cause. And now this Zealot named Simon bar Giora has begun organizing within Jerusalem, in our very midst!"

Ananus, a former High Priest who was the most senior of the elders there, flicked a fly off his robe and added to the discussion. "Josephus is right in one respect – we must stand up to the Zealots, or we have lost control not only of Judea but of all Israel. We must start right here in Jerusalem, where even I can no longer walk without an escort from the Temple police. Nor should we romanticize these Zealots. They are provocateurs, and they are increasingly indistinguishable from the Sicarii."

No one in the room was unaware of the dangers posed by an alliance with the Zealots and the Sicarii – hired killers who skulked around Jerusalem hiding daggers in their cloaks, attacking their victims from behind, and then disappearing into the crowds. The wealthy, the powerful, those who most benefited from Roman rule, appeared to be the chosen targets of the Sicarii. Ananus himself succeeded to the position as High Priest after the assassination of his predecessor, Ananias, who was also his father. The Sicarii had come to represent anyone who betrays, steals, or murders. Even Judas, the infamous betrayer of the Christos, was now routinely referred to as an Iscariot.

Manasseh, who had obtained his wealth processing and selling salt from the Asphaltites Sea southeast of Jerusalem, asked who was going to protect Jerusalem if they were all to be assigned to military posts in the provinces. "I have been thinking about that," said Josephus. "Clearly we need Yosef ben Gorim in Jerusalem. He is our most experienced military officer. Ananus should also stay to stand guard at the Temple and hold the Palace if he can from the Zealots, now that Herod Agrippa has deserted us."

"He did not desert us," contradicted Philip. "He and his sister Berenice were thrown out of Jerusalem by the Zealots. Nor should we lament his absence. A man who has received his entire training at the court of the Emperor Claudius is no fit leader of the Jews at a time like this. He is more Roman than Jew and no one will follow his orders."

Josephus did not bother to defend Herod Agrippa II. If the war did not go well, Agrippa might never return to Jerusalem. Josephus was happy enough that no one objected to the suggestion that Yosef ben Gorim and Ananus be assigned the defense of Jerusalem – especially Ananus, a man who was ruthless and just a few short years ago broke all Jewish laws and custom by sending a Christian and some of Ananus' political opponents to their death. Ordinarily, Josephus would not care to trust any power to a man like Ananus, but these were perilous times and Ananus would assuredly do his utmost to preserve the Temple. The Temple of Jerusalem was no typical edifice; it was the emotional bond that tied all Jews to each other and to the Lord God, who had promised them the "land of milk and honey" on which they could build their Temple.

With consensus on the defenders of Jerusalem, the provinces were easily divided according to those who were originally from the area and most familiar with its topography and its people. Manasseh was an obvious choice to defend Perea, adjoining his salt beds on the Asphaltites Sea. Philip was given Samaria. Yohan the Essene was assigned to Emmaus and the cities directly north of Jerusalem. Costobarus and his brother Saul were assigned to Idumea. Josephus's family was from Gamala in Galilee, and he was naturally posted to the city of Jotapata in Galilee to organize defenses there.

"There is every reason to think," said Yosef ben Gorim, "that the Romans will enter from the north and attempt to take Galilee first. You will likely be the first to be tested, Josephus. Working in our favor is the fact that Nero has done nothing to support the military, other than the Praetorian Guard. Moreover, his generals are old. Galba and Otho are already close to the age of retirement. Galba in particular is wedded to his governorship in Hispania – he'll not easily give up his fortune from the silver mines there. Vitellius is still young, but I doubt they can spare him from Germania. Still, I hope he will be given the task, as he is a general who needs to be loved by his men and buys their affection with coin. Such a man is likely to be a lax disciplinarian."

"It is the Flavians I worry about the most. Flavius Vespasianus would have to be called out of retirement by Nero, but he by far has the most combat experience of any of the Roman generals, active or otherwise. He distinguished himself during the invasion of Britannia, and he knows how to lay a siege. Moreover – and here is our greatest danger – his son could easily be given command of the legions near Alexandria. The father and son could join forces and attack us from the south as well as north. Given the present disorganized nature of our defense, we may not be able to conduct a fight on two fronts for very long. Our safest strategy is not to engage the Romans directly, but to wait them out. Wall off our cities and stockpile food so that the population can survive for many months. Insure there is a steady supply of drinkable water and do not rely on water that can be cut off by the Romans. If we can withstand a lengthy siege, we can eventually come to terms with the Romans."

Yosef ben Gorim paused for a minute to collect his thoughts. "Remember this – the Romans are not going away. This is not a fight we can 'win' and hope to expel the Romans from Israel permanently. The best we can hope for is a stalemate, inflicting such damage on them that they will agree to negotiate. Fighting a rearguard action against the Zealots, who mistakenly think that we Jews, of all the people in the world, will be the ones to succeed in expelling the Romans, is going to drain our resources. In this regard, Josephus is right. We must find a way to neutralize the Zealots since we cannot bring them to their senses. I am afraid to say this, but the Zealots will never learn the folly of their beliefs until they are steeped in Jewish blood. If they agree to help in your defense, use them on the front lines where they will draw the brunt of the Roman attack. Perhaps then they will learn."

There was a further discussion about how to obtain supplies and the various ways in which they would communicate with each other. Ananus closed the meeting with a prayer, invoking God's help in protecting each of them and ensuring the survival of Israel and the Jews.

Josephus repaired home to his wife and parents. He did not relish telling them of his imminent absence. If tragedy were to come to Jerusalem, he would have much preferred to stay with his family and spirit them out of the city to safety if necessary. His wife, however, would hear nothing of this. "You have an obligation to Israel first," she said, "as an educated man and a member of the ruling class." Josephus could not disagree with this, but if he was to have any hope of success, he would need to use every bit of education he had received in order to face the Romans. His body gave a slight tremble every time he thought of the ordeal ahead, but if it was God's judgment that he die at the hands of the Romans, far better that he do so as a military commander than as a learned scholar.

He left Jerusalem within a few days, and was given an allotment of ten horses, 500 men, and a collection of spears and arrows that trailed behind in a wagon. His troops, such as they were – they were mostly retired military men or Temple police – were expected to forage along the way to feed themselves. In every village people would come out to greet his "army" and cheer them on. The Jews, he thought to himself, had very little understanding of what really lay ahead of them.

The road to Jotapata ran through Judea and then Samaria, and it was becoming increasingly difficult to find food, even though this was the middle of the growing season and his path lay through some of the richest farmland in all of Israel. Brigandage was on the increase, as the Zealots scoured through the country like a swarm of grasshoppers. Increasingly his progress was halted by roadblocks created by self-appointed toll seekers. At first Mathias, his subaltern, would cry, "Make way for a member of the Sanhedrin!", but this no longer impressed or frightened anyone, and it was only when Josephus would deliver with his spear a smart slap on the back to one of these men that the miscreants would back away.

Progressively, Josephus began to despair of his mission. As they entered Galilee, and saw the villages despoiled by marauding gangs of Jews, Josephus realized that the nation was not even worthy of being saved. "This is a judgment upon us, Mathias," he would say. "The Lord God has found our generation wanting and sinful, and we now must pay the price. That is why he has visited both the Zealots and the Romans upon Israel."

"I tell you that we shall not last more than forty-seven days before I am captured and executed by the Romans." Why he chose that number Josephus could not say. These ideas would come to him, usually as visions or dreams. He had believed even as a teenager that he could foretell the future, and he had convinced others of his gift for prognostication. He was especially skilled at interpreting dreams, but he also paid attention to animals and their interactions with man. He kept a keen eye out along the roadside for any unusual sighting that would give him hope, such as a white lamb that had strayed from its herd, or an eagle with an injured wing, unable to fly. No such omens appeared.

"You must not talk like that," Mathias would say to him, and of course Josephus knew he was right. With everyone else, he kept a hopeful countenance and uttered nothing but promises of victory. He kept his misgivings to himself, however much they were augmented by further proof of anarchy in the countryside. As he rode on his horse to Jotapata, he focused his mind on the task at hand. "We must think and act like the Romans," was his fundamental principle. All else followed, but how was he to train an army to be as disciplined and skilled as the greatest fighting force in the world? Especially when he had but two or three months before a Roman legion arrived at the gates of Jotapata.

His only source of hope was the reflection that, if he had to choose any better place in Israel to defend, other than Masada, it would be Jotapata. The city of about 60,000 people lay atop the thin crest of a hill which fell off abruptly on three sides. The only easy access to Jotapata was along the ridge of the mountain top from the north. He could defend this area by building a wooden rampart across the ridge, fortifying the existing stone wall and gate.

He thought he should waste no time, so he called forth a courier to write down his introductions and instructions for the elders of Jotapata. He did not want them surprised at his arrival, and he could only hope that his presence would be welcomed. In the meantime they could begin chopping down trees in the countryside, crafting as many arrows as they could, fortifying their food and water supplies, and inducting as many young men as were fit to defend the city with him.

It was nearly a week before his troops reached the gates of Jotapata, and to his relief they were opened to him with crowds of citizens lining the streets, cheering them along the way to the synagogue courtyard. He was greeted by the chief priest and various officials, who made it clear that they had already shut the city up months ago to ward off the depredations of the Zealots. "We have had no truck with them or their kind," said a certain Sameas of Galilee, who appeared to be the leader of the principal political sect in Jotapata. "They are thieves who prattle on about excessive Roman taxation, but then extort from our merchants more than the Romans ever did."

"We may need their help in the end," said Josephus, especially after learning that the city had raised only 2,000 men to augment his meager resources. "The Romans will be here soon with at least 10,000 men, as well as a horse brigade of 500. If you cannot raise more help within Jotapata, I will take it on my own responsibility to bring in the ablest Zealots and ensure they concentrate on fighting the Romans rather than harassing the Jews."

It was virtually non-stop work that kept Josephus's mind off his forebodings. He left himself only four hours of sleep at night, plus a periodic nap during the heat of the day. All his waking time was spent familiarizing himself with the narrow roads of Jotapata and inspecting the progress on the wooden palisade to the north of the city. He had quickly despaired of finding additional fighting power within the city itself, and sent out scouts to entice any roving Zealots to come to the defense of the city.

He expected little from this effort, but much to his surprise word traveled through the countryside and dozens of volunteers would show up each day asking for permission to defend Jotapata. Josephus would make them swear to do nothing to harm the citizens. He then put them to work on the palisade, or in finding food in the countryside, or in procuring large vats of olive oil. Within a little over a month he had a force of 6,000, and had begun to have experienced soldiers drill them in spear throwing and use of the bow and arrow. The presence of so many men allowed Josephus to reassign many of his original defense force from Jerusalem to police duties in the city, a task to which they were more accustomed in any event.

Josephus sent regular communications to Jerusalem regarding his progress and received periodic notes of encouragement back, but with no promises of additional help. Notwithstanding the Sanhedrin's misgivings regarding the king, Josephus had maintained friendly personal relations with Herod Agrippa II over many years, and he saw fit therefore to send him a letter to learn if there was any news as to the intentions of the Romans. He received a reply within a week.

Greetings from King Herod Agrippa

My Good Friend Josephus,

It is with a warm heart that I received your recent letter and learned of your excellent work in defeating the rebels, Zealots, and others who have brought chaos to Galilee. You know better than anyone how treacherous these men can be, having spent so much time in and out of Galilee trying to defend our rule there, only to be rejected by all of these parties and factions. Long may your name be revered by all of Israel for coming to the aid of our people at a time of such distress! I have every faith in your military and leadership skills, dear Josephus, as I have in your courage and honorable intentions in upholding the rights and privileges of our noble family, descendants of Herod the Great, may his memory endure forever.

I have been in communication with friends in Rome and learned that the defeat of the Roman legion at Bet-Horon was a deep shock to the Roman administration and the military. Such a defeat has not been experienced by the legions since the time of Augustus.

The Emperor Nero is said to be despondent over this occurrence and has terrified the Senate and the military with threats of retribution for this loss. For a long time he was unable to make any decisions, and then when he did approach experienced generals (at the advice no doubt of his Greek eunuchs), he was rejected by all of them. He thus has turned to retired general Flavius Vespasianus. He has had to induce Vespasianus with an enormous monetary gift, but in due course the general accepted the commission and is making preparations for his departure.

I very much regret telling you this, as Vespasianus will not be deterred until he has avenged the death of thousands of Romans at Bet-Horon. As of yet, there is no indication that any other senior commander will accompany Vespasianus, and we may only hope that his son, Titus Flavius, is not enjoined to accompany his father. From all I have been told, the son has a streak of cruelty that does nothing to bring credit to the Roman military. Please, therefore, do nothing to get on the opposite side of either of these generals. I may travel back to Judea with Vespasianus and supplement his army with mine; together we shall bring these robbers and traitors to justice.

For the moment, my sister and I have decided to travel to Rome to appeal personally to Nero to negotiate a truce so that terms can be discussed. We have never wanted a separation from Rome, which has brought us many benefits. This evil is the work of fools and opportunists, and my sister and I feel we are in the best position to convince Rome of the need to avoid further violence. Keep this information close to your bosom for the moment.

May your endeavors be blessed by the Lord God. I shall write to you, my old friend, from Rome.

Herod Agrippa

Josephus folded up the scroll slowly, his heart beating furiously. Herod Agrippa had been out of Israel for far too long. He no longer understood the mood in Israel after Bet-Horon. Men were eager to take on the Romans and confident of defeating them. It was laughable to think Herod Agrippa could raise an army of men to support him; certainly not when he was riding side by side with an invading Roman army. Josephus very much feared that he would be on opposite sides of both Vespasianus and his old friend Herod Agrippa if they chose to attack Jotapata.

There was worse news in Herod Agrippa's missive. Vespasianus would almost certainly select his son to accompany him as well. What Vespasianus gained from all of this was uncertain; money, to be sure, but possibly glory. There hadn't been a real Triumph in Rome since Augustus came to power, a Triumph, that is, that came not just with a captive king or new territory, but with real wealth. Wealth such as Jerusalem offered. The Temple treasury alone would provide a stunning display of gold during a Triumph along Rome's Via Sacra. Vespasianus would more than likely start at Jotapata and destroy all of Galilee, Samaria, and Judea until he reached his greatest conquest – Jerusalem.

And then the thought occurred to Josephus, that perhaps there was something much higher at stake for Vespasianus. With Nero murdering his own family one by one and having no decent heirs, and with the Senate now completely disgusted with the rule of mentally defective and capricious emperors, the Julian dynasty might well be coming to an end. A new dynasty would take its place, and the throne of the emperor of the world would be open to anyone with the military might, the money, the love of the people, and the audacity to claim the purple. Surely Vespasianus, with the glory of his conquest of the Jews, and with the money in hand from the Temple, would be far ahead of any contender.

As for Titus, he wanted to shine in his father's resplendent glory, and he likely wanted the experience of battle that would set him apart from all other generals. And if his father did in truth become Imperator Flavius Vespasianus Augustus, his son would become Titus Flavius Caesar, his heir apparent.

Josephus realized now how high the stakes were. He understood clearly why Agrippa and Berenice were leaving the country. This was not a military campaign to avenge the deaths of a few thousand Romans and restore hegemony over a small corner of the world. With just the right circumstances working in favor of Vespasianus, such as Nero deteriorating ever-more into megalomania, this was a fight for control of an empire.

Chapter Twenty

One morning at the very height of spring, the city of Jotapata was greeted with the faint sound of horns bleating in time to the pounding of drums. Far off in the hills could be spotted a cloud of dust which grew larger as the sun approached midday. The Roman legions were at long last at hand. Josephus ordered the gates closed; the outer barricade was nearly complete but would now have to do. Panic spread through the city as throngs of people rushed to the outer walls to glimpse the agents of their impending doom. Women shouted fearfully for their missing sons who had been outside the city foraging for food or wood. It was too late for them now to defend Jotapata, though Josephus hoped some of them would rally together to organize a rear attack on the Roman forces.

Josephus ordered the crowds back from the walls so that his men could set up defense stations. "Go back to your homes and your businesses," he commanded them, in as calm yet stern a voice as he could muster. "You are as safe here in Jotapata as anywhere in Israel, including Jerusalem. We have all been preparing for this moment. Every citizen of this city, including every child, knows exactly what to do. Now is when we will show the Romans once again the strength of the Jewish people. Remember Bet-Horon!"

At the mention of Bet-Horon, a loud cheer rose from the men swarming along the walls. The Zealots who had entered Jotapata in the past few months were particularly vocal, shouting "Bet-Horon, Bet-Horon!" over and over. Their shouts soon took on the same cadence as the drums from the Roman legion, less than an hour from the city. The Zealots had taken to wearing black armbands to distinguish themselves from all other fighters, as if they wished the honor and glory of their victory over the Romans to redound only to themselves. Josephus argued in vain with them to remove these armbands, but they had no leader to talk to, and seemed to decide things spontaneously. The Zealots refused to consider themselves part of an integral defense of Jotapata, and they barely recognized Josephus's authority. It was yet another canker of doubt that plagued Josephus's inner thoughts.

"Is it Vespasianus?" asked Josephus of Mathias. Josephus no longer had the sharp eyesight of youth to see far into the distance. "It is the Twelfth Legion," said Mathias. "That is the only standard I can see. Besides, there is no eagle on their standard. It must be only the Twelfth. Whether Vespasianus or Titus is leading them, who can say? Perhaps Cestius Gallus has been allowed to lead them and redeem his reputation."

Josephus thought that very unlikely. Once in disgrace, a general often was lucky to head off to retirement if not ordered to commit suicide. Besides, he had heard that Cestius Gallus had taken very ill after the Bet-Horon debacle and may not even be alive. He would know soon enough. Jotapata was situated on a mountain of limestone with caves leading to points of egress into the low hills that formed the countryside around the city. He had stationed trusted sentries at each of these caves, partly to defend the weapons and food stored there, and partly to alert the city to an impending attack by the Romans should they discover the cave system. Most importantly, the caves were access points for the network of spies that Josephus had set up to report to him anything they could learn about the Romans, and to send communications back to Jerusalem.

As the Romans grew closer to the city, Josephus could make out hundreds of horsemen in the vanguard. Behind them was the regular army – row after row of soldiers in the legions, marching in order to the tempo set by the drums. Josephus expected the Romans to spend some time setting up camp and then to organize siege-works such as battering rams and catapults. His first surprise was the speed with which they created their camp. They arrived in the early afternoon, worked all night, and by the next night they had a completed camp located to the north of the city and facing the main gate. The Roman camp was surrounded by a barricade and sentry towers, and featured two main roads which criss-crossed in the center. The tent of the commanding general was located at this meeting point of the roads. Latrine facilities were located in one corner of the camp, and cooking facilities in another.

The organization and efficiency of the Romans was incredible for Josephus to behold. Everyone knew the role they had to play. The army preferred to feed off the land, so contingents of soldiers were assigned to forage for vegetables, meat, and fruit. All soldiers were required to drill daily, regardless of weather. The practice reaped enormous benefits when the army was engaged in battle. It was not an army that fought man to man unless it absolutely had to. Its strength was the precision of so many men moving in one direction, shifting together at the call of a horn or whistle, or organizing into its famous "turtle" formation, in which 100 men would be covered by their shields over their heads and all four sides, moving as a unit, impervious to spears and arrows.

"It is Vespasianus in charge," reported Mathias, based on information he was receiving from spies located outside the city walls. Josephus expected his arrival at some point, but he did not expect him to be so aggressive in launching an immediate attack. Within a few hours of the camp's completion, Vespasianus had the entire city surrounded by his troops. No one could get in or out, and this was a permanent cordon until the siege either succeeded or failed. By that afternoon, Vespasianus sent several hundred men to attack the main gate. The attack failed. Josephus was able to fend off the Romans with arrows and spears, but Josephus suspected this was an expedition to probe Jewish capabilities and resolve.

This did not serve as cause for anyone else in the Roman camp to stand by and watch. People at the camp remained busy even when fighting was underway at the walls of the city. From the moment the engineers arrived, they commenced work on a road that extended from over the hills many miles away, ending directly at the walls of Jotapata. It was another example of Roman organization and efficiency. Josephus knew how difficult it was to build one of these roads – the effort involved leveling the land, laying a gravel foundation, hauling the heavy stone blocks that were to be used as the road surface, and then placing the blocks in position and smoothing the surface. He did not understand how something this monumental, something that was to last for centuries, could be built in just five days. He was to learn soon enough the importance of this road to Vespasianus' campaign.

Josephus held his incredulity to himself. He wanted to keep the Romans off-guard as much as he could, so during the first week he organized daily sallies against the Roman camp. This was something Vespasianus did not entirely expect – a day-after-day assault on his base of operations. Roman camps were designed for the unexpected, however. The sentry posts alerted the entire camp of any approaching assault, so that the raids were met with arrows and spears from the Roman side. Josephus was not able to make any real progress with these raids, but he received attention from the Roman command and a small degree of respect.

All of this was preliminary, as far as Vespasianus was concerned. The real work commenced in the second and third weeks. The Romans began constructing a wooden ramp sloping upward to the height of the east wall. Josephus was determined to repulse this work as much as possible, since a ramp once complete made entrance into the city as easy for the Romans as if the gates had been opened. He instructed his archers to rain arrows on the engineering crews. He sent Zealots out from the city to harass the workers day or night. Casualties began to rise on both the Roman and Jewish sides, but Vespasianus had 10,000 men at his disposal and was not concerned about losses at this point.

The work on the ramp stalled now and then, but was always recommenced, and the ramp rose higher until it approached the battlements. Josephus countered this by raising the walls, adding more stones and bricks for the Romans to mount. This posed yet more delays for the Romans, because now the slope of the ramp had to be adjusted, with its start located further away from the wall. Undaunted, the Romans made the adjustments in less than a week. "I am not watching humans at work, Mathias," said Josephus, "I am watching a machine. Nothing is done individually. Everything is coordinated and executed with great speed and accuracy. Which army of the world could possibly match this?" Josephus was thinking of his own difficulties merely in raising the walls: finding the stones, lifting them in place, and so on, with an end result that looked primitive and vulnerable compared to anything the Romans did. It frustrated him, but other than Mathias, he spoke to no one about these misgivings.

When the ramp was once again at the height of the walls, a large lumbering machine came over the hills down the Roman road, which was made precisely for such transportation. The battering ram was rolled up the ramp and began its work attacking the walls to create a breach by which the Romans could invade the city. Josephus used every technique he could think of to deter this effort. Arrows aimed at the crews operating the battering ram killed men from time to time, but those men were immediately replaced. He had one giant of a man lift an enormous stone and aim it directly at the metal tip of the battering ram. It was a direct hit, and the metal tip went rolling down the side of the hill. The Jewish defenders on the walls of the city cheered. By the next morning the tip had been repaired and the ram was back in operation.

Nothing seemed to deter the Romans. If the ramp was set fire, it was doused out within a few minutes. Josephus tried boiling oil, pitched over the walls on top of the men operating the battering ram. It deterred the workers, to be sure, but it incensed Vespasianus. He ordered his engineers to build three towers, one on each side of the ramp, and one straddling the ramp. Each of these towers was constructed to a height greater than the walls themselves. Now the Romans had the advantage of height. They poured arrows on the defenders, forcing them to abandon the wall battlements, thereby allowing the Romans to remove the battering ram and begin work again on raising the height of the ramp itself. At long last the ramp exceeded the heights of the walls.

Several weeks had gone by with Jotapata under siege. The Romans were frustrated and increasingly eager to breach or scale the walls and put an end to Jewish resistance. Josephus was gaining a reputation for determination and imagination that had not been seen in other commanders in the Judean wars. The situation in the city, however, was desperate. Jotapata had no natural source of water, so Josephus had arranged for all the cisterns to be filled throughout the winter. The water was running out, and word had reached the Romans of this fact. Josephus tried to counter this by having women wring their laundry out on the city walls, so the Romans could see the way the Jews were able to waste an obviously-abundant resource. It was at this time that Vespasianus was inspecting the ramp, when he was hit in the shoulder by an arrow. The wound was not serious, but it infuriated the Roman soldiers, who were devoted to Vespasianus and his son Titus. They were anxious for action, even if it meant street-to-street fighting. They wanted to show the Jews what real warfare was like. The stage was now set for a decisive moment.

It came about unexpectedly for the Jewish defenders. A traitor from Jotapata was allowed an audience with Titus. He told him conditions in the city were rapidly deteriorating. Water and food were nearly out, and people were demoralized. The men were exhausted from the fighting, and as a consequence they took to sleeping all at the same time, in the small hours of the morning, when they expected nothing from the Romans. Titus decided to act on this information.

He organized a small raiding party that he himself led. The raiding party used the ramp to lower themselves over the walls. They knew precisely where to head to reach the guards of the gate, all of whom were sleeping, as predicted. They quickly and quietly slit the throats of these guards and then opened the gates. Outside of the gates, over 8,000 Roman soldiers were standing at attention, prepared to enter the city of Jotapata, and raze it to the ground. Thousands of Jewish men, women, and children would not survive that day.

Chapter Twenty One

It was the screams of the women that woke Josephus up. Those screams, and the sound of babies crying and shrieking, were sure signs that Jotapata was under attack from within. It was an unearthly mixture of horror and terror that Josephus was utterly unprepared for, and never forgot, despite witnessing similar cruelties several months later when Jerusalem fell.

"Come sir. Come quickly! We must get out of here now!" It was his orderly, Yohan, urging him to leave. Josephus grabbed his robe and sandals and ran to the balcony overlooking the city. What was happening, he wondered? To the east he saw fires starting to burn in the homes and businesses south of the synagogue. The screaming and tumult was concentrated there. Then he understood immediately. The Romans had found a way to infiltrate Jotapata. "Call the troops, Yohan. We must defend the city and repel the Romans."

"That has already been done, sir. The Zealot battalion is engaging the Romans in the streets. Others will join them soon. But you must come with me to the caves. If you are captured by the Romans, all is lost."

Josephus felt the taste of fear rising up in his throat. He had felt this before, at other times of danger, and was always ashamed of his cowardice. This was unworthy of a soldier, much less a commander and leader of men. Yet it was certainly true if he was caught, the city would crumble. He was the leader holding everything together – that is how he looked at things. He must give way to reason; he was a scholar and thinker, and reason must prevail. He was not running away out of fear.

Yohan had assembled over a dozen men on the floor below. He asked Josephus to explain the situation to them. "Soldiers," he said, "we are under attack, and street fighting is now beginning to thwart the Roman invaders. In times such as this, the military leadership cannot engage in street fighting, as we will lose all communication, cohesion, and ability to lead. Yohan is taking us to a prepared cave where we can lead the defense of the city."

Yohan quickly opened the door, instructing Josephus to stay

with him at all costs. He quietly melted into the light mist, but his form was still visible from the other end of the street, so that no one was left behind who did not purposely stray. He knew the city well, weaving from street to street, staying away from the main road, and heading inexorably to the west. The reddish glow in the mist behind them pulsed brighter now and then, as did the sounds of despair and agony that reached their ears. "What is happening to my children?" one man uttered, and then suddenly he vomited on the wall of a building. Two men surrounded him, picked him up, and dragged him along.

"We can help our children and wives and parents only one way now, and that is by reestablishing our leadership in a safe location," said Josephus. It was a rational thought. It gave some hope to most of them as they continued on their zig-zag route to the western part of the city, but no man was entirely free of a sense of shock and foreboding.

Twice Josephus thought they were under attack themselves, because it was difficult to tell friend from enemy. People would exit buildings without warning, some of them wandering the streets as if insensible to what was happening around them. Perhaps they were panicking, Josephus thought. If he hadn't been running for his own life, he couldn't say for certain how he would have responded. He could have easily acted like a crazed animal when it was trapped and faced certain death.

It took Yohan about fifteen minutes to find the building he sought. When he ushered his group in through the door, they discovered others were inside, already heading to a lower level in which was located a door in the floor that hid a stairway to a cave below. The door was normally covered by crates, which confused Josephus when he thought about who would hide the door again once they were all inside the cave. "Never mind that now sir," said Yohan. "There is food and water stored in the cave for several weeks' survival. We must get there at once before the Romans reach this house."

The Romans weren't going to reach this house, hoped Josephus. Perhaps Yohan was too pessimistic. Did not he see how valiantly the Zealots fought at the start of the siege? And how they repulsed the enemy? Nevertheless, Josephus followed the others one at a time down a short ladder into the cave.

The cave had narrow walls at first, barely able to accommodate three men passing down the path at the same time. The floor sloped unevenly downward, but as the men descended deeper into the cave, the walls broadened out, leading ultimately to a large cavern that had no exit. There was light occasionally along the pathway, but Josephus could not determine where it was coming from. He estimated that the walkway was well below the city walls, and that the cavern was located along the mountainside toward the west of the city. The light most likely seemed to originate from shafts that occasionally opened up to the outside. Whether the shafts could also allow others to enter the cave was unclear, as they were high enough up that someone would need a long rope to accomplish an entrance.

The air was moist but very still; it offered no circulation, but it was breathable. It was when they reached the cavern that Josephus comprehended the extremity of their situation. Beside the fact that there was no exit, the food that was stored in amphorae was hardly enough to feed the number of men assembled. When everyone had finally reached the cavern, Josephus counted heads and came up with thirty nine who would have to share food and water that might last just four or five men only a few weeks.

"We can get additional supplies from back in the city," said Yohan. "I will serve as your communicator to the outside, and as the tide of fighting turns back in our favor, I will seek out more food. I'm sure several other men here will volunteer to help me work from the house above the cave, while you and the others stay safely here in the cavern."

"That is very commendable of you, Yohan," said Josephus. He had noticed Yohan before as just one of his orderlies, but now he took a closer look at him. He was barely out of boyhood. He must be eighteen years of age at most. He was taking on an enormously important and dangerous mission. Josephus wondered how such a young man could display intrepidity worthy of a seasoned soldier. Yohan had gotten themselves here safely and had already established a sense of responsibility unusual for his age.

Josephus realized the one man he really wanted at his side was not there. How Mathias became separated from him he could not understand. He was in the same room with him when he went to sleep. On the other hand, what could Mathias do to help him? This was no fit area to conduct a war campaign. The idea that somehow he and his officer staff could mount a defense of the city from this cavern was ludicrous. How long would it be before everyone in this cavern understood the same thing?

Josephus called his men together. There were fourteen of them, including Yohan. He explained the situation in detail for them, putting as positive a sheen to their situation as he could muster. He needed three or four of them to go with Yohan and act as scouts, foragers for food, and an advance guard to defend the cave should the Romans discover their lair. Once the fighting died down, they could begin to send communications to the defenders of the city. Josephus expected to be out of the cave in two or three days at the most. Three men volunteered to accompany Yohan to the house above. "Take your swords with you," he reminded them.

He then assembled all the other men, who by now understood Josephus himself was with them in the cave. He explained the situation to them, maintaining a positive tone and assuring them he was taking charge of the defense of the city from the safety of the cavern they were in, from which he would extricate them in a manner of days. In the meantime he needed to organize the living situation in the cavern.

The light at the front of the cavern was very dim, but toward the rear it was nearly dark. "Those who wish to, may stay and sleep in the walkway. During the day there is more light there, though the air is not especially fresh anywhere in this cave. At night it will be utterly dark and you will see nothing in front of you. You will have to navigate your way by feel alone. I recommend that once night falls we all remain where we are and sleep as much as we can until dawn. Several of you were quick enough to grab some pitch torches and flint, and there were two more in the house above. We will use these at nighttime sparingly and briefly, largely to light your way to the food."

"We have several amphorae of water, wheat, bread which has gone hard but is still edible, and salted fish and meat. I will ration these in small portions. Even though we should be free to leave this cave in a few days, we must prepare for a lengthier stay. We have an advance guard staying in the house above who will search for additional food for us tomorrow or the next day as the opportunity arises."

"There is no running water in this cave and no place for our shit and piss. I assure you it will become very uncomfortable very quickly for all of us if we do not control our sanitary situation immediately. I want one of the bread amphorae to be emptied and the bread stored safely in a clean cloth. The amphorae will then serve as one giant communal chamber pot. We will find a way for you to step up over the amphorae to use it, and we will have select times during the day or night when it will be available. All your waste needs to go into this pot, and make sure the lid is kept on tight."

With these rules in order, the group settled down to an existence of boredom mixed with the tension of uncertainty as to what was happening on the streets of Jotapata. Before nightfall Josephus took a walk up to the entrance to the cave. As he approached, he could hear the faint sounds of yells and orders being barked in the street above them. It was men making the noise this time – not women – and he couldn't tell for sure, but it sounded like Romans talking in Latin. He hoped this was not the situation and knocked on the door to the cave to get the attention of Yohan or any of the other men. Nothing happened. Josephus found he could not lift the door for whatever reason – he hoped it was hidden under crates – so he knocked again, this time louder. Still no response, so he tried two more times, each time risking a louder knock. He got the worried sensation that they all might be trapped in the cave if they couldn't find a way to budge the door, but on the fourth attempt he heard scraping noises, and the door was slowly opened with a thin glow of lamp light illuminating the face of one of his officers.

"Oh, it is you, sir. You best stay where you are. The fighting has advanced to all parts of the city. We are staying quietly in the house, not to draw any attention to us. If the Romans begin house to house searches, we will hustle into the cave as quickly as possible. We have rigged up a way to allow a light plank to fall over the door and keep us all hidden. The fighting does not yet appear to fall in our favor, sir."

Josephus had nothing to say to this, so he muttered some platitude about courage and then ordered the man to leave the plank covering the door "just in case." He did not wish to contemplate having to move the crate, which might not be possible no matter how many men pushed from below. Josephus returned to the cave, and when queried about what was happening above, he replied things were going to plan and his advance guard was out searching for food, having already communicated to the defense forces where he – Josephus – was located. It was all a necessary deceit, Josephus felt.

The men settled into the darkness that was now gripping the entire cave. Few risked trying to move from where they were in such a condition, and every few hours Josephus ordered a torch to be lit to allow the men to work their way back to the amphorae that served as a chamber pot. Eventually most men settled into some form of sleeping, judging by the fitful snoring, and Josephus found himself as well drifting into unconsciousness.

That night was the first night he had his dream. He had had such dreams since childhood. They were visions, in his opinion. They were so lifelike that the great surprise to him was when he woke up and realized he hadn't already been awake. A dream such as this was always the same, night after night, and he remembered the first time he understood they were prophetic. He noticed how the dream, if interpreted properly, told something about people he knew or about himself – something that was to occur in the near future. He was around ten years old when he discovered this secret and this power that he had. As dream episodes occurred, he became better at the interpretation of them, and by fifteen his family and friends were convinced he had the gift of prophecy.

At that time Josephus could have traveled Judea, Idumea, Galilee, and elsewhere, playing the role of a Jewish prophet such as Hosea or Daniel or Isaiah. He never chose to do this, mostly because his dreams were not about religious matters and afforded him no grand insight into calamities befalling Israel. His dreams were too specific as to people, place, and time.

This dream was more difficult to understand then most, though it was just as real. He was standing in a forest when he noticed a young girl cornered at bay near a plum tree, surrounded by three ravening wolves. The plum tree was shriveled and the plums were diseased and rotten, several of them having fallen to the ground, surrounding the child. The girl was but a child. She was neither terrified nor cowering, but instead she was facing up to the wolves with shouts and gestures. Somehow this kept the wolves from attacking.

As happens in dreams, the scene shifted and he suddenly ceased to be himself and instead was transformed into an Ur-ox. This was a real creature; he had seen one once in the arena in Rome on his only visit to that city, early in Nero's reign. He had met Nero as well, as part of a delegation of Jewish notables selected to petition the Emperor for more religious freedom for the Jews. It was the Ur-ox, however, which made the greatest impression on him. It was a species of cattle, but easily twice the size of any bull he had ever seen, and much bigger than any ox. It was as tall as a horse, and the two horns which curved first down and then up from its massive head were each of them longer than any man's stretched-out arms.

The Romans adored such spectacle involving wild and exotic animals, and this particular beast was said to have been captured in the vast forests of Germania, where it still roamed. Some said the Ur-ox was common even in Israel in the distant past, judging by bones of the animal that had been uncovered. King Herod had placed an unearthed pair of Ur-ox horns in his palace as a symbol of his strength. The Ur-ox in the arena had been starved for days and was given free rein in the arena to hunt down slaves for food. As it was gorging on human flesh, a charioteer emerged with arrows and shot several into the hide of the animal. It bellowed in rage and pain and charged at the chariot, nearly overturning it. Several more chariots were called forth, and the Ur-ox was burdened with yet more arrows. This was still insufficient, and a group of gladiators was summoned to at last fell the beast with spears. Its death throe panting could be heard throughout the arena, so large was the animal, and the crowd sat silent and mesmerized as the Ur-ox lay throbbing and snorting on its side, blood leaking out from its nose and wounds, before it finally died. Nothing had gone according to plan, but the crowd loved the drama nonetheless.

But why was he, Josephus, an Ur-ox in this dream? He came charging at the wolves, impaling one on his horn and tossing its body into the air with surprising ease. The other two he gored and trampled to death. He remembered distinctly the deep feeling of anger he felt inside him as he rushed to destroy the wolves and save the life of the girl. When she was free of danger, he lay down beside her. Her reaction was strange. She smiled with a slight look of condescension, as if he owed her this favor. There was no word of thanks, no comforting hand on his tired body - merely a smile, as she gathered up several of the pock-marked plums about her and held them closely to her breast, treating them like the most precious gems in the world.

He woke up with a yell and in puzzlement. Sometimes his dreams were relatively easy to understand, other times he struggled to interpret them. Always, though, he discovered the secret before the event that was predicted had occurred. And always, he immediately felt compelled to tell his family about his dreams, who had learned soon enough to pay attention to what he was saying. In the cave, however, the men around him lacked such familiarity with Josephus and woke up in alarm at a man shouting about his dream. They calmed him down and listened to his tale repeated several times - about a girl under a plum tree, three wolves, and an Ur-ox. Only a lunatic thought this way, but none of them wanted to think that of Josephus. He was clearly in command of his senses at other times, and every man had his safety invested in Josephus' leadership and skills. No, he could not be a lunatic. He was just overwrought on occasion with strange dreams.

Josephus slept soundly after his dream and woke up again as faint light was beginning to fill the cavern. He remembered immediately the dream he had that night, but he still could not fathom what it meant for him. Was he to travel to Germania? Was he to kill three men? Was his wife safe in Jerusalem, despite terrible dangers to come? He did not know what to think, but time would give him the answer. It always did before.

He stretched and stood in the line that had been forming at the chamber pot. He noticed that the entire cavern was steeped in the odor of feces and piss. It was unpleasant but not overwhelming, perhaps more objectionable for its persistence than its strength. What was wrong with the lid, wondered Josephus? When the seal that protected the food was broken, the lid no longer was air-tight, and Josephus had to figure a way if possible to create another seal. He then noticed when it was his turn at the head of the line, that the men had been shitting on the ground near the pot and scooping the feces into the amphora. This made perfect sense, in retrospect. It was possible to stand on something and piss safely into the pot, but the risking of falling in when shitting was too real. Consequently the whole area around the chamber pot reeked and was causing a problem as well.

Josephus understood better the difficulty of housing thirty-five men in such close and incommodious quarters. They were definitely going to need to vacate the cavern in the next day or two before the place became unbearable and unlivable.

He supervised the distribution of small amounts of food and water to the men, but chose for himself to visit the door to the cave first. This time there was an immediate answer, and he asked to speak directly to Yohan. He wanted an honest assessment of the situation.

"It is not good sir," said Yohan when he reached the cave door. "We tried to leave the house to see if there was any escape for you, but by the middle of the night the Romans were in complete command of the city. The Zealots put up a fight, as did many of the soldiers you assembled, but what surprised the Romans most of all was the resistance by the women. Romans are not used to fighting women, and all throughout Jotapata women picked up swords and clubs and fought off the Roman soldiers. There are the bodies of women on almost all the streets of the city, and hundreds of our soldiers were slaughtered near the gates."

"It was Titus himself who found a way into the city. I believe we were betrayed by someone who led him through the caves. He has led the attack, and they say he is covered with Jewish blood. Now they are hunting for males my age and dragging them away even if they don't resist. Orders are to crucify all of them, and the crosses are now going up outside of the walls to the city. The men who tell us these things are running in panic to escape, but there is no escape, and we never tell anyone of the cave below our house."

"As for all others – the children, the old people, the remaining women – they are being rounded up to be sold in the slave markets. The Romans are searching every home for gold and other valuables, and they are torturing people to get them to show them where they have hidden their coins. We hear whole families are submitting to death from their parents or their friends rather than face capture by the Romans. Just on this street alone we know of one old man who slew his daughter and three children and waited for the Romans to capture him. He, of course, did not kill himself – no Jew would do such a thing."

"One other thing. Fires are beginning to burn throughout the city. I don't think they are deliberately set by the Romans, at least not yet. They won't decide to destroy the city until they are sure they have found every denarius and aureus. But there is no predicting when that will be. Some Roman soldiers have come down this street, but they have not begun house to house searches in this sector of the city. We are going down the street to the empty houses here to find food; I don't know how much more we can do in the daylight. If the Romans come in force into this area, we will join you below immediately. This cave is our best chance for escape. We can wait them out until they are done with the city and then escape to the countryside one night."

Yohan passed several baskets of fresh food down the ladder. Josephus asked him to find some long lengths of rope; there might be some way to fling them up to the surface openings, though that prospect of escape was probably very slim. He also asked for more torches if possible. He had no other advice to give to the boy other than to thank him for what he was doing.

After the cave door closed on him, Josephus stood mutely at the bottom of the steps. He had felt all the blood leave his face and was slightly dizzy. The sense of fear was returning; he could taste it traveling up from his stomach to his gorge. He had long ago said to himself that he would rather die as a soldier and a patriot than be slaughtered by the Romans, but now that the reality was facing him he was terrified. He did not want to die. It was all that simple; he did not want to die. He wanted to find a way out of this, but there was no way out he could see. And his position as general of the troops defending Jotapata made it impossible for him to create a way just for himself. That would be cowardly. He must lead these men, the last of his troops, to whatever fate awaited them and share that fate with them. And that meant death.

Chapter Twenty Two

osephus controlled the trembling in his legs and arms as he walked back to the cavern. The men began to follow him silently, sensing ill fortune had struck them. He determined to share all the news he had with them this time, and called them all around. He told them the situation as described to him by Yohan.

The terror that had gripped him now spread to everyone in the cavern. He was gratified to see he was not alone in his fear. He felt himself less of a coward. Some men fell to keening and beat their head on the ground, moaning, "We are going to die." Josephus took some of his soldiers and pulled these gentlemen to their feet. "If we are going to die, we will die like men and take as many Romans with us as possible."

Other men, however, lamented the loss of their wives and children, and the fact that they would never know if they were handed into slavery, killed by the Romans, or killed as a mercy by someone in their family. These men were inconsolable. Josephus could do nothing for them because his pain over his wife and parents was as great, even though for now they were safe in Jerusalem. He had no way to instruct them to flee that city before Vespasianus and Titus reached the northern gate, and it was too late to escape.

Josephus called his own men together to review their options. The general sense was that they should die like soldiers, not like trapped animals. The challenge was how to engage the Romans in combat and so improve their chances for a decent and quick death, if it came to that. Out of necessity, they had to get out of the cave and into the open street to at least have a chance. The cave itself posed a two-sided situation. The narrow walkway and the single ladder up to the door made it difficult if not impossible for an attacker to launch an assault without suffering at least as many deaths as the defenders. On the other hand, the men in the cave could not escape once the Romans were assembled en masse in the house above. They concluded that strategically their best option was to flee the caves now, while they could still mount a proper defense in combat.

Would the rest of the men in the cavern agree to this? They were

farmers, shopkeepers, scribes - not soldiers. Josephus called everyone together and discussed with them this last remaining option.
"But we will die at the hands of the soldiers – we are not skilled to
fight anyone, much less Romans!" This was the sentiment of several
of them who wanted to wait things out. "This is a secret place. We
can stay here for weeks if we eat sparingly."

Someone else pointed out something that seemed mundane but
obviously important. "Has anyone noticed the odor coming from
the cesspool in the back? It is becoming stronger by the hour. How
much longer can we take such conditions? It will become impossible
to sleep here or even breathe." Several people chided him for feminine weakness. Josephus kept his silence, but the fact concerned him
and convinced him even more they must evacuate their hiding place.

"We are leaving," he announced to the company. "My soldiers
and I will take what chance we have fighting the Romans. Anyone
who wishes to join us may do so, and those who do want to take that
risk may stay here, where there is food. No one will betray your
presence in this cave. But if you decide to leave, we are leaving now.
Gather your things immediately."

About a dozen of the men got up and began reaching for their
robes, swords, and other belongings. They were interrupted by a
noise of a scuffle occurring at the cave door. Josephus rushed down
the walkway with his weapon and urged his soldiers to follow him.
One of the four men of the advance guard was at the bottom of the
stairs, his sword in his right hand and his left hand hanging on to the
foot of Yohan, who could be seen slashing away at several Roman
soldiers above him. Suddenly Yohan was yanked up by two men
grabbing on to his armpits, and the door was slammed shut.

"You're Cyrus are you not?" asked Josephus. "Yes sir. We were
caught by surprise when nearly ten Romans stormed into the house.
I was already on the lower level along with Yohan, and I immediately ran to the cave door, as was our plan. I barely made it down,
as you can see. I am sorry about Yohan. I don't know what they will
do to him, but they may want to interrogate him."

Cyrus lowered his voice so none of the others could hear. "They
were asking for you, sir – by name. Vespasianus himself must be
wanting you." Josephus mulled this information over in his mind
for a minute. Vespasianus must be looking for a human trophy to
use in his victory parade in the Roman Forum. The Romans considered this a singular honor to bestow upon a defeated yet valiant foe.

The victim never looked at it that way, and Josephus was already thinking how to use this as a bargaining advantage. Would the Romans allow the others to go free if Josephus turned himself over to them? Perhaps he should trade his life and those of his soldiers to allow the farmers and other non-military men to go free.

The more immediate problem, however, was defending the cave, or there wouldn't be any opportunity to make trades with the Romans. The Romans have already no doubt called for reinforcements. They will strike soon while we are off our guard. Josephus called for all of his men to assemble at the stair ladder and position themselves in pairs a sword's distance from the pair in front of them. He wanted the Romans to fight through a sequence of defenders and absorb the maximum amount of losses as possible. Perhaps then they would agree to negotiate rather than lose over thirty men in trying to capture one person.

All they could do was wait.

Over an hour went by. The men were tired of standing but dared not sit. The attack could come at any time. Josephus began to think the Romans had extracted some information from Yohan or any of the other two of his soldiers in the house. They must know something now about the layout of the cave and the walkway. They realize they have the advantage of resting their troops while we must stay on alert, thought Josephus, or they are thinking of some other strategy. Josephus tried to stay one step ahead of them, but he could not see what exactly they would do next.

Yet another hour elapsed. It was now mid-morning. Josephus had forgotten about breakfast, and so he gave the order for the civilians in the cavern to receive their morning ration of food and water. He instructed the men to mix some of the fresh food he had received from Yohan into the ration; there was no sense in wasting it.

The cave door now opened from above. The soldiers in the walkway were instantly on alert. The attack had come, but to everyone's surprise the soldiers threw seven bodies down on the men below. All of the victims were women. Some had their breasts ripped off or big gashes in their vaginas. The lucky ones died of a single sword stroke to the heart. The cave door slammed shut once again.

The men disentangled themselves from the bodies with disgust and shock. Josephus ordered that the bodies be brought to the back of the cavern near the amphora that served as a latrine. He now knew exactly what the Romans intended to do. There was no campaign by Vespasianus to capture Josephus alive rather than dead. That was just a conceit, or if there was such a campaign, the Romans did not yet know Josephus was in this cave. The Romans weren't going to spend a single life of their own to kill or capture any of the men in this cave, because they didn't need to. The cave was being converted into a living tomb, and the bodies of the dead women were thrown in to prolong the agony of the men who were destined to starve to death if they were lucky. The unlucky ones were going to succumb to any number of diseases that would arise from festering bodies thrown in the midst of the living. The cave door would never again be opened except by accident far into the future, if someone by chance stumbled upon it.

A certain numbness took root in Josephus's soul. It was as if he were among the dead already, now that he realized his fate. He really didn't care what happened to him. In fact, no one might ever know. He was to obtain no glorious death in a losing battle, but on the other hand he was spared the indignity of a public execution in Rome or on a cross overlooking Jotapata.

Josephus sat down quietly against a wall, his head in his hands, a picture of despair. He saw no need to explain himself and no need to lift the spirits of the other men. They would comprehend their tragedy in due course, on their own. Nothing he could say would now ameliorate their condition. For hours he sat there, nearly motionless, his soldiers walking back to the cavern listlessly, no one giving orders, and no one saying much of anything. The disappearance, essentially, of Josephus as a leader, as a man who could always be counted on to save them, took away the last hope any of the men had. Hours went by, and as night fell, someone lit a torch and let it stay lit, offering at least a flicker of light to such a forlorn assemblage. Men reached in to the food storage at will, taking as much as they wanted, as all discipline had disappeared from the group.

Josephus slumped along the wall and fell asleep. He had the dream again, and he woke as was his habit, crying out with the urge to describe to the men around him what was happening to him. No one could make any sense of this – the abandoned child, the plum tree, the savage wolves, and the Ur-ox as rescuer. Many of the men had never heard of an Ur-ox and were even less inclined to consider Josephus as an entirely sane man. On the other hand, it was a dream, and everyone understood the illogic that lay behind most dreams. But why would someone repeat such a dream two nights in a row?

Later that night, it happened as Josephus knew it eventually would. One of the bodies erupted, spewing out gore and bile from the innards of the poor woman. With the putrefaction came an ungodly odor that burned the nostrils and made sleep impossible. The cries of the men to Josephus were impossible for him to bear. "Help us!" they demanded. "What are we to do?" they wanted to know. Josephus was at the end of his patience with these helpless men. He staged his own eruption of bile, directed verbally at all those he was expected to save.

"What did you think would happen," he thundered. "Are you all imbeciles? Can you not see that the Romans have entombed us here for eternity? You have been buried alive, your only consolation being that you can move about and eat while the food lasts, if the maggots do not get to it first. And then it will be your turn. The maggots are waiting for you; they are waiting for all of us. They have an eternity, while we have a month or two at most. The fortunate ones will be those who die first, from disease or hunger, whichever you prefer. And if you are smart, you will stop drinking water immediately. It only hastens your agony, while lack of water will hasten your death."

Josephus stood up for the first time since the morning and walked over to the torch, seizing it aloft. All eyes were on him. "Now," he said to the group, "you might as well get used to the reality of the tomb." With that he stomped out the torch light on the ground, and in the total blackness of the cave he stumbled over men back to his spot against the wall.

No one slept well the rest of that night, and no one dared relight a torch. The morning of the third day dawned. Josephus stirred himself only to use the chamber pot. He selected some salted fish from an amphora but refused any water. He could not very well drink after the lecture he had given them the previous night. Besides, he wanted to show them how a man of integrity and strength died. He had not anticipated the effect of salted fish on his mouth, which dried out quickly and called for water with great insistence. Josephus resisted and tormented himself purposefully, in his stubbornness, anger, and despair.

So went the entirety of the third day, and in the late afternoon a second body exploded, sending a further noisome pestilence into the noses of the doomed men. The compounded effect of decaying bodies, along with the reek from the chamber pot, was now too much to bear for any man. Josephus considered the effect, in his own mind, as a form of torture. We are being tortured to death, he said to himself. The only hope they had is that eventually all the seven bodies would be fully decayed and that odor would cease. Perhaps then they would get some sleep and be able to die in a small degree of comfort.

It was not to be. On the morning of the fourth day, the cave door opened and a body was quickly shoved down to the floor, with the door snapping shut just as quickly. It was the body of Yohan. His back and legs were a lacy mesh of blood and bone from a severe whipping. Four fingers were cut off from his right hand and his genitals had been removed. He appeared to have died from loss of blood, probably left hanging on a whipping post until he expired.

"Why did they do this to him?" asked Josephus. "He was too young for this. He was a very brave man, braver than any of us here." Josephus sincerely mourned his orderly. Others had Josephus to save them; he had had Yohan to save Josephus. He was his last hope, not that he put much faith in being saved under the circumstances. Still, it was at least some hope, and the difference between some hope and no hope was the difference between the flickering light of a torch at night and the cave's being thrown into complete blackness.

Josephus crawled along the floor of the cave, scraping with his fingers as he went by. He had done this before. He was looking for any place with dirt, any place he could possibly bury his young friend, but there was nothing but solid rock and some gravel. The cave had been carved out entirely by water and offered nothing but hard surfaces and an occasional seam of limestone.

One man yelled out spontaneously, "We are no longer among the living. We cannot breathe, we can barely eat or drink, there is no one who even mourns our death. I shall not endure this any longer and die like an animal. Here is my sword. I am an honest and devout Jew, and I could never kill myself, but I beg you – anyone here – please kill me! Be quick about it. And if there is anyone else who wishes to join me in a death with dignity, ending this shame and agony, I will kill them first. I promise it!"

He crawled about on his knees from man to man, looking into their eyes, pleading for an end to his suffering. No one knew what to say to him. He therefore looked up to the roof of the cave. "Lord God, I beseech you, put steel into the heart of at least one man here.

Let them fear not that they are murdering me. They are not; they are delivering me from death everlasting, an ignoble death. It is suicide that is murder; it is murder of the soul, and as a Jew I cannot kill myself. But if your Law forbids suicide to any Jew, then surely death at the hand of one Jew to another in these terrible circumstances cannot be against the Law. It is an act of kindness and a rebuke to the wicked who enclose us in a living tomb."

"Please God! Let there be one man of strength here to help me!" He crawled this time to Josephus, looking at him straight in the eyes and saying nothing. "I will help this man," muttered Josephus. "I will help this man," he repeated, in a louder voice. He stood up. "I will help this man. He has the courage to ask for deliverance from evil, and he is right – what I will do is not murder. Yet you must all understand something else. This man's death will add yet one more body to decay in our presence. It will prolong our struggle. Is that what everyone wants? Would it not be better if as many of us as possible chose this same solution for ourselves?" Here he took the sword of the man and raised it on high. "I will do this for this man, but I want a favor in turn. I ask that someone here do the same for me. I offer you no forgiveness, for it is not an offense against the Lord God or me that you do this. I offer you my thanks instead."

Several of Josephus's soldiers stood up alongside him. "I will do this too," they said. A few of the others joined the group, and then more still, until three-quarters of the men in the cave had agreed to participate in a pact of death. The remainder of the group were reminded that the mounds of decaying bodies they would then face at the end of this ritual would provide an environment so deadly that their problems would become insuperable. Several more joined the pact, until ultimately all did. The last to agree faced the inexorable truth that they could not survive on their own. They gave in out of emotional exhaustion as well; they simply didn't care what happened to them. Meeting death now rather than a month later was merely making a non-emotional, rational trade-off.

"How shall we do this?" asked one person. One man who gave his name as Moshe proposed a solution. "We all agree as Jews we cannot commit suicide, so our only option is to take turns dispatching each other. We sit in a circle and draw lots. Whoever's number comes first is the first to be slain, by the individual to their right. He who sits to the left of the first to die then slays the individual on their left, and so on. When we reach the top of the circle, the survivors again proceed in sequence, slaying the person on their left, until one last individual is left alive. That person either surrenders to the Romans, if they will let him, or starves alone in this cave. It is the only solution that is fair."

An older man stood up. "My objection is not that this is unfair, but that I myself will fail to deliver an efficient death to someone else. I have come to terms with my death. I am older than most of you, so perhaps it was easier for me, but I want no more of this dire existence. Let death come now and quickly. But I have been a woodworker all my life. Perhaps if I had been a farmer I would have familiarity with killing animals, but I have no experience in killing animals, much less a human. That is my fear; that I will do a bad job for someone."

Josephus asked Cyrus to stand up. "Cyrus, you have been a professional soldier most of your life. Tell us the quickest way to kill a man, with the least amount of pain."

"In the arena there is something called a mercy killing," replied Cyrus. "This is how I would want to die if I were a gladiator. It is a quick thrust of the sword into the heart from below. The man is usually dead in a minute or two. You must, however, know how to reach the heart without being blocked by the ribs. An equally quick method is a sword thrust down the back, with a twist that severs the spine at the neck. This produces nearly instantaneous death, but it is more difficult to accomplish. You must have practice."

"I suppose for someone who is not comfortable with the sword there is always the alternative of the garrote. It is easy to fashion; we need a cord or belt and a small peg of some sort. If constructed properly, the garrote works as well as hanging if, again, the spine is cut at the neck. Even if you fail to do this, the man being strangled will struggle for a few minutes for breath, but he will lose consciousness in two or three minutes if someone else holds him down."

"Let me suggest something to you here. There are five or six of us who are soldiers and who are skilled at killing a man. I propose that we be excluded from the circle and go last, creating in a sense a circle among ourselves. As professionals we can then assist you in this task before us. I would even do most of the work. All I ask is that you hold the sword with me, or you tighten the belt while I hold the man down. You participate in some way to your capacity, while I deliver a professional kill. No one should suffer needlessly under this proposal."

Several heads nodded in agreement as this idea was set forth.
Cyrus added one other thing. "I want to make it clear that I am
proposing this as the proper thing to do, not as a way to avoid being
slain myself. All of us as soldiers have seen death time and again.
We are prepared for our death every time we step into battle. It
could happen to us at any time. Now happens to be the day that fate
or the Lord God has appointed for me and for all of us. So be it. I
assure you, this is far better for me than to linger day on end in this
cave. I have seen many a man die on the cross, and while it is the
nails that bring the greatest pain at first, it is the unending thirst that
torments them at the end. No amount of water quenches that thirst.
That is what will happen to whomever is last standing in this cave.
The water appears copious now, but it will dry up and run out, and
then you will experience true suffering. It is far better to go to your
death quickly and with less pain."

One more man stood up. "I am relieved at this idea of the soldiers going last and helping the rest of us. It gives me confidence
that I am in good hands when my turn comes. But I am so terrified
of dying and so anxious about finding any way out of this, that if we
wait much longer I will not be able to go through it. And once we
start this – once the first man dies – there should be no turning back.
We are all committed to go through with this, in respect for the man
or men who went before us. It would be a grave sin against them
to change the rules after they have died. I would like to hear each
man present say on their sacred oath that once we start, there is no
turning back."

"I think that is an excellent idea," said Josephus. "I agree – once
we start, there is no turning back. I say this on my sacred oath.
There – I have said it. Who will go next?" Josephus turned to the
man to his left, who said, "On my sacred oath, once we start, there
is no turning back." So it went around the room. Every single man
confirmed his agreement to see his way through to his death and
that of the others with him. There was a palpable relief in the room
once the last man delivered this oath. There was no more wavering,
no more speculation. It had been decided.

Josephus had been thinking about how to create a lottery to
see who would set the circle of death in motion. He came upon
the idea of carving numbers into the circles of stale bread that were
abundant in one of the vases. He reached for his knife and began
the work, asking anyone who wanted to observe, to check his

numbers, to make sure all were correctly included, and to assure that the discs selected were close in size. The bread was certainly hard enough to allow for carving a clear, deep number. When the discs were completed he put them in an empty vase and asked every man but his soldiers to select a number. From this the men then assembled in a circle in the order of the number they had chosen. There were seven men left out of the circle -- Cyrus and Josephus (who had seen some fighting but was not as proficient at battle as the others), and five other of his soldiers who were veterans of the slaughter that occurred in wars. They would serve as the execution squad until all the civilians were dead. Now came the moment to decide at what point in the circle the killings would commence. Josephus returned all the numbered discs back into the vase.

"Who shall select the number that starts us off," asked Josephus. "Let he who wanted to die first choose the number!" someone shouted out. The man who had pleaded for someone to kill him, and who had kept silent since then, stepped up to the vase. "Lord God," he prayed, "I beg you allow us all to face death bravely." He pulled out number 17. Everyone mentally counted to themselves around the circle until their gaze fastened upon number 17. He had gone pale and started crying, and so did number 19 and 21 and others who saw now the sentence of death that had been passed down to them.

Cyrus stood up and approached the unfortunate first selection. "Are you ready," he asked. The man who held number 17 in his trembling hand could not reply or even nod. Cyrus and number 16 helped him to his feet. The rear of the cavern opposite the chamber pot had been selected for the executions. It was largely in darkness and away from the men in the circle. Two other soldiers joined Cyrus and number 16. As they led number 17 away, they could hear Cyrus ask, "How would you like this done?" Whispering through his sobs and tears, the man asked to be killed with a blow through his spinal cord. Each man in the circle was listening acutely to every sound that came from the corner of the cavern. There was a series of rustling and shuffling noises. Then a brief silence. Then a loud snapping sound, and gurgling, followed by the sound of a body thumping on to the ground. Then more silence – a prolonged silence as Cyrus made certain the man was dead. The circle next saw Cyrus and another soldier carry the body past them and out to the opening of the walkway, where it was agreed they would deposit the bodies. Nobody would be using the walkway after this grisly ritual anyway.

There was no turning back now. Number 16 returned to his place in the circle, his lower lip trembling, with tears running down his eyes, even though there was no evidence he was crying. Another of the soldiers approached number 19 with the same request: "Are you ready?" He too needed help getting up, as did most of the others. There were no objections raised by anyone as over thirty men went to their deaths; the oath they took was surprisingly effective at giving each man the assurance that there was no way out, no miracle rescue to occur, and no possibility of backing down, no matter the reason. The bodies piled up; the circle kept getting tighter and tighter; the same quiet sobbing and weeping struck every man, with some men expressing regret over things they did not do in their lives, and many others going to their death with a prayer on their lips. The soldiers were very efficient. The group had been delivered to their deaths in little more than an hour.

It was now the turn of the soldiers and Josephus. All of them but Josephus were splattered with blood. They did not need a circle to determine priorities. They found the first seven numbers from the pieces of bread scattered about the floor of the cave and chose accordingly. Josephus was confident he would not be number 7, the last man standing. He had felt it was his time to die and he had accepted that. He had spent days coming to an acceptance of his death, and it was almost painful to contemplate any other outcome now. He chose number 6.

An intense weariness overcame Josephus. It had been building all morning as events progressed. He was prepared for his death, but a strange thought kept occurring to him: what had been foretold by his dream? He could not get this out of his mind. He could not go his death without knowing what the dream meant. His body was calling him with greater and greater insistence to go to sleep, as if everything would be revealed in one last dream. He resisted and he struggled against it, as number 7 accompanied number 1 to the execution ground, but the soldiers decided that area was slippery with blood and too difficult to maneuver effectively. They had nothing to hide among themselves, and they took pride in their professionalism. It was quickly decided therefore to move the executions into the open, at the center of the circle. And so they did. The body of number 1 was dragged off to the distance, and Cyrus took his place. He had chosen death by a blow to the heart; his executioner was skilled and Cyrus was dead in less than a minute.

At last it was left to Josephus and number 7, a man named Reuben. He proposed something unexpected. "I do not want to be the last man standing, Josephus. I could not bear to be alone in this chamber of death. I could not bear it. Please – I beg you – trade places with me. You have much more strength than I do; everyone has seen your courage as a general leading our soldiers. Nor does this break your oath. You and I will still see this through to the end, as we promised the group. It will just be different paths to the end, however." Reuben grabbed hold of Josephus's tunic. "Please Josephus, do this for me as a last favor to one of your colleagues."

Reuben was crying at this point. "Are you ready to die?" was all that Josephus could say. "Yes I am ready to die," said Reuben. His eyes showed gratitude and relief. "How do you want this done?" asked Josephus. "I wish to have the thrust to the heart, like Cyrus. Position yourself like this," Reuben said, as he maneuvered Josephus so that his back was against the cave wall. "I will do all the work. I will stand in front of you. Hold the sword out like this. I will position the point at the correct entry spot, and I will thrust myself against the blade. The wall will hold you up. All I ask is that you do two things. First, when the blade is inside, twist it around a bit to make sure it splits my heart open. Second, my body will want to slump. Try to hold me up as long as you can. Are you ready?"

Josephus steadied himself against the wall, his feet apart for balance. He held the sword out as instructed and tensed his body, though the weariness in his bones was stronger than ever. He wanted to sleep. Reuben balanced the point between his ribs and directly facing his heart. Josephus looked into the eyes of a man about to kill himself in front of him, and with a lunge that Josephus did not expect, Reuben impaled himself on the blade, pinning Josephus to the cave wall. Reuben's eyes rolled up into his skull as he left out a prolonged but soft moan. Josephus remembered to twist the blade back and forth, and a short while after he did so, a gush of blood spewed forth from Reuben's mouth and onto the face of Josephus. Reuben's body slumped, and Josephus tried his best to hold him up, but the weight was too much for him. Reuben slipped off the blade and fell to the floor, where he showed no sign of life. Josephus could not remember if he saw the man die or not; exhaustion took hold of him at that moment, and Josephus slumped to the floor as well, unconscious and unaware of the dead man beside him.

Chapter Twenty Three

osephus! Josephus! Wake up. What has happened here? It
is Nicanor. Come Josephus, wake up for me please!"

Josephus was angry. He was dreaming again, and he
was transformed into the Ur-ox at the moment when he was venting
his fury on the wolves. Something was shaking him but it was not
time yet. He was still dreaming, and the little girl hadn't thanked
him. She never thanked him. Why couldn't she express some gratitude just this one time?

"He is still breathing, centurion," said Nicanor to the officer who
accompanied him to the cave beneath the cellar floor. "We must get
him out of here." Nicanor was holding a cloth to his face. The air in
the cave was too foul to tolerate. The air did not move, and neither
did any of the bodies strewn about the floor, obviously freshly killed.
"Who did this?" wondered Nicanor mostly to himself, though the
centurion had the same question on his mind. Some group of people
– certainly not one man – must have gotten into this cave just before
Nicanor and his escort of soldiers had arrived. But where was the
other entrance? In a cave such as this there could be multiple ways
to get in and get out that were not easy to see right away. Roman
soldiers couldn't have done this; there were no missing groups of
soldiers this many days after the city had been taken. This had to
be a blood feud of some sort. But what was the commander of the
Jews doing here?

The centurion had two of his men lift Josephus and carry him
past the mass of bodies in the walkway. As they were approaching
the wooden staircase Josephus began to stir. His dream had ended,
and he was now babbling about the dream itself. Something about
a little girl and wolves and an ox. They got him to the cellar where
there was some fresh air and he was a bit more responsive, but they
needed to lay him down on a cot in the living area before he appeared to be fully awake.

"Do you recognize me, Josephus?" Nicanor had grown up
in Gamala, and his family was close to Josephus' family. He and
Josephus had been boyhood friends. Nicanor had spent most of his

career in the employ of Herod Agrippa, as had his father before him. It was easy for Nicanor to switch his services over to the Roman administration in Syria when Herod Agrippa II lost control of Galilee and the northern cities, and that meant that Nicanor would find ready work with whomever the Roman general was that would be sent to subdue the Jews. His task at the moment, given to him by General Vespasianus, was to find Josephus if he was alive and identify the body if he wasn't. The Romans had a small obsession with the leaders of the armies they defeated, because these men could serve a purpose as trophies, or they had to be killed or neutralized in some way to prevent further uprisings.

There had been reasonably sound intelligence, extracted by confessions, that Josephus was trapped in a cave below a house in the western sector of Jotapata. Nicanor was confident that this man was his friend whom he hadn't seen in years, but it was only after the centurion had brought him water and a cloth, and they had removed the blood caked on his face, that Nicanor could be certain that this was Josephus.

He was fully certain once Josephus returned to coherence, of a sort. "She never thanks me in this dream, Nicanor," said Josephus. "I don't know why that is. And this is the first time you have appeared in this dream. That complicates things."

"This is not a dream, Josephus. We are in the house above the cave where we found you. There are over thirty bodies down there. Do you know what happened?" Josephus sat up. They handed him a cup of undiluted red wine, which seemed to jolt him back to consciousness. "What are you doing here Nicanor? Why did you bring me out of the cave? I have an oath to die there. This is not right, Nicanor. I made a promise on my honor to everyone. There is no going back." Josephus stood up and began wandering around the room. He spied the staircase that led to the floor below and began to head back down to the cellar, saying repeatedly that he had taken an oath.

Nicanor nodded to the centurion, who ordered two of his soldiers to bring Josephus back up. Nicanor propped Josephus back up in a chair. "Do you have any fruit, Nicanor? I would love some fruit. Some plums, or figs?" The man was clearly not fully sensible, but he was making progress. The centurion inquired from his staff as to where they could find fruit. Jotapata had been sacked; few stores had any useful merchandise at all, but one of the soldiers carried some figs and dates, and passed those along to Nicanor. Josephus plunged into the fruit and drank some water. He looked quizzically at Nicanor. "If this isn't a dream, Nicanor, what are you doing here? And what am I doing here? I don't belong here? I shouldn't be alive."

"I work for General Vespasianus now, Josephus, after Herod Agrippa left the country. He has come back as well, but General Vespasianus wants my services at the moment, and most importantly, he wanted me to find you. I'm glad I did."

Josephus laughed slightly, and then laughed a little bit more. "Well that is funny, Nicanor. I have spent days and days trying to think of a way to avoid being killed by the Romans, and here you are, my friend from many years ago, rescuing me so I can be properly killed." Josephus laughed again and then grabbed Nicanor by his tunic and looked him straight in the eye. "Do you know what, Nicanor? I don't care. I am a dead man now. I took an oath."

A look of comprehension mixed with horror passed across Nicanor's face. "Do you mean all those men killed themselves?" The centurion turned and looked at Josephus when he heard this. "We did it by a lottery, Nicanor," replied Josephus. "I am the last man standing, and I have an oath to die for them all."

"Who was the officer in charge of this sector?" shouted the centurion. "Find him!" His soldiers began scurrying around. Nicanor stood up and began pacing around. A lottery! Of course, it made sense; Jews do not kill themselves. These men had killed each other. He understood that, but he had never heard of something like this happening in Israel. More than thirty men dead, each at the hands of one of the others. He had no idea how this was going to be explained to General Vespasianus. It had to be handled carefully, for the protection of both Vespasianus and Herod Agrippa. News of this nature could take on mythical importance.

Unfortunately for Nicanor, it was too late. The Romans who had been in the cellar began talking among themselves. Several of the soldiers walked back down to the cellar to see for themselves. The officer in charge had been found and brought to Nicanor and the centurion to report. "We heard there were some of those Zealots down there. We captured three of them and obtained some information from them that it was going to be impossible for us to bring them out without a heavy loss of life ourselves. It was the way the cave was constructed. So we decided to starve them out. We threw a few bodies we found on the street down into the cave as an incentive for them to leave, but at least as of today no one had given up. We were following orders, sir. I think I handled it properly. I saved the lives of my men. This man here? I've never seen him before. We heard nothing about any commanders or generals being there. No one said anything about how many people were there, not that it mattered. We would have had to pull them out one at a time through that staircase."

"And the man without any genitals and fingers. What did he tell you?" inquired Josephus. He was more alert now, though still operating as if in a fog. "He was very rude to us, he was," said the soldier. "He called us names. My men responded – that's all that happened. He told us nothing. The other one told us what he knew, which wasn't much because he had never been in the cave in the first place."

Josephus rubbed his forehead with his hand. He wasn't surprised about Yohan – that boy had courage beyond anything he had seen, though in looking back, he realized every man in that cave had courage beyond what they possibly could have expected of themselves. As for him – did it really matter if he died at the hands of Vespasianus? He didn't care how it happened, as long as he paid his debt to his fellow sufferers.

"Yohan was tortured to death, Nicanor. Did you know that? They were all tortured to death in that cave. I thought that to myself at the time. People will need to remember that. It was what many of us worried about, as we were walking to our execution. A lot of those men said no one would know or remember anything about them. You need to make people remember, Nicanor. They should remember me, too, after I die."

"I want you to tell me what you can about what happened, Josephus. You can do that on the way to the Roman camp. For now we need to get you into some fit clothes to meet the General and find you a horse or a donkey, because you are clearly unable to walk across the city."

"Oh no you don't, Nicanor! These are my fit clothes." Josephus looked down at the dried blood on his tunic and his legs. "This is my burial shroud, Nicanor. The General can see me in this."

A donkey was found for Josephus and Nicanor walked alongside him as they began to journey across town and out to the Roman camp. Josephus relayed what he could remember. It came out in bits and pieces, as he recalled certain things, and there was no order or sequence to his memories. Nicanor could not fathom the ordeal these men had been through. He understood more fully Josephus's insistence that he not change his clothes – they were a symbol to him of honorable behavior undertaken in extraordinary circumstances.

For his part, Josephus would pause now and then as he comprehended the destruction he was seeing all about Jotapata. In the western part of the city there were still bodies on the streets. Slaves in crews of four or five traveled with an open cart, dumping bodies into the cart as they went along, fighting off flies and rats and dogs that were feeding on the flesh of the dead. The odor of death was everywhere, but it was the sweet odor of fresh air that Josephus noticed most of all.

As they reached the open camp, Josephus was required to dismount. News had already spread to the Romans that Josephus had been found. The Romans had developed a hatred for this man whose stubbornness and tactics had resulted in many unnecessary Roman deaths. There were also rumors about a suicide pact of some sort, but no one had any details.

As he entered the gates there were jeers from the soldiers lining the main road that led to the center of the camp, where the officer tents were always located. "Take him to the yoke," they shouted. "The yoke!" The yoke was a crossbeam normally used to team a pair of oxen. It was positioned at a height somewhat below the chest of an average man, and defeated armies were required one by one to stoop and walk underneath the yoke as a sign of their defeat and submission to Roman might.

Nicanor and the centurion with his soldiers paused at the gate. They bound Josephus's hands behind him and began the slow march to the center of the camp. "The yoke! The yoke!" the crowd of soldiers demanded. They fully expected Josephus to be humiliated this way – it was always the tradition for a victorious army. The yoke was located just outside of the general's tent; the crossbeam was positioned atop two sticks holding it up, and it was usually adorned with something symbolic to the legion involved.

The soldiers followed the procession and at last the yoke could be seen. Josephus didn't notice it at first, though his Latin was good enough to understand what the soldiers were saying and he was expecting something of the sort. The world was still a type of dream to him – the bright sun, the smells, the colors. He was drinking all that in, because it was so unreal and not appropriate to a man who was condemned to death and had just emerged from his tomb. It mattered little to him whether he walked under or around the yoke, until he saw it. There, atop the crossbeam and adorning the yoke, was a massive pair of horns from a bull.

Josephus ran free from his escort, calling back to the centurion "Untie my hands." When he reached the yoke, he looked again at the centurion, who was running up to his charge to reassert control. The soldiers surrounding them turned silent; this was highly unorthodox behavior. "Untie my hands, I said." Josephus said this in perfect Latin, in his most authoritative voice, spoken as a man used to giving orders. Nicanor had caught up to them by this point and asked the centurion to untie the prisoner's hands. "He will cause no harm."

Josephus ran his hands up and down the enormous horns mounted on the yoke. He had to feel it for himself, to know it was real. It was becoming very clear to him now. He began to see his way to the solution he had been seeking for days. "Whose is this?" he demanded, looking about at the centurion and then at the soldiers who were assembled in a large crowd around the yoke. They had been expecting a humiliation but were very uncertain what was happening now.

"Where did you get this? Who found this? I need to know. It is very important. Whose is this?" Josephus was pleading to the crowd for the answers he sought.

"It is mine." A man of moderate size emerged from the tent at the center of the camp. He was wearing an ordinary soldier's tunic and sandals. The soldiers all around went completely silent and stiffened their postures.

As Josephus approached him, the centurion and another soldier rushed up to protect the General. "It is an Ur-ox, isn't it," said Josephus. "I know this animal. I have been dreaming about him for days. He was telling me something important, and I thought it was about me, but it wasn't. It was about you. It has been about you all along."

Josephus paused and looked more closely at the man. "Which one are you – Vespasianus or Titus?"

"I am Vespasianus." He pointed at the yoke. "I captured that Ur-ox when I was a youth posted in Germania. He was a magnificent animal. He has been my personal symbol ever since." Vespasianus pointed to a standard that was fluttering above his tent; it depicted a bull with the distinctive curved horns of an Ur-ox. "And you are Josephus. Bring this man to my tent."

Vespasianus turned on his heels and returned to his tent. "Serve him some wine," he ordered. "Nicanor, you can stay. Centurion, thank you for your efforts; you will be rewarded. You are dismissed."

"You may sit down, Josephus. You have given us much trouble, much trouble. I am not entirely sure what to do with you, though I do know what my troops would have me do."

"I fully expect to die at your hands, General Vespasianus," replied Josephus. "I am prepared for it. Today would be preferable. I have an oath to fulfill."

"What oath is this?" inquired Vespasianus. Nicanor informed him of what he had learned of the death pact in the cave. Vespasianus let out a low whistle as the story was told. He looked to his right at a man who was sitting at the back of the tent. It was his son, Titus. "They could be brothers," thought Josephus. "They have the same, stocky, muscular torso, the prominent forehead from partial balding, the flattened face and nose. They remind me of those working dogs with short, stout legs. Very appropriate too for Vespasianus."

"Well, well, Josephus, you have had quite the ordeal. I think we will have to disappoint our men. You have already gone under the yoke by being in that cave. There will be no public humiliation for you today. But I may have to disappoint you as well. We may have to postpone your execution. Tell me more about your dream."

Josephus was eager to discuss his dream. It was his entire purpose for being there, now that he understood fully its import. He recounted the exact details of the dream for the General, who listened with rapt interest. Josephus proceeded to plot out the position of the characters on the table top, using his fingers as if he were sketching out a plan of attack on a military map.

"Here is the plum tree. It is sere and dying. Its purple fruit is rotten and sterile. It symbolizes the imperial throne, which is full of corruption. It tells us that the Emperor Nero is near the end of his reign. He will be overthrown and forced off the throne.

"The young girl is Roma herself. She is unstained and unafraid. But she is under attack. The three wolves represent three different contenders for the throne. They may hold power briefly, but ultimately they will all be defeated by the Ur-ox, which obviously represents you. You will be Emperor, in the end. You will not seek it out. You will let the three others fight among themselves in a civil war. Then others will demand that you take on the responsibilities of government. Your troops will demand it of the Senate, and the Senate will in the end confirm you as Emperor. As your first born son, Titus will become Caesar to you as Augustus, in other words, your heir. It could not be more clear."

Vespasianus sat down on a portable military stool and rubbed his nose for a second. "This could be a fairy tale you are telling me, Josephus. When did you have this dream? Did you tell anyone about this?" Josephus explained his long history with dreams and visions, and their predictive power. He explained that this dream began the first night he was in the cave, and many people there heard him describe the dream in the exact same detail, since these dreams repeat themselves always in the same way.

"Yes, well, all of those people in the cave are dead, aren't they? That's unfortunate for you that no one else can establish whether you were dreaming or are simply making something up." Josephus replied that it did not matter to him whether anyone else believed in either his dreams or his predictions. What mattered was whether the prediction came to pass, and they always did in some form or another. "My only regret, General, is that I shall not live to see you ascend to the imperial throne, which could happen this year or next."

"You do want to rush to your death, don't you? Perhaps, Josephus, you should consider that your debt has been paid. The old Josephus died in the cave, and you are the new, resurrected Josephus. You should become one of those Jews who worships Jehoshua, the Christos. He was resurrected just like you. On the other hand, that may not be such a good idea – Nero is too fond of tormenting those Christians. In any event, there is no other way to confirm you have prophetic powers, which is regrettable."

"Do you have papyrus and a stylus for writing, General?" Titus had some on his desk and brought them over. Josephus continued: "I am going to write a number down that only you shall see. It represents a certain number of days from one event to today, when I was captured in the cave. At the start of your campaign, I predicted to my aide-de-camp Mathias that that number of days would elapse before our defeat and my apprehension. I told only him, partly because I was embarrassed. A commander should not be predicting his own defeat. Find this man Mathias, ask him if I made such a prediction, and how many days were involved. I have lost track of the date, given all that has happened to me recently, but I wouldn't be surprised if this prediction has now come to pass."

Josephus got up, brought the paper to Vespasianus, and showed him the number 47.

"It looks like I have another commission for you, Nicanor. Find out if this man Mathias is still alive and bring him to me. As for you Josephus, you will be confined to our barracks prison for the time being. I know you won't be committing suicide, but I want your oath as an officer that you will not be conspiring to have someone else kill you. I may have some use for you, and you may have more work to do for the benefit of your people. And whatever you may think of us Romans, Josephus, there are some of us who worry about such things as the prosperity of the people we conquer. We are not all of us here to tax every Jew into poverty. You might inquire about my record as governor in Africa if you want proof."

"I give you my word, General, that I will not arrange my own death."

Josephus was led off to his prison cell. Nicanor did not take long to find Mathias. All officers had been rounded up and kept captive in one area of the city, pending their trials. The expectation was that all of them would be executed by crucifixion. Mathias was surprised when he was dragged out of his prison cell one morning, and even more surprised when he found himself standing in front of Vespasianus himself.

"You are Mathias, the aide-de-camp to Josephus? I want you to tell me exactly what Josephus said to you at the start of the campaign, about how long it would last."

"Your Excellency," said Mathias, "he told me on the first day of the siege that 47 days would elapse before he would be captured and executed. I don't know where he got the number, but for obvious reasons I kept that conversation to myself for fear it would otherwise demoralize the troops. I have told no one about it since."

"He was wrong on one thing," said Vespasianus. "He was not executed, but he is being held in our prison cells here. I think I will not return you to the city but instead hold you here as well, on condition that you make sure Josephus stays alive. You will have some time to be with him during the day. Keep him busy. I heard he is a scholar. Get him to start writing something. We'll provide him with the materials. If you do this, we will see about commuting your death sentence."

Vespasianus had Mathias imprisoned in a cell near Josephus. The General was now alone with his son Titus. He reached for a paper in his folders and held it up to Titus. "You see that, Titus -- the number 47? It has been exactly 47 days from the start of the siege to his capture. He has the gift of prophecy. That is all we need – proof of his talents. Whether his story of the girl, the wolves, and the Ur-ox is true is not as important. People need to believe it is true – that is what matters. We will bide our time on this and see how things develop. It doesn't take a prophet to predict that Nero cannot last much longer. He has antagonized everyone in Rome and lost almost all of his political support. He is only being propped up now by the Praetorian Guard. There will come a point when I will want you to subtly spread some information about Josephus and his prophecy to the troops. I want them all to believe it by the time we are ready to move."

Vespasianus could see his son virtually drooling with anticipation at the possibility of rising ultimately to the throne when Vespasianus died. He didn't like the way Titus was infatuated with power. He needed to learn restraint and the art of making friends. Vespasianus already had friends positioned all around the Empire – he had served in many different countries. Fools like Galba and Vitellius made their way through politics by bribing people, and once you started doing that, the money was never enough.

Oh yes, Galba and Vitellius were wolves. That's what made the dream so believable. It had the perfect symbol for men like that. Who the third wolf was, he wasn't sure yet. Someone would rise to the temptation.

He had one more thing to do. He called for the head of his personal guard. "I want a detail of two men posted permanently at the yoke every hour of the day. That is six men in total each doing eight hour shifts. The yoke is not to be touched by anyone. You are responsible for anything bad that happens to it."

He could take no chances now. It was not the yoke he was interested in – it was his Ur-ox. It had brought him good luck over the years. It was now about to bring him the greatest prize the world had to offer – the throne of an Empire. Of course, he had the prophecy on his side. Vespasianus believed implicitly in the prophecy. He believed in it immediately as Josephus described it. He felt it in his soul, and not in his mind, and it took every ounce of self-restraint he could muster to avoid showing any hint of his excitement about the prediction. He would be Emperor. There was no doubt. He now had the prophecy on one side of him and the Ur-ox on the other. But he had to keep Josephus alive and well, available to be put on show publicly when necessary. And he had to keep his Ur-ox protected.

The Fates were now completely supportive of his ambitions. But he never forgot the advice he was given by the Emperor Claudius when he was planning out the campaign to conquer Britannia: the Fates always appreciate help now and then from the mortals whom they favor.

PART FIVE

The defining event of the first century is now about to take place – the siege and destruction of Jerusalem – which sets Western civilization on a course that will embrace a tiny cult of worship among Jews, allowing it to develop into the religion of Christianity. None of this is evident to the players at the time, who include Flavius Vespasianus, a contender for Emperor of Rome; his son Titus; the Jewish scholar Josephus; and those Jews who attempt to defend Jerusalem from Roman attack. They have two leaders, Yohan of Gischala and Simon bar Giora. These two come down to us in history either as Jewish patriots or as reckless criminals who prey upon the long-suffering Jewish people who are left defenseless at the hands of a band of Jewish marauders known as The Zealots. An estimated one million Jews will die horribly in the fall of Jerusalem and the loss of Israel, and their descendants are about to commence the long exile known as the Diaspora.

The Zealots

Jerusalem
Years 69 to 71

Chapter Twenty Four

"The Lord will never be willing to forgive them; his wrath and zeal will burn against them. All the curses written in this book will fall on them, and the Lord will blot out their names from under heaven."

Yohan of Gischala held up the sacred Torah for his men to see. They were packed into the synagogue courtyard of Yohan's city, Gischala, which they were defending from the Romans encamped outside the city gate. After the fall of Jotapata, it was the last major city in Galilee left standing. Should Gischala succumb to the Roman siege, the way was open for the legions of Titus and Vespasianus to advance to Jerusalem itself.

Yohan looked out at his ragged excuse for an army – men with every conceivable sort of weapon, from swords to knives to clubs to shovels. Men with no discipline, most of whom had a history as brigands, thieves, and even murderers; and too many of whom had been practicing their criminal arts on the citizens of Gischala. These were men who would follow Yohan of Gischala anywhere, for he had stirred up their hatred of the Romans and incited them to rebel against Roman rule. There had been enough instances of Roman cruelty, arbitrary justice, excessive taxation, and now outright slaughter of the Jews, that it did not take much to convince these men that armed insurrection was the only answer. They listened avidly to every word of his rhetoric, they followed him into battle, and they had some successes against the Romans, but they suffered more defeats than they had successes. They had ravaged the countryside of Galilee and Samaria in search of food, and they raped respectable Jewish women with the same eagerness as they would the much-despised Samaritan women. These were men who would otherwise be massacred by the Jewish population of Galilee and by the citizens of Gischala if the people ever were given the opportunity. Unfortunately, that opportunity never arose, because Yohan's army spent more of their time terrorizing the Jewish population than attacking the Romans. Yohan called his army The Zealots, because he assured them they were destined to purify Israel of Roman wickedness. These were the men Yohan of Gischala was about to betray.

Yohan returned to the verse he had just cited from Deuteronomy. "'The Lord will blot out their names from under heaven.' So says Moses. So say I. The Romans are weakening every day. They scrounge the fields looking for food, but there is none. We have it all. Where are their famous military engines to batter down the gates of Gischala? They have none strong enough, or we would have seen them by now! They have given up the fight, and when the time is right, we shall rush forth from these gates and destroy them all!"

"The Romans shall be blotted out of human memory. They shall face the wrath of the Lord Almighty, and who shall be the agents of the Lord God?" "We shall!" shouted the men in unison. "We shall! We shall!" They shouted over and over, and from his balcony, Yohan laid out his hands in a command of silence. "Let us praise the Lord God!" With that, Yohan began singing the one verse of scripture which always ended his perorations. Quickly his army raise their voices into a mighty sound.

"For out of Jerusalem will come a remnant, and out of Mount Zion a band of survivors. The Zeal of the Lord Almighty will accomplish this."

His men fully believed they were the band of survivors, destined to save Israel. They were about to learn otherwise.

Yohan returned to his private quarters. He motioned to one of his closest aides, Benyamin, to join him. In the privacy of an anteroom, he received Benyamin's report. "Titus is offering us his right hand in peace. It is the most sacred oath a Roman commander can make, and he will therefore live up to his promise. If we allow him to take Gischala without a fight, he will guarantee the safety of its residents. There will be no pillaging. We and all of our men must surrender to him, but he will impose no reprisals on any of us. Once the war is over, which for him means once he and his father, Vespasianus, have taken Jerusalem, we can go free."

"And if we do not accept his terms?" asked Yohan. "Then the battering rams will be brought to the gates immediately," said Benyamin. "They are within a day's travel from here. Titus will begin building up earthworks around the city walls as well. One way or another, he will find a way into the city."

"You were instructed to accept his terms, but we need time," noted Yohan. "What did he say to our condition of surrender?"

"He understood that tomorrow is our Sabbath, and he knows full well that Jews cannot work on the Sabbath, even if it is the labor of surrendering to an opposing army. Therefore, he has agreed to our one condition that our surrender will occur two days from today."

"Very good work, Benyamin," said Yohan. "You and I shall be leaving tonight, quietly, with the list of the commanders that I have given to you. We will ride hastily to Jerusalem and then to Idumea to seek help. I told the men just now that the Romans have no means of battering down our gates, but we both know that is not true. What we need is time to get help, otherwise we will lose Gischala. Just as we leave, you are to deliver this same message to one of the men who will be left behind, one who can be trusted to explain our absence properly to the army. He is to keep their morale up until we return."

Benyamin was no fool. He could see this flight to safety for what it was – a cowardly desertion by Yohan and those closest to him. He doubted the men left behind in Gischala would be fooled either, and once the siege began in earnest, most of them would desert the city as well. The people remaining would open the gates eagerly and welcome Titus as a hero, giving him possession of all of Galilee. As for himself, he preferred to take his chances with Yohan of Gischala. The man was a survivor.

Benyamin's instincts were correct, even though the plan did not unfold as desired. Somehow word traveled throughout the army of the Zealots that Yohan of Gischala was leaving immediately for Jerusalem. By the time Yohan and his closest lieutenants were mounted and ready to leave Gischala, over a hundred men were prepared to join them, and most of them had forced women, and even children, to accompany them as hostages.

As Yohan and his commanders fled Gischala in the dark of night, several hundred people followed him. Their trek across the desert south to Jerusalem was dire, and quite a number did not survive the heat and lack of water. Yohan was disinterested in the fate of these stragglers, or even of the men who had previously been his followers and were now as desperate as he was to reach the safety of Jerusalem. He was only interested in getting away as fast as he could from Gischala before Titus discovered the deception, and he was right in doing so. Titus was furious when, two days later, he discovered Yohan of Gischala had fled the city. Titus did not like being played for a fool, and he was fortunate that hardly anyone in the Roman legion he commanded knew about the negotiations with Yohan. Titus sent his fastest mounted soldiers to track down Yohan but it was too late; the man had reached Jerusalem and was now safely inside the city. He had left many stragglers wandering after him across the desert.

What Yohan discovered in Jerusalem was a situation quite to his liking. The city was in complete panic at the prospect of Vespasianus and his son arriving at any moment outside of the walls of Jerusalem. Civil order had broken down, as the wealthy and many members of the Sanhedrin had fled Jerusalem, or in many cases, had fled Judea altogether. Refugees were flooding into the city from Galilee and elsewhere, and in their number, as occurred in Gischala, were many men of dubious background who began to take effective control of the streets.

Yohan made sure that his lieutenants spread the word about his heroic defense of Gischala, and how he had braved his life to rush to Jerusalem to warn the city of the impending besiegement. He vowed publicly to help in the defense, using the knowledge he had gained in fighting the Romans in the past few years. He had rumors spread about that he was instrumental in the defeat of the Romans at Bet-Horon, the battle which had forced Nero's hand and prompted him to send Vespasianus with four legions to finally subdue the Jews.

Any stragglers from Gischala who attempted to contradict this campaign of deception, which threw a luster of temerity and heroism over the personage of Yohan of Gischala, were silenced by his allies. Yohan helped his cause considerably by making up stories about his past, and he was such a convincing deceiver that he fooled the one man in Jerusalem who should have known better – Ananus, the former High Priest.

Ananus was one of the few religious elders who had not fled the city. He had stayed behind because it was his assignment to defend the Temple from the Zealots, just as Josephus had been assigned by the leadership to defend Jotapata. Both men failed at their jobs.

This was the mistake Ananus made, one that Yohan of Gischala was poised to exploit.

"How did it happen?" he asked Ananus when they first met. By this time Yohan was hailed as the virtual Hero of Gischala, and Ananus was inclined to unburden himself to someone of his own stature – a leader and military commander. "They overran the city, these Zealots," said Ananus. "There were several thousand of them who came mostly from the south, but their forces were augmented by men from all over. Some of them had military experience, but most were adventurers and louts."

"They coveted the Temple grounds as the most secure position in the city; and with the Romans evacuating the adjacent Fortress Antonia, they assumed that those two structures would be unassailable by the Romans. They may be right, from a strictly military viewpoint. We had less than one hundred Temple police to repel them, and our forces were simply insufficient. They quickly took command of the outer courtyard, and shut down the market, so there is now no organized place for anyone in Jerusalem to obtain food. Within a few days they overran the inner courtyard."

Ananus continued: "What they have forgotten about is the religious significance of the Temple to Jews everywhere. Their mere presence in the inner courtyard is profane, because not all of them are Jews, and they have even allowed women within the sacred areas. As to whether they have dared to enter the Holy of Holies, I cannot say, but surely it is only a matter of time."

"And to show you what manner of men these are, they chose a new High Priest by lot, a farmer who knows nothing of rituals, a feeble-minded tool who does whatever they tell him. They dress him up in expensive priestly robes and parade him around the city as a new religious authority. I don't know what is more appalling - the buffoon the Zealots have chosen for High Priest or the impious nature of their presence in the Temple itself."

Yohan nodded his head gravely as each charge of impropriety and religious sacrilege mounted. He commiserated fully with Ananus, despite the fact that he himself had commanded a collection of Zealots in Gischala. He asked why a counter-attack had not been contemplated. "We simply do not have enough men in Jerusalem for that," was all that Ananus could reply.

Left unsaid was the fact that the problem wasn't enough men – Jerusalem was crawling with men, residents, pilgrims for the

Passover, and others, who would be willing to wrest control of the Temple away from thieves and murderers. The problem was that no one was willing to follow Ananus. He had already estranged himself from the Pharisees with his vicious and entirely illegal arrests and executions of their leading citizens. He could certainly not count on the support of a growing group within Jerusalem – the followers of the Christos. They too had lost their leader in the pogroms that Ananus had instituted eight years earlier. When Ananus was officially ousted by the Romans from his position as High Priest, it was the ultimate disgrace, which resulted in his losing allegiance from the Temple police. Ananus was an orphan politically and religiously, who had only a notable family name to recommend him. He was a perfect instrument upon which someone like Yohan of Gischala could play any tune he desired.

"Perhaps I can organize a defense for you," suggested Yohan with a convincing tone of ingenuousness. Ananus perked up. "My lieutenants are battle-skilled with professional military experience," he continued. "There are enough men in Jerusalem with military background that we could form an opposing force quickly, at least equal in number to the criminals inhabiting the Temple. Certainly we would be superior in skill and tactical talent."

This was very much to the liking of Ananus, and it was contrived that they would join forces and place them under the military leadership of Yohan. Recruiting and other preparations were begun immediately. At first the Zealots within the Temple grounds were unsuspecting, but their spies within the city informed them of the activities that were underway, and it was decided that a pre-emptive attack by the Zealots would be sufficient to repel the effort of Ananus (for there was no thought yet that he had any accomplice in these efforts).

This attack had to be brought forward hurriedly by the Zealots, when it was discovered that Ananus was in the final stages of preparing an assault on the Temple. He would have had the aspect of surprise on his side, had he not decided that each one of several thousand recruits had to be individually purified before they would be allowed to step foot into the inner courtyard. This was, of course, a religious nicety that the Zealots had not bothered to observe; and before the purification ceremony was complete, it was the Zealots who carried the element of surprise, by issuing forth from the courtyard gates to the marketplace grounds where

Ananus' troops had assembled. The slinging of arrows and spears quickly gave way to bloody hand-to-hand sword fighting that resulted in hundreds of deaths. No side gained a decisive advantage, and both eventually retreated, Ananus realizing how difficult it would be to extract the Zealots from the sacred grounds, and the Zealots realizing in turn that over time Ananus would be able to recruit sufficient numbers of troops to overrun the Temple and put to death every one of them.

It was in a sobered mood that Ananus once again consulted with Yohan of Gischala, who argued that the citizen's army might have had better success if more time had been spent on training and military preparation rather than religious sanctification. Ananus was despairing as well because of the possibility that bloodshed might be spilled on the grounds of the inner courtyard in order to defeat the Zealots, an unforgivable insult to the Lord God. Worse still, the Holy of Holies might be penetrated. Was there any way, he wondered, that negotiations might work in extricating the Zealots from the Temple?

Yohan proposed that he himself should conduct these negotiations to discuss what terms might be suitable to the Zealots. "Perhaps," he suggested, "they might be willing to occupy only the Fortress Antonia or man the city walls." Ananus was agreeable to these negotiations, as long as Yohan took a solemn oath to represent only the interests of the citizens of Jerusalem, under whose authority the assault forces had been organized. "I swear to defend only the interests of the people of Jerusalem, under my solemn oath and in the sight of the Lord." Thus was Yohan committed to the cause.

Bearing an ensign of truce, Yohan was admitted to the inner courtyard, where he asked to meet with the leaders of the Zealots. Five men approached him who served as a collective leadership of the Zealots. They were familiar with Yohan of Gischala, and one of the men had already met him.

"My interests are the same as yours," Yohan began. "We both want the ouster of the Romans from Israel, and if necessary we desire to inflict on them the most painful defeat so that they will never again step into this land. If you know of my reputation, you know I am devoted entirely to the interests of Israel and to our independence so that Jews can once again live in covenant with the Lord God, unhindered by outsiders."

"I am here representing Ananus, who now has several thousand volunteers preparing to assault the Temple. He is receiving more recruits every day. It is only a matter of time before the doors to the inner courtyard are breached, or these men scale the tower walls. Your very lives are already forfeit as we sit here." Yohan could see by their eyes, which flickered back and forth nervously one to the other, that he had touched on the very point which they most feared. The Zealots had taken over the Temple and the Fortress Antonia as impregnable redoubts, anticipating it would be the Romans they would be fighting. They never expected to be fighting fellow Jews within the city.

"If you know anything of Ananus, you must know that his primary interest is preserving the sanctity of the Temple. He wants you out of these grounds and he wants the priesthood of the tribe of Levi restored to its traditional rights. He is so obsessed with this that he has entered into secret negotiations with Vespasianus to open the gates of the city to him so that he can undertake your removal. Ananus believes the Romans have much more advanced and purposeful assault machines that can quickly penetrate the courtyard wall. Vespasianus has 10,000 men at his disposal, and he can so quickly overwhelm all of you, that what bloodshed there might be, if any at all, would be minimized. Your deaths would then be assured, probably by crucifixion."

The look of alarm on the faces of his negotiators was even more profound with this revelation, but there was another look as well: anger. "What sort of Jew is he," shouted one of the men, "that he would willingly turn Jerusalem over to the Romans? How naïve can he be to expect that, after nearly four years of war, the Romans will simply walk away from the treasure that lies within these walls and not tear down the walls afterward?"

The other men seconded these sentiments, saying that with this information, they would never leave the Temple and willingly turn it over to a traitor such as Ananus. "But remember," cautioned Yohan, "even without the Romans he is going to come after you, and he ultimately will defeat you. I would have been right by his side, until he informed me of these negotiations with Vespasianus. Like you, I cannot countenance the thought of any Roman walking through the Damascus Gate into the city, now that we are rid of them. There is a way, however, to defend Jerusalem from the Romans, and at the same time, thwart Ananus."

"You need reinforcements. I propose that we send word to the Idumeans to the south, asking for reinforcements. Once they hear of the duplicity of Ananus, they will rush to our defense, because otherwise, they are completely exposed to an attack by the Romans if Jerusalem falls. Idumea will be the last province of Israel to be conquered if Judea, Samaria, and Galilee have all fallen, and they will be easy prey if no one is available to assist them."

The Idumeans were renowned for the fierceness of their fighting. They considered themselves Jewish, but their practices of worship were not the same as might be found in Jerusalem - the Idumeans were nomadic, traveling the countryside with their sheep and goats as the seasons warranted. Among all the Jews, the Idumeans were considered the closest to the Arabs. They had the same weathered look and dark skin of the Arabs, reflecting their life outdoors in the desert, and they had similarly high expectations of hospitality from their friends, no matter when they might show up. This too came from a life spent in the desert, where hospitality from strangers was often necessary for survival. The Idumeans naturally expected to be greeted with fulsome expressions of welcome when they reached the southern gate of Jerusalem.

"I appreciate," continued Yohan, "that you do not know me well enough to trust me. Therefore, I suggest that together we write the letter to the Idumeans and that you send your own courier with the letter to Hebron. Any reply will remain sealed until we all can meet – the six of us – to hear the response."

The Zealots, fired up as they were by rage, heartedly agreed to this proposal and the letter was dispatched by courier before Yohan returned to Ananus. Yohan reported back to Ananus the most important news of all – that the Holy of Holies had not been entered. This did not diminish the desire of Ananus to remove the Zealots from the Temple, but it certainly confirmed for Yohan that the man's principal concerns were religious, not military or political. Yohan was now completely steeped in double-dealing and kept counsel only to himself about his proposal to the Zealots. The lie that he started, however, began to spread outside the walls of the Temple, so that the people of Jerusalem were plagued by uncertainty whether Ananus was really going to turn the city over to the Romans. Ananus, for his part, could not understand how such thinking had arisen and tried as best he could to deny the rumors. He was, however, but one man against many with suspicions.

Several days later, Yohan innocently informed Ananus that the Zealots had an answer for them, when in fact they had received a sealed message from the Idumeans. He therefore hastened back to the Temple, where he learned with the Zealots that the Idumeans were already on their way to Jerusalem with reinforcements, intent on overthrowing Ananus and strengthening the Zealots in their defense of the city.

The distance between Hebron and Jerusalem was comparatively short, and the advance troops of the Idumeans were at the southern gates of the city shortly after their letter had arrived. Much to their surprise, the gates were closed to them, and under order of Ananus they were not to be opened. This was an affront to the Idumeans at many levels: a refusal of hospitality that was otherwise traditional among Jews, a privation on their troops due to the scarcity of food and water, and a suggestion that the Idumeans were not to be trusted with the defense of the capital city.

As the days progressed, with Jerusalem remaining closed, the ire of the Idumeans mounted. Ananus was at a loss as to their presence in the first place, but he was certainly wary enough of their presence to let them in. Who had called them? He had no idea that the Idumeans were there because he – Ananus – was considered a traitor who was working to destroy Jerusalem and Israel from within. The poisonous suspicions that had been sown by Yohan were now working corrosively to undermine any hope for the city when and if Vespasianus arrived and mounted a siege.

Ananus ensured that a vigilant guard stood watch over all the gates and towers of the city, alert to any potential attack by the Idumeans. He did not anticipate a blow from within the city. The opportunity came to the Zealots a week after the Idumeans were forced to encamp outside the walls of Jerusalem. A fierce thunderstorm arose in the middle of the night. The persistent lightning and high winds were such that Ananus allowed most of the guards to seek shelter. Sensing their chance, the Zealots stole out of the Temple, slew the few remaining guards at their posts, and opened the gates of the city to the Idumeans. The resulting slaughter perpetrated by the Idumeans was out of all proportion to the insult they had received outside the city walls. They rampaged throughout Jerusalem, indiscriminately killing women, the elderly, and children. They were later to blame their behavior on the Lord God, saying they were only the instruments of His fury at the mistreatment they received. They cited as evidence the thunderstorm, unusual for that time of year, and which provided the Zealots an opportunity to overcome the guards at the city gates.

The Zealots welcomed their conquering allies and established for themselves free reign over the city while the Idumeans were rampaging among the population. The Zealots in particular sought out Ananus, and finding him hiding in a fish-mongers shop, they dragged him forcibly to the inner courtyard of the Temple so that he might defile the sacred altar with his own blood.

Ananus was to meet his death a short walk away from the spot where, on his own orders, the Christian leader Yakov the Just had been flung off a tower to the stone pavement of the Gentile courtyard, where he was dispatched with a blow to the head.

No such mercy was shown Ananus. He was strapped to the sacrificial altar, and a large axe was aimed straight at his groin. He was cleaved in two clear up to his stomach. His intestines spilled out and blood drained slowly down the altar. He screamed in agony for well over two hours before expiring from his ordeal.

The Zealots bade their dull-witted counterfeit High Priest to cut out some of the intestines of the victim while he was still alive and lift them up as a burnt offering to the Lord God on High. The wind and the rain kept extinguishing the flame of the offering, which was never consumed by the fire properly.

Had they been as religious as they professed, the Zealots might have interpreted their mockery of an offering to the Lord God as an ill omen. Certainly, judging by what befell all of Jerusalem when the Roman legions arrived, the Zealots came to believe the offering was not well received by the Almighty.

Yohan of Gischala might have told them that. Indeed, he did tell them that, when he said, "the Lord will never be willing to forgive them; his wrath and zeal will burn against them." No one at the time thought this admonition could possibly apply to Jerusalem itself.

Chapter Twenty Five

Mews of the fighting among the Jews within Jerusalem reached Vespasianus quickly. His commanders and centurions were eager to march to Jerusalem and begin the siege at such a propitious moment. Vespasianus thought otherwise. "Let them continue to fight among themselves and destroy themselves. Let us see how long this lasts. It makes our ultimate task lighter by the day. In the meantime, we have cities and villages to the south of Jerusalem to take so that Jerusalem will then be completely surrounded."

A more personal consideration was that he wanted to meet up with his son and give the legion that Titus commanded a respite, since they had borne the bulk of the recent fighting. Accordingly, he invited Titus up to Caesarea Philippi. They hadn't seen each other in a few months, but Titus looked more fit than ever. This military life definitely suited him. He might well turn into a better general than his father, thought Vespasianus.

After catching up on some family talk, including news of what Domitianus, the younger brother of Titus, was doing, Vespasianus said that it was time to have a private chat while they had the opportunity. "Everything is going according to our plan and in agreement with the prophecy of Josephus. We now have had three wolves appear who were all eager to lead Rome, and two of them have been devoured. That leaves the last one for us to finish."

"Galba was the first wolf to appear. As governor of Hispania, he had access to revenue from the silver mines, and he also had an enormous fortune which he had inherited from his father. Why he was stingy with money was never easy to understand, but sometimes these rich men are like that. They worry constantly that they will lose everything overnight. This miserliness was his undoing, because the real reason he was proclaimed emperor by the Praetorian Guard was that they were promised by Galba's supporters that they would receive a substantial bribe."

Vespasianus continued: "Perhaps no one told Galba about this, but when he got to Rome, he refused to pay anything to the

Praetorian Guard. These men bided their time, while they watched Galba put people to death without a trial and ignore the legions overseas which had also supported him. Eventually, two of the legions in Germania had had enough, and they refused to renew their oath of allegiance to Galba at the start of this year. I think that finally scared him, so he announced he had appointed a successor, Calpurnius Piso."

"He must have thought that this would reduce the pressure on him, because he was already an old man when the Senate approved him as emperor, and now people could concentrate their attention and complaints on his successor. The problem was this – and it will be a real problem for us as well. The Praetorian Guard now have it in their mind that they decide who is to be emperor. This was exactly what people predicted when the Guard assassinated Caligula and then found Claudius and thought he was enough of a fool that they could control him. They were wrong about Claudius, but they were right that the Senate will accept anyone the Guard announces as their emperor. Moreover, they've shown they can be bribed by anyone who is wealthy enough and wants the power of the throne. The Guard were fully expecting to be bribed for accepting the appointment of Calpurnius Piso as heir, but again Galba was too cheap, or maybe too principled, to placate the Praetorian Guard. "

"The Guard now had been insulted twice: no payment when Galba came to the throne and no payment when Galba announced he had appointed a successor, Piso. So what happened? Galba's trusted friend, Salvius Otho, who I think you met the last time we were in Rome, began secret talks with the Praetorian Guard, and obviously money now changed hands, because the Guard declared it had a new emperor, Otho."

"This is where I feel sorry for Galba. He was trying to do the right thing. He was trying to reduce the power of the Praetorian Guard to create a new government for the Empire. But I just think he could have done that in steps – paying the Guard what they demanded, but gradually replacing them or even giving some of this power back to the Senate. Then he made another mistake: he decided to meet Otho in front of the Praetorian Guard, not knowing they no longer supported him. Instead of deference, the Guard surrounded him and killed him with multiple sword wounds, as if he was Julius Caesar. Then Otho had Galba's head cut off so he could display it around the Praetorian camp."

"I never had any respect for Otho in the first place, but I have to tell you, Titus, that I could not support this man as emperor based on how he treated Galba. There was no cause for such disrespect. The man had a noble career serving Rome, and as I said, that was all he was really trying to do, however flawed his approach may have been."

"Fortunately, it never got far enough for me to have to declare for Otho, and I will say he did redeem himself at the end. Once he became emperor, he still had to deal with the German legions, who refused to support him and were now openly declaring for their commander, Vitellius. Otho decided he needed to suppress this revolt personally, and he brought his legions, including the Praetorians, up to the Po, where he rushed into battle. His men fought well, but Otho did not have full strength – he was too impatient to wait for his troops from the Danube to arrive. He lost this battle and had to retreat."

"Here is where, as I said, he redeemed himself. His other legion arrived, and he could have forced another battle, where he had a good chance of emerging as the victor and defeating Vitellius, but instead he decided to abdicate. He believed that any future battles would result in unnecessary bloodshed on both sides, so he retired to his tent and stabbed himself in the heart."

"I don't know how well the Praetorian Guard took this, but it was said that some of them were so in awe of Otho's noble sacrifice that they jumped on his funeral pyre. I doubt that very much – not these men, but in retrospect they should have all done so, because when Vitellius got to Rome, he dismissed them all and replaced them with his personal guard from Germania, many of whom don't speak any civilized language, either Greek or Latin. This is actually an interesting idea; it makes it much harder to bribe them, and they can't participate in our politics very easily."

"I've known Vitellius for a long time. He is a sybarite of the first order. He spends all his time dining, enjoying the choicest wines, and ordering that the rarest food be brought to his table by the military. Like Galba, he has been very arbitrary in his arrests and executions, including some senators. He is absolutely the worst choice for emperor because he has no interest in government and no capacity for it. His troops from Germania are very undisciplined precisely because he has been entertaining them with dinners and games for the past five years."

"Everything you are telling me, Father," said Titus, "suggests that the time is ripe for us to do something. All of these men are far worse in skill than you are; the Senate must be desperate to find someone with competence who will refill the Treasury and put an end to arbitrary rule."

"I agree," said Vespasianus. "But we must make everything appear as if this is not our idea – that I am not coveting the job. You have to remember, we are not Roman patricians or connected even by marriage to any notable Roman family. As far as the Senate is concerned, we are of peasant stock. They are quite happy to accept our military services, but would not normally entertain the idea that I am acceptable as head of the government. Things must be arranged so that they are begging for me to take the throne."

"Here is what I want you to do. You need to have two or three of your lieutenants pass the story around about the dream that Josephus had and his ability to predict the future. Prepare Josephus carefully in case anyone asks him about this prediction. I am sure he will want to cooperate; he has every reason to see me in Rome as head of the government. At some point, probably within a month, I want the legions I command to declare for me as emperor. I will give you the signal, but I want the legions to truly believe in what they are saying. They need to believe that the government in Rome is corrupt, that these successive emperors have been very bad choices, and that the gods have ordained me as the next emperor. The more they believe, the better, because they may have to fight for us."

"I am leaving Caesarea Philippi to travel down to Alexandria. I want to spend some time with Tiberius Alexander. I need his support and I need it early. He has the respect of the Senate – he is a very capable governor. And Egypt has command of Rome's grain. That is yet another important asset we must have. It doesn't mean we can bribe or threaten the Senate by withholding grain, but it does mean they don't have to worry about interruptions in the grain supply if they choose me."

"I then expect the other legions in Syria, Anatolia, and elsewhere in the East will declare for me. I want to be seen as the candidate from the Eastern half of the Empire, where the wealth really is. And that is where you come in again. I'm going to leave with you the responsibility of conquering Jerusalem and finishing up this campaign in Judea. You have the ability, you have an able group of commanders under you, you will have four legions, and you will be my heir and successor to the throne. People will respect that fact, but you must succeed here. We need the wealth of Judea to help refill the coin chests in the Treasury. Plus, we need a Triumph that will be unlike any seen before in the Forum. We need to raise Rome's spirits as we start our government. Try to take Jerusalem with the least amount of destruction here as possible, but do what you have to in order to get your hands on their treasure. That is one of the things we are implicitly promising the Senate, and we must deliver on that promise."

"I will leave Josephus with you. He will probably be of benefit to you in any negotiation you have to do with the Jews. I think he is trustworthy. He is looking for us to be his patrons in Rome, so dangle something valuable in front of him to keep him interested and on our side."

"I think, Titus, that will be all we need to discuss privately for the moment. We have quite a few tribunes and centurions waiting to have dinner with us, so let us not disappoint them."

Chapter Twenty Six

s Titus continued to subjugate one city after another in Judea, having side-by-side with his father already completely conquered the northern provinces of Israel, those who opposed him fled south to Jerusalem. One such man was Simon bar Giora, an opportunist and adventurer similar in nature to Yohan of Gischala. Yohan, however, associated himself with the Zealots, and at least had a cloak of religiosity to cover his misdeeds. Simon was not interested in moral scruples, since he had none. Those who stood in his way would find themselves impaled one night on the sharp end of a dagger. In normal circumstances, Simon would ply his various crafts of extortion, bribery, theft, and murder in a limited sphere, as a common criminal. In the chaos that engulfed Judea with the advent of the rebellion against Rome, a man like Simon had a much broader scope from which to work.

It helped considerably that he had leadership qualities. Such skills could be of tremendous use at a time when criminals of all sorts had free reign of the country and when otherwise honest men might commit unthinkable and unspeakable deeds out of hunger or some other form of desperation. Simon bar Giora, by virtue of his behavior, the example he set, the string of successes he enjoyed, and his rhetoric, attracted several thousand such men to his cause, whatever that cause might be. For most, it was survival at the expense of others; for some it was the opportunity to amass wealth; and for a few it was the chance to perpetrate gross crimes, such as murder for the sheer delight it brought to them.

It was at the height of the indiscriminate massacres by the Idumeans that Simon bar Giora slipped into Jerusalem with several thousand followers, as the gates to the city were now open for anyone wishing to enter who professed a desire to defend Jerusalem against the coming siege by the Romans. The Zealots, who had previously been confined to the Temple's inner courtyard, now had access not only to the Upper City of Jerusalem, which constituted the western sector, but to all other areas that lay at a lower level, namely the Lower City and David's City. Yohan of Gischala was rewarded for his duplicitous devotion to the Temple Zealots by being named their leader. As Yohan and his Zealots joined the Idumeans in their plunder, Simon bar Giora was not going to sit by quietly while such enormous opportunities were being exploited by others.

Instantly he and his men began their own campaign of terror against the population of Jerusalem. Neither Simon's forces nor Yohan's had any real connection to Jerusalem nor the people they were intimidating, then threatening, and finally torturing in order to find hidden coins or jewelry. The two armies – ostensibly there to defend Jerusalem from an enemy that hadn't even appeared yet outside the walls of the city – began to compete to find the richest homes, the secret stashes of wealth, and the hidden supplies of food, which were already in short supply. Competition quickly led to conflict, and in a very quick time, the two forces were battling openly in the streets of Jerusalem. They agreed on only one thing: they policed all the gates of the city not only to prevent allies arriving who would aid their new enemies, but more importantly, to prevent the citizens of Jerusalem from leaving, lest these "defenders" were robbed of their prey.

The fighting escalated from hand-to-hand combat in the streets and alleys of the city to more elaborate military tactics, employed chiefly by Yohan of Gischala, who had the advantage of using the military machines left behind by the Romans at the Fortress Antonia when they fled the city. These devices were used to pour down upon the lower parts of Jerusalem a barrage of large rocks. Yohan's men were completely unfamiliar with the use of these machines, which were the most advanced of their kind in the world, and consequently the destruction sprayed over large areas of the city, hitting civilians far more than Simon's forces, adding considerably to the state of misery that already afflicted the people of Jerusalem.

The Idumeans were caught up as well in these attacks, and as the prospects for plunder were diminishing quickly, and the possibilities for food were vanishing, most of the Idumeans were allowed to flee the city and return to Hebron. Simon's forces were desperate to destroy the machines that were the source of such terror, and they were successful in setting fire to a few of them before Yohan ordered his men back to their defensible position in the Temple compound. Yohan found himself back to his original position before the Idumeans arrived to save him, but this time he was not facing as weak a foe as Ananus. Simon bar Giora was a formidable adversary, prone to use any tactic necessary to advance his goal, which was complete domination of the city.

One such tactic was to destroy the city's supply of grain, intended to allow the population to withstand a siege of many years duration. The purpose of this tactic was to deprive Yohan and the Zealots of food, but the end result was to deprive everyone in Jerusalem of food altogether, not just the Zealots, but also Simon and his men, and the population in general. The city was a month or so away from mass starvation, and it was at this time that Titus arrived from the north with four Roman legions under his command.

Chapter Twenty Seven

Titus carried with him two letters, the first having arrived as he and his four legions set out for Jerusalem. It was a message from the Senate of Rome, sent via a Senatorial courier. Under pain of death, only the addressee could open and read a message from the Senate, and Titus had to use his personal signet ring to stamp his seal into hot wax – thereby establishing his identity – before the courier would hand over the parchment scroll to him.

To the Noble and Honorable Titus Flavius Vespasianus Secundus
Greetings from the Senate and People of Rome,

> *Be hereby notified that the Senate of Rome, on behalf of the People of Rome, has bestowed upon Titus Flavius Vespasianus, your father, the titles of Princeps, Imperator, Pontifex Maximus, and Caesar Augustus. Full imperial power has been granted your father so that he may properly manage our government in Italia and in all the provinces of Rome.*
>
> *The Imperator has requested of the Senate that we approve you as his heir to his offices and titles, and therefore, following due consultation and discussion, the Senate, on behalf of the People of Rome, has voted you, Titus Flavius Vespasianus Secundus, the title of Caesar. The Senate grants you hereby all such powers and authority which may be appointed you by the Imperator, at his discretion and in consultation with the Senate. Further, in the circumstance of the death of the Imperator, the Senate authorizes you to succeed to the titles of Princeps and Imperator and Pontifex Maximus, and to assume full imperial power and management of the government as a worthy successor to your father.*
>
> *So decreed by the Senate and People of Rome.*

Quintus Pompeius Barba
Secretary to the Senate of Rome

Titus fondled the scroll in his hand for several minutes upon receiving it; it was such an insignificant thing, yet it granted unimaginable power – the power of life and death over millions of citizens, freemen, and slaves in a vast Empire. Occasionally, Titus would pull the scroll out from a safe place in his military bag of papers, not quite sure it was real, and wonder once again at the magnitude of the power he was to wield. And whenever he felt this way, he would pull out a private message he had received a few weeks earlier from his father, who had been wintering in Alexandria, while waiting for an opportunity to sail with his legions to Rome.

To Titus Flavius Caesar Vespasianus

Hail, from Imperator Titus Flavius Caesar Vespasianus Augustus,

My son,

> *I write privately to tell you news of our efforts in Rome. I expected to travel to Rome in the spring, if the situation was propitious, and press our cause. The government of Vitellius was bearing out all I had foretold and feared: important military and economic decisions were placed on hold, while Vitellius entertained as often as five times a day at obscenely rich banquets. And this, while Rome's treasury in the Temple of Saturn was virtually depleted. He began indiscriminately to order the deaths of important Senators, for the most specious of reasons. The alarm within the Senate, having suffered through similar barbarisms from Otho and Galba, not to mention Nero and Caligula, was at such a pitch that some of them would no longer wait for my arrival. Thus, one of our supporters, Marcus Antonius Primus, commander of the VI Legion, marched from Pannonia to Rome and met Vitellius and his troops for battle. Yet, there was no battle. Vitellius& own troops rebelled and chased him back to Rome, where he was murdered. The Senate, I suspect with considerable relief, voted me full imperial power the next day.*
>
> *I have requested your appointment as Caesar and my heir, and you should receive notification from the Senate of this appointment in a few weeks. I caution you, my son, to avoid any ostentation upon your appointment as Caesar. There will be time enough later for such show. Focus all your attention on Jerusalem, so that you may return to Rome with accomplishments of your own, and that the people may say you are a worthy successor to my government.*

And note this well: you and I now bear a burden such that few men in the world must carry. Governance is a burden, not a pleasure. Power is an illusion, as you shall discover, and the abuse of power is the easiest of temptations to which one may succumb. Do not the examples of Galba, Otho, and Vittelius bear out the truth of this? I have no small ambition; I have worked to achieve this goal of governance, but I have done so with my eyes open to the responsibilities, and may I repeat, the burdens of such high office. It is the Imperator who works for the people, not the other way around. Always remember this.

Write to me about your progress. I know the press of battle makes it difficult to do so, but write to me.

Your father,
Imperator Vespasianus

Titus kept both letters together and never read one without reading the other. As much as he wanted to revel and gloat over the first, it was the second that mattered to him. He had watched his father progress in a treacherous world. He had watched him make friends and keep his friendships, as his father often said that loyalty received from others is earned only as loyalty is extended to others. Titus was determined to accomplish that which his father had asked him to do: give him Jerusalem. He knew his battle would begin, not when the first skirmish occurred, but when his legions arrived at the gates of Jerusalem. It was then that the psychological battle commenced, and Titus wanted all of Jerusalem to understand the might and majesty of Rome even before a single arrow was fired.

The people of Jerusalem, enfeebled by hunger and desperate for salvation from two oppressive tyrants within the city, flocked to the western and northern walls of the city to witness the spectacle of the arrival of the Roman legions. The sequence of Roman martial progression was meant to impress, if not intimidate their enemy. To the beat of drums and the sound of trumpets, the mercenaries were the first to appear – the non-Roman soldiers representing various local kings and other rulers who hated the Jews and were willing to participate in their destruction. They were followed by the engineers who prepared the roads, built the earthworks against the walls, manned the machines, erected bridges, and otherwise accomplished prodigious mechanical tasks that were beyond the ability of any other nation's army. After that came the soldiers carrying the baggage and tents of the commanders, followed by the commander himself – Titus Flavius – impressive in his burnished breastplate, plumed helmet, and red cape. The spear-holders followed, hundreds of them; then the horsemen of equal number; and next the massive machinery, many dozens of which included different types capable of hurtling boulders, boiling oil, and fire, or of ramming walls and gates down.

None of this constituted the real army yet. That was to follow, led by the tribunes, and reporting to them their centurions, and below them the decurions, and then thousands of foot soldiers, marching six abreast, after which came the soldiers carrying the standards and the eagles, bedecked with the trophies awarded the legion from previous battles. Following up on all this military might were the servants to the army, the baggage trains, and the most fearsome of all – the slave traders, who were poised to profit once the city was sacked. It was the sheer number of slave traders that frightened the opponents – it showed the confidence the slave traders had, that their time with the legion would not be wasted.

And this was but one legion. Titus had three more at his disposal, some of which were marching to the west of the city and some outside the city, such as at Emmaus. It was thought by the people of Jerusalem that this display would be enough to cause the two opposing sides in Jerusalem to set aside their animosity, join forces, and defend Jerusalem as they continually claimed was their purpose for being there. For a week or so there was a truce and some evidence of accommodation in the face of a common enemy, but this peace disintegrated quickly, and fighting between Yohan and Simon continued with renewed vigor.

Titus having been convinced by his father that, given time, the enemy would weaken themselves substantially, surveyed his field of operations to determine his strategy for taking the city. He had with him Tiberius Alexander from Egypt, who was much older and with more experience at military sieges, and who had now fully thrown in his lot with Vespasianus. Titus also intended to employ Josephus if he had the opportunity to negotiate for the city's surrender.

Chapter Twenty Eight

Call my staff together"! Titus shouted this out to no one in particular, but as he had been surrounded by orderlies during the entire procession to the gates of Jerusalem, it was easy for them to pass the word along to the legion commanders. It had been decided days before that Titus would camp with his personal legion, the Tenth Fretensis, and that his camp would be positioned to the northeast of the city, on an elevated area known as the Mount of Olives. Tiberius Alexander was the first to arrive at Titus' tent, which had been quickly and efficiently set up by the engineers, as one of their first responsibilities upon arrival at Jerusalem.

"How do you like your viewpoint, General?" asked Tiberius Alexander. "At least I have one," replied Titus. He and Tiberius had known each other for years, since Titus' legion was normally assigned to Cyrenaica in North Africa. They hadn't been tested in battle together, because Egypt was completely subdued, but Tiberius was impressed with what he had seen of Titus from the few months Tiberius and his legions had been deployed in Galilee and Judea.

"I much prefer some mountains and hills to work with strategically and tactically, Tiberius. The sands of Egypt and the flatness of the landscape offer little scope for military imagination." Titus and Tiberius Alexander were standing outside his tent, looking south. "I had forgotten how mountainous Jerusalem was," added Titus. "I've only been here once before, and while naturally I made mental notes of the military possibilities of a siege of the city, things always look different when you are faced with the actual task."

"Ah – here is Rutilius," noted Titus. Appius Rutilius Alba was the Chief Engineer for the campaign, and as such had a rank equal to the legion commanders, including Tiberius Alexander, who was ten years older than anyone else on Titus' staff. Titus asked, "what do you think of placing our siege works on the east wall? Ordinarily I would prefer to hold the high ground and not be boxed in at the bottom of that valley that runs from here to the wall, but if we could breach the wall near to the Temple Mount, we could avoid all the trouble of attacking the two outer walls to the north." Titus was in the process of removing his ceremonial breastplate and leg grieves as he asked this question, and gave out a small sigh of relief when he was disencumbered of his armor.

"I would not recommend it, General," said Rutilius. "It does not look like there is any flat ground there, which we are going to need if we are to maneuver our machines. I could overcome that by building a leveling platform for the machines, but we would still be exposed to attacks from atop the wall. Besides, this section of the original wall built by Herod the Great cannot simply be battered down; the stone blocks of the wall are too thick. Herod built this wall to last at least as long as the Pyramids."

By this time Gnaeus Numicius Caeca had arrived. He and Tiberius Alexander were in charge of the legions positioned to the west and the north of the city. "I would like to get a closer look of the ground down there," said Titus to the group. "Then I want to see the position of both of your camps. Where's my horse? And I want Mathias to come with us."

One of Titus' aides immediately went to prepare his horse. "Are you certain of the loyalty of Mathias?" asked Tiberius Alexander. "We haven't known him very long." Titus had gone inside his tent to fetch his sword belt, and Tiberius had followed him. "He's been enormously helpful since Jotapata, and Josephus has vouched for him," said Titus. "I think both he and Josephus are too deep into our campaign to extricate themselves – they would not be accepted in Jerusalem, since many view them as traitors. You have to admit we must rely at some point on those Jews who know the city well. There is an added benefit – Mathias can ride a horse."

Titus strode out of his tent. He mounted his horse and waited momentarily while four men from his personal bodyguard rode up to accompany him. With Tiberius Alexander, Numicius Caeca, and Mathias in tow, the group slowly rode down the rock-strewn hill of the Mount of Olives and past a garden of olive and lemon trees that was popular with the public, and known as Gethsemane. "Don't get within arrow range!" shouted Titus to the rest of his reconnoiter party.

As they reached the bottom of the hill and began slowly pacing their horses across the valley floor, the enormity of the eastern wall impressed Titus. He had not appreciated the height of this wall, and how difficult it would be to pound through it, or scale over it. He could see men and women atop the wall – no doubt still observing the arrival of the Roman legions and their work in establishing their three base camps. He couldn't make out their faces, however; that is how high these walls were. All he could see were people scurrying about between the crenellations. He led his party further south, hoping to see any sign of weakness in the structure.

As near as Titus could tell, the wall was one solid mass of gigantic stones from the north to the south of the city. There were no gates, no areas that had been repaired, and no visible structural faults. He had reached the midsection of the wall, where behind it lay the Temple Mount, the highest ground in Jerusalem. Towering above them was the Great Temple itself, firing glints of gold rays in the afternoon sun.

The Temple was a worthy prize, thought Titus, as he contemplated the riches that must be housed inside, and which he was personally determined to bring to Rome for his triumph at the Forum. It was Numicius who first spotted trouble. "Fall back, Fall back!" he shouted to the group, as he maneuvered his horse away from the eastern wall.

Titus wasn't sure which he heard first – Numicius' warning, or the shouts of dozens of Zealots issuing forth from the eastern wall. More than anything afterward, Titus remembered at the time of the attack his incredulity at the sight of fighters seemingly materializing from stone. There had to be a door there, but where was it? It was only later that he realized there was an indentation in the wall that, by a trick of the light, did not appear evident from a distance.

Numicius and Tiberius Alexander were already slowly clambering back up the Mount of Olives, and Titus' bodyguard was inclined to do the same, but the General stood his ground, perhaps frozen not in fear, but in surprise at this attack. The Zealots were swarming out, armed with swords, lances, farm tools, and cudgels. It wasn't clear that Titus' reconnoiter party was going to escape them, because the Mount of Olives was rocky ground, and the horses had to proceed gingerly to avoid injury. Dismounting would have been even more foolhardy; Titus and his team would be outnumbered ten to one, within minutes.

Tiberius rode up to Titus, and grabbed his arm. "We've got to get out of here, General. Head north with us, along the valley floor. Maybe we can outride them!" Titus shook off Tiberius' grasp, and to the surprise of everyone, took off in the direction of his attackers, who were now about a minute or so distant. Instinctively, Titus' bodyguard rode off with him, and Mathias followed.

Now it was Tiberius' turn to be amazed, as were the Zealots, as Titus slashed and jabbed his way into the thick of the attack. His bodyguard quickly caught up to him and surrounded him, carrying on the counter-assault on his behalf. Mathias assisted where he could, but he had no weapon and was forced to kick at his opponents, and use his horse to break up their advance.

The Zealots were clearly surprised at the ferocity of the counter-attack, and perhaps it was the screams of their compatriots that caused them to fall back, as Jews were either being trampled by horses or pierced by Roman swords. Tiberius saw his opportunity, with the temporary retreat of the Zealots back to the wall. He and Numicius rode up to the group and, with the help of the bodyguard, brought Titus to safety by riding north along the wall at a rapid pace. By the time they were able to reach camp at the top of the Mount of Olives, Tiberius Alexander was furious. He dismounted and nearly pulled Titus off his horse and back into his tent. Everyone outside could hear what transpired.

"That will never happen again!" Tiberius was screaming at Titus. "You will never leave this tent without full combat armor, and a complete contingent of bodyguards. You almost had yourself killed out there, taking a completely unnecessary risk, and endangering our entire mission. Don't think I am blameless in this; I should have been wary enough to forbid this little adventure from the start."

"Perhaps you were right about Mathias," rejoined Titus, in a subdued tone. He was not used to being yelled at by anyone, but he didn't dare raise his voice to Tiberius Alexander. "He should have told us about the door at the base of the wall."

"Do not start blaming your subordinates. Mathias proved his loyalty today. He came to your defense and he had no weapon. He would have been the first to be pulled off his horse and slain, if the Jews hadn't fallen back and given us an opportunity to escape. I'm sure you know I will give you the best military advice I can, and follow your orders immediately. But I have sworn to your father to protect you, so let me repeat: you will not leave this camp ever again without your personal armor and a full contingent of bodyguards. Are we clear on that point?"

"Yes, Father," was all Titus could say. This little exchange seemed very odd to the Greeks listening outside the tent, or to a Jew like Mathias, who could not imagine a subordinate speaking with such vehemence and reproach to a superior. To a Roman, however, it was completely understandable. Romans valued family more than anything else in the world, and within the family, the father, the *pater familias*, was all-powerful. When Vespasianus charged Tiberius Alexander with the safety of his son, and when Tiberius took an oath to fulfill this responsibility, Tiberius became Vespasianus, in effect – the father to the boy. Titus had no option but to obey him on matters involving his own safety.

The consequence of Titus' folly became apparent the very next day. The Romans had not yet completed construction of any of their three camps, and Yohan of Gischala took advantage of this by ordering an attack on the base camp atop the Mount of Olives. Titus happened to be monitoring the progress at the northern camp, but he watched from a distance as hundreds of Jewish attackers poured out from the northern gate and began climbing up the Mount of Olives. Worse still, the Romans in the camp were beginning to panic, and did not show their usual discipline in organizing a defensive posture.

"I followed your advice," Titus later said to Tiberius Alexander. "I ordered our legion at the north camp to prepare for a mounted assault from horses. I had my personal armor on, as I promised you I would, and I had twenty four guards around me at all times. We attacked from the north of the Mount of Olives and quickly drove Yohan's men down into the valley. They were trapped and utterly defenseless. We slaughtered all of them – over a hundred men."

Tiberius Alexander congratulated Titus on this success and said nothing further. He might have argued that this foray could have been undertaken by the commander of the horse brigade, but he thought better of it. Titus had the tenacity of his father – he was never going to be deterred from personally leading his men in battle. Moreover, he had that one quality that distinguished a great Roman general from an ordinary one: he was not willing to ask his men to take on any risk which he himself would not undertake, and he proved this quality time and again by standing side-by-side with his men in battle.

This willingness to take on mortal risk was to serve Titus well, when he needed to rectify the greatest mistake he made in the campaign – his misguided assault on the Second Wall. "We will simply have to work through their defensive positions in the north," said Rutilius Alba to Titus after it was clear an assault on the eastern wall would never work. "The other wall – what the Jews call the Third Wall – should be easy for us to surmount. For the most part, it is an earthen structure with a wooden barricade mounted on top. I can build several towers that will allow us to destroy the barricade from above. The next wall is more formidable. The Second Wall is all stone, and much older. We are going to have to use the battering rams to get through, but once through, you will have direct access to the Fortress Antonia and the Temple Mount, from inside Jerusalem."

Rutilius' advice, at least regarding the Third Wall, proved correct. It was on the fifteenth day of the siege that the Romans were able to surmount the Third Wall. They were surprised to find hardly anything on the other side. Not only was the land largely empty, since the expansion of Jerusalem to the north had been for the purpose of constructing farms rather than apartment buildings, but there were few Jewish defenders to offer the Romans any resistance.

"Destroy it." This was Titus' simple order to Rutilius Alba, whose engineers promptly dismantled the entire Third Wall, which allowed Numicius Caeca to move his camp closer to the Second Wall. Rutilius brought up his battering rams and commenced smashing into this wall day and night. Eventually a small opening was created, leading to what appeared to be a market place.

Titus insured he was on hand when the opening was accomplished, and he ordered his soldiers to head through the breach and establish a command post from which the Romans could take control of all the land and buildings between the Second and First Walls. This was a mistake. This sector of Jerusalem was under the control of Simon bar Giora, and he surprised the Romans not only by the fierceness of his defense, but by his mastery of street fighting tactics. The Romans who first went through the breach were slaughtered, and those who followed found themselves under attack on nearly all sides.

Once again, Titus chose to personally intervene to save the situation. He ordered up a unit of archers, and they joined him on the roof tops of apartment buildings, where they could fire arrows at the attackers. The strategy worked. Simon's men were eventually routed by the Romans, but the Romans were still in a precarious position.

"I will not make that mistake again," said Titus to his commanders. "Widen the breach. I want 5,000 of our soldiers to get through quickly and take control of the situation." It took Rutilius Alba several days to accomplish the engineering work, but once done, the Romans poured through the Second Wall and within weeks had forced the Jews to retreat to their final line of defense, behind the First Wall – the original wall of ancient Jerusalem.

Titus called for another meeting of his general staff once his army had progressed to the point where they could attack the Temple Mount. They assembled at the base camp on the Mount of Olives. "Let's get out of this heat," said Titus to his staff. "There is a pleasant, shady spot just south of here called the Garden of Gethsemane. We'll talk there." Titus had taken to spending his spare time in this garden, accompanied by his complete bodyguard, as he had promised Tiberius. It was an isolated and relatively cool area, where he could think about his next steps, and look across the valley to the Temple itself, his ultimate prize.

"It is time," said Tiberius Alexander, "to try a little diplomacy, and if that doesn't work, we need to anticipate a very long siege that will starve them out." "Starvation is not a worthy strategy for a Roman army," said Numicius Caeca, "but in this case, I think it is our best option. These Jews are obstinate; we've found that to be the case in every city we were forced to conquer up north. Even if we use diplomacy, it is not clear that anyone in Jerusalem can make a decision. From what we hear, Yohan and his Zealots spend more time fighting Simon than they do fighting us."

"Let's hope that continues," said Titus. "It's to our advantage if the Jews destroy themselves so that we don't have to do that for them. We should certainly use diplomacy first, and see if they are willing to consider terms of surrender. Mathias, do you think Josephus can be given safe access to the city?"

"I doubt it, General," responded Mathias, who was now considered a member of the general staff. "As much as Josephus would love to have access to the city, to find out what has happened to his parents, his wife, and his children, I doubt that the Zealots would wait more than five minutes before they killed him."

"I will have our towers ready in a few days," added Rutilius. "They will be taller than the First Wall, and Josephus can address the crowd from there. At the very least, he will be able to talk directly to his people, and not to Yohan or Simon. He may have more success that way. The refugees who are escaping the city tell us the situation is absolutely dire. Bodies are piling up on the streets as people die from hunger. I know it is not the Roman way to resort to starvation during a siege, and that we would much prefer the glory of fighting our way through, but let us remember it was the Jewish defenders who destroyed their own grain supplies. Starvation is already here for the Jews, whether we like it or not."

"True enough," added Titus. "Let us summarize our strategy. We have assault towers ready to be in place near the Fortress Antonia within a few days. We will have Josephus offer terms to the Jews before we begin an assault. We have to decide how hunger and thirst will play a role in our campaign. As Rutilius says, those factors are already present in this campaign. If diplomacy doesn't work, then it seems we should take advantage of the situation already existing. If the Jews have chosen to starve themselves into submission, let us not resist their efforts. Rutilius, can you build a barricade all around the city? We don't need to recreate the Second or Third Walls – we merely need a way to prevent refugees from thinking they can escape the siege, once it is obvious it is going to be prolonged into the summer months. And there will be refugees – lots of them."

Rutilius agreed his engineers could surround the city and make escape impossible. Titus asked if everyone concurred with the strategy, and there was assent all around. Titus passed out some figs and dates, and offered his staff some light red wine. "We should enjoy this pleasant spot, even if the Jews cannot," said Titus. "When this campaign is over, this may be the last decent space left standing in all of Jerusalem."

Mathias sat glumly, and declined to eat and drink. It was all very good for the Romans to talk about how the "Jews" had decided to starve themselves, but everyone knew the truth. The Jews – the everyday inhabitants of Jerusalem – had nothing to do with these decisions, with the Zealots, or with the men from outside the city who came to defend it. Yet they were the ones paying the greatest price of all – giving up their lives in defense of an independent Jerusalem that many realized was not possible in the face of Roman might and determination.

Mathias worried that what was being decided today in the Garden of Gethsemane could lead to the death of hundreds of thousands of Jews. He had to impress upon Josephus the importance of making his diplomatic efforts a success. It was the last chance for his people to avoid complete destruction.

Chapter Twenty Nine

he only way through the Fortress Antonia was to go over it or under it, so massive were the marble blocks used in its construction. The logical approach was to try to scale the walls and overcome the defenders, so Titus ordered the construction of siege works tall enough to reach the top of the towers of the fortress. While this work was underway, he sent Josephus up one of the towers being built, and instructed him to plead with the Jews to give up their resistance. Dodging arrows, Josephus addressed his fellow Jews in Hebrew and in the loudest voice he could muster:

> "I too am a Jew," he began. "I defended our country in Jotapata and was prepared to die for Israel. I too respect that which makes us unique: our covenant with the One God. Yet, where is the worship and respect we owe the Lord God? Do you see any sacrifices being made at the Temple? Is the Temple any longer purified, or has it been stained already by too much blood?"

> "I have been told again and again by Titus that he does not wish to destroy Jerusalem, and he does not wish to damage the Temple, one of the great glories of the Jewish nation. In this regard, he is of the same opinion and attitude as Caesar Augustus and Tiberius, both of whom revered and respected the Temple. Look about you in the inner courtyard. Do you not see the plates of gold contributed to the Temple by both Augustus and Tiberius?"

> "Since the time of Pompey the Great we have lived under Roman domination. No Jew pretends to prefer such a condition to our own complete independence, but tell me if there is any nation which borders the Great Sea which enjoys its own independence. There is not one. Not one nation has been able to withstand the might, the skill, the determination, the courage, and the sheer power of the Roman military. Why do you, Simon bar Giora, and you, Yohan of Gischala, believe you are any different?"

> "Mars, the god of war, resides in Rome and nowhere else. For those who believe in such a god, he favors none other than the Romans. For those like us who believe in the One, Invisible

*God, how long do you think He will abide in the Holy of Holies?
How much profanity will He tolerate, or is it not true that He
has already turned his back on the Jews and now demands
retribution for our sins? How else do you explain your failures
to deny the Romans control of the first and second outer walls?
How do explain your continued failures to interrupt their
progress with their war machinery? Why is it that the pool
of Siloam, which provides the city with the cleanest and purest
water, has now dried up?"*

*"Foolish men! You think you can defeat the Romans, yet your
world shrinks day by day, and you continue to deny to the people
of Jerusalem, the people you say you defend, the right to do what
they want to do, which is open the gates of the city to Titus, who
has promised no retribution and who wants nothing less than to
restore the city to its previous splendor and importance."*

*"You have tormented the people of Jerusalem with your endless
war upon them, your murdering rampages, your extortions,
and now you have brought the greatest calamity upon them
– famine! We know the horrors which are now afflicting the
ordinary people of Jerusalem. We see people desperate for even a
grain of wheat, who manage somehow to escape the city and come
begging to the Romans for sustenance. Their faces are gaunt,
their stomachs are bloated, and their strength is dissipated. Is
this the victory you have promised them? And be assured,
these torments are coming to you, Simon bar Giora, and Yohan
of Gischala. They are coming to all of you who profess to be
defenders of Jerusalem."*

*I beseech you, Simon bar Giora and Yohan of Gischala, end this
suffering! Send out emissaries so that Jerusalem and Rome may
work toward an honorable peace. And make no mistake: Titus
will pursue this war with vigor and determination if you do not
come to terms. Do so now!*

Those citizens who had the strength began scrambling to the
walls to hear what Josephus had to say. In their extreme difficulty
they wished for nothing more than the restoration of the city to
its previous condition before the Zealots and other renegades
took control of Jerusalem and before Titus instituted his siege. To
the men who promised devotion to Simon or Yohan, Josephus

appeared as a traitor to Israel, taking food from the Romans and doing their bidding. They mocked him and hooted derision at his comments. He was intermittently assailed by arrows, some of which were able to reach him, and one of which struck his shoulder. Still, he spoke on, relating the many instances in Jewish history where a king would come to terms with an oppressor rather than expose the people to ruin.

Simon and Yohan instructed that the gates of the city be secured even more tightly, so that none who might be tempted to listen to the falsities they felt were being uttered by Josephus would be able to go over to the Romans. Yet the people were in such distress that many were now determined to escape Jerusalem at any cost. Even death at the hands of the Romans seemed preferable to the slow torture of starvation, and some entertained the notion that they could obtain food from outside and return to the city to feed their family. Consequently, hundreds of people began assembling their smallest but most precious objects for their journey outside of the city. The favored approach was to swallow pieces of gold, so as to hide this wealth from the robbers or from those who manned the gates. The gatekeepers could be bribed to let someone through, only to have that person assaulted, robbed, and killed a short distance outside of the city. Even more precious than gold, however, was food – fights would break out over mere crumbs from a piece of bread.

The bloated bodies of the dead, especially of children and the elderly, began to be brought daily to the southern tower and dumped over the walls. A tremendous mound of bodies formed there, the stench of decay becoming so powerful that people moved away from the area. Eventually, though, people became too weak to continue hauling bodies such a distance, and the corpses piled up on street corners. Entire houses were abandoned when families perished one after another in quick succession. Rats and flies and maggots became the true rulers of the city, forcing Simon's men to find refuge in houses free of dead bodies and forcing Yohan's men to retreat to the Temple compound and Fortress Antonia.

Titus watched the stream of fortunates who managed to escape the city appear each morning outside the gates, scrounging the fields for a blade of grass. At first he let many of them run off into the desert. Then, instead of finding supplicants each morning, he began to find bodies of Jews around his encampment, their bellies slit open and their bowels strewn about. Upon investigation, he learned that the mercenaries and slave traders associated with the legions were assaulting these people and slaughtering them in search of gold coins that they might have swallowed.

Titus vowed publicly to execute anyone he found perpetrating such a crime. He consulted with his commanding officers about the deteriorating situation in his camps, caused by the regular stream of hundreds of Jews a day who managed to escape or bribe their way to freedom. Not only were these people becoming a burden for the army and a distraction from the business of pursuing the siege, but they were undermining discipline. Moreover, as was pointed out by many of the tribunes who reported to Titus, none of his efforts at reason, at negotiation, and at leniency, had produced the slightest positive effect on the Zealots or on Simon or Yohan. Any other city, and any other nation, would have long since surrendered to avoid the extremity of death by famine.

Titus determined that he could no longer be lenient with the people of Jerusalem and that he must put a stop to the exodus that was occurring in larger numbers each day. Accordingly he ordered one such escapee to be crucified in full view of the Zealot guards and anyone else who manned the walls and towers to the north of the city. Rather than produce a sense of fear, this scene was met by mockery from Yohan's men, and so the next day dozens more were crucified, and this dreadful example was expanded day by day until at one point 500 or more men and women were mounted on crosses, their doleful cries reaching the ears of their friends or relatives who had not imagined that a greater distress could befall them than famine. Indeed, for some of them, crucifixion was not deemed a greater distress; it was considered a merciful release from their agonies due to hunger and thirst, and so hundreds continued to seek escape from the city. The Roman soldiers, out of their wrath for all Jews, would have expanded the crucifixions to the horizon, if it were not for the lack of precious wood to make the crosses.

Titus ensured that none of this impeded the work of his crews readying the assault on the Fortress Antonia. At length the siege works were complete, allowing the Romans to scale the tower of the fortress, but only a few at a time could do so. These few would be met with almost certain death at the hands of the defenders, until enough Romans who followed them would be able to overwhelm the Jews. No man was willing to sacrifice themselves in such a way, and Titus realized he would have to use every ounce of rhetoric to convince some few soldiers – and only a few were needed - of the nobility of such a sacrifice.

He wrote to his father describing the resulting attack on the fortress. He felt it necessary to put on paper - to memorialize - what had occurred.

To Imperator Titus Flavius Caesar Vespasianus Augustus
Greetings from Titus Flavius Caesar Vespasianus,

Honored Father,

I present to you Jerusalem, all its wealth, and all its people. I have ordered a week of sacrifices be offered to the gods in thanksgiving that we have been delivered of the arrogance and single-mindedness of the Jews. I wish to banish them altogether from Judea, if at all possible, but first we must as Romans acknowledge the bravery of the men who brought us this difficult prize.

As you know, the problem in this siege has always been to take command of the Fortress Antonia. It is too substantial to pull down or batter through, so we built a siege tower of equivalent height, and from there I looked across to the stone pavement of the roof of the tower opposite us. It was certain death for the first few men we sent over there; I saw that at once. I thought carefully if there were any alternatives to such a sacrifice, but I could find none. If we were ever going to take Jerusalem, we had to control the Fortress Antonia.

We selected the best thirty men of each legion and I called them together. I explained our tactical situation: how the quickest route to victory lay over the wall facing us. The likelihood of survival for the first group of men to reach the fortress was poor, but the opportunity for eternal honor was commensurately as great. I reminded them of their oath as soldiers, and as many were veterans, I exhorted them to think well and hard on the sacrifices other legions have made and the glory they achieved - achievements - that are still being commemorated today in the Forum of Rome.

My men know me well. They knew I would have eagerly joined them in this action. Tiberius Alexander had absolutely forbidden it, however. He said that a wise general may win many a battle by the display of courage at the right moment in the right situation, but that a foolish general will only gain defeat by committing himself to near-certain death. I bade the men think carefully on their decision and then stepped to the side, waiting.

No one spoke up. I saw the fear in their eyes, and I did not blame them. I was almost at a point of despair when someone stood up. "I will scale the wall. I choose death voluntarily for your sake, commander, and may others take strength from my courage and my resolution." His name was Sabinus—a Syrian—a small man of thin frame but of such fierceness as I should never wish to meet in an enemy. I cried for him in front of all to see; I cried as I held him with an arm around his shoulder. At length, only eleven other men were willing to join him.

We set two ladders across our tower to the other side & the fortress tower - and Sabinus crawled slowly over the ladders, his sword held high. He charged at the Jews the minute he reached the fortress, and there he was met by forty defenders at least, but they were so stunned at his aggression that they fell back to one corner of the tower roof. I swear to you, Father, we would have carried the day, if there were any way we could have gotten our men over there more quickly. When the Jews saw how long it took for others to reinforce Sabinus, they regained their courage and shot Sabinus through with so many arrows that he could not survive. We lost several more men as well, including those who were still on the ladders when the Jews managed to dislodge them and plunge them to their deaths.

Once again my men were despairing of ever entering the city, and their anger was so great that I worried as to the consequences when we finally were able to gain access to the fortress. It was at this point that the gods showed their favor toward us. My engineers had been inspecting the fortress walls all about for any sign of weakness, and they thought they had found one. At the conjunction of the Tower that we were besieging and the wall that traveled off to the east, there was one large stone at the base that seemed to be poorly laid, so that the stones above it were not level and cracks had begun to appear in their surface from the weight bearing down on them from above. If we dug the earth away from that one stone - a keystone, as it were - we might cause a collapse in the entire wall at that section.

I ordered our engineers to begin the work of digging away the support under this keystone. While this was underway, I called together the soldiers once again. The exploit of Sabinus was the only topic of conversation throughout the legions, and many of our men felt great shame at not displaying the same degree of courage as did Sabinus. They also now harbored such a hatred for the Jews, who had put us through so much difficulty with this siege, that their rage was boiling over. I thus had many more volunteers to attempt to cross over to the roof of the Fortress Antonia.

It took a matter of days, but my engineers were now very confident that their original estimation was correct. As they dug beneath the keystone, they could hear the gnashing of the stones above, and they were obliged to prop up the keystone with heavy timbers lest it come crashing down on us. This gave me the opportunity to time the collapse of the wall with the assault on the tower roof. The moment I chose was two nights later, when the moon was about to be reborn and darkness would be our ally.

At my signal the wooden props were pulled away, and we all watched and listened expectantly. Do you remember that one earthquake we had in Anatolia when you and I and Domitianus were stationed there? The sound starts low, as if off in the distance, and then builds, and suddenly there is a sharp crack! This is exactly how it happened, as we watched the entire side of the wall along the fortress disintegrate. A gaping hole opened up for us, with access to the outer courtyard, which the Jews call the Gentile Courtyard.

I ordered my men to attack simultaneously from above and through the breach in the wall. This time we were successful in getting reinforcements to the tower, and within ten minutes our men were swarming into the outer courtyard. This is where the worst fighting of the entire campaign took place. The courtyard is not big enough to house more than a few thousand men, and in such close quarters, it was not possible to mount a brigade of archers. Combat was entirely man-to-man, but we had the advantage because I had given each man the password for the night, and by this means, in the darkness, they could announce themselves to each other and avoid error. The Jews were not so fortunate. They slaughtered as many of their own as they did of our soldiers.

We were able to push the Jews into the inner courtyard, and at last I could see our way to the Temple itself. A fire had broken out in the inner courtyard, and this was yet another distraction for the

Jews. They tried to put it out, but it grew greater and fiercer, and the Jews were hard pressed by our own men rushing at them now with both swords and spears. I began to worry about the safety of the Temple. I know you wanted to preserve the Temple at all costs, so as the fire grew hotter and closer to the Temple, I ordered our own men to begin putting it out.

I have mentioned previously their loathing for the Jews. I cannot call it lack of discipline or insubordination after such a long campaign, with so many losses among our companions, but not many men took up my order to extinguish the flames. They fought on, and in their fury slaughtered many Jews, but somehow the fire at last reached the Temple itself. One of my centurions thought one of our own men may have tossed a burning slab of wood through one of the windows of the Temple, thus setting it alight. I don&t know the truth of this, but within minutes flames were leaping out of the roof of the Temple. It crumbled so quickly that I was astonished, and I worried that any of the treasure in gold and silver or gems might be melted along with the Temple. Fortunately the Jews secreted their wealth outside of the city just before we arrived, and a Jew led us to this trove after the fighting was over. I think you will be pleased with the result.

It took several more weeks to finally subdue the city. We had to place siege works against the Upper City and pound our way through. This is where Simon bar Giora made his last defense; Yohan of Gischala had already given himself up to us. At long last, though, we were able to capture Simon bar Giora in a cave. While I cannot hand to you the Temple itself, in its glory and beauty, I can give you the two leaders of the Zealots. They will adorn our Triumph, and I shall keep them safe until then.

They will join several hundred thousand prisoners we have living in the New City, most of whom will now be sold into slavery. The provinces will be happy, as will all of Rome and Italia. I have ordered the destruction of as much of Jerusalem as possible. I would like to treat of Jerusalem the way we treated Carthage, but I do not think that possible. There are too many Jews living abroad who could return and repopulate the city. Besides, we need the city as a strategic link to Arabia and to Egypt. It shall, however, be a place of desolation for many years to come. Even now, you cannot walk on any street without coming across bodies bloating in the sun. We are disposing of at least several hundred thousand bodies in a non-stop cremation to the south of the city. The stench is appalling, and I order the fires to be extinguished on days when the wind blows from the south over the whole of the city. As you can imagine, very few of our soldiers desire to work at this task, so we have appointed slaves to this effort.

I will send you detailed inventories of the gold, silver, jewels, slaves, and other treasures we have obtained with this victory. It may take a few more months. I will be obliged to winter here and join you in Rome in the spring. There are still more Jews to be taken in the southern provinces, and over a thousand are said to be holed up in a place called Masada. This will keep us busy for a while.

With respect and veneration, I am,
Your son.
Titus Flavius Caesar Vespasianus

Chapter Thirty

ow many prisoners do we have now, Fronto?" Titus was asking his chief quartermaster for the latest numbers on the captured and the wounded among the Jews. It was Fronto's assignment to sort out what would happen to these people and to work with the many slave traders on disposing of them.

"There are nearly 3,000 in the Temple courtyard alone. They have been there a week and we need to decide what to do with them," said Fronto. "It is difficult in that space to feed them and deal with all their excrement, plus too many are beginning to die of disease. They will lose any value to us if this keeps on."

"But they are all condemned men anyway," stated Titus, almost as a question. "How much money are they worth and to whom?" Fronto was quick to answer. "I've had several agents for various arenas look them over and express an interest in taking groups of them for sale. They are almost all certainly fighters. We found them in the Upper City and scooped them up in groups, with their weapons, so I don't think we've made too many mistakes – as long as they are healthy, they should be able to put on a good show in the arena."

"Perhaps I could use them," said Titus. "I need 700 Jews to be shown in the Triumph, but I was going to find them in the thousands of people we have penned up in the New City. They all need to be robust and good specimens as soldiers – I don't want the people of Rome thinking our adversaries were small and weak. They also have to be handsome – the women always like that – and they need all their limbs and have no major blemishes on their body. I thought that after the Triumph they could all be sold off as slaves, but what you are telling me is we could make more money selling them as gladiators."

Fronto nodded his assent. "I will go through the men in the courtyard first and isolate those who fit your description," he said. "If I need any more I will find them out in the New City pens. They could be given a small brand on their leg to show they are later to be sold as gladiators, not slaves."

"I know you've done that sort of work before," said Titus, "so I am sure you can do a good job. Now as for the rest of the men at the courtyard, I'm also going to need some for the games I am hosting the rest of this year here in the East, before I return to Rome. The two biggest arenas will be in Antioch and Alexandria, and I think I will need 200 men in each arena to fight to the death. There should be no problem with that – they are all condemned anyway."

Fronto passed a hand before his eyes and Titus could sense his exasperation – he must be watching his profits disappear with 200 men here and there put to death for free. So Titus said, "It is not as bad as all that. You'll still have at least 2,000 men to sell to whatever gladiatorial school or arena you want. Fatten them up – you'll get a good price for them. I authorize you and your squad to take ten percent off the top as your fee."

Fronto brightened up immediately. Titus continued. "Besides, your real money is going to be in slaves. How many people do you have who can be sold immediately?"

"Not many, sir," said Fronto, and then coughed a bit – "Pardon me," he said, "I meant to say Caesar." Titus smiled to himself; everyone around him was having trouble adjusting to his new, exalted title that had been granted to him by the Senate, now that his father was officially Imperator Flavius Caesar Vespasianus Augustus. Fronto added: "There are too many that are sick or weak. The slave traders are all pushing down their normal price, saying the risk is too great that they will die before they get to wherever they are to be sold."

"Aren't you feeding them?" asked Titus. "I give them what I can, but the food shipments from up north are very slow in getting here," replied Fronto. "We always have to feed our own men first." Titus responded, "You're the quartermaster – I authorize you to find out what the delays are. There is plenty of grain stored in Caesarea Philippi; I know that for a fact. There is much more up in Damascus and Antioch. Tell whoever is in charge of these shipments that I want enough grain to keep these people alive; I want it at reasonable prices; and I want it here in ten days, or that individual will answer to me personally."

Fronto had to admit that such a plan would certainly impress the slave traders, if not dismay them. "We should aim to have most of these people shipped out in a month at the latest," Titus continued. "I think we need 50,000 in Italy alone, 20,000 in Greece, and perhaps another 30,000 for the farms in Gaul. Find out if any of your agents want to cover other provinces in Africa, Hispania, maybe Britannia." Fronto nodded his head in agreement.

"But Caesar," he said, "the Egyptians need at least 10,000, and they only want young men for their mines. Anybody over seventeen isn't going to last more than three months in the heat, they say. They think they can get as much as a year's service out of boys aged twelve to seventeen. They'll pay very well."

Titus winced a little bit at the thought of wasting young men like that, but this was war. How many of that age had already died of the famine? 50,000 at least. He gave Fronto his consent: "Give them as many as they want," he said.

Titus leaned back in his chair, put his hands behind his head, and stretched his feet out. He could use some sleep – he could use a lot of sleep. He always felt this way after a battle, but he had all these ceremonies to attend to, of which only the Triumph really interested him. It was going to be a Triumph such as Rome had not seen in a hundred years. He wondered if he would ever get any sleep, now that he was Caesar, heir to the throne. It was only now that Titus was comprehending the burden that was ahead of him. At first, a year ago when his father told him about the prophecy, Titus was giddy with the thought of inheriting such power and wealth. Now he was not so sure. Now he could see spending the rest of his life in meetings, going over government decisions, making judicial rulings, visiting the provinces, being nice to Senators (including the ones he didn't like), worrying about the state of the Treasury, fighting off any more rebellions, hosting dinners for kings and ambassadors, and so on and so on. It was too dreary to think about. Being a general had been a lot more interesting. Now he would have to worry about other generals wanting to take power away from his father and him.

Titus brought his mind back to the business at hand. "You say we have at least 200,000 people out there in the New City. You know our routine. Everyone who is an adult over seventeen but not over forty five, is to be sold if they are healthy. Anyone over forty-five is to be released back into the city, though how they are going to live there in a city that is virtually destroyed I do not know. Children under seventeen should be sold with their parents, where possible, but break them up in you have to. You negotiate the prices, but sorry – no direct commission for you on slaves – only on the gladiators I mentioned earlier. You know the rules – the legion gets the money and then most of it goes to Rome."

"And if they are unhealthy?" asked Fronto. "Keep them separated from everyone else," said Titus. "Don't let them back into the city, but let's try to keep them alive. I don't want Jerusalem to die out completely – it is still on important trade routes, to the Nabateans at Petra, for example, and then to Alexandria. We need some adults young enough to have children. A lot of these sick people will die, but just enough should live that we can keep a small population of Jews in Jerusalem."

"Oh, and make sure you have the dead brought immediately to the South Gate. That's where the cremations are being done, as I am sure you can smell from time to time. And if you get any hint of an epidemic developing, I want to know immediately. We are really racing against time, trying to get all these people sold in a month before disease strikes. It's inevitable we will have an epidemic if we wait too much longer than a month."

With the killing done, and the really nasty work of cleaning up Jerusalem and disposing of the population ahead of him, Titus wanted to keep his soldiers isolated from the Jews, and so they were restricted to camp unless they were part of the security detail patrolling the city. He had organized an awards ceremony to take place in a few days. All those who showed exceptional heroism were to be publicly recognized in front of all four of the legions, and they were to receive promotions as well as cash awards. All his men were looking forward to it, and he saw outside his tent a delegation of his lieutenants who were here to review the list of those recommended for recognition.

As Fronto was leaving, however, Titus's aide-de-camp entered, informing him that a ruler of a minor kingdom on the Euphrates, which had lent mercenaries to the campaign, was here to pay allegiance to Caesar, congratulate him on his promotion to the government, and as a "minor" note, request an increase in the allotment given him from the spoils of the war. The aide pointed out it would be rude to let a fellow-ruler wait outside, and that Rome might need his help on some other occasion, and so on and so on. Titus was certain his aide could think of a few more reasons why he had to go through this diplomatic game rather than do something interesting for his army. He sighed. This was but a taste of what awaited him when he arrived in Rome.

Chapter Thirty One

arnabas sat quietly in a chair on the first floor of the Christian community center. He had been there an entire day and still had not slept nor moved much from his seat. He simply didn't know what to do. He had not the strength to think of the future, and it was difficult even to think of the present. For the first time in many months he was not hungry. He had eaten, not well but adequately in the camps set up in the New City, and the Romans had given him a few days ration of food when he was released. But he had not touched the food since. His inclination was to return to his habits during the siege: eat nothing unless he absolutely had to, for there was no telling where the next meal may come from. He had found some oil lamps on the first floor and had wandered around in the back rooms awhile, just to make sure there were no dead bodies. He, Lysander, and the other elders had insisted on removing the dead before the bodies began to putrefy. That carefulness is probably what saved their community center. The Romans simply burned down any building which had bodies inside; it was so much simpler than dragging them out to the incineration grounds south of the city.

Since there were no immediate empty grounds around their building, Barnabas and the other survivors took the bodies to fields near the Hippodrome in David's City. At first they would travel by night with their shovels; two men, and later women, were responsible for pulling the bodies along on a cart. Eventually they did this out in the open, when no one cared what anyone was doing, unless it was the robbers, but even they had given up finding anything of value weeks ago.

Some people said they could tell if a robber was a Zealot, or a supporter of Simon, or a simple thief taking advantage of the collapse of social order. Barnabas wasn't one of those people. A thief was a thief; they acted all the same to him and never bothered to justify why they were stealing or why they were torturing people in the vain hope that they could find something valuable.

What was he to do all alone in this building? It was his home now, so he supposed no one could evict him from the premises; but there were nearly 200 people who used to work or live or worship in these spaces, which had become quite small relative to the size of the group. And this did not count at least fifty or more pilgrims who had come to Jerusalem for the Passover and who had been trapped here once the siege began. Not that Christians really celebrated the Passover anymore, but these Christian pilgrims were here to commemorate the crucifixion that happened nearly half a century ago. They came in greater numbers each year, mostly from the north – from Antioch, Damascus, Ephesus, Corinth, and increasingly from Rome and now Alexandria. Christianity was spreading throughout the Empire, which completely amazed Barnabas. This was the work, he concluded, of a few of the Twelve who traveled beyond Samaria and Galilee to explain to others the miracles they had witnessed. Some of them had accepted the resurrection story – Barnabas had begun to think of it in big capital letters: THE RESURRECTION STORY – because it had become so important to some people and had become so elaborate. It was almost as elaborate as what he called THE BIRTH STORY, the tales about Jehoshua, with an imaginary father named Yosef and his mother, Miriam, traveling on a donkey to Bethlehem, and a birth in a stables, and then visits from Magi, and later travel into Egypt. What silliness, thought Barnabas. It was as if people were trying to make everyone deliberately forget about Jehoshua's being born in Galilee. Why, he himself – Barnabas – grew up in Galilee and met the family of Jehoshua in Nazareth, where the Master was born and raised. Barnabas got to know some of his brothers and sisters quite well, not counting Yakov, of course, who chose to stay in Jerusalem and become one of the Christians.

What would Yakov think of all this? Would he say that he was fortunate to have died before all this happened? Not, of course, dying in the way he did, but at least not having to live through the past spring and summer, when the world literally felt like it was coming to an end?

Yakov probably wouldn't say much; he wasn't a man for complaining. He would simply carry on making people comfortable, helping the pilgrims in their distress at being separated from their families, and assisting those who were facing death from hunger or illness. If anyone asked him about why so many pilgrims were coming to Jerusalem from so far away, having the most peculiar ideas about Jehoshua, Yakov would say: "It's all because of Paulus," and he wouldn't be judgmental about Paulus as so many others were. As Barnabas himself was. Barnabas never fully liked the man, certainly not when he was oppressing them in the very early days, and only a little less when he had become one of them. Paulus was the same argumentative and opinionated person every time Barnabas had met him; Paulus had his own ideas about Jehoshua and his mission, and he was never wrong about his own ideas. That was Paulus exactly – the man who was never wrong.

Yakov would say, "Don't be so harsh, Barnabas. Paulus does many good things for us and others. In his soul he is a very kind man – a noble man, even. He talks of love in the way Jehoshua used to talk of love, and they could both make the idea and the emotion behind love very real. The rest of us do not have this gift. So let him be. Let him do his work."

Barnabas would stay quiet after receiving such advice, tinged as it was with admonition. That was Yakov's gift: he could quiet people down and smooth over differences. Simon Petros was like that, so were Kediah and Miriam of Magdala, and to be frank, anyone who knew Jehoshua. Barnabas had felt the change in himself as well. After several years accompanying Jehoshua around Galilee and then Samaria and Judea, Barnabas had simply lost the anger that was inside of him. The sheer force of the personality of the Master molded and shaped the people who met him or followed him. Barnabas had thought more and more about this transformation in himself, and he had realized it was a distinguishing characteristic of the leadership of the Christian community in Jerusalem. We didn't have any fight in us, Barnabas used to think. He would argue this with Miriam and Lysander and Philip and a few others, and they would smile and tell him it was unimportant, and that fighting was not what the Master wanted. Then Barnabas would not have enough fight in him to say anything further, and things would go on just as they always did for them in Jerusalem.

That lack of anger may be why so many of them reacted the way they did when they heard about the death of Simon Petros in Rome and how he died. The horrible way he died, like the Master, only more shamefully, in front of thousands of people. Everyone was shocked with this news, but Philip wasn't surprised, and Miriam wasn't either. They seemed to have expected it and gave the impression it was some glorious thing to die that way for the Master. That was when Barnabas really, truly had nothing to say, because he felt weakness inside of himself – the weakness that came from not knowing with a certainty that he could do what Simon Petros had done, which was die for the Master.

Barnabas was simply not a man who relished suffering, and he had seen so much of it in the past months that he was more than ever convinced that it was the one great bane of human existence. Not suffering in itself, which was a natural condition that all men must bear, but the suffering that one or more men imposed on others. That cruelty he could no longer abide. There was no excuse for it, there was nothing really human about it. He could not understand men who took pleasure in inflicting pain on others, which meant that he couldn't understand the Romans at all. He therefore loathed those who perpetrated such evil. Could he take the next step and welcome suffering imposed on himself – "turn the other cheek," as the Master would say? He would bear it if he was trapped and had no other choice, but before he met the Master he would have fought his way out if he could. But even then, he would not endure such suffering and then find some form of redemption in it, as did Simon Petros. Simon Petros would feel he somehow owed this suffering to the Master. And that, thought Barnabas, was how he was different from Simon Petros. Barnabas could never feel such a debt to the Master, nor was he sure he would welcome such a death even if it guaranteed him eternal life with the Father

He heard a slight moving of the door. He had locked the door, which was never done until the troubles started. Someone was trying to get in, and Barnabas thought instantly of robbers or murderers. He looked about for something to use to defend himself, but then he heard a voice: "Is anyone in there?" It sounded like Lysander but he couldn't be sure. "Who is it?" asked Barnabas. "It is Lysander. Is that you, Barnabas?"

Barnabas was surprised at how relieved he was to hear Lysander's voice. He hadn't realized the loneliness and isolation he had felt the past day – he had been too lost in his thoughts and experiences. He lifted the latch quickly, and there was Lysander standing next to a Roman soldier. It was not what Barnabas was expecting at all.

"He is the decurion for our street," said Lysander. "His name is Virgilis, and he has helped me. He represents no danger." Barnabas realized he was rather dumbly blocking the door, perhaps out of habit, so he stepped aside and welcomed the two into the room. "Everything has been cleaned out," said Lysander, looking around. "Hardly any furniture, no food. Have you been upstairs?" Barnabas admitted he had not, and Lysander gave him a sharp look, as if Barnabas was acting irresponsibly, which Lysander definitely would have concluded had he known Barnabas had been there for two days.

"Virgilis, do you mind if we make sure of things upstairs? It won't take a moment and you needn't accompany us." Lysander bolted up the stairs as Barnabas followed him. Virgilis took the seat Barnabas had vacated. Lysander barely looked about the room, which was also virtually empty, but immediately headed to a corner and got on his knees. He fiddled with the floor boards for a minute, and prying them open, he exhaled a sigh of relief as he lifted a series of scrolls and parchment papers up from their hiding place. "The Father in Heaven is looking out for us," whispered Lysander to Barnabas. "I was very fearful of losing these more than anything." Lysander put them back into safekeeping and replaced the boards. "They will be safe here now. Fire was our only remaining danger but I think that risk is gone. Let us go down to Virigilis; we must get back to the New City."

Barnabas did not understand what the discovery meant, but there was something about Lysander's energy and command of the situation that made him feel he must comply. Besides, he saw now that it was not healthy simply sitting in a room doing nothing for over a day. They closed the door behind them but did not bother locking it; there was no one about anymore on the streets, though Barnabas was still frightened that evil men might be lurking anywhere. Virgilis did not understand Galilean, so Lysander explained to Barnabas in their local language what was happening.

"I identified myself to the centurion responsible for our confinement. I explained that I was a leader within the community of Christians and that I could help them identify all the Christians in the New City. I would be able to remove the burden from the Romans of caring for them. He had certainly heard of the Christians from the terrible things Nero had done, but he had to find out from his superiors whether Titus felt the same way about us. Apparently both Vespasianus and Titus are more tolerant of us, so I have been given permission to look through the camps and identify the Christians. I assured him none of them was involved in the fighting, and in any event, we are only allowed to remove those who are age forty five or older. I suppose you have heard that almost everyone younger, unless they are ill, are being sold, and their children are going with them."

Barnabas had heard some rumors to this effect, and had thought that such divisions would destroy their community. "I must agree with you there," said Lysander. "It will destroy Jerusalem as well. However, I do not believe Titus will be able to enforce this policy completely. There are simply too many people involved. Second, Jews will eventually come back to Jerusalem from abroad and re-populate the city. Our immediate hope is that our communities to the north will want to send some families to move here."

Barnabas had been looking about the streets as they walked across the city. What would normally take them an hour to get to the Damascus Gate was going to take five hours, and they would be lucky to return in time before darkness. Barnabas was beginning to think they would stay in the camps that evening, so enormous was their task. "Why would anyone want to move here?" said Barnabas in response to Lysander's comment.

"No one will move here the way it is. The Romans are going to be shipping food down here regularly all winter. What they told me that they want us to do is to plant some winter crops before it is too late. They will give us land near the Hippodrome. I think Titus at first wanted to empty the city completely, but then he realized, even after so many deaths, there are hundreds of thousands of people who need attention. He cannot simply let them die of starvation; he has to take some responsibility for us, or his new administration – that of his father, really – will begin governing with a terrible stain on their reputation. Nor can he resettle all of us; that would disrupt the other major cities in the East. He has to have us become self-sustaining as quickly as possible. He also has to empty out the New City, because that is going to become one gigantic garden to help feed the population here."

Lysander and Barnabas, with their escort, walked slowly through the main streets, stepping over the rubble, and avoiding the corpses that still remained. "I am afraid," said Lysander, "that the Romans are going to need slaves to clean up this city. I suspect that also will be the task assigned the men under forty five, before they are shipped abroad. The slave traders aren't going to like the delay in getting their profit, but it has to be done. You and I and others of our age, with some strength left, will probably have to help as well.

One big priority will be to get the fountains working again, where possible."

"How many of us do you think are left," asked Barnabas. "How many Christians, do you mean?" queried Lysander. "No," said Barnabas. "You know what I mean. How many of us? How many are still alive who knew Jehoshua?" Lysander knew exactly what he meant. He had been fighting a rear-guard action for years now, trying to maintain some sense of what the Jerusalem community of Christians had stood for. They had been the ones who knew Jehoshua personally. They were the people who followed him on his mission, who heard his teaching first-hand, who knew the truth about him. They were dying out, and his was an important question.

"Philip and Miriam are now gone," said Lysander. It was a simple statement of fact. Barnabas and Lysander and a few others had accompanied them on the cart to the burying ground in David's City. They had both succumbed to the famine. Javan and the two children had survived, but the children were disconsolate at the loss of their step-mother and uncertain what new horrors were before them as slaves. Kediah had died less than a year after the death of her husband, out of sorrow, bitterness, and loss more than anything; she had fortunately not lived long enough to see the destruction of Jerusalem. "There might be five or so more of us who followed him who are still around," added Lysander. "We haven't heard from any of his other brothers and sisters for years. Nor have we heard from any of the Twelve."

Barnabas listened quietly to this summary. Lysander was probably correct; their generation was dying out – the people who knew Jehoshua personally - and now the war with the Romans had accelerated that process. "What is going to happen when we all die," asked Barnabas. He meant what is going to happen to the legacy of Jehoshua, but Lysander understood the question well enough.

"Why do you think I placed the scrolls and other writings in a safe place?" replied Lysander. "It is important that we have that written record preserved. That must be our priority now. Even if we cannot rejuvenate our community, even if our community is destined to die out along with the rest of Jerusalem, we must preserve the written record. I am going to send copies of everything we have to the communities abroad. We have all of my scrolls, plus the history written by Marcus in Alexandria, plus a few more things people have written, including some of the strange stories about his birth, such as that one from Corinth. Each of the communities must receive this material, or at least the material we trust. Personally I would not send copies of the letters from Paulus, because I don't trust his interpretation of things, but it is probably too late to stop those ideas. Paulus has written to everybody long before us. We will just need some money to buy the parchment and hire a scribe; if need be, I will copy all of it myself. But one way or other, we have to get the truth distributed as much as we can."

It was several hours before the three of them reached the Damascus Gate. Decidedly, they would be spending the night in the New City, sleeping on the ground again and probably taking most of the next day identifying as many people as they could, including those Christians visiting from abroad who wished to be released back to the community center. As they stepped beyond the Gate, both Barnabas and Lysander took a glance at the execution grounds. Amidst so much destruction, Golgotha seemed unchanged. Why not, thought Barnabas? A place of death such as Golgotha thrived at a time when an entire city was turned into a charnel house. Isn't that what war was? Death spreading itself over a wider and wider landscape? Yet this was the place the pilgrims most wanted to see. They would get on their knees and crawl their way up the rocks to reach the summit of this hill. The Romans would force them off, but the attempts would continue.

Barnabas remembered one letter from Paulus, where he quoted from the prophet Isaiah. "Death, where is thy sting?" Barnabas could answer that. He had just spent hours walking and stumbling his way through what was once a great city, only now the smell of death was everywhere. That's where the sting of death was, and it was certainly to be found wherever men waged war.

Barnabas also knew that the story had not ended. He had heard Jehoshua talk many times about eternal life with the Father. He had seen him conquer death by raising men from the tomb. Death did not have the final victory. Not even the Romans had the final victory. That is, ultimately, what Barnabas believed. He also had to concede that it was what Paulus believed, only Paulus was much better than anyone else at explaining it, even if Barnabas did not agree with everything Paulus wrote and didn't like the man personally.

Barnabas believed these things, but could he act on them? He was back to thinking about his great weakness. He stopped and looked over his shoulder one last time at Golgotha. Where would he get the strength of someone like Simon Petros to embrace such a death? It was all very good for Lysander to copy the writings he had and send them everywhere, but unless he – Barnabas – or other men like him, were willing to embrace death with the confidence that it was a small price to pay for eternal life, who would believe whatever was written on a piece of parchment?

Chapter Thirty Two

lavius Josephus caught himself daydreaming again. Perhaps it was the vista over the Forum from his new apartment in Rome. He found the view captivating – people moving about constantly, business being done, sacrifices being made at temples. The colors of the buildings literally changed as the day progressed and the sun moved over the sky. Josephus would start to think about the strange circumstances of fate that brought him here: his capture by the Romans in Jotapata, his dream regarding Vespasianus achieving the throne, and now his position as almost a member of the Flavian royal family.

His dream suggested that Vespasianus would come riding out of the East with his legions and take command of Rome. It didn't quite work that way, though the outcome was the same. Vespasianus bided his time in Alexandria, giving Vitellius plenty of time to anger the Senate, who were the recipients of his summary justice, and allowing more and more of the provinces in the East to demand that Vespasianus be named Emperor. In the end, Vespasianus didn't have to leave Egypt at all. Once Vitellius' own troops murdered him, the Senate was eager to hand the throne to the one man who could provide stability to the Empire. More than stability – Vespasianus would be able to bring an astounding amount of gold and jewels to the Roman treasury from the conquest of Jerusalem, but not before first placing all this wealth on display in the Forum at his Triumph.

And such a Triumph it was! That too was something Josephus was also day-dreaming about, so wonderful had the experience been. He had just written to his wife in Jerusalem about it – thank the Lord God she was safe, as were his parents. Now he had just penned a letter to his parents as well, but wanted to proofread it one more time.

Greetings from Flavius Josephus to Matityahu ben Jonah
Honored Father,

*I have been in communication with Lucilius Bassus, and he writes
to me that you and Mother are safe and are well-provisioned, even
though food is still scarce in Jerusalem, and despite the fact that so
many thousands of Jews died or were exiled as a result of the recent
war. I said a prayer of thanks at the local synagogue when I heard
this news; and I said to the Emperor as well that, as procurator,
Lucilius Bassus deserves commendations for his work in restoring
Jerusalem and extirpating all hint of the folly which overtook
the Zealots and so many others who believed they could challenge
Rome's might.*

*I have been given permission by the Emperor to use his familial name
of Flavius as my own. This is, of course, meant as no disrespect to
you or our family, but as you can appreciate, to advance in Rome you
need a Roman name, and there is none higher nor more esteemed
in the entirety of the Empire than Flavius. I am proud to claim the
Emperor as my patron, and the use of his personal name is a rare
honor that has brought me much respect in Rome.*

*The Romans are a very religious people; they believe fervently
in signs and portents that can occur in many ways - birds in the
sky, animals seen in the forest, or dreams. That is why so many
people here, especially among the nobility and the wealthy classes,
ask me regularly about my dreams, since I have a reputation from
Vespasianus himself for experiencing visions of the future. I tell
people I receive such visions very infrequently, and they are often
difficult to interpret, but still they press me to tell them whether a
marriage will be successful, or a business venture profitable, and
so on. Domitianus, the younger son of Vespasianus, is especially
persistent, but I must disappoint him. I do not tell him that I might
have had a frequent dream about him, in which the outcome is
very unfavorable, because it will only discourage him, and because
I simply cannot be certain yet what this dream is saying to me. One
can make an excellent living being a soothsayer to the upper classes
of Rome, but it would be a dishonorable career, and I have chosen
instead to maintain my professional honor and personal pride.*

*I make my living here as a writer and an interpreter whenever the
Emperor needs to meet with someone who speaks only Hebrew.
Despite the substantial destruction in Jerusalem, there is still*

a large and thriving community of Jews in many cities, such as Antioch, Alexandria, Corinth, and Rome. These Jews occasionally do important business with the government, so the administration here in Rome must still deal with them. I am also thinking of writing a memoir of my experiences during the war. Time has proven me correct: men like Simon bar Giora and Yohan of Gischala misjudged their abilities and that of our nation, and they brought us to ruin. The Lord God has punished such people severely, though all of us have suffered as a consequence. I think a written history of the war needs to make clear the role these Jews played in bringing destruction on our nation, and that we should never again dare to think we can challenge an empire such as the Romans have built.

I do not see how any Jew could doubt what I am saying if they had been in Rome for the Triumph that was presented by the Senate for the Emperor and for Flavius Titus. I do not believe any such spectacle has ever been seen before anywhere on the earth - not even Rameses II could have mounted something this magnificent. I will try in words to describe for you and Mother the splendor, the grandeur, and the glory that was presented to the Roman people, but my words will be poor failures in comparison to witnessing the actual event. I doubt I shall ever see such a majestic sight in my life again.

Imagine first the Roman Forum - narrow lanes, many temples and shrines at different levels, large basilicas for court and legal business, vendors selling precious goods in the forum stores. Every lane along the procession route is lined with people who have been waiting there for two days or more. Every roof and vantage point in the surrounding hills is filled with cheering Romans. Over a million people are able to see this occasion in history. The day of the Triumph is a national holiday, with feasting arranged for everyone, even in the poorest villages in Italia.

I was a guest of the Imperial family and was able to witness much at close range. The procession of wealth was seemingly endless. The parade included boxes filled with the finest gems and jewelry, and then many treasure chests overflowing with gold bars and coins, all destined to replenish the Roman Treasury. Statues of the main Roman gods and goddesses were carried aloft by attendants in the finest purple robes with golden ornamentation. These images were *crafted out of the rarest marbles, or bronze, or ivory, and each of them was accented with gold crowns, as well as precious gems for their eyes. The workmanship was exquisite - the ablest Greek carvers and artisans must have been hired for this - and bear in mind these statues were created just for this occasion.*

Following this display were the gigantic tableaux featuring scenes from the war. Some of these were as high as a four story building. The woodcarvers who made these scenes recreated the Temple, the Fortress Antonia, the inner wall, a complete miniature view of the Upper City, and many other such marvels, so that anyone who has lived in Jerusalem would recognize them instantly. There were even scenes of some of these buildings on fire, and the final tableaux showed Titus in his position of authority in the ruins of the Temple.

That made me long even more for the Jerusalem that does not exist anymore, but I cried without shame when the Jewish captives were marched into the Forum. They were dressed in rare robes of embroidered cotton, and I know they were picked for their beauty and physical strength, but I wept unabashedly when they were paraded by the Emperor, as I knew their fate was to die in the arena from wild beasts or gladiator fights. My only solace was that those two deceivers, Simon bar Giora and Yohan of Gischala, were next on display. They were locked in wooden cages, carried on carts, and had been subjected to every imaginable torment and insult from the people, who would have killed them if they could. They were naked except for a loincloth, and their bodies were covered with vegetables, honey, rotten fruits, and of course considerable human excrement, all of which the crowds had flung at them along the route. I felt no sorrow for these men, only shame as a Jew that such brigands and miscreants should be the cause of so much suffering for our people.

A large golden statue of Victory entered the parade route in the Forum and announced the arrival of the two men everyone had come to acclaim: Emperor Vespasianus, and his son Titus. They were in two separate chariots of ivory, ornamented with gold, and they had golden laurel wreaths on their heads. The second brother, Domitianus, rode along as well, on a white horse with purple raiment.

Vespasianus and his two sons reached the temple of Jupiter Capitolinus, where they mounted the steps, preparing to offer sacrifices to Jupiter in thanks for their victory and signaling the solemn conclusion to the Triumph. Before they could do so, however, it was customary in these triumphs for the leader of the enemy to be slain before the crowd. Yohan of Gischala had been granted life imprisonment by Titus, which was most merciful of Titus, considering how Yohan had betrayed him at Gischala. Still, it was Simon who was the crueler of the two men, and it was therefore Simon bar Giora who was pulled from his cart and dragged violently across the Forum pavement. He was then led to an area of execution, and at a signal from Titus, as the victor in the campaign, two men held tightly to Simon&s arms while a third came from behind and strangled him to death with a cord. As his body slumped to the ground, a tremendous cheer rose from the crowd, and Vespasianus, shrouded in incense, lifted the sacrificial meat of a lamb to the heavens in final supplication to the gods that Rome continue to benefit from their protection.

While this signified the end of the procession, the true festivities had only begun. The rest of the day was devoted to feasting. Every citizen of Rome was entitled to a full banquet meal, and for non-citizens food was laid out in the Forum, if one was willing to wait in a very long line. The tableaux were on display in the Forum, and on the Rostra, where speeches traditionally are made, the jewels and gold were open for all to see, heavily guarded of course. I trembled when I saw our golden candelabra placed there, along with much else taken from our Temple sanctuary. There are many Jews who live in Rome, and I could tell which they were when a look of shock crossed their face as they realized the desecration that had occurred to the Temple.

I suppose it is no use bemoaning these circumstances at length, as it is mostly our own fault as a people that we allowed ourselves to be so divided by religious factions. I truly believe the Lord God has abandoned us, at least temporarily. Barbarians will say it is proof that Jupiter is a superior god to the One God that no longer resides in the Holy of Holies. I cannot say that; as a Jew, I know only the One God. I simply do not know where He now abides or whether He does so anywhere on earth.

At the very least, after seeing the display of this Triumph, I do not believe any nation or any force that we know of can ever overcome the Romans or defeat their Empire. This empire shall last at least a thousand years.

If the Lord God is listening at all to our prayers, he will allow us to coexist as part of this Empire. He will give us the wisdom and humility to avoid deception and the vain belief that anyone else can conquer it.

Please tell Mother I love her, I am doing well, and read this letter to her. I miss you both and am looking for an opportunity to return to see you as soon as possible. If your circumstances in Jerusalem worsen, you must write to me immediately and I will see what I can do to move you away from there. I am writing separately to my wife and am making the same promise, and I have asked her to take care of you and Mother when she can.

I submit to you my filial respect and obedience and my eternal affection for you both.

Flavius Josephus

Flavius rolled the parchment up and sealed the scroll. He had the use of the imperial messengers, so this letter would reach his parents within a week. He truly hoped his Father would listen to his advice, write back, and request help in leaving the city. There was no future for him or anyone else in Jerusalem, so why should his parents at their age struggle with the basics of finding food and water?

But his Father was a stubborn man and would never leave Jerusalem. Or maybe stubborn wasn't the right word, thought Josephus. Maybe it was better to say that his Father, like most Jews, loved Jerusalem so much that he would never abandon it. It was the Promised Land, after all. As for Josephus, despite all his daydreaming about life in Rome, and the splendor of the Triumph, and his fortunate situation as an aide to the Emperor, his most frequent day-dream found him back in Jerusalem, before the war, worshipping at the glorious Temple, giving the honor and respect due to the One, Invisible God. Josephus was, in the end, not very different from his Father after all.

PART SIX

It took three long years for Rome to "mop up" Jewish resistance, with the Jews putting up a final stand at the desert fortress of Masada in the Year 73. The scene now shifts six years later, in 79, first to Rome, where we meet Olympias, the daughter of Crispus and Chrysanthe. She has settled in Rome with her husband, a wine merchant, and their three young boys. She and her husband live a secretive life as Christians in Rome, mindful of Nero's persecutions, even though Emperor Vespasianus has been tolerant of Christians and left them in peace. Olympias is among those who help Christianity find its roots in Rome. In contrast, Jerusalem remains in charred ruins, with Rome unwilling to spend effort or money to restore the city after its destruction. By the year 79, Rome does agree to restore the Sanhedrin and the position of Nasi, which is offered to Gamaliel's grandson, Gamaliel of Yavneh. He begins the arduous task of rebuilding Judaism, whose followers are flung to all areas of the Roman Empire and beyond, and whose home – the Temple of Jerusalem – will remain in ruins and unbuilt even up to this day.

Olympias

Vatican Hill and Jerusalem
Year 79

Rome

Chapter Thirty Three

ct as if you come to this tomb frequently. If anyone stops us, say you are a member of the Matucius family. You are visiting the remains of your grandmother." Olympias took a sideways glance at her visitor. Ampelios, from Antioch, was all she was told about him. He was Greek, with somewhat regular and handsome features and a full head of sandy hair sometimes found in men from the northern part of the country. Maybe he was Macedonian in origin. She gauged him to be about thirty five years old, slightly younger than herself, and he had the rough hands of a day laborer. Not a farmer, she thought, but someone who uses tools – perhaps a stone mason. That would probably explain his shortness of breath; there was something wrong with his lungs, and at his age it was likely caused by his work. She had seen this sign before in stone masons and anyone else who worked around dust.

She slowed down. Ampelios leaned against a stone marker. "We shall rest," Olympias told him, as if it was her need to stop now along the Via Triumphalis. She didn't mind. She had time, and it was always better to stay along the main roads in the cemetery and to act naturally. A roar came up from the crowd in Nero's Circus. "Someone has just met with an accident," she told Ampelios. The crowd liked accidents best of all, more so than even their colors winning a chariot race. The Via Triumphalis ran southeast from the Circus. In an hour or so it would be filled with people heading home from an afternoon at the races. They would be sporting the colors of their team: red, green, white or blue. Most of the young men would head to the taverns, and then eventually fights would break out in different parts of the city, usually the Blues from the Subura fighting the Greens from the Esquiline Hill.

Two of her three sons, Leontios and Sophos, were at the chariot races. Admission was free for those poor enough and willing to sit out in the sun at the highest seats in the stands, so they had left early to wait in line for entrance. Rome normally held chariot races at the Circus Maximus, but the entire structure had burned down in the Great Fire fifteen years ago. Indeed, the fire had started in the wooden stalls under the stands at the Circus Maximus. Nero had been forced to put up an alternative structure here on Vatican Hill, next to the cemetery, and far away from the dangerous conditions across the Tiber in Rome. Vatican Hill was a relatively empty space, except for the cemetery that had been there since the time of the Republic. Some of the tombs and markers were so old that Olympias could no longer read the inscriptions. Her Latin wasn't that good anyway, and Romans abbreviated their written words so frequently, and with no apparent rules or reason about the process, that Olympias often would be mystified by even the newest tomb.

Walking amidst the streets and lanes of this cemetery was still one of her favorite pleasures. Cemeteries were strictly regulated under Roman law. It was a death sentence for anyone who desecrated a tomb, and the wealthier families competed with each other to erect the most elaborate mausoleums, with expensive carved marble figures of the deceased, surrounded by cupids. Sometimes the family founder would be shown in a religious procession, displaying his piety and reverence for the gods. In Greece, where Olympias grew up, there was never this much devotion to the dead.

Still, the cemetery was like a private park or garden open to the public. Even Nero, when he built a country villa on Vatican Hill, had a lane installed that led directly to the cemetery. Olympias enjoyed the flowering trees at this time of year, the bright green buds on the giant yew trees, the rivulets of water that ran down channels built to direct the overflow from rains, and the benches placed at those spots which afforded splendid views of Rome across the Tiber. The twitter and singing of birds during the spring mating season added the last touch of perfection to the scene.

The Via Triumphalis sloped upwards on a crest leading to the top of Vatican Hill. Olympias afforded as much time to her guest as he needed to regain his breath. The spectators at Nero's Circus would let out cheers and shouts from time to time, lending a peculiarly Roman character to their visit. No other civilization – certainly not the Greeks – fancied elaborate spectacles and gruesome contests as much as the Romans.

Olympias rose, and her guest took his cue from her, rising to his feet. They resumed a placid pace up the road. Olympias assured Ampelios they were close now, and soon they took a turn to the right. Via Cornelia, thought Olympias. Fortunately it was unmarked, but a sharp-eyed visitor could easily remember landmarks along the way. Olympias never showed anyone this spot unless referred to her by Linus, and even then they had to be visitors temporarily in Rome, preferably from the eastern provinces.

Via Cornelia was unpaved and narrow. The trees and monuments afforded more than shade; it was somewhat dark down this lane. Past two or three more intersecting lanes, and Olympias looked behind her to be sure no one was observing. Some of the caretakers, who also acted as guards and police, had begun to recognize her, even though she would take alternate routes when she could. No one would suspect much if she was visiting a tomb on her own or with her family, but to be visiting the same place time and again, each time with a different person, evoked suspicion. Her family could not possibly have that many relatives.

Seeing no one in front of or behind her, she quickly walked into a building on the right and motioned Ampelios to follow her. Down a narrow walkway was an empty room on the left and a little further on a larger room to the right. The light was very dim here, and she cautioned to watch for the stairs as she led him to the larger room. Once inside, she brought out an oil lamp and lit it. She set it down on the ground. It afforded a slightly brighter view of the chambers in the wavering light of a single flame.

There were niches for urns along the wall, and two particularly large urns on one wall. Along the floor was a sarcophagus with a simple stone top. It had one mark on it – that of the Egyptian ankh, which was a symbol throughout the Empire for eternal life.

Olympias got on her knees in front of the sarcophagus and motioned Ampelios to do the same. "Petros," was all she told him. Ampelios sunk his head to the ground, nearly touching the top of the tomb. He grabbed the lid with both hands, as if he intended to lift it. Olympias had seen this before. People wanted to raise the lid, perhaps to see the remains of Simon Petros, but she suspected other reasons predominated. Increasingly Christians were seeking out this tomb for cures, given the reputation Simon Petros enjoyed as a healer when he was alive.

Ampelios took a cloth from his robe and coughed quietly into it. The solemnity of this place never failed to etch itself upon the emotions of those who were allowed to visit. Invariably people said nothing or whispered a question or two. Many cried. Ampelios lay his handkerchief on top of the tomb and placed his hands over it. He lowered his head and fell into silent prayer.

Olympias' thoughts turned to her own prayers. "Please, Simon Petros, make sure that Demetrios is safe. It has been three weeks since he left on his trip, and I know that is not a long time not to hear from him when he is traveling, but I worry nonetheless. Please keep Emperor Vespasianus safe. He is no friend to the Jews but he has not made things worse for us Christians. He has stopped the persecutions that Nero initiated; that is the main thing. And help me guide Leontios. At fourteen he is at an age where his friends can influence him far more than we can as parents. Make sure he does not meet with the wrong friends."

Olympias leaned back and then rose quietly from her knees. She retreated to another corner of the room and sat down. Ampelios was lost completely in his devotions and supplications. She would give him time. She would rather walk back when the races were over and crowds could provide them anonymity. The mausoleum was utterly quiet, despite it being open to the hallway through which they entered. The Matucius family, however many were interred in the urns that lined the walls, rested solemnly. Ampelios rose to his feet, carefully folding his handkerchief and placing it in his robe. He would keep that handkerchief all his life, Olympias predicted. She had never been raised to be superstitious like that, but living among the Romans had heightened her sense of the mysterious, and the stories of miracles performed by Jehoshua and Simon Petros undermined her reliance on the rational. It was when Heiron took ill at age five that she realized for the first time that she would have given anything if someone had offered Demetrios and her an amulet or potion that would guarantee Heiron's life. He survived that scare, and at seventeen had now joined his father in their import and export business. Olympias never forgot the lesson from that experience, and so she watched with sympathy as pilgrims came to Rome seeking a healing from the remains of Simon Petros.

Olympias walked over to the door of the crypt and looked left down the hallway. She could see no one. Motioning to Ampelios but saying nothing, she walked quietly out to Via Cornelia. No one was on this small lane as she and Ampelios began the walk to the Via Triumphalis. Ahead she could see people walking in both directions on the Via Triumphalis; this was a good sign for them. The races were over or nearly over, and the crowd from Nero's Circus was beginning to leave for home.

"I believe I know your husband, Demetrios," said Ampelios. "He is in the wine business, is he not? I met him when he last came to Antioch on a purchasing trip. He visited our community there, which has grown quite large. He works for Avram ben Moses? The shipping merchant? I thought I recognized the description of Demetrios when Linus mentioned him."

Olympias confirmed his questions. "He is on another trip to the east at the moment, otherwise he would be happy to meet you. I don't know if he is intending to visit Antioch on this trip, however. I haven't heard from him in nearly a month."

"There is nothing unusual in that," added Olympias. "If there had been any trouble, I would have heard from him or from Hannah, Avram's mother. She checks with him periodically when he is on these journeys to make sure he is safe. She has been close to my family for years, when I was growing up in Corinth and when her husband, Moses ben Hezekiah, was still alive."

"That must be why you settled here on the Vatican in the Jewish community," suggested Ampelios. Most Christians who met Olympias and Demetrios were curious about this fact, since the Christian community was located on the immediate outskirts of Rome and not across the river. "Moses wanted us here," answered Olympias. "He and his wife may have been Christians, but his business relationships were mostly with the Jewish community. Demetrios came here to establish a business in Rome, and this is where he was going to get financing and book cargo space on the merchant ships. His specialty in this market is wine, and when he needs to find buyers for some of the more expensive amphorae, he can travel in to the city to meet with wealthy Romans. It helps, of course, that he is Greek and not Jewish, when it comes to selling the wines. I think that is one reason Moses selected him for the position, but as he always told us, there was never any question that Demetrios was the right man for the assignment. He has a natural sense for the business."

"We grew to like it here," added Olympias. "As you can tell, there is much more of a country feel here than in the city. Heiron, our son, adapted very quickly, and we have been able to find a good educator for him and our two other sons. It was not expensive when we first moved here, but that has changed considerably in the past fifteen years. When Nero built a villa nearby to the cemetery here, it became fashionable for aristocrats and wealthy merchants to move to Vatican Hill. Then, of course, the Great Fire escalated the exodus, as over 100,000 people were made homeless. Demetrios and I began to wonder if perhaps this area was becoming like Rome itself – crowded, dirty, dangerous at night. Now we are almost certain of it, with the destruction of the Temple in Jerusalem and the arrival of so many Jews from that city. People estimate that as many as 30,000 Jews have come here since Vespasianus became Emperor and Titus lay siege to Jerusalem."

"But I think he has been good for our community," said Ampelios. "That is our impression in Antioch. He does not demonize us as Nero did."

"That is true," agreed Olympias. "We don't believe in worshipping the emperors as the Romans do, but it does not hurt us to pray for the health of Vespasianus. I doubt, however, that any of the Jews around here would agree with anything we say about either Vespasianus or Titus."

"You were here, then, when he died?" Ampelios had changed the subject, but it was a question everyone who visited asked. Olympias was conscientious about telling her visitors enough without revealing too much. The greatest secret held by the Christian community in Rome was the one she had been willing to reveal to him: the location of the tomb of Simon Petros. Only three people in the Rome community knew where to find it: Linus, as head of the Christian believers since the death of Simon Petros; Olympias; and someone else he would never identify. He had many reasons why he had asked Olympias to carry this burden. She was a faithful and reliable member of the community; she was Greek and less liable to be suspected of being a Christian; her husband was a successful businessman and also less likely to be suspected; and she lived very near the cemetery.

She had agreed to this responsibility, but it had been the most difficult burden she ever had carried. Particularly when Nero was alive, there was always a dread in her mind that she would be arrested and put to the torture. Most Christians succumbed to the torture and confessed to crimes they did not commit, but they also gave up names of others who were Christians. Once Nero had died and the terror had died down, those who survived but who had caused others to go to their deaths had been abandoned by the Christian community, but Linus and the other leaders were constantly asking if this was the right policy. If they were truly repentant, was it right to completely cut them off from an eternal life with Christos? Was this not a judgment that only Jehoshua and his Father could make? Olympias was on the side of leniency and forgiveness, if only because the secret which she carried on behalf of the whole community had made her think more closely about the frailty of humans in the face of such wickedness as torture.

"Those were terrible, terrible times," she said to Ampelios, thinking out loud. "Most of us had not expected the ferocity of Nero's condemnation, though Simon Petros had warned us. It wasn't exactly the Great Fire for which we were blamed. Almost two years had passed before Nero began arresting us. The truth was, he needed a diversion from all the criticism he was receiving for building the Domus Aurea – his Golden House. The expense was phenomenal: it featured the finest marbles, paintings, sculptures, glass windows, mosaics, tile floors, and fountains. An enormous lake was established in front of the Domus Aurea, and beside the lake was erected a colossal statue of Nero, entirely nude and expensively gilded. On that basis alone he was probably going to be condemned for bad taste – and this was a man who prided himself on his artistic sensitivity."

"But that wasn't the worst of it. The land he used was just south of the Forum and some of the most valuable land in all of Rome. He completely razed the buildings in that area to make way for his palace. And then when the public found out he wasn't even going to live in the house – it was only for his artistic endeavors and to be used on state occasions – the condemnations and jests were plastered on every wall in the city. I suspect he was quite shocked at the response. Even the Senate, which has difficulty saying no to any emperor, was against him."

"But why attack the Christians?" asked Ampelios. "You are not particularly numerous or noticeable." "Nero made us noticeable well before the fire," said Olympias. "He was angry at us for some reason, so there was official animosity already in place. But frankly, we made it worse. Many of the Jews who moved here from Jerusalem were familiar with the harassment we received from

Ananus, the Chief Priest, who put Yakov to death. They would mock and taunt our young boys, only a few of whom were Jews. Most were Greeks or Romans, and they were subject to claims that Christians were killing babies, eating their flesh, and drinking their blood. I didn't take this very seriously – none of us parents did. Unfortunately some of our young men decided to retaliate by throwing swine feces at the Great Synagogue in the city. That, as you can imagine, led to outright attacks on Christians in the street and on our community center. For a while, our Assemblies weren't safe to attend."

"Because we were such a small group, and the Jews were so numerous, it was easy for them to spread lies about us throughout Rome. We got the reputation for being barbarians and odious people. We were a very easy target for Nero. One day the average Roman didn't know we even existed, and the next day we were a threat to families everywhere because we practiced cannibalism. The Romans are such superstitious people they will believe anything – the more outlandish the easier it is for them to accept. People literally thought we were practicing secret rites of human sacrifice right here in the center of the civilized world."

"And that's when the arrests and tortures began?" said Ampelios. "And the result was easy to predict," he continued. "Christians began admitting to every despicable accusation, once they were tortured. And, of course, they implicated their families and many others. People will say anything under torture."

"The government then announced that all these accusations were true because of the confessions they had from the Christians," responded Olympias. "It made it completely unnecessary to hold trials or dispense any of the 'justice' for which Rome is supposedly famous. People were taken straight from prison to their deaths right here at the Circus." Olympias nodded her head in the direction of the structure which, as new as it was, dominated Vatican Hill.

She fell silent and Ampelios sensed she was reliving the memories of those horrors. He tried to come up with something to say that might be comforting. "It is said in Antioch and elsewhere that the Christians went to their death singing and praising Jehoshua and the Father. It strengthened all of us to hear of such courage."

"You may well think that in Antioch," retorted Olympias, with a tone of asperity. She then thought her guest did not deserve such a reaction. He was only trying to understand what had happened in

Rome. "I'm sorry," she went on. "I didn't mean to sound that way. If it helps people in Antioch or in other communities to think upon our bravery as Christians facing the torments placed upon us by the government in Rome, let them think that. But the truth is, which you may keep to yourself if you wish, we are not gods here. Our people spent their time in prison singing praises to Father in heaven, that is so, but on the day of their execution there was none of that. Most of them were led down to the cells in the circus to prepare for the 'entertainment' to follow. The first group were led to the center of the arena, to the crosses that had been erected on the Spina that runs down the middle of the race course. The Romans try to use their imagination for these events: our friends, our family members, were crucified in every way possible: on T's, on X's, impaled on sharpened poles, upside down, sideways, covered with honey or tar. It was all very well-orchestrated. Each person had four Roman executioners assigned to them, and one at a time they were crucified, the crowd encouraged to applaud the next, cleverest way to torture someone to death."

"Then the real entertainment began. Women were dressed as Amazons, with one bare breast, and hunted down by female gladiators. Then a group dressed as animals would be ravaged by bears and lions. Young girls and boys were tied to a chariot, and then races would be held to see which team won. For those who survived being pulled seven times around the arena, gladiators would dispatch them with a sword through the neck. If that wasn't entertaining enough, toward the end of the afternoon gigantic elk were driven into the arena, each with an infant tied between its antlers. The animals would be goaded with spears and fire to thrash and buck their way around the stadium until the babies were dead, and then the animals would be slain too."

"I told you no one is a god here. No one went to their deaths willingly. Our people were dragged and pulled into the arena, stabbed and whipped so that they would 'perform' for the crowd. The cries of agony from those who were crucified, which included Simon Petros, were as real as those from condemned criminals. Christians pleaded for mercy; they huddled in fear; they denounced Jehoshua if it would save their lives, but it was too late. The crowd had already paid their money and expected a show. And that is certainly what they got – unlike anything ever seen in Rome before, many people said."

"Toward the end the crowd had stopped cheering. I heard people saying it was too much, that Nero had gone too far with such a spectacle. Those who brought children complained that there was no warning about the entertainment including children being slaughtered. I'm not naïve enough to think that the crowds became more sympathetic to Christians, but this entertainment did not help Nero. I'm not surprised that a little over two years later the Senate turned on him and demanded his suicide."

"I don't know how you could have done that – how you could have witnessed such a thing," said Ampelios. "My wife could not have faced such a trial." "I had no choice," replied Olympias. "I owed it to my friends who had been caught up in the investigations. When Simon Petros first began to suspect the environment had turned dangerous for us as Christians, he ordered those who had families with children to move to a different area of Rome. He wanted us to cease socializing with each other. Demetrios and I already lived in trans-Tiberim on the Vatican, so it didn't matter to us. Once he was imprisoned, Simon Petros refused to receive any visitors; he knew that would only implicate us. That is how I escaped detection, and I thank the Father that no one gave up my name or that of Demetrios under torture."

Ampelios asked, "Is it true that Paulus was also executed along with Simon Petros? This is what people say in the East." "That is not so," said Olympias. "Paulus was released from his house confinement at least a year before the Great Fire, but he was also exiled from Rome. His colleague Aristarchus was released at the same time and returned to his family in Greece. As to Paulus, we heard he went to Gaul or other western provinces. But we have received no information since he left Rome, which is exceptionally unusual for Paulus. He could not live without writing; that is why so many of us were worried about him. Then came the persecutions, and people had others things to concern them than Paulus. I suppose you have not heard from him recently in Antioch."

"We have not," replied Ampelios. "No one has heard from him in several years. Even in Jerusalem, they have wondered if Paulus has decided to organize new communities in the west. But, of course, the Jerusalem community of Christians is very much smaller than it used to be after so many were killed by the Jews and then the Romans. And the Christians there have not been able to find a leader to replace Yakov. Lysander is trying, but he is too old for the responsibility, which is a serious setback. You are most fortunate to have Linus to lead the community here."

"I agree," said Olympias. "He is a remarkable man. He has held our community together despite our losses. He has also welcomed new members. I find that the most amazing thing of all. Why would someone want to join a religious group that has been made illegal?"

"I suppose it all depends on what you teach about Jehoshua," said Ampelios, but then he paused. "I really don't know what your teachings are in Rome. Do you follow Paulus, or do you follow Yakov and others from Jerusalem?"

Olympias thought a minute before answering. Without a doubt the absence of both Paulus and Simon Petros, as painful as that has been, afforded an opportunity to finally settle this dispute. "For a while," she said, "we had both ways of thinking taught in Rome. We were in fact two different communities;, one led by Simon Petros and another by a follower of Paulus. The two of them rarely talked to each other, and when Paulus was under house arrest, I don't think Simon Petros saw him more than twice during his whole stay here. Now, however, for our own safety, we have been forced to come together. Animosity works against us; we cannot afford for one group to divulge the names of the members of the other group to the Romans. Now we will have to find a way between the two philosophies, or perhaps merge them together somehow."

They had come to the end of the Via Triumphalis. The walk down had naturally been easier on Ampelios, but he seemed more animated as well. Perhaps it was the experience of seeing the tomb of such a renowned healer. Perhaps it was the conversation. The air had turned cooler, and Olympias was eager to get home to her three boys. She had confidence that Heiron would maintain good order, but it was an exceptional thing to allow Leontios and Sophos to attend the chariot races. It was the one entertainment in Rome that Olympias felt suitable for older children. The gladiatorial contests were too violent and were in any event usually restricted to adults. The theatre had become more salacious in recent years under Nero, and both Demetrios and Olympias decided no longer to take their children there, though she suspected Heiron might slip out to the theatre now and then since he was an adult and had money of his own. She only hoped he was staying away from taverns and, even worse, the brothels that seemed to be on every street corner in Rome.

Olympias pointed out the tavern down the next street, where they had first met. "Do you see our meeting point down the road? From there it is easy to find the bridge across the Tiber. Do you know your way in Rome to where you are staying? If you get lost, just ask for directions to the southern gate on the Appian Way. Someone there can give you instructions from that point."

"I wish to thank you for this opportunity," said Ampelios. "I am afraid, though, that I don't even know your name." "Nor shall you," said Olympias. "Even new members to our community use false names. We cannot afford the risk of anyone knowing the real identity of the other members. Only Linus is known to all, but he is certainly known to the government as well. I, for one, hope to remain in the darkness, yet live my life in accordance with the principles of Jehoshua so that I may receive eternal life. But I thank you for your company, and I remind you that what you saw today must never be revealed to anyone – not members of your community, not to new converts, not even your wife."

Olympias turned her back on her guest and began heading up the Via Triumphalis, the way in which she had just come. She found it better to leave her guests abruptly rather than go through lengthy farewells, or have to accept any money, even though occasionally when she would visit the tomb of Simon Petros she would find money left behind by pilgrims whom she, Linus, or the unknown third person, had brought there.

She bundled up her robe and hurried home. She wanted to make sure the three boys had all made it home safely.

Chapter Thirty Four

Jerusalem

amaliel of Yavne scrambled up the blocks of marble and rubble that were all that remained of the Temple of Jerusalem. He searched for one particular spot – the highest point possible amidst the ruins – and there he would sit, looking out at the city. If he half closed his eyes, he could imagine the Jerusalem of his youth. He would pretend he was on the top of the highest tower in the Temple complex, and below him were at least a thousand people stirring about the courtyards, buying and selling food and other goods because it was market day. In the distance he would see the red tile roofs of apartments and places of business, an endless series of buildings that stretched south and west and east from the Temple, to the very walls of the city. There would be municipal fountains here and there throughout Jerusalem that would provide fresh water. If he sat long enough, he could imagine the odor of burnt meat reaching his nostrils; the priests at the Temple altar below him were offering up a sacrifice of lamb to the Lord God.

Then he would open his eyes fully and see the reality below: a city destroyed by war, with most of its buildings so badly burned or damaged that they were unusable. The Temple itself was utterly demolished, and it was now nothing more than massive blocks of marble strewn about, one piled on top of another in a haphazard way. The Romans had promised that there would be no Third Temple; the Temple of Jerusalem, the physical focal point for the Jewish religion and for Jews everywhere, was never going to be allowed to be rebuilt.

With the terrible destruction that had occurred, there would normally be many thousands of homeless people to feed and clothe and shelter in some way. But the Romans had solved that problem with their usual efficiency. Beyond the hundreds of thousands of people who were killed during the war, an even greater number of Jews were marched off into slavery. It was said that at least 30,000

Jews had been bought by families in Rome, and perhaps as large a number were sent to work on farms in Italia and Gaul. Even before the war there were sizable Jewish populations in all the major cities in the Empire, but now things were different. There seemed to be more Jews living outside of Judea, Galilee, Samaria, and Idumea than existed in the country of Israel itself. What other nation existed largely outside of its own borders? People were beginning to call it the Diaspora – the nation in exile.

Gamaliel could not spend his time today day dreaming atop the ruins of the Temple. He must continue with his campaign to unite all the different religious sects that existed in Israel. It was the only way, in his view, Judaism could survive, particularly after the Romans destroyed the religious leadership of the country. His father was among the members of the Sanhedrin who were executed by Titus after Jerusalem fell. His father was fortunate; he was beheaded. Others members were tortured to death, some by having their skin peeled off while they were still alive, or in the case of one rabban, being wrapped tightly in the Torah and then set on fire.

Ten years after these events, the Roman procurator for Judea, Lucius Flavius Silva, authorized the reestablishment of the Sanhedrin, which had been outlawed. Perhaps the Romans were tired of running what was left of the country by themselves. Gamaliel was a natural choice to serve as Nasi. His father, Shimon ben Gamaliel, was Nasi when he was executed, and his grandfather, the revered Gamaliel the Elder, was president of the Sanhedrin as well. With so few religious or political leaders alive anymore, Gamaliel was not at all surprised that the Romans turned to him to help fill the vacuum.

How to attain his goal? There were the two principal religious groups, the Pharisees and the Sadducees, who had shared power in the past. Would they be willing to do so again? The Pharisees were as much a political power as a religious group; they believed in strict adherence to the Law of Moses, and to enforce their views, they tended to dominate the Sanhedrin. As a Pharisee himself, Gamaliel knew that he would be viewed suspiciously by the Sadducees, and that the Pharisees would expect him to restore their traditional dominance on the Sanhedrin. They would expect this arrangement because there was no hope that they as Pharisees would ever be allowed to share religious responsibilities with the Sadducees, who had been ordained by Moses himself to forever provide the candidates for the priesthood.

The problem, Gamaliel discovered, had solved itself – or rather, had been solved by the Romans. There was no Temple anymore, and so there was no central source of power in Israel for priestly influence. Without any priests needed to manage the Temple, the marketplace in its courtyards, and the sacrifices and prayers offered not just in daily services, but also on important holidays like Passover, the Sadducees had lost their fundamental purpose. Being a descendant from the tribe of Levi, as the only tribe that traditionally was allowed to provide priests, was no longer of value.

The other practical fact was that there were so few Pharisees and Sadducees of any stature left in the country. Those who had survived the massacres by the Romans had fled Jerusalem, so a reestablished Sanhedrin was hard to form, not because it was difficult to find the right political and religious balance, but because there simply were not enough qualified candidates. It made Gamaliel think that the honor of being asked to form a Sanhedrin, and likely being chosen as the new Nasi, was rather hollow.

Yet he had to do something. The country could not rely forever on the Roman judicial system to solve all legal and religious problems. Whether or not he liked Flavius Silva – and Gamaliel did think as a procurator Silva was much fairer than the men before him, who had to take some responsibility for pushing Israel into rebellion – Jews would never fully trust an occupying power to provide impartial and informed judgments, especially on religious matters. Even the Romans realized this.

Perhaps the Christians could help. This is where Gamaliel was heading – to the Christian community center, which had received some damage but was still functional. His request for an invitation to speak to one of their Assemblies had been accepted, though reluctantly. They were a secretive and distrustful group of Jews, he thought, but perhaps he could persuade them to help in the rebuilding of Israel.

He was met at the door by Lysander, one of the few members left who had known Jehoshua personally. He was also "keeper of the scrolls," so to speak – a man who had an acknowledged ability to remember precisely and record exactly what Jehoshua had spoken and taught. Gamaliel had never seen one of Lysander's scrolls – they were limited only to distribution to other Christian groups – but he understood they were the definitive texts used by the Christians, along with some other documents such as a biography of Jehoshua written by Marcus of Alexandria. Gamaliel would like to see these documents out of curiosity, but also out of a sense of scholarship. His father and his grandfather had been noted scholars on religious matters, and it seemed to Gamaliel that perhaps now was the time, fifty years after the death of Jehoshua, that the Jewish religious authorities ought to look more seriously at this man as a prophet.

Not that there was widespread agreement on whether Jehoshua was indeed a prophet, but clearly his reputation had not diminished over the years. Gamaliel's grandfather had been right after all: there was no sense in suppressing the Christians. If the Lord God intended for Jehoshua to serve as a prophet, time would prove him to be a prophet. Given the destruction of Jerusalem and the Temple, Gamaliel believed some new thinking by the Sadducees and the Pharisees was in order.

Lysander appeared to be seventy in age at the least. He might have shrunk over time, as happened to the elderly, but Gamaliel thought from his dealings with him that his mind was fully functioning. He had the wrinkled face of an old man, and his hair had thinned, but his eyes were bright and inquisitive. He gave one the sense he was listening not only to you but to others around him at the same time, as if he might pick up some interesting and worthwhile information that he could store in his very precise memory. It was slightly unnerving to Gamaliel to think that everything he said would be restated exactly by Lysander, even many years later. He first noted this phenomenon when Lysander told him, word for word, what his grandfather, Gamaliel the Elder, had said at a meeting with the Christians thirty years ago. But this was one of the reasons he liked talking to Lysander; he was one of the few men left in Jerusalem who remembered his grandfather.

"Welcome, Gamaliel," said Lysander to him. "We are just beginning our Assembly. You do not mind sitting through the services, do you?" Gamaliel said not only did he not mind, he considered it an honor. He understood that the Christians in the past were very open about outsiders attending their religious services, but that they had naturally become secretive given how they had been treated by the Jewish authorities and now by the Romans.

Upstairs, Gamaliel was surprised to see less than 25 people in the Assembly hall. This was a room that easily seated 100 and had done so in the past. Maybe he was hoping for something more favorable for the Christians in Jerusalem – that they had escaped the

Diaspora imposed on the Jews. But apparently that was not the case, because all he saw were elderly people. Where were the married couples? The young people eligible for marriage? The children? Gamaliel knew where they were – they had been led off by the Romans to distant cities, sold as if they were cattle. The people here in the Assembly Hall were the remnants of what was once a living, thriving Jerusalem. They were like all the elderly people he met in the city: they were the majority who lived here now, spending their money and time writing to various friends in other cities, asking if they knew if their children or grandchildren had "moved" there. The lucky ones received some confirmation, but most were left in perpetual doubt. They would die with that doubt and the heartache it entailed.

"The teaching today is about Jehoshua's sermon to the multitudes in Galilee. I know you have all heard this discussion before, but there is such wisdom in Jehoshua's words that we can never tire from his message." The speaker was another elderly person – a man named Ithiel – Gamaliel knew nothing else about him, but settled in to listen to his comments. Ithiel was speaking from a scroll, quite possibly one of the scrolls from Lysander covering Jehoshua's words.

"And Jehoshua began teaching to his disciples, but the crowds that followed him were so large that he climbed to the top of a hill so that all might hear him. Sitting down, with his disciples close around him, he said:

'Blessed are the poor in spirit, for theirs is the kingdom of heaven.'

'Blessed are those who mourn, for they shall be comforted.'

'Blessed are the meek, for they shall inherit the earth.'"

These words were fresh, thought Gamaliel, but they were familiar at the same time. Where had he heard or read them before? Not for nothing was his training steeped in the verses of scripture – in reading and discussing the books of Moses, the Proverbs, Lamentations, the words of the prophets of Israel, Ecclesiastes. He was a Gamaliel after all, and in his earliest memories he was sitting at the table with his grandfather, learning about the scriptures. He thought first of this statement by Jehoshua: "Blessed are those who mourn, for they shall be comforted." Jehoshua wasn't the first to say those words. Isaiah has said them much earlier: "The Lord has anointed me to comfort all who mourn," remembered Gamaliel. And earlier in that very chapter, Isaiah says he has come "to proclaim good news to the poor."

And that comment about the meek, continued Gamaliel in the discussion he was having with himself in his own mind, surely that is from Psalms: "But the meek will inherit the land and enjoy peace and prosperity."

Was it not said in Proverbs: "The hunger for righteousness exalts a nation"? Jehoshua had altered this somewhat: "Blessed are those who hunger and thirst for righteousness, for they shall be satisfied." Gamaliel also remembered from the book of Enoch: "Blessed are you, righteous and elect ones, for glorious is your portion."

And so it went. There wasn't any saying of Jehoshua's that was being discussed by Ithiel that did not have some antecedent in Jewish scripture. Surely, Jehoshua was well-learned in the scriptures, so much so that he could summon up references to diverse sayings and writings, yet make them sound new and meaningful. What could be objectionable about that? Why were so many people opposed to him, especially the powerful and important individuals who were considered leaders of the Jewish community?

Gamaliel remembered his grandfather speaking somewhat favorably about the Christians. His father, on the other hand, was not as kind. The Christians were troublemakers: Jehoshua challenged the law; he was a blasphemer who compared himself to the Lord God; he did not accept the covenant between the Jewish people and the Lord God. Was he even a Jew? This last point was the most important of all. If, as Gamaliel suspected, Jehoshua was one of a long line of Jewish prophets, yet his teaching was in part alien to traditional Jewish scriptures and thought, what did this interpretation say about the Jewish religion? What changes were Jews supposed to embrace?

Ithiel had finished speaking, and Lysander was now leading the group in a ritual involving eating bread and drinking wine. Gamaliel had heard about this ritual, and witnessing it in person, he found it quite inoffensive. In fact, it lacked some of the visceral attributes of a Jewish ceremony, especially the smell of meat being sacrificed on an altar. In that regard, Gamaliel thought what the Christians were doing was weak in comparison, and rather odd, at that. If Jehoshua required that his followers honor him by commemorating a dinner, but if the commemoration itself was meant to substitute for the traditional Jewish sacrifice to the Lord God, was Jehoshua suggesting that he himself was the sacrifice? It could certainly be interpreted that way, especially considering how Jehoshua had died. If he was indeed a Jewish prophet, who came to warn Israel to reform lest punishment be dealt the Jewish people by a vengeful God, then perhaps his death was merely the price paid by any whom the Lord God sends to prophesize.

But there seemed to be something deeper to it, as if Jehoshua did not believe in the law or the covenant. He wanted to replace these, with what was unclear, but it was certainly threatening to those like the Pharisees who sometimes worshipped the law more than they did the Lord God, or to the Sadducees, who cherished their privileges as priests more than they cherished the law. Yet these Christians were the people whom Gamaliel had come to reconcile with the Pharisees and the Sadducees, and for that matter, the Romans.

Lysander had brought the service to a close and now was introducing Gamaliel, who was quickly reviewing in his mind what he intended to say. He thought he would emphasize their common heritage as Jews, and would perhaps speak to the lessons from Ithiel, who discussed teachings from Jehoshua that were thoroughly imbued with sacred Jewish scripture. But as with his meetings with the Pharisees and the Sadducees, he opened with a prayer.

Gamaliel then said, "Thank you, Lysander, for this welcome to your community. Lysander has spoken of my mission today – of an opportunity that has been given to all of us as Jews, and as citizens of Jerusalem, to regain control over our community and our city. It is an opportunity to restore the independence we had before the war with the Romans. It is an opportunity to reduce the Roman presence in Jerusalem and Judea, and the first step is to reestablish a judicial body – the Sanhedrin – which will be composed entirely of Jews who will decide legal and religious issues for our community."

"As to why we should do this, I believe the need is best expressed through our traditional prayer of Shema, which all of us recite as we lie down to sleep in the evening and as we awake in the morning:"

Hear, O Israel, the Lord is our God, the Lord is One!
Blessed be the name of His glorious kingdom, forever and forever.

You shall love the Lord your God with all your heart, with all your soul, and with all your might.
And these words I command you today shall be in your heart,

And you shall teach them diligently to your children,
And you shall speak of them when you sit at home, when you walk
along the way, and when you lie down and when you rise up.

That I will give rain to your land, the early and the late rains,
that you may gather in your grain, your wine and your oil.
And I will give grass in your fields for your cattle and you will eat and
you will be satisfied.

Beware, lest your heart be deceived
and you turn and serve other gods and worship them.
The anger of the Lord will blaze against you, and He will close the
heavens and there will not be rain, and the earth will not give you its
fullness,
and you will perish quickly from the good land that the Lord gives you.

I am the Lord, your God
who led you from the land of Egypt to be a God to you.
I am the Lord, your God.

Gamaliel chose a slow cadence in which he sang this prayer, in the hope it might remind his listeners of that which they all had in common. His instincts were correct; slowly the people listening to him began quietly joining in his prayer. He was deeply moved to hear the members of this Christian community sing this prayer with him, and for many it did indeed bring back moments from their childhood with their parents, or memories of prayers sung at their synagogue.

"Our heart has been deceived," said Gamaliel after a few moments of silence following the prayer. "We have deceived ourselves. We thought we could defeat an earthly power through military means – through death. Only the Lord God can inflict death. We divided ourselves into religious factions: Pharisees, Sadducees, Christians, Essenes, and others. We turned Judaism into many parts and then decided that our part was superior to all others. The Lord God did not address his promises just to the Pharisees, or to the Sadducees, or to the Christians. He addressed his promises to all of Israel. It is we who have pretended that there are multiple Israels."

"And what is the consequence of erecting so many false gods?

For those who were the most desperate to defeat and destroy the Romans, for the Zealots and the assassins, the Scarii, the Lord God has led them to utter ruin. His judgment has been harsh and must be a lesson to us all. But is the price we paid for our idolatry any less? How often do I hear someone say that they have suffered a living death, condemned to live alone while their spouse, children, sisters, and brothers toil in a strange land under the yoke of a foreign master?"

"The Lord God has indeed closed the heavens against us. Can we not learn from this lesson? Is it not time to set aside our differences and live again as one people? I plead with you to send me one man, or two, or three, to join in establishing a new legal court for Jews in Judea. The time is right for us all."

"Look about you in Jerusalem. The desolation is everywhere. Half of our population has been sent into exile, many to the new Babylon, to Rome. Their suffering is no less than that of our ancestors who lived in thrall to the pharaohs of Egypt. Yet, we can give them hope! In Egypt our ancient forefathers had only the expectation of reaching a land of milk and honey. We, however, now inhabit that land."

"But for the hope of so many Jews who live in foreign lands, Israel must be made whole, and Jerusalem must be restored. We cannot rebuild the Temple – at least as yet we cannot. But we can make Israel one nation, no matter how many Roman procurators and prefects and sub-prefects and legionnaires are sent here by Caesar, and no matter which Caesar occupies the imperial throne."

"Help us to reach unity. Help me to be a unifier. Such is my prayer to you. If Israel is allowed to remain in ruination, there shall be no hope for the families viciously taken from us. If you choose not to help me, at the very least, choose to help them!"

Gamaliel finished speaking and thought he had done as well as he could. He did not expect much of a response, and he assumed the community of Christians would discuss this idea and respond in a few days. He did not anticipate an immediate reaction and was surprised when people raised objections.

"Why should we participate in a Sanhedrin that will pass judgment on religious matters, when we believe that no authority but our own leaders can judge such things? We would only be lending credibility to those who should have nothing to say in respect of our beliefs and practices." These comments came from Ithiel, the man who delivered the lesson for the service.

"And what if there are disputes with other groups or people?" asked Gamaliel in response. "There must be some group who can decide on the proper interpretation of scripture. That same group will have the resources to do scholarly work on ancient texts and to help with the distribution of copies of scripture. Surely this will help all of us?"

"We do not need your help," was the response he heard, expressed one way or the other, by several people. He was surprised at the desire of these people to remain isolated from their fellow Jews. He decided to address the matter directly. "Why are you so intent on continuing the differences of the past? It must be obvious that no one has benefited from such separations."

A woman stood up. She appeared to be in her mid-fifties. She was small in height and had kept her head covered with a scarf. Gamaliel could see that she wore a fine necklace of golden beads, alternating with colored stones, and that she must at one time have been a woman of substance. How did she hide such a valuable item from the Romans during the siege and sack of Jerusalem? They were most thorough in sniffing out precious jewelry, even if it meant using torture.

"You say no one has benefited from keeping all Jews separate. I was with Kediah, wife of our dear, lamented Yakov, when he was thrown off the tower of the Temple and then clubbed to death on orders of the High Priest. Where were the members of the Sanhedrin when that atrocity happened? You say they are going to look out for our interests, but they chose to look the other way when Ananus decided to murder Christians. Where was your father when that happened? I had to restrain Kediah when her husband was killed, or she would have willingly run out to the courtyard and joined her husband in death."

"That execution was merely the culmination of many years of repression visited upon our community, dating back ultimately to the execution of Jehoshua himself," she continued. "I am too young to have experienced the earlier days of arrests and tortures and executions that occurred not just in Judea, but in Galilee and Samaria. But I was not too young to absorb the lessons our elders took from these experiences: always stay hidden and do not trust the Jewish authorities. The only reason we are listening to you today is out of respect for your grandfather, who was a friend to us and at least understood us. We respect also his grandfather, the blessed Hillel, who inspired Jehoshua to reframe the law of Moses, to simplify it, to modernize it, and to make it meaningful in our lives, rather than the instrument of control and punishment that it has become today under the very same authorities you ask us to support in a new Sanhedrin."

"It is not for me alone to speak for everyone here. I can only speak for myself, in saying that no Christian can possibly serve on the Sanhedrin and serve Jehoshua the Christos at the same time." Many others in the group spoke or even shouted out affirmations for the sentiments this woman expressed. "Salome speaks for us all!" one person shouted out. Gamaliel was now despairing of making any progress with the Christians, but he thought he at least must not let her accusations against the Jewish leadership go unanswered.

He raised up his hands for silence. "It is true that many Jews held their tongues during the atrocities perpetrated by Ananus. Nor did he single out the followers of Jehoshua when he was searching for victims. As to my father, he protested these actions by Ananus, and he protested to the Romans as well when a new procurator finally arrived in Jerusalem. The result was that Ananus was quickly deposed, and ultimately he was killed by the Zealots when he defended the Temple during the siege."

"I cannot explain the behavior against you by men such as Caiaphas and Ananus," continued Gamaliel. "Nor is it just the Levites, and the priesthood which they control, who have organized repression against your community. The Sanhedrin in the past has not had a good record in this regard. But I ask you to think of it this way: a Sanhedrin which is composed in part of Christians will not find it easy to continue repression against Christians. Instead, it will be forced to consider Christians as equal members of the Jewish community. A Christian will receive the respect due any other Jew."

The same woman who spoke up about Kediah rose to her feet again. "Why did you come here expecting to find Jews? Who told you we are Jews? For those of us who are old enough to have been there, the day Yakov the Just was thrown off the Temple roof was the day we ceased being Jews."

Gamaliel was so stunned to hear this sentiment that he didn't know what to say. He had grown up believing that someone who was born Jewish would always remain a Jew; being a Jew was not like a garment that could be thrown off when it became old or uncomfortable. He had never heard anyone renouncing their identity. At a later and quieter moment, he would be able to think carefully about what he was hearing. Was the force of the persecution of Christians by Caiaphas, Ananus, and even Saul so fierce and destructive that its victims found themselves no choice but to renounce their religious identity? Or was there something in Jehoshua's teaching that led Jews to such an extreme measure?

For the moment Gamaliel was being "rescued" from this awkward situation by Lysander, who rose and addressed the community, saying that his guest would be leaving soon and perhaps in the next Assembly the community of Christians would decide what to do about this offer to join a new Sanhedrin. Lysander called for a final prayer, after which the small group disbursed, while he escorted Gamaliel down the stairs and said his farewells at the door.

Gamaliel had little illusion that he would be called back. He walked absent-mindedly through the streets of Jerusalem, looking up every so often by habit for the scintillating gilt tower of the Temple, only to remind himself that this landmark no longer existed. He could see how Jerusalem was coming to terms with the permanent destruction wreaked by the Romans. Only a handful of the water fountains he passed worked. The smell of sewage wafted along the streets. The Romans, who prided themselves on their municipal improvements, declined to repair much of the basic damage done to the city. More businesses and stores were abandoned than were in use, and entire apartment buildings had turned into shells for lack of tenants.

Gamaliel had intended to return home, but without thinking he headed back to the ruins of the Temple. He found himself scaling the large blocks that once constituted the inner sanctuary. He sat down at the very place from which he began his journey today. The day had turned cloudy, the sky threatening to rain. From this vantage he could not see the destruction that characterized Jerusalem now. He could continue the pretense that all was normal, as it used to be, before Vespasianus, Titus, Simon bar Giora, Ananus, and the others fought over the city and destroyed it. He could avoid the sense of despair that hung heavily over the city wherever he walked.

His wife complained about his frequent trips to this mountain of stone blocks, and she was right to do so. He was spending far too much time up here, throwing himself into the past, ignoring the reality that awaited him below, when he reluctantly decided to climb down from his perch. But high atop the Temple ruins, he could escape the cruel reality that he was one of the few religious leaders left in Jerusalem. The senior members of what was once the Sanhedrin had all been executed. He had escaped execution only because the Romans had allowed him and his family to flee to Yavne while Jerusalem was under siege. It was just as well none of his friends was left in Jerusalem; they would all consider him a traitor, like Josephus. Josephus, in fact, had fled to Rome, where he had ingratiated himself with Vespasianus. He had even taken on the surname of Flavius, to show his affinity with his new patron.

Maybe he should take his family to Rome as well, Gamaliel wondered. He was tired of scrounging for safe drinking water, and his wife exhausted herself hoping to find some place that would sell fresh meat or vegetables. Worst of all to a man of Gamaliel's stature, with a religious pedigree unequaled in the entire city, it was dispiriting to consider that there was no religious life left in Jerusalem. The few synagogues that functioned would rarely wish to waste money on sacrificing meat that was needed for survival. None of them had the money to support students who would study the Torah and carry on the rabbinical traditions.

Judaism had died when the Temple fell. Such was the case in Jerusalem as well throughout Judea, Idumea, Samaria, and Galilee, based on the extent of the destruction that had occurred in the countryside. It was left to the hundreds of thousands of Jews who lived dispersed throughout the Empire to keep the sacred traditions alive. But what could be expected from them? Half of them were slaves. Most of the rest had been resident for centuries in cities like Alexandria, Antioch, Corinth, and Rome, and had probably lost their identity as Jews. The only Jews he had met who had any sense of purpose or hope for the future were the Christians, and not only were they eagerly awaiting the End of Time when Jehoshua would return, they didn't consider themselves Jews anymore.

Judaism was a dying religion, as far as Gamaliel could tell. He knew it was wrong to despair, but when the Lord God had withdrawn his favor because the Israelites had broken their covenant with him, what hope could there be for Jews anywhere? That is why he spent so much time in this place high atop the rubble of Herod the Great's Temple. It was the one place where he could imagine that there was a future for Israel in a world dominated by Roman gods and Roman legions. He could imagine such a future – but in his despair he thought it was only a pretense, a false god. The One God, the Almighty God, the Invisible God, the one Jews called Adonai because his real name was too sacred to be written or spoken – in Gamaliel of Yavne's opinion, that God had abandoned the Jews. Perhaps he would bestow his favor on others, but as Gamaliel stepped down from his peak and descended back into the tragedy that constituted what was left of Jerusalem, he felt in his soul that the Lord God no longer walked beside him.

Chapter Thirty Five

You are going to have to talk to him, Mother," said Heiron. "Leontios is friends with the wrong people. They think it's a game to target and harass Christians. He needs to know now." Olympias knew this day was coming, but she had also delayed talking to Leontios as long as she could. He was fourteen, old enough to know but perhaps not old enough to understand. His age was one reason she hesitated. The other was a family concern – perhaps it was best if Leontios had this discussion with his father. "Could it wait until your Father returns from Asia?" asked Olympias. Heiron thought it could not.

She had to trust Heiron. He was seventeen and acting *in loco parentis*, as the Romans would say, in his father's absence. He was already managing the wine-import business when his father was on trips overseas, making sure shipments were met at the port of Ostia when they arrived and ensuring they were brought safely to the warehouse. Heiron was not old enough yet to meet with prospective clients, but he at least was presentable and mature enough to deliver wine to existing clients in Rome, some of whom were powerful Senators with respectable family lineages. His position didn't mean he needed to meet these powerful people – often he was dealing with slaves when making deliveries – but it certainly meant that Heiron had the reputation of the family in his hands at times like this.

Leontios and his younger brother Sophos were already asleep. It had turned dark over an hour ago, and they had seen almost all of the 24 chariot races staged that day at Nero's Circus. Heiron had a simple meal prepared for them when they got home, and by the time Olympias had returned from her visit to the cemetery with Ampelios, the two boys were already tired.

Olympias decided she would talk to Leontios in the middle of the night if he woke up. Sometimes he did, but sometimes boys at that age would sleep right through the night if they had had an active day. Olympias was a two-shift sleeper, like many other adults in Rome, and she would be up in the deepest hours of the night for a short while, and then she would sleep again until dawn. She liked those dark hours of silence, when she could lie next to Demetrios and perhaps enjoy his company. She knew for a certainty that once he returned, she would be enjoying his company night after night for quite some time – Demetrios referred to his ardor as "catch-up time" for all the intimacy he had missed while being away.

Her initial sleep this night was troubled, and she eventually woke up at her usual time, but as a result of a nightmare. She had dreamt Demetrios had been captured by pirates and his captors had demanded an enormous ransom for his release. They would not, however, accept cash but instead required payment in wine. She and Heiron counted up all the amphorae of wine they had in the warehouse, but they kept getting the count wrong, and would have to start over again and again, never coming to a number that would be large enough to release her husband. It was like running in place and getting nowhere, only the stakes were enormous, and she woke up in a sweat, frightened that Demetrios would never return.

She had suffered from this dream before, and it seemed to occur whenever she showed guests to the tomb of Simon Petros. She lay in bed awake, trying to calm her beating heart, telling herself it was only a dream. The only connection she could make between this night vision and Simon Petros was the manner in which Demetrios and Linus managed to retrieve his body.

She sat up and walked around the bedroom a bit, before deciding she was not going to go back to sleep immediately. She walked out to the small garden next to her apartment building and sat on a bench in the cool night air. One bird was beginning to sing – dawn was probably an hour or so away. Nothing calmed her spirits as much as these hours when the birds during spring would talk to each other just before dawn. The chirping would start with one bird, and then another would awaken, and in her mind it was the best music imaginable. Why they chattered so she did not know, other than perhaps to teach their young how to communicate. She remembered the birds in Corinth doing the same thing, but then summers in Greece became so hot that the birds seemed to flee or stay in hiding the rest of the season. In Rome, however, the birds were different; they would sing all year long. It was one of the compensations for no longer living in Greece and seeing the broad expanse of sea on a daily basis, which she knew now she took for granted while growing up.

She never spent much time regretting leaving her home in Greece. Her parents were both dead, her brother Alcaeus had retired to the countryside to take up farming, and her sister Theodosia had made a bad marriage to a drunk and a fool. She stayed with him because she had five children and because there was no other family left in Corinth to take her in should she decide to risk leaving him. Theodosia would write to her from time to time, pouring out her woes, and all Olympias could tell her was that if necessary, Demetrios would stop in Corinth on one of his business trips and arrange for passage for her and the children to Rome. Her husband wouldn't be able to reach her from so far away, and she could start a new life, but Theodosia never was able to agree to such a plan. Perhaps her situation was not truly dire, though Olympias thought much had to do with the children. They were getting too old now to disrupt their lives in such a way.

The other small problem with this plan was that Theodosia had never turned to Christianity as her parents had hoped. Olympias was the only one of the three children who could be described as actively involved in this new religious cult, as the Romans called it. Olympias had risen to a position of leadership in the Roman community of Christians because she could read and write, and was able to communicate regularly with the other communities in Greece and elsewhere. She could never write a letter like Paulus, filled with interpretations of both Jewish scripture and Jehoshua's teachings, but then Paulus was unique. He was Jewish with an educational background in Jewish scripture and a knowledge of Greek culture, and he had traveled everywhere. It was now so many years since they had heard from him that Olympias assumed he was dead, and Linus once confided to her the same thought. Fortunately, they had saved all his scrolls and letters he left behind when he was released from house confinement in Rome, so they had a good record of his thinking. With Simon Petros gone, Linus had begun using some of these scrolls for his own sermons during their services, which still had to be conducted in secret. At least the community did not have to remain in the caves to the south of the city that had been their safe haven during the time of Nero's purges. Olympias and Demetrios did not enjoy having to travel such a distance.

If anything, their Assemblies were now taking place frequently on Vatican Hill at a house Linus had found that could accommodate their growing community. It was near to where Olympias and her family lived, and while that location was highly convenient, Olympias was slightly nervous about the change. The Christians in Rome had always conducted their activities in the city itself or the ghettos just south of the city walls. She didn't want her peaceful enclave on the other side of the Tiber becoming known as a refuge for Christians. During the next persecution – and one never knew in Rome which emperor would be friendly or not to Christians – she preferred to live anonymously and quietly away from the Christian community. It had saved her life during the last repression.

This precaution was one difference between Simon Petros and Linus. Simon Petros was always fearful of Roman persecution, and he constantly urged caution among his community, even to the point of requiring Christians to use false names when they met. Linus was much less cautious, which seemed to come from having a more cheerful personality than Simon Petros. Still, Linus was no fool. On important matters he was extremely secretive, and if bad times returned, Olympias was confident he would be every bit as effective as Simon Petros in preserving the community as much as possible. He was, she thought, a very worthy successor to Simon Petros in that respect.

The other part of Linus' character that she admired was his ability to get along with other Christian leaders. Perhaps this ability was merely the consequence of the first generation of Christian leaders dying out; the old philosophical arguments between men like Paulus and Simon Petros did not seem as important to Linus and other leaders of today. She thought, though, that the secret of Linus' success was the respect, if not reverence, he showed to this first generation. He was impartially deferential to all who came to visit Rome, and he did much to preserve the memories of the men and women and children, for that matter, who perished under Nero's persecutions.

Olympias remembered all too well the night Linus showed up at their door with a plan to retrieve the bodies of as many of the Christians as they could who had died at Nero's Circus. The first day of the games had ended, and Linus in particular wanted to steal the body of Simon Petros and give it a proper burial. Such an action was completely against the law, but somehow Linus had befriended the slave whose job it was to cart bodies out of the arena each night when the games ended, and to throw them into a pit filled with animal carcasses. What Linus needed, which Demetrios had, was a cart that could be disguised to hide bodies.

In the end, and considering how little time Demetrios had to prepare, the plan went quite well. Demetrios filled a cart with amphorae of wine, covered them with a tarpaulin, and left room in the center for a few bodies. He, Linus, and a third person willing to take such a risk, positioned their cart along one of the side roads leading down from the Via Triumphalis. It was a dry night with only a crescent moon, and the darkness helped their plan considerably. They waited in silence and darkness until they heard the cart driven by the slave turn the corner off the Via Triumphalis. Quietly, they maneuvered their wine cart into the center of the narrow lane, and since it was too dark to see into the distance, the slave's cart rammed into this unexpected obstacle and nearly overturned. As it was, several mangled or dismembered bodies fell out.

The slave realized he was in deep trouble, but Linus and Demetrios were entirely apologetic and solicitous, promising to help put things right as quickly as possible. The accident was, as far as the slave was concerned, an unexpected bit of good fortune. What strangers would possibly want to touch the bodies of criminals executed in the arena? But there was more good luck in store. Demetrios opened up one of his urns of wine. It was an especially excellent vintage – a rich red wine with exceptional fruitiness, such as the slave had probably never enjoyed. It might not be of the quality that the Emperor would serve, but no Senator would turn it down. With a bit of bread, two mugs, and some water, Demetrios escorted the slave over to a tomb that they sat upon, enjoying their repast, while Linus and his friend went to work.

With grunting and various visible signs of labor, Linus and his colleague went about the grisly business of moving bodies off and on the slave cart until they came across Simon Petros, whom Linus could identify in the dim light by his wounds and feeling the beard on his face. Some of the bodies were ram-rod stiff, and that made it very difficult to disentangle one from another, so Linus decided to set the body of Simon Petros into the wine cart and leave all the others back with the slave. It was, Linus later said, a very painful decision for him to make, since he recognized other friends in that cart and desperately longed to give them all a proper burial. But they were already taking too many risks, and he remembered the saying of Jehoshua regarding saving one lost sheep even if it meant losing the others. They had come to save Simon Petros, and he wanted to ensure they accomplished that goal.

The slave was already finishing his third cup of wine and feeling very good about the circumstances in which he found himself. The wine cart with its safely hidden cargo had been moved out of the way, and the slave cart and mule were properly restored for him to be on his way. Demetrios led his new friend back to his cart, allowing him one final swig from this nectar of the gods that he had been enjoying. Everyone said quiet but gracious good-byes, as Demetrios prodded the mule to get going down the hill. Where exactly the slave cart and the other bodies wound up was not clear, but Demetrios expected it was at a slaughter house nearby where the unfortunate victims would be dumped with the bodies of horses, cattle, chickens, and other animals carried off the streets of Rome each morning.

In any event, as Linus told them, their work was still half done. He had scouted out another place in the cemetery where common burials took place, usually for local Jews, since Romans preferred to cremate their bodies. They had but a few hours before dawn when they could dig a decent grave that would be indistinguishable from all the others, except for a marker that Linus left a foot beneath the top soil. He and Demetrios also memorized the location by several trees nearby, and about six months later, they came and recovered the body and brought it to a proper sarcophagus that became the final resting place of Simon Petros.

She had never told this story to anyone. Only she and Demetrios needed to know, and it was unimportant for the boys to find out, because they were not being asked to become Christians. She heard quiet voices inside the apartment and decided to see who was awake. It was Leontios and Sophos, discussing the previous day's excitement, which was apparently too great to allow them to sleep.

"Leontios, as long as you are awake, I want to talk to you. Perhaps we can go for a walk when the first light appears." Leontios grunted his consent. He didn't spend too much time thinking about the suggestion. This talk was probably going to be just another one of those mother-to-son discussions about his "future" and what he intended to do with his life. He went on conversing with Sophos, comparing the strategy of the Green team in several of the races to the losing tactics of the Red and White teams. Sophos had been a supporter of the Blue team, because he hadn't yet seen many races, and because the Blues were the favorite of most youth whom he knew. Some of their charioteers had been racing for over three years, which was well beyond the date when a typical charioteer would be either dead or retired with a terrible injury. Leontios was doing his best to change his brother's allegiance, based on the argument that superior strategy and tactics in the end would win out.

Olympias returned to her seat in the garden, mulling over what she would say to Leontios. He was such a difficult person to talk with. He was the tallest and thinnest of her three boys, already taller than his older brother. He took after his father, having in-herited his handsome looks and reserved demeanor. Leontios was relatively unemotional as well, and the last time she remembered him crying was when he was a baby. If he hurt himself, he would pick himself up and stoically carry on through the pain. She was never quite sure what he was thinking, and his tutor, while giving him high marks for learning to read and write, thought he had "too big an imagination," whatever that meant. Because Leontios confided in no one in the family, Olympias couldn't imagine what his imagination was creating.

When the sky was just beginning to lighten, Olympias beckoned Leontios to join her, and he dutifully followed. He talked on and off about the races of the day before, as they followed a path up the hill, behind the stables where Nero had kept his prized race horses. Olympias had her own destination in mind – a rocky out-crop that afforded a splendid view over the Tiber and into the city. She wasn't sure Leontios had ever been there. When they reached the spot, the sky to the east was beginning to turn dark purple and red. The city below them across the Tiber was still in darkness, but speckled with yellow lights from municipal torches illuminating the main streets. They watched in silence as the ribbon of black which separated Rome from their suburb turned dusky brown. The Tiber then turned purple and red, reflecting the colors of the sky.

What had started as an arc of color directly to their east fanned out to encompass half of the sky before them. Stars dwindled into oblivion, and the sky gradually turned pink, accented by rows of purple and red clouds that seemed to be stationary sentinels in a ce-lestial brigade. "Look Mother," said Leontios excitedly, "the Temple of Jupiter Optimus Maximus!" A hem of scarlet first outlined the roof of Rome's largest temple, but soon the entire roof was aflame, and then other buildings came into focus: the Temple of Saturn, the small dome of the Vestal Virgin's temple, the Forum of Julius Caesar, and then much further to their left, the Pantheon.

The first hint of yellow was now surfacing due east of the city, and in a manner of minutes would suffuse the eastern half of the sky and chase the pink and purple shades away. The buildings of the city were taking on a golden tone, as was the Tiber, whose slow current was now visible as yellow wavelets along the surface. Olympias well knew from visits to this locale that this was the time when the sky was most enlivened by color, and when the city was at its most sublime. For a few exceptional minutes, every major building was turned into gold, while parts of the sky were turning into their daytime shade of blue. It was a most satisfying, ever-changing, and never-tiring spectacle, and Olympias was glad her son, who rarely showed much emotion, was visibly awed by the spectacle.

Leontios continued to point out various landmarks as they emerged from their nighttime shrouds. His knowledge of the city, thought Olympias, was quite exceptional, and she asked him where he had obtained such a thorough familiarity with so many buildings. "My friends and I walk about the city all the time," he said, giving Olympias the opening she was hoping for. "I don't think I have met these friends. Who are they?"

"Oh, there's Erastos, and Nicostratus, and Epaphras, and a few others. I don't remember how exactly I met them; I think Epaphras introduced the others to me. In the Greek part of the city, these are the boys you need to know."

"Why is that?" wondered Olympias. "They just are," said Leontios. "They know things, more than some adults do. They know how to get around and how to get into places."

Olympias was very anxious to start a conversation about the places these boys could get into, but she thought it would set Leontios on edge and perhaps ruin the rest of the conversation.

"What happened to your friend Gershom, from around here? You've known him for a very long time." Leontios paused for a minute before answering, as if he was calculating out how many years he really had known his boyhood friend. "Gershom has turned out to be too bossy. He wants to control everybody around him, and he demands that people address him formally. Besides, all his friends are Jews who live on Vatican Hill. With Epaphras and his friends I feel I am a part of the Greek community in Rome."

"I hear Epaphras and his friends don't like Christians very much." Leontios did not respond to this question with alarm. "Nobody likes the Christians very much, Mother. Who could possibly worship an executed criminal?"

"We do. We're Christians." Olympias thought it best just to deliver the announcement without any emphasis.

"Who is a Christian?" asked Leontios. "What do you mean?" He was showing honest puzzlement, as if the thought of actually knowing a Christian was completely alien to him. "Our family is Christian, Leontios," said Olympias, and this time the magnitude of the fact was beginning to occur to him. His eyes opened wide and he looked his mother straight in the eye. "We can't be Christian! Christians do terrible things!" Leontios said with absolute alarm.

"People say terrible things about us, Leontios, but you know they are not true. We do not eat babies, we do not sacrifice humans on an altar, we do not burn people alive in their homes."

"Why are you telling me this, Mother. How can I possibly be a Christian! I know hardly anything about the Christos, other than the awful things his followers do."

"You are not a Christian, Leontios. Only Father and I are Christians. We are not expecting you to become one unless you wish to do so. It is, frankly, too dangerous now to be a Christian, and we cannot force that danger on our children. But we were both Christians before we met each other. We continue to support the community here."

Leontios thought very carefully about this revelation. He was quite relieved to understand he was not a Christian and could deny it truthfully if anyone asked him. Still, it was enough of a shock to accept the fact that his own parents followed this crucified Jew. He thought back to their weekly absences, which he had been told were to attend some temple service. Those must be the times they go to worship the Christos. His mind was now completely confused. His parents were his parents; he had always accepted their "rightness" and their honesty. It was just who they were. They didn't lie to him – except this deceit was a massive lie that he now had to digest and possibly forgive. Maybe they did it to protect him; that was a possibility, especially when he was younger and it was a time when Christians were being executed in Rome. That fact brought to mind another question.

"Did you know any of those Christians who were executed?" He was very curious, because it would explain those long periods of secret crying that his mother used to have. "I knew many of them,

Leontios. They were very close friends to me. I watched every day of those "games," until every last one of them had been tortured to death. It was the most dreadfully horrible thing I have ever witnessed. It was also why your Father and I decided to keep this secret from you – to protect you."

Now, Leontios felt he was getting some honest answers. Things began to make sense, and the "rightness" that he had felt was the essence of his parent's love for him was fully restored. They had kept things hidden from him, and probably from Heiron and of course Sophos, who must still be too young to understand such things, just so that the three of them could be protected. It wasn't right that the three of them should be punished for the crimes of their parents, but he couldn't think of them as being crimes if his Mother was right – if the stories about the Christians were all rumors. He was fourteen now – almost an adult – and he could take a little pride that his Mother was confiding this secret to him. That must be the reason she brought him up here – and he had thought they were going to have another dull talk about his future. Except, this talk really was about his future, only in much more important ways than he had imagined.

"The reason I am telling this to you, Leontios," said Olympias, "is that it hurts us when you and your friends attack and insult Christians. We know the truth about these people, who are all friends of ours, and we can tell you the truth if you wish to know it. But even if you don't, you must accept our judgment that this behavior is very harmful and must stop."

A slight shiver of anger crossed Leontios' brow. Heiron must have betrayed him. Of course, who else would know what his friends did! How much his mother knew was another question, but he had to assume she knew the worst. "We were just having fun, Mother," was the best he could say. "It didn't mean anything."

"But it did mean something, Leontios," answered Olympias. "It continues the lies and the persecution. We have protected you all these years by keeping you separate from the Christian community, and now you must protect us."

His mother's request had a surprisingly salutary effect on Leontios' thinking. It made him feel like a responsible member of the family, and no longer just a child, since he was being asked by his mother to do something for her and her friends – something important. "I will get my friends to stop, Mother. Somehow, I'm not sure how, but I won't participate if that makes you feel better."

Olympias put her arm around the shoulder of her son and said nothing in response. The morning chill was beginning to lift. The red globe of the sun was now nearly completely above the eastern horizon, and the sky was almost entirely restored to blue. They could spot out details in the city and see ships moving along the Tiber. The ferry between Rome and the Vatican Hill had begun to operate.

"What does it mean to be a Christian, Mother?" Leontios asked this question with a simple directness. Olympias had no difficulty responding. "Belief in the Christos provides us eternal life after death. Not the sort of life after death that the Romans or we Greeks talk about, but a true, meaningful, and blessed life. Jehoshua was a very wise man who spoke many truths that are pertinent to all men, not just to Jews, Greeks or Romans. He taught us not only about eternal life, but about how to live the most human life possible. And because he conquered death itself, as an example for all of us, he will return with God at the End of Time to judge us all. If we have lived a decent and moral life according to his principles, we will be accorded a place in heaven with Jehoshua and his Father. Those are the things we believe."

Olympias knew that these beliefs would be quite too much for Leontios to accept at this time, but it was the best explanation she could provide. "He must be very powerful to have conquered death, I suppose," said Leontios. "But if he was so powerful, why could he not have conquered the Romans when he was alive?"

"He decided not to," was the best Olympias could produce in the face of such an important question. "He could have defeated the Romans, but he wanted to set an example for all of us. He always said that we must accept the violence of others if we are ever to conquer violence. I know that sounds difficult to understand, but there is much wisdom in it. When he returns, which might well be in my lifetime or yours, he will demonstrate his power for all to see."

"Do you mean he will destroy the Romans, even the Emperor?"

"Yes, if the Romans have been evil, and if the Emperor has been evil, he will destroy them," responded Olympias.

They sat silently together, each with private thoughts about their conversation. Olympias looked at the magnificence of Rome and contemplated the End of Time. Perhaps it would happen soon, as Linus and others said, or perhaps it would take many lifetimes. By then, Rome would be changed. The evil and corruption of the soul that gripped this city, and the entire Empire, would be purged.

Christians would abound, and temples would be converted into Assembly halls. The gods of this world would be overthrown, and the One True God would be the only subject of worship. Morality would govern personal behavior, and laws would not be needed to control and punish people. The threat of eternal punishment would be sufficient. Instead of the hatred and fear which infested the world, love would reign. Was not Jehoshua's greatest commandment that we love others as we would wish to be loved? And as love spread throughout the Empire, peace would follow in its wake.

She could imagine all this clearly, and thought she ought to redouble her efforts to bring her friends into the beauty and wisdom of The Way, as Paulus used to call it. Only then could they be saved, and only then could true moral change come to the entire Empire.

Leontios looked at the same scenery. He imagined a day when Jehoshua the Christos would return to earth and conquer the Emperor and every legion under his command. He was by no means sure he believed what his Mother was telling him about Jehoshua, but if she was right, it would behoove him to be on the winning side of this coming battle. Perhaps he should look more carefully into this Christianity that his parents followed and supported.

And if she was right, surely the Christos would need warriors on his side to ensure victory in this battle. He could see himself in that role. He would be one of those preparing the way for the arrival of the Almighty Lord! Leontios would sweep away his enemies for him!

It was a delicious thought for a boy steeped in the martial dreams of conquest that sometimes stir the souls of young men. And Leontios knew just where to start in such a campaign. He would start with that weasel, Gershom! He thinks he knows everything, and he thinks he is superior to everyone! He deserves what is coming to him. It would be his own fault, and besides, though Leontios knew very little about this Jehoshua whom he intended to follow in battle, he did know one thing – the Jews were responsible for his death. Everyone said so. Gershom deserved what was coming to him!

Perhaps his friends like Nicostratus, Epaphras, and Erastos would join him in his campaign. He was sure they could be talked into redirecting their games of harassment toward the Jews and away from the Christians. They would have to be a bit more careful – there were many more Jews in Rome than there were Christians.

But there were far more Greeks in Rome than there were Jews. If it ever came down to a real battle, the Greeks would win. Gershom deserved whatever punishment was coming to him. So did all the other Jews who were like Gershom. The Jews who felt superior to everyone else. The Jews who killed Jehoshua. They all needed to be wiped out.

Leontios reached over to his mother's hand and gave it a gentle, loving squeeze. He smiled at her with that slightly wistful grin he sometimes had, and she smiled back. And he thought to himself - how proud she would be when she saw what he could accomplish as a Christian!

APPENDIX A

Historical Fact vs. Fiction

ehoshua: Conflagration takes place during the period 57 CE to 79 CE, which includes the seminal event of the first century for both Jews and Christians, the siege and fall of Jerusalem to the Romans. This tragic event should properly be viewed as the return of Rome to control over Jerusalem and all the Jewish provinces; the Romans first took command of the area in 63 BCE when Pompey the Great invaded and added these provinces to the Empire. There are several story lines in this book leading up to and then extending beyond the collapse of Jerusalem, which happened from 67 to 73 CE. There are a mix of fictional and historical characters in this telling of the events. You will want to consult Appendix B, which lists all the characters, and which highlights those who were cited in historical or biblical texts. In contrast are those characters I created and who are entirely fictional.

Appendix A does the same thing for the reader, by identifying in each chapter the circumstances and story lines that are historically derived, versus those that are entirely fictional. The circumstances which are biblical come mostly from *Acts of the Apostles*, which describes the missionary work of St. Paul (Paulus), St. Peter (Simon Petros), and several of the apostles. I use the gospels for references to the teachings or sayings of Jesus (Jehoshua). The principal historical source is *The Wars of the Jews*, written in the late first century by Flavius Josephus. I have already discussed his book at length in the Foreword, but suffice to say that Parts Four and Five in this novel owe their strategic and tactical details to Josephus' descriptions of the sieges at Jotapata and Jerusalem. There are quite a number of modern biographies on Vespasianus and Titus that were consulted to understand these two Roman emperors. The extant commentaries on them, provided by their contemporaries such as Suetonius, are useful for coloration but have to be treated with suspicion, as it is hard to tell in these biographies what is factual and what is salacious gossip.

Part One – Aristarchus

Paulus was regularly running into legal difficulties with the Roman authorities in the cities he visited. Often these were the result of conflicts he had with Jewish religious officials who felt he was teaching heresy. Sometimes these run-ins ended in violence, and one such instance resulted in Paulus' arrest following altercations and stone-throwing near the Temple in Jerusalem. Paulus held Roman citizenship, it is presumed through his father, since men could obtain citizenship by serving a term in the Roman army. In any trial that would involve capital punishment, such as inciting riots, he had the privilege through his citizenship of appealing to Rome. Theoretically, such an appeal could be made to the Emperor himself, but just as often the appeal would be scheduled for a high Roman court. Paulus filed such an appeal and was held in a Roman prison in Philipi Caesaria for a rather long time, two years, awaiting his transfer to Rome. All of these events are documented in *Acts*.

We do not have any history regarding the trial, other than that he was sentenced to house arrest. House arrest implies he was guilty of something. What we understand of the Roman legal system is that the defendant was responsible for interrogation and cross-examining witnesses, as well as presenting the case. His lawyer was there to ensure his legal rights were respected by the court. The judge, or praetor, had colleagues called triumvirs who sat in on the trial and who provided him legal advice and opinions on the verdict; but the praetor himself determined guilt, innocence, and sentence. Capital punishment was usually doled out immediately if that was the sentence. I have placed this trial in the court of the Praetor Peregrinus, who would normally handle cases from the provinces. All of the court officials and the dialogue are fictional.

In my telling of this story, the verdict is interrupted by a surprise witness, Gaius Cornelius Plautis, an official of the Office of the Pontifex Maximus. This is an entirely fictional character and circumstance, but I use this scene to introduce the types of complaints and charges the Romans often leveled against the Christians. In the story, Cornelius Plautis is sent on a mission to Galilee and Judea to learn about Jehoshua and the Christos cult. He uses the trial to accuse Paulus of being a leading figure in a cult that practices human sacrifice and worships a condemned criminal who was nothing but a magus (magician) practicing common tricks learned when he studied in Egypt.

There is hardly anything in the written record that tells us what the Romans thought about Jehoshua and the Christians, because when Constantine converted to Christianity around 330 he ordered all negative commentary on the religion destroyed. His officers were obviously very thorough in doing so. However, one interesting document survived, because it was written by a church leader named Origen. He wrote a rebuttal to a pagan work whose author had criticized Christianity. That pagan work was called *The True Word*, and was written around 280 CE by a Greek writer called Celsus. Origen's rebuttal is titled *Contra-Celsum*, and in it he quotes at great length from Celsus in order to be clear what it is he is refuting. *Contra-Celsum* is therefore our leading source on what Romans thought of Christianity, and I use these and other charges that we know were thrown at the Christians as the basic argument put forward by Cornelius Plautis.

The Pontifex Maximus, or High Priest, was an office always held by the Emperor (and continues to be held by the Pope in Rome). One source at the time says that Emperor Nero was interested, if not fascinated by Jehoshua, and had a statue of him installed in his palace, along with other gods to whom he prayed. I use this information to create a scene where Aristarchus is invited to the Emperor's palace and sees what happened to that statue. Aristarchus is the same figure found in Book One, and is a real figure known as a traveling companion for Paulus.

This chapter finishes with Aristarchus seeking and finding Simon Petros in Rome, in order to ask him to accept Paulus as a guest in his house. Simon Petros refuses, and instead brings Aristarchus to meet with Diodorus, the head of a rival sect of Christos-worshippers in Rome who follow the teachings of Paulus. Diodorus is fictional. This scene represents two facts we know are true: Simon Petros did not get along personally with Paulus, and they had different beliefs about Jehoshua, his resurrection, and the meaning of his life.

Part Two - Chrysanthe

This section explores the development of the Christmas story as we now know it. The central characters are Crispus and his wife Chrysanthe, plus their three children. Crispus is a figure identified in *Acts* as a leader in the Corinth church. His wife, their children, and the other characters in this section are fictional. We learned in the previous section of the criticisms, accusations, and charges the Romans, Jews, and others threw at the Christians. These statements began circulating very early in the history of the church, perhaps just ten years after the death of Jehoshua, and certainly in response to the rapid rise of the cult of Christos-worship.

It becomes very interesting to juxtapose these charges against the claims made in the gospels. The gospel of Mark might have been written as early as the 50s. He places the birth of Jehoshua in Nazareth, and he says nothing of the Christmas story. The gospels of Matthew and Luke date from 80 to later. We learned in the Foreword to Book One, *Signs and Wonders*, that in between these three gospels, a gospel now lost to us circulated, today called the Gospel of Q. This gospel very clearly was the source of much of the material in Matthew and Luke, since they match up so closely side by side that it had to be more than coincidence that the sequences of their stories were the same. Moreover, they both carried the Christmas story, which obviously must have been sourced from Q.

The Gospel of Q, therefore, had to be written between 50 and 80, give or take a few years, and it was unknown to Mark. The author of Q might have been the originator of the Christmas story, or was merely passing it on as truth. The more interesting question is, what happened between 50 and 80 to cause such a story to circulate, and the answer most likely centers on the increasing fierceness of pagan and Jewish opposition to the Christian cult, culminating in the purges in Rome in the 50s, and Nero's persecutions in the 60s. In that context, the Christmas story can be seen as a logical rebuttal to all of the criticisms raised by the pagans, and a few raised as well by Jewish opponents. If we line up these rebuttals one by one, the origins of the Christmas story spring out as immediately obvious:

Pagan and Jewish Criticisms	Christian Response
Mary (Miriam) was a harlot and Jehoshua was her illegitimate son born from a liaison with a Roman soldier named Pantera	Miriam was impregnated by the Holy Spirit and gave birth as a virgin; Joseph married her and became Jehoshua's earthly father
Jehoshua was not of the House of David and could not therefore be the Messiah (Meshiach)	Mary was from Bethlehem, the seat of the House of David, as proven by her need to travel there for the census
There was no earthquake or celestial event at the birth of Jehoshua to signify a king had been born	There was a bright star in the sky directly over the stable in which he was born
Jehoshua was nothing but a cheap magician (magus) performing tricks that people interpreted as miracles	The three greatest magi of their age understood the kingship and divine nature of Jehoshua, and at his birth came to the stable to worship him
He learned his magic in Egypt, the source of all superstition	The Holy Family was forced to flee to Egypt due to the threat from Herod the Great, and thus Jehoshua spent his early years there
Jehoshua died disgracefully as a condemned criminal, the worst sort of person to worship	Jehoshua's death was part of the divine plan by God, whereby his son took human form, suffered a terrible death, and redeemed mankind from Original Sin

The principal Roman criticism centered on Jehoshua's shameful execution as a criminal. The Romans were mystified that anyone could worship someone of that status. Indeed, the surprising thing about Roman opinions regarding crucifixion, judging from the writings we have of that time, was that Romans thought the worst part of crucifixion was not the pain involved, but the disgrace suffered by the victim. I go into this in greater detail in Book One, but crucifixion victims were not given a proper burial, and their soul therefore was not able to travel after death to Elysium. To the ancient mind, this was the ultimate shame anyone could suffer at their death. A second assumption Romans, or non-Christians in general, entertained was that Roman legal practices ensured a fair trial. Therefore, Jehoshua really was a criminal, simply by virtue of the fact that he suffered capital punishment through a state execution.

The Christians, of course, made a virtue out of his shameful death and created elaborate descriptions of Jehoshua as completely blameless for his own death, which was eventually described as being orchestrated by the Jews. It was necessary, in other words, for Christians to establish that Jehoshua's trial was decidedly unfair; hence the need for the Roman prefect, Pontius Pilatus, to wash his hands of the affair during the verdict. These rebuttals show up in the latter gospels of Matthew, Luke, and John, and the theory that Jehoshua's death was part of a divine plan to redeem mankind from his sinful nature is found in Paulus' epistles. The Christmas story is perfectly tailored to provide Christians with answers to the criticisms that were beginning to spread around the Empire. In this section, I describe the story as something that was concocted initially for children, but later came to be accepted by adults as truth.

Part Three – Yakov

Yakov (James, i.e. James the Just) is one of the most interesting and important figures in early Christianity, but little is known of him. Perhaps his fame would have been greater had the Jerusalem community of Christians not disappeared after the first century. Yakov is identified in the Gospels and *Acts* as the brother of Jesus, but we know little of him beyond that, and the fact that he led the Jerusalem church after his brother's death. He was martyred in the 60s at the hands of the High Priest in Jerusalem.

A great deal is made of St. Stephen, the first Christian martyr, who was stoned to death, according to *Acts*. Much more should be made of Yakov as yet another martyr at that time, but it isn't, because Christianity has found him an awkward figure, best left undiscussed. This reticence has to do with the fact that the *Gospel of Mark* has an awkward passage where Miriam, the mother of Jehoshua,

Yakov, and all the other brothers and sisters, greets Jehoshua when he comes up to Galilee, and attempts to have him restrained or incarcerated, presumably for mental instability. This incident caused Jehoshua to state that a prophet is without honor in his own country, and it explains to some degree Jehoshua's requirement of his followers that they abandon their families and follow him instead. Equally awkward is the fact that Jehoshua even had any brothers and sisters, much less that many, with no father about to account for them.

As Christianity matured and Jehoshua evolved into God and the Son of God, it seemed necessary for the church to purge any discussion of his brothers and sisters. No one wanted to pursue the idea of God's nieces and nephews. Therefore, the Catholic Church devised the idea that Yakov and all these supposed siblings mentioned in Mark were in fact cousins to Jehoshua. This trick was predicated on the fact that the words *brother* and *cousin* are similar in Aramaic. The Catholic Church abides to this day by this ruse and insists Yakov was the cousin of Jehoshua.

The death of Yakov by stoning on the grounds of the Temple is described in *Acts*. There is an alternative and more elaborate description of his martyrdom in a passage written by Heggesipus in the third century CE. It tells of Yakov being throw off the roof of the Temple and then being clubbed to death as the *coup de grace*. I use the second version of his martyrdom in this chapter. The conclusion of the chapter ends with a scene of Yakov's wife, Kediah (who is entirely fictional), renouncing her Judaism. There is no historical basis for this scene, but the evidence does mount from this point forward that relations between Christians and Jews deteriorate.

Part Four – Josephus

I provide an extensive discussion of Josephus in the Foreword, covering his role in the Jewish wars and as an historian. In this section the focus is on his work as military commander of the defense of Jotapata, and his introduction to Vespasianus. The material used in this section is largely provided by Josephus himself. In his history *The Wars of the Jews*, Josephus provides political and military details on the defense of Jotapata, a small city near Cana in Galilee that was well fortified on a hill and barricaded on three sides. Josephus talks about himself entirely in the third person when discussing his role as general and commander of the Jewish forces. As one might expect, he gives himself high marks for his role as commander, suggesting that any other individual would not have lasted as long against the Romans. The six weeks of the siege exposed the residents and defenders of Jotapata to privations, but nothing as extreme as happened to Jerusalem. Nonetheless, the Romans found a way into the city (Josephus says it was due to a betrayal by a Jewish informant), and then sacked Jotapata.

Josephus and some of his followers took refuge in one of the caves under the city. They were determined not to surrender, but conditions became so abysmal, and their capture seemed inevitable, that a proposal was put forward that they slay each other, since Jews are forbidden by their religion to commit suicide. This proposal was carried out, and Josephus was, seemingly by chance, the last man standing (and therefore presumably subject to capture and crucifixion by the Romans). The lottery method selected for this ritual execution has long been the subject of discussion by mathematicians, who describe the matter as the "Josephus Problem", which relates specifically to whether a participant, given the selection method used, could work out in advance what position they should be in to become the last man standing. There is, it turns out, a solution to the problem.

Josephus relates how he had a lifelong ability to predict the future through dreams, and that he used this ability to convince Vespasianus that Josephus would be better alive than dead. I invent a dream that would interest Vespasianus personally, but other than that, Part Four recounts exactly what Josephus described in his book, with some texture and color added.

Part Five – The Zealots

Part Five describes the climactic siege and destruction of Jerusalem by Titus, the son of Vespasianus. Again, the tactical and strategic military actions taken during this siege are described in great detail by Josephus, who has now turned to helping the Romans, and therefore I use this detail as the framework for this section. The principal challenge in describing the siege is to decide how much of Josephus' antipathy toward the defenders of Jerusalem one should accept. By the time of the siege, a group known as the Zealots had developed into a quasi-military force, under the leadership of Yohan of Gischala and Simon bar Giora. The Zealots have a reputation among historians as being insurrectionists and guerilla fighters against the Romans; their intention was clearly to drive the Romans out of all of the Jewish provinces. They had been a nuisance for the Romans for decades, including the time when Pontius Pilatus was prefect; but by the time of the siege of Jerusalem they had succeeded, along with other Jewish rebel forces, in defeating the Roman legion at a battle near Bet-Horon in Judea. This prompted Nero to mount a counter-attack under the direction of General Vespasianus, who had four legions at his command.

One man's insurrectionist is another man's patriot, and there was certainly considerable support and sympathy for the Zealots among the Israelites. Jewish historians look at the Zealots with more favor than Josephus, who described them as more interested in committing pillage and rape among the Jewish population in Jerusalem than in actively defending the city. This opinion is contradicted by evidence that the city's defenders were eager to rush out of the city gates and attack the Romans in their camps; but this action might be explained by the fact that forces other than the Zealots were manning the defensive battlements of Jerusalem.

Mindful of these pitfalls, I generally side with the opinions of Josephus, since he has proven to be accurate when it comes to matters that can be tested on archaeological grounds. The Zealots are not given a favorable treatment in this chapter. One thing is for certain; they weren't given favorable treatment by the Romans. Most adults left alive after the sacking of Jerusalem were enslaved or sent to die in the arena or in the Egyptian mines. It is difficult to write about this war without chronicling the suffering of the Jews, which will continue to be chronicled in coming books in this series, as the Diaspora commences from this point.

Part Six – Olympias

Olympias is a character from the start of this book who is now older and with a family, resident in Rome. She and her husband are Christians who practice their faith surreptitiously, given the unfavorable view of the religion by the authorities and the persecutions that occurred under Nero (but were fortunately not continued by Vespasianus or his sons). The circumstances in this section are fictional. We do not know what really happened to the body of St. Peter after his martyrdom on the Vatican Hill. The Catholic Church has done considerable scientific research on the human remains that lie underneath St. Peter's Basilica, and the Church claims it has very good reason to believe these remains are actually those of St. Peter. The case that has been made is reasonably convincing, partly because the bones lie directly under the high altar of the Basilica, they were reverentially treated, they show some indications the person had been crucified, and they appear to have been the object of centuries of pilgrimage and adoration. There are also written records describing the shrine to St. Peter that had been built by Constantine the Great, and was positioned directly where the new St. Peter's Basilica was built in the fifth century. This sequence seemed like excellent material to weave into a story involving Olympias.

These scenes are juxtaposed with a shift back to Jerusalem, a city now in ruin. Gamaliel ben Yavne, the grandson of Gamaliel in Book One, has been asked to organize a new Sanhedrin by the Roman authorities (this is an historical fact). I use this situation as an opportunity to explore relations between a Jewish leader at the time and what was left of the Christian community in Jerusalem. The outcome is not propitious for future relations between the two groups, and it is a disappointment to Gamaliel, almost as much a disappointment as the disappearance of the Jerusalem in which he had grown up. The meeting he has with the Christian community is entirely apocryphal, and I am only speculating what might have happened had there been such a meeting.

The book ends with a return to Rome. Olympias must deal with her second son, who needs to be informed that his parents are practicing, believing Christians. I use this scene to hint at one of the most shameful aspects of Christianity, and that is its long history of anti-Semitism and persecution of Jews. Anti-semitism will continue to be a theme surfacing in later volumes in this series.

APPENDIX B

Characters in *Jehoshua: Conflagration* in Order of Their Appearance

(Historical and biblical characters are in **bold**; all other characters are fictional}

Part One – Aristarchus (From Corinth to Rome, Year 57)

1. **Aristarchus** – A young traveling companion and scribe to Paulus, mentioned in *Acts* as a Greek Macedonian from Thessaloniki, and sentenced to house arrest with Paulus

2. **Paulus** – A Jewish Pharisee known originally as a persecutor of Christians and later as a convert to Christianity; creator of the Pauline theology of Christianity; also known as Saul of Tarsus ; in modern times known as St. Paul or Paul of Tarsus or the Apostle Paul

3. **Jehoshua** – also referred to as Jehoshua the Christos, Jehoshua the Nazarene, childhood name of Yesh, teenage name of Jehu; in modern times known as Jesus Christ; in this book a figure of worship, remembrance, or veneration

4. Captain Tychon – Shipmaster of the vessel taking Paulus and Aristarchus to Rome

5. Gaius Nicomedes – brother to Aristarchus, a former traveling assistant and secretary to Paulus

6. Porcius – A tour guide who offers his services to Aristarchus at the Roman Forum

7. **Nero** – Nero Claudius Caesar Augustus Germanicus, Emperor of Rome from 54 to 68; grand-nephew of Emperor Claudius, who adopted Nero as his heir

8. Eumilia – A prostitute in Rome

9. Renita – Eumilia's madam

10. Laelius Disertus – An advocate, or lawyer, assisting in Paulus' defense at his trial in Rome

11. L. Trebonius Cassianus – Praetor Peregrinus, or chief judge handling Rome's trials of overseas cases; also a former Chief Augur of Rome

12. Enoch ben Irad – A Jewish witness against Paulus at his trial

13. Iram ben Enoch – A Jewish witness against Paulus at his trial, and son of Enoch ben Irad

14. **Lukas Kyrillos** – A young travelling assistant and scribe to Paulus; in modern times known as St. Luke the Evangelist, and Luke the author *of Acts of the Apostles*

15. **Marcus Antonius Felix** – Roman procurator for Judea from 52 – 58 or 59 ; tried Paulus for sedition and kept him incarcerated in Caesarea for two years until Paulus was transferred to Rome on appeal to the Emperor

16. **Pontius Pilatus** – Roman prefect for Judea from 26 to 36 or 37; patronized by Emperors Tiberius and Gaius Caesar (Caligula), but later dismissed for malfeasance and cruelty; in modern times known as Pontius Pilate, who sentenced Jehoshua to death

17. Gaius Cornelius Plautis – An agent of the Office of the Pontifex Maximus; an unexpected Accusator against Paulus at his trial

18. Pantera (or Jehoshua ben Pantera) – A common surname assigned to Jehoshua and used by non-Christians for at least two centuries after his death; Pantera was supposedly a centurion stationed in Galilee and was the father of Jehoshua through a sexual relationship with Jehoshua's mother, Miriam

19. Hermogenes – A Greek clerk serving Emperor Nero on administrative matters

20. **Simon Petros** – A Jewish follower of Jehoshua; one of the original Twelve disciples; also known as Kefas (Aramaic for the Rock, a nickname given to him by Jehoshua) and as Simon the Healer; in modern times known as St. Peter or Peter the Apostle; the first pope of the Catholic Church

21. Adriel – Wife of Simon Petros in Rome

22. **Bartolomeo** – One of the original Twelve disciples of Jehoshua, recruited by Philip and always mentioned in conjunction with him; also referred to as Nathanael (in the

Gospel of John); known in modern times as St. Bartholomew or the Apostle Bartholomew

23. Tomas – A Jewish follower of Jehoshua; one of the original Twelve disciples; known in modern times as St. Thomas or the Apostle Thomas, and further, as Doubting Thomas because he lacked faith in the resurrection

24. Diodorus – A Christian in Rome and leader of a sect that followed the teachings of Paulus (as distinct to those of Simon Petros)

Part Two – Chrysanthe (Corinth, Year 60)

1. Chrysanthe – A member of the Christian community of Corinth

2. **Crispus** – A member of the Christian community of Corinth and mentioned in one of the Epistles of Paulus; in this book, husband to Chrysanthe

3. Alcaeus – Son of Chrysanthe and Crispus

4. Olympias – Elder daughter to Chrysanthe and Crispus

5. Theodosia – Younger daughter to Chrysanthe and Crispus

6. **Apollos** – A leading figure in the Asia Minor Assemblies (churches), who, like Paulus, traveled from one city to the next, preaching the Good News of Jehoshua; mentioned in *Acts of the Apostles*, but little is known of his preaching or theology and whether it differed from Paulus'

7. Mother Sophia – High priestess of the order of Dionysos in Corinth ; also known as Eunike

8. Chloe – A member of the Christian community of Corinth; oldest friend of Chrysanthe

9. Hannah – An older member of the Christian community of Corinth; married to the wealthy merchant Moses ben Hezekiah; also referred to as Sister Hannah

10. Rebekah – A young girl in the Christian community of Corinth

11. Jael – A young girl in Corinth who taunts Alcaeus about being a Christian and being circumcised

12. Master Zibiah – A Jewish rabban in Corinth, who educates Hannah about Jewish scriptures

13. Neophytos – A client of Mother Sophia, who in his old age joins the Christian community in Corinth

14. Idaeus – Another client of Mother Sophia; was murdered by her with the help of Neophytos

Part Three – Yakov (Jerusalem, Year 62)

1. **Yakov** – Yakov the Nazarene; Yakov the Just; brother of Jehoshua; in modern times known as St. James or James the Just

2. Ehud ben Aliazar – A young boy from Nazareth featured in a dream sequence with Yakov and his brother Jehoshua (Yesh) as children

3. Avram ben Aliazar – Brother to Ehud ben Aliazar

4. **Miriam** – The mother of Jehoshua and Yakov; in this book featured in a dream sequence; in modern times known as the Virgin Mary or Mary the Mother of God

5. Abram ben Hosah – A Jewish priest at the Temple accused of embezzlement on trial with Yakov in front of Ananus ben Ananias

6. **Miriam of Magdala** – A Jewish follower of Jehoshua, originally from Magdala, a small town in Galilee within walking distance of Nazareth; in modern times known as Mary Magdalene

7. Javan – A Jewish tinsmith by trade and husband of Miriam of Magdala

8. Kediah – a Jewish follower of Jehoshua; born in Nazareth and a childhood friend of Yakov, Jehoshua's brother; later married to Yakov

9. Lysander – A member of the Jewish community of Christians; especially known for his exact memory and ability to chronicle precisely the sayings of Jehoshua

10. **Marcus** – A Greek scholar in Alexandria, of Jewish descent; a chronicler of one of the first biographies of Jehoshua; in modern times known as St. Mark or St. Mark the Evangelist, author of the *Gospel of Mark*

11. **Philo of Alexandria** – A Greek scholar in Alexandria, of Jewish descent; known for his philosophical writings, which established him as a leading neo-Platonist of his day; known

also as Philo Judeaus; presumed in this book to be the teacher of Marcus

12. **Salome** – A member of the Christian community in Jerusalem; along with Miriam of Magdala, one of the earlier followers of Jehoshua and described in the Gospels as one of the women who visited Jehoshua's tomb

13. **Miriam, mother of James** – A Christian who accompanied Miriam of Magdala and Salome to the tomb of Christ, according to the *Gospel of Mark*; not to be confused with Miriam, the mother of Jehoshua and Yakov

14. **Ananus ben Ananias** – Son of the High Priest Ananias and a member of the Anan family of Sadducees; himself later a High Priest and defender of the Temple during the Roman Siege of Jerusalem; responsible also for the martyrdom of Yakov the Nazarene, the brother of Jehoshua

15. **Caiaphas** – Yosef Caiaphas, High Priest at the Temple in Jerusalem; member of the Sanhedrin

16. **Gamaliel** – A prominent Jewish religious leader and thinker of the first century in the Christian era; the president, or Nasi, of the Sanhedrin; also known as Rabban Gamaliel, Gamaliel I, the Blessed Gamaliel, and Gamaliel the Elder; he was the grandson of Hillel the Elder and the grandfather of Gamaliel of Yavne

17. Yonathan ben Ananus – A cousin of Ananus ben Ananias and a member of the Sanhedrin

18. **Porcius Festus** – A Roman procurator for Judea, from 59 to 62 (the dates are uncertain); successor to M. Antonius Felix

19. **Lucceius Albinus** – A Roman procurator for Judea, from 62 to 64; successor to Porcius Festus following his unexpected death; Albinus' delay in arriving in Judea gave Ananus ben Ananias an opportunity to purge his enemies from the Sanhedrin and to execute Yakov the Nazarene

20. Greek mendicant – A beggar searching for coins in the Gentile Courtyard of the Temple

Part Four – Josephus (Jotapata in Galilee, Year 67)

1. **Josephus** – A Jewish historian of the last half of the first century; also known as Titus Flavius Josephus (his Roman

name) and Yosef ben Matityahu (his Jewish name); defender of Jotapata during the Jewish war with the Romans, later a client of Emperor Vespasianus and his sons; author of *The Wars of the Jews* and *Antiquities of the Jews*

2. **Yohan the Essene** – A Sanhedrin member appointed to defend Emmaus in the war with the Romans

3. **Yosef ben Gorim** – A Sanhedrin member appointed to defend Jerusalem in the war with the Romans

4. **Mannaseh the Merchant** – A Sanhedrin member appointed to defend Perea in the war with the Romans

5. **Philip ben Josimus** – A Sanhedrin member appointed to defend Samaria in the war with the Romans

6. **Costobarus** and his brother **Saul** – Sanhedrin members appointed to defend Idumea in the war with the Romans

7. **Gaius Cestius Gallus** – A Roman legate in Syria from 63 to 66, with pro-consular (governor) authority over all Jewish provinces; led a legion into Judea in 66 to restore order and was ambushed by Jewish insurgents at Bet-Horon, with great loss of life and materiel by the Romans

8. **Simon bar Giora** – A leader of Jewish insurrectionist forces in the Jewish Wars; presumed as well to be a Zealot, or revolutionary

9. **Herod Agrippa II** – Grandson of Herod the Great and son of Herod Agrippa; educated in Rome at the court of Claudius, who gave him kingship over the Jewish province of Perea; Agrippa II proved to be unpopular and fled with his sister Berenice back to Rome at the start of the Jewish Wars; he is sometimes referred to as King Herod but should not be confused with either of his regal ancestors

10. Mathias – A military sub-altern to Josephus

11. Sameas of Galilee – A defender of Jotapata

12. Yohan – A military orderly to Josephus

13. Cyrus – A professional soldier and defender of Jotapata; trapped in the cave with Josephus

14. Reuben – A professional soldier and defender of Jotapata; trapped in the cave with Josephus

15. **Nicanor** – A childhood friend of Josephus ; later in the employment of King Herod Agrippa II and then in the employment of Vespasianus

16. **Servius Sulpicius Galba** – Served briefly as Roman Emperor in 69 during the Civil War of that year

17. **Aulus Vitellius** – Served briefly as Roman Emperor in 69 during the Civil War of that year; assassinated by his Praetorian Guard; was succeeded on the throne by Vespasianus

18. **Vespasianus** – General in charge of the Roman siege and attack on Jotapata and of the campaign against the Jews; later appointed Imperator by the Roman Senate; also known as Titus Flavius Caesar Vespasianus Augustus; in modern times known as Emperor Vespasian

19. **Titus** – Son of Vespasianus and his heir to the throne of the Roman Empire; commander of a legion during the first stage of the Roman campaign against the Jews; later commander of the entire campaign that resulted in the siege and destruction of Jerusalem; also known as Titus Flavius Caesar Vespasianus Augustus; in modern times known as Emperor Titus

Part Five – The Zealots (Jerusalem, Years 69 -71)

1. **Yohan of Gischala** – Defender of Gischala during the Roman campaign against the Jews; a prominent leader of the Zealots; later defender of Jerusalem during the siege by the Romans; ultimately sentenced to life imprisonment by Titus

2. Benyamin - A military orderly to Yohan of Gischala

3. **Simon bar Giora** – A defender of Jerusalem during the Roman siege of that city; a leader of the Zealots; ultimately executed in the Roman Forum during the Triumph staged for Vespasianus and Titus

4. **Fronto** – Chief quartermaster to the legions under the command of Titus; responsible for the disposition of all Jewish prisoners condemned to serve as slaves or die as gladiators

5. **Bartolomeo** – One of the original Twelve disciples of Jehoshua; recruited by Philip and always mentioned in conjunction with him; also referred to as Nathanael (in the

Gospel of John) known in modern times as St. Bartholomew
or the Apostle Bartholomew

6. **Domitianus** – Titus Flavius Caesar Domitianus Augustus,
    Emperor of Rome from 81 to 96; younger brother of Titus and
    son of Vespasianus

7. **Lucius Calpurnius Piso Licinianus** – Named by Emperor
    Galba as his heir in 69; murdered that same year by Otho's
    soldiers

8. **Salvius Otho** – The second of the three emperors in the year
    69 ; succeeded Galba after his assassination; Otho himself
    was forced to resign the throne by his Praetorian Guard later
    that year and committed suicide in response

9. **Tiberius Julius Alexander** – A procurator of Judea from 46
    to 48, of Jewish descent from an Alexandrian family; Tiberius
    Alexander was a Roman provincial administrator with
    military experience, who supported Vespasianus' claim to the
    throne and assisted Titus in the siege of Jerusalem

10. Appius Rutilius Alba – Chief Engineer for the Roman legions
    at the siege of Jerusalem

11. Gnaeus Numicius Caeca – A Roman general responsible for
    one of the legions participating in the siege of Jerusalem

12. Quintus Pompeius Barba – A Roman official who acted as
    secretary for the Senate of Rome

13. **Marcus Antonius Primus** – A Roman general instrumental
    in ousting Vitellius from the throne and opening the way for
    Vespasianus to assume the role of Emperor

14. **Sabinus** – A Syrian soldier employed in the Roman legions
    during the siege of Jerusalem ; cited by Josephus for his
    exceptional bravery in storming the Fortress Antonia

15. **Barnabas** – A traveling companion to Paulus and proselytizer
    to the Gentiles; a possible cousin to Marcus of Alexandria; in
    modern times known as St. Barnabas, an apostle listed in *Acts
    of the Apostles*

16. Virgilis – A decurion in Jerusalem at the time of the siege; a
    decurion was a local person of wealth or stature who assumed
    administrative responsibilities for Rome

17. **Matityahu ben Jonah** – Father of Flavius Josephus

18. **Lucilius Bassus** – The Roman legate (i.e. governor with full

military power) appointed to Judea in 71 by Vespasianus ;
responsible for finishing up all Jewish resistance in the war,
culminating in the siege and capture of Masada

Part Six – Olympias (Vatican Hill, Year 79, later Jerusalem in the same year)

1. Ampelios of Antioch – A member of the Christian community
   in Antioch; a pilgrim in Rome desiring to pray at the tomb of
   Simon Petros
2. **Linus** – Second bishop of Rome after Simon Petros (St. Peter);
   thus the second Pope
3. Demetrios – Husband of Olympias, on business to the Eastern
   provinces
4. **Gamaliel of Yavne** – Nasi of the Sanhedrin following the
   destruction of Jerusalem; son of Shimon ben Gamaliel, who
   was executed by the Romans after the fall of Jerusalem;
   grandson of Gamaliel the Elder; also known as Gamaliel II
5. Ithiel – A member of the Christian community in Jerusalem
6. **Lucius Flavius Silva** – A Roman procurator of Jerusalem
   around 79 to 80
7. Heiron, Leontios, and Sophos – Sons of Olympias and
   Demetrios, from oldest to youngest
8. Gershom – Young Jewish friend of Leontios
9. Erastos, Nicostratus, and Epaphras – Three young Greek
   friends of Leontios

APPENDIX C
Timeline

Reigns and Terms of Office of Rulers
During First 50 Years of Christianity

Year	Roman Emperors	Judea/Samaria	Galilee/Perea	Temple High Priests
4 BCE		Herod the Great		
2 BCE				
Christian Era				
2		Herod Archelaus		
4	Augustus	4 BCE - 6 BC		
6	27 BCE - 14 CE			
8		Coponius		
10		(start of Roman rule)		
12		Marcus Ambivulus		
14		Annius Rufus		
16			Herod Antipas	Ananus ben Seth
18			4 BCE - 39 CE	
20		Valerius Gratus		
22		15 - 26		
24				
26	Tiberius			Yosef Caiaphas
28	14 - 37			18 - 36
30		Pontius Pilatus		
32		26 - 36		
34				
36				
38		Marcellus		
40	Gaius (Caligula)			
42	37 - 41		Herod Agrippa I	
44			37 - 44	
46		Cuspius Fadus		
48	Claudius	Tiberius Alexander		Ananus ben Nebedeus
50	41 - 54			46 - 52
52		Ventidius Cumanus		
54				Jonathan
56		M. Antonius Felix		
58		52 - 59	Herod Agrippa II	Ishmael ben Fabus
60	Nero		48 - 70	56 - 62
62	54 - 68	Porcius Festus		Ananus ben Ananus
64				Joshua ben Gamaliel
66				
68	Galba/Otho/Vitellius			
70				Phannias b. Samuel
72	Vespasianus			
74	69 - 79			
76				
78				
80	Titus/79 - 81			

APPENDIX C
Timeline

Reigns and Terms of Office of Rulers
During First 50 Years of Christianity

Year	Sanhedrin Nasi	Historical Events	Jehoshua Chapters
4 BCE		Birth of Jehoshua?	
2 BCE	Hillel the Elder		
Christian Era	31 BCE - 9 CE		
2			
4			
6			
8			
10	Shimon ben Hillel		
12			
14			
16			
18			
20			
22			
24			
26		Jehoshua Ministry	
28		Execution of Jehoshua	*Jehoshua*
30			*Lamech the Trader*
32			
34			
36			*Miriam of Magdala*
38		Jewish Pogrom in	
40		Alexandria	*Marcus*
42			
44			
46			
48	Gamaliel the Elder		
50	34 - 50	Council of Jerusalem	*Gamaliel*
52			
54		First Trial of Paulus	*Paulus in Ephesus*
56			
58		Jewish/Christian Riots	*Aristarchus*
60		in Rome	*Chrysanthe*
62		Martyrdom of Yakov	*Yakov*
64	Shimon ben Gamaliel	Nero Persecutions	
66	50 - 80	Siege of Jotapata	*Josephus*
68			
70		Siege of Jerusalem	*The Zealots*
72			
74			
76			
78			*Olympias*
80	Gamaliel II of Yavne		

APPENDIX D
Maps

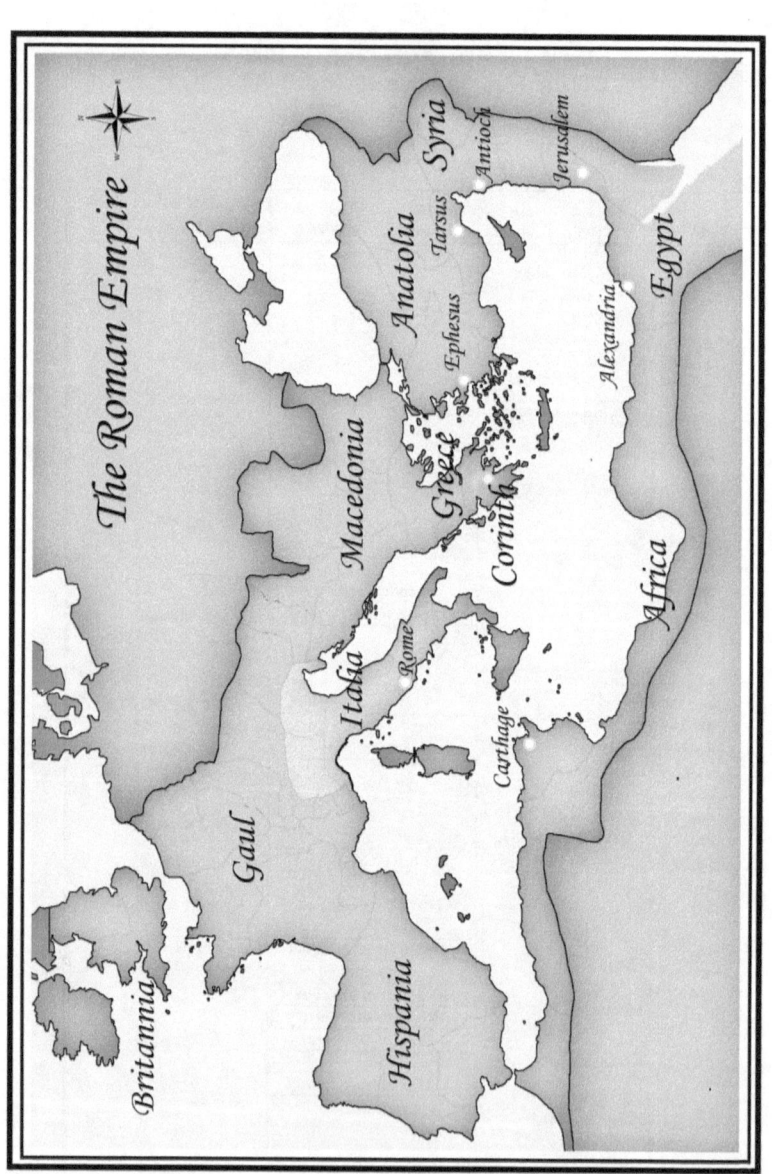

MAP OF THE ROMAN EMPIRE

MAP OF THE FORUM ROMANUM

APPENDIX D
Maps

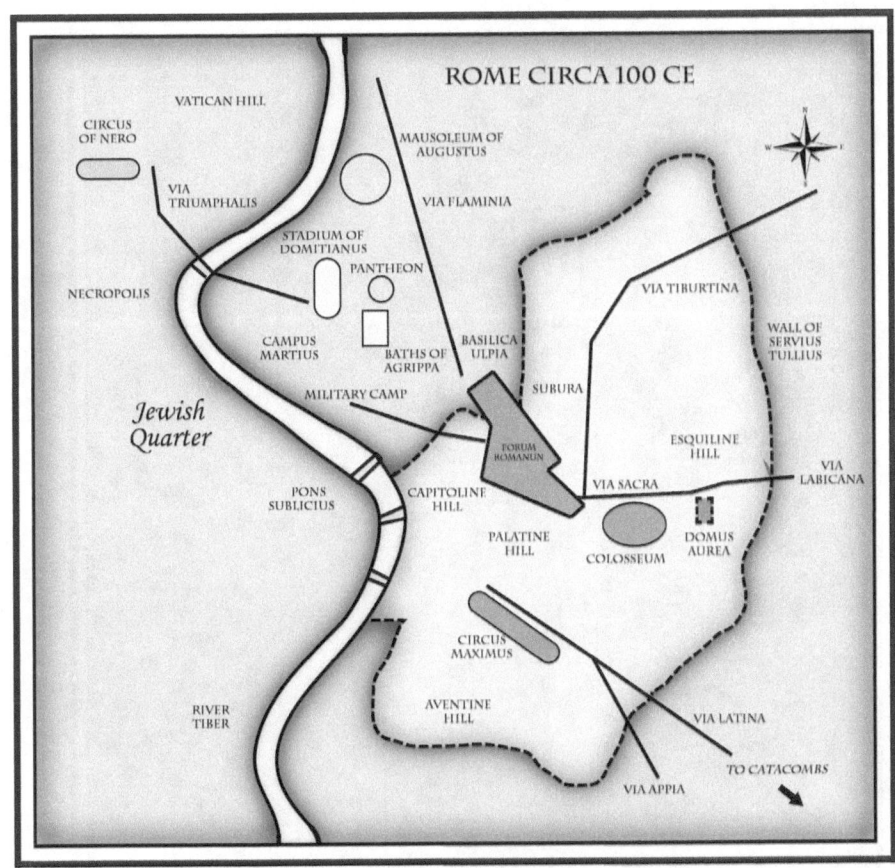

ROME CIRCA 100 CE

APPENDIX D
Maps

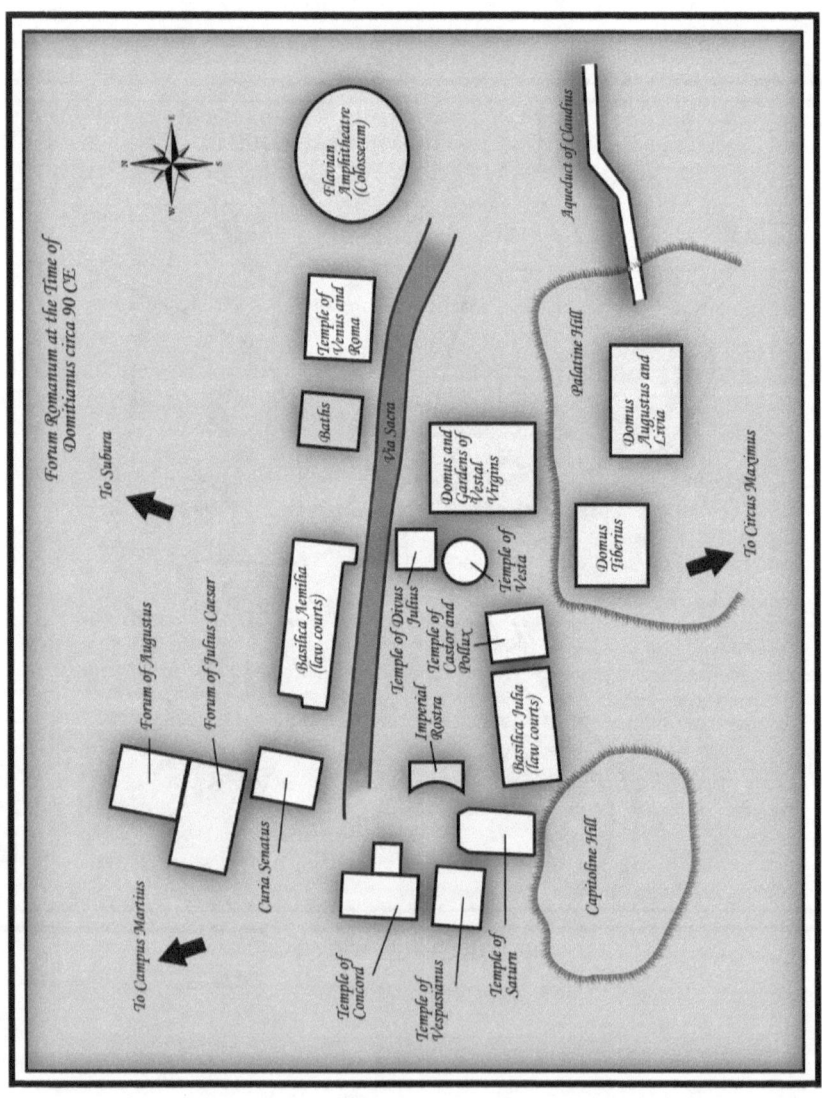

APPENDIX D
Maps

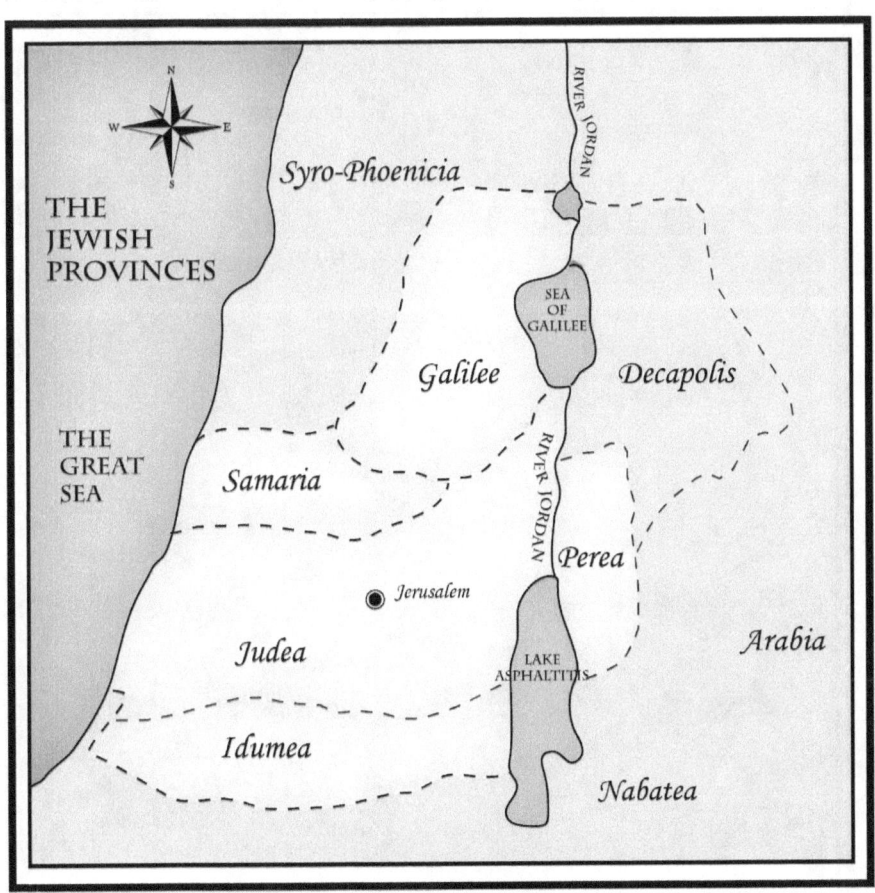

MAP OF JEWISH PROVINCES OF ROME

APPENDIX D
Maps

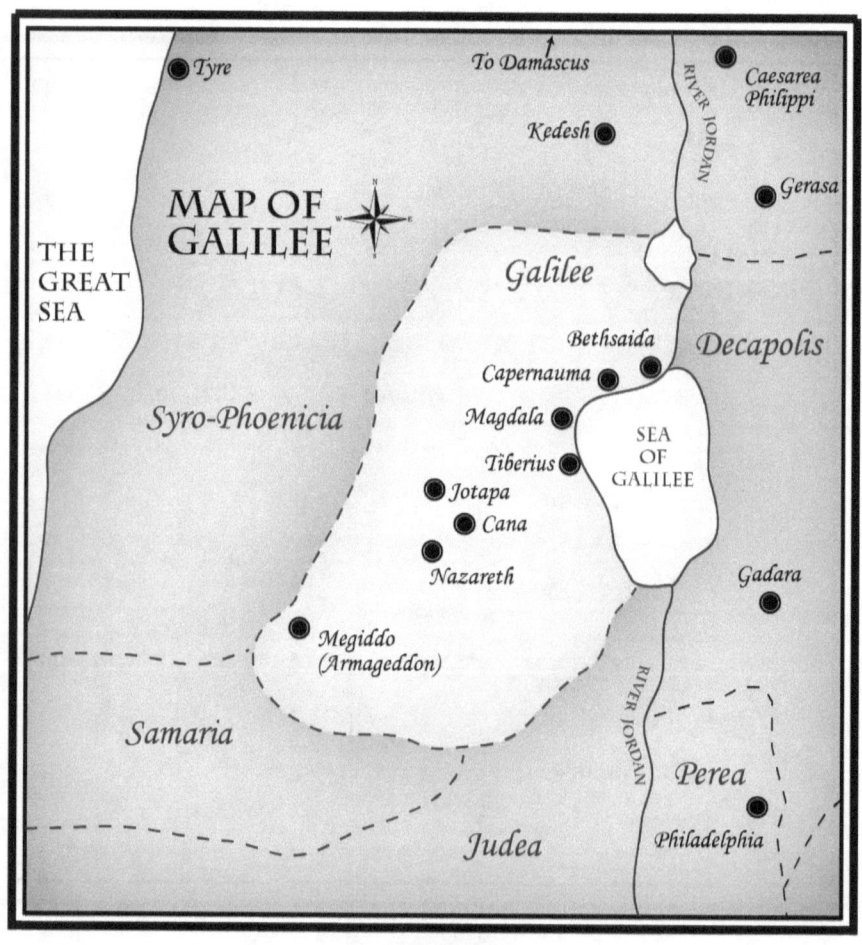

MAP OF GALILEE

APPENDIX D

Maps

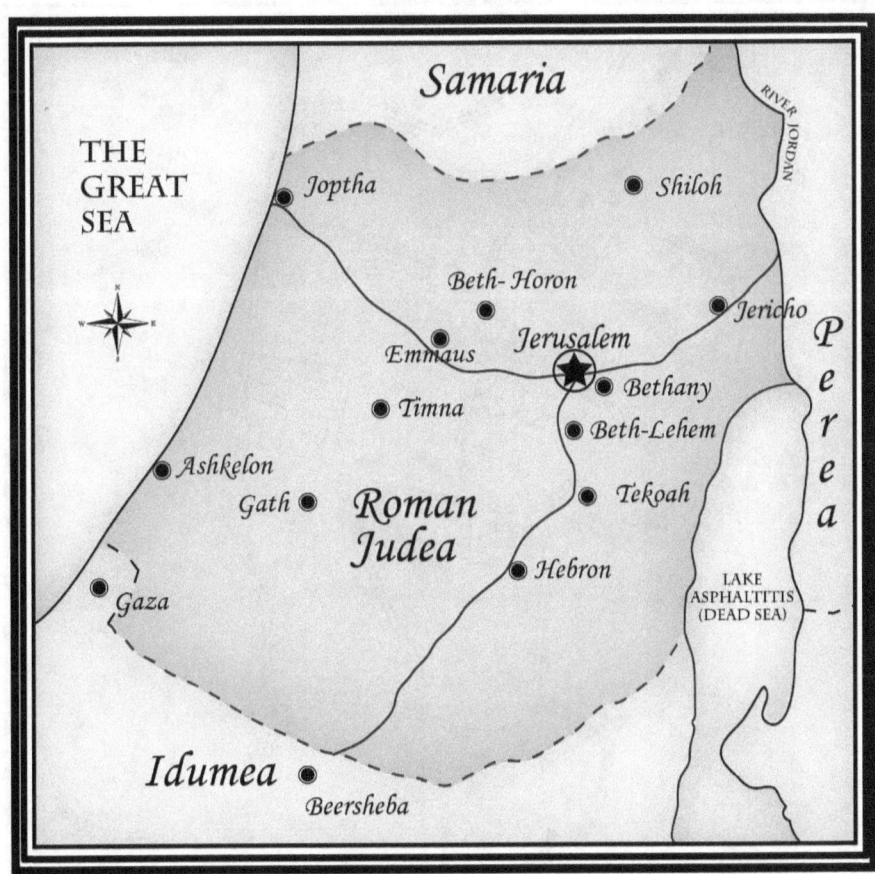

MAP OF ROMAN JUDEA

APPENDIX D

Siege of Jerusalem

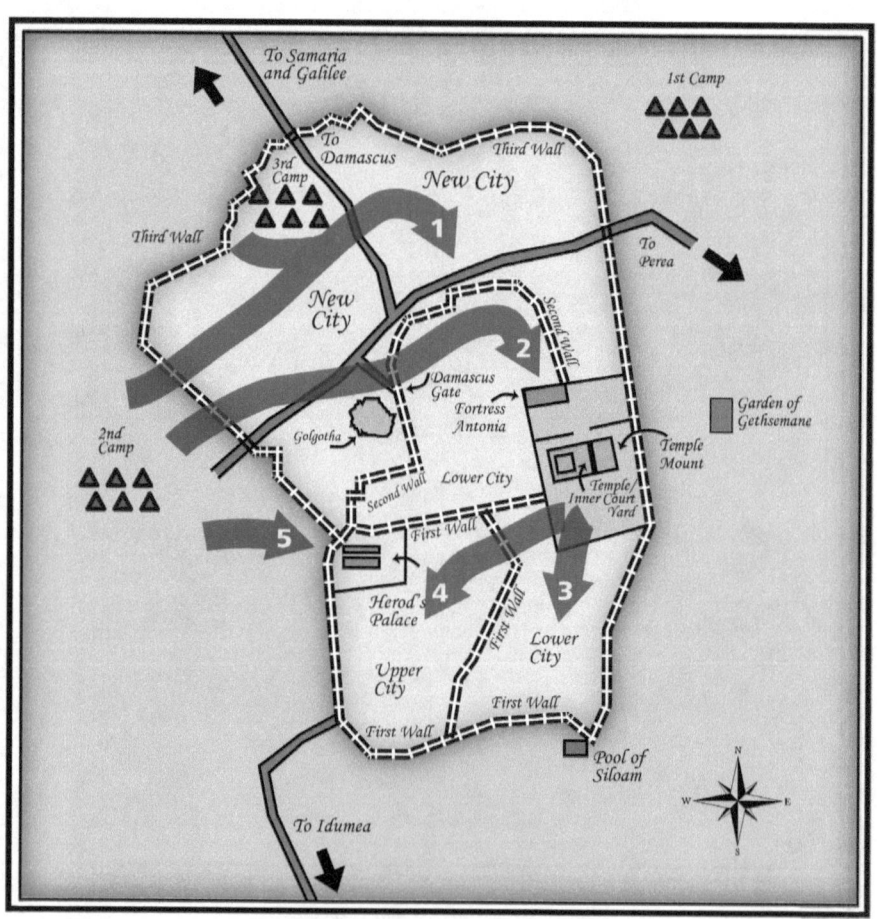

ROMAN SIEGE OF JERUSALEM, 70CE

APPENDIX E

Synopsis and Summaries of Parts One through Six

Jehoshua – The *Jehoshua* series of novels covers the history of early Christianity, using an historical fiction format. This format allows for historical characters and circumstances to be blended with fictional characters and events. Christianity has been an inspiration for many such novels: *Ben-Hur, Quo Vadis,* and *The Robe* are among the more well-known. These novels treat Jesus Christ with reverence, and an underlying theme in these books is the redemptive aspect of Jesus' death on the cross. On the opposite end of the spectrum are purely secular novels by such authors as Nikos Kazantzakis, Gore Vidal, and Norman Mailer, who take a more fantastical approach to the stories about Christ, his passion and death, and his mission.

The *Jehoshua* series is somewhere in between these two approaches, though author Garrett Glass creates circumstances in his novels that are certainly closer to the purely secular model. There are no miracles in the *Jehoshua* novels, but Jehoshua (Jesus) is treated respectfully, as are his followers. The goal of the author is to understand how these early followers of Jehoshua came to believe in his miracles and the resurrection, to the point they would accept death rather than denounce their beliefs. Why, for example, did communities of worship of Jehoshua and remembrance of him sprout up so quickly in all the important cities of the Roman Empire? How did this happen in the face of opposition from Jewish establishment leaders, and persecution by various Roman governments?

Jehoshua: Signs and Wonders, the first in the series, explores these issues from the execution of Jehoshua through the first twenty five years of the Christian movement. This book explores how stories regarding the resurrection began to circulate, how the closest followers of Jehoshua were forced to live in fear and secrecy, and how their principal oppressor, Paulus (St. Paul) turned into a supporter with a distinctly different message from those followers living in Jerusalem.

Jehoshua: Conflagration takes us through the next twenty five years of history. Historical and biblical figures appear in this novel, as do many fictional ones, all of them dealing with momentous changes and events. Jewish provinces under Roman control become the scene of bitter insurrections against the Roman administrators. The Jewish leadership is split into groups which have different solutions for dealing with these uprisings. At the same time, some Jewish leaders are highly suspicious of the "cult" of Jehoshua worshippers which is growing not only in Jerusalem but in many other Jewish and Gentile cities. As these developments boil over, the throne of the Roman Empire is suddenly vacant with the forced suicide of Nero and the lack of a clear successor. Civil War among the Roman military leadership adds yet another destabilizing aspect to the problems in the Jewish provinces. Through all of this we can see emerging a small Jewish sect called the Christians, poised to take advantage of the dissolution of the Jewish religious establishment and to commence an extraordinary journey that will lead ultimately to Christianity replacing the Empire itself. The story would be completely unbelievable were it told to any of the participants at the time, and *Jehoshua: Conflagration* puts us as readers into the minds and feelings of these participants so that we can get an understanding of how unexpected the success of Christianity truly was.

Part One – Aristarchus – Year 57, From Corinth to Rome

Paulus is *en route* to Rome by ship, as a prisoner heading for trial under the charge of insurrection and public disturbance. He is accompanied by a young traveling companion, Aristarchus. The ship is damaged in a storm and forced to take shelter on an island, but the vessel is reparable and no one is injured. Upon arrival in Rome, Paulus and Aristarchus are held in custody for a short time until the trial is ready to begin, in the court of the Praetor Peregrinus, who hears cases involving foreigners. In Roman courts, the accused questions the witnesses, and Paulus is successful in drawing from the witnesses against him admissions that they did not see Paulus instigate any riots – they only saw the damage done by the riots. Further exculpatory statements from Paulus' witness, and from the Roman procurator in Judea, lead to a verdict of *absolvo*, which would otherwise allow Paulus to go free. But a Roman administrator from the office of the Pontifex Maximus – that is, the Emperor Nero in his capacity as head of the state religion – is given permission to testify against Paulus on another matter completely: the charge of religious impiety. A long list of accusations against the sect of Christians is brought before the court, and as a consequence Paulus is placed under house arrest in Rome until a further trial on these charges is arranged. Aristarchus is sent to seek help from Simon Petros, but yet more complications arise when Simon and his wife reveal they have no intention of housing Paulus. Aristarchus must come up with a last-minute solution to ensure Paulus can avoid further trouble with the authorities.

Part Two – Chrysanthe – Year 60, Corinth

We meet Chrysanthe and Crispus, two leaders of the vibrant community of Gentiles and Jews in Corinth who venerate the memory of Jehoshua the Christos. So absorbed have these two been in their leadership roles in the community, that they ignore warning signs of trouble with their son Alcaeus. The trouble erupts when Alcaeus is detected secretly engaging in the pagan rites associated with the Greek god Dionysos. This shocks Chrysanthe in particular, who eventually discovers the cause of Alcaeus's disaffection. Working with others within the Christian community, she is determined to deal with the problem and protect her two younger daughters from experiencing the same doubts and challenges as Alcaeus. The result is an innocent pantomime for the children of the community – a small play that is destined to have unexpected long term implications for the worshippers of Jehoshua.

Part Three – Yakov – Year 62, Jerusalem

Ananus ben Ananias, following the death of his father Caiphas, now succeeds to the position of High Priest at the Temple. Two other events occur at the same time which conspire to hand unchecked power into the hands of Ananus. The first is the death of Gamaliel, the Nasi of the Sanhedrin and a protector of the small group of Jews now called the Christians, who worship Jehoshua of Nazareth as the Christos. The second is the death of the Roman procurator Festus. His successor, Albinus, must unexpectedly remain in Alexandria for several months before taking on his new role in Jerusalem. With no one to stop him, Ananus decides to continue with his father's policy of persecuting the Christians. He organizes a rump session of the Sanhedrin, orders the arrest of the Christian leader Yakov of Nazareth, and brings him to trial on capital charges. Protests from the Jews to Albinus at this arbitrary and illegal action by Ananus will eventually cost him his job as High Priest several months later, but not until he has done terrible damage to the group of Christos worshippers in Jerusalem.

Part Four – Josephus – Year 67, Jotapata in Galilee

In the Year 66, Jewish resentment at Rome finally boils out of control. The spark is an incident involving a perceived sacrilege by Gentiles who sacrifice birds on the sacred grounds of a synagogue, in contravention of Jewish religious doctrine. Rome does nothing in response to Jewish complaints, and as a result riots erupt throughout the Jewish provinces. The riots are a ready-made opportunity for those who have long been resisting Roman rule, chiefly the insurgents known as the Zealots. They create an organized military resistance, and when the governor of Syria brings his legion down to restore order, the Zealots ambush the Roman troops, putting to death 6,000 soldiers, capturing the legion's aquila, or ceremonial eagle, and forcing the Romans to abandon Jerusalem and all of the provinces. This is the greatest loss of Roman troops and territory in at least fifty years, leaving the Emperor Nero in shock. He commissions the most experienced general he can find – Flavius Vespasianus – to retake Jerusalem. Vespasianus will invade a year later from the north, through Galilee, and meets his first serious opponent at Jotapata, under the unlikely command of a Jewish religious scholar, Josephus.

Part Five – The Zealots – Years 69 to 71, Jerusalem

The defining event of the first century is now about to take place – the siege and destruction of Jerusalem – which sets Western civilization on a course that will embrace a tiny cult of worship among Jews, allowing it to develop into the religion of Christianity. None of this is evident to the players at the time, who include Flavius Vespasianus, a contender for Emperor of Rome; his son Titus; the Jewish scholar Josephus; and those Jews who attempt to defend Jerusalem from Roman attack. They have two leaders, Yohan of Gischala and Simon bar Giora. These two come down to us in history either as Jewish patriots or as reckless criminals who prey upon the long-suffering

Jewish people who are left defenseless at the hands of a band of Jewish marauders known as the Zealots. An estimated one million Jews will die horribly in the fall of Jerusalem and the loss of Israel, and their descendants are about to commence the long exile known as the Diaspora.

Part Six – Olympias – Year 79, Rome and Jerusalem

It took three long years for Rome to "mop up" Jewish resistance, with the Jews putting up a final stand at the desert fortress of Masada in the Year 73. The scene now shifts six years later, in 79, first to Rome, where we meet Olympias, the daughter of Crispus and Chrysanthe. She has settled in Rome with her husband, a wine merchant, and their three young boys. She and her husband live a secretive life as Christians in Rome, mindful of Nero's persecutions, even though Emperor Vespasianus has been tolerant of Christians and left them in peace. Olympias is among those who help Christianity find its roots in Rome. In contrast, Jerusalem remains in charred ruins, with Rome unwilling to spend effort or money to restore the city after its destruction. By the year 79, Rome does agree to restore the Sanhedrin and the position of Nasi, which is offered to Gamaliel's grandson, Gamaliel of Yavneh. He begins the arduous task of rebuilding Judaism, whose followers are flung to all areas of the Roman Empire and beyond, and whose home – the Temple of Jerusalem – will remain in ruins and unbuilt even up to this day.

Appendix F

Definitions of Religious Terms and Groups

The Spirit – Paulus is the principal user of the term "The Spirit". In Latin the term was *spiritus,* and in Greek *pneuma.* Paulus would have understood the term in its Greek usage, but more especially, as used in Jewish scripture (our Old Testament). In this sense, the *Spirit* conveys a sense of God's presence, perhaps in a person, place, or dwelling. It can also imply a blessing from God. Christian usage originally emphasized the aspect of the blessing as a gift, for example when the apostles were visited by the *Holy Spirit* on Pentecost, who endowed them with a gift of speaking many languages. The term *Holy Spirit* is a Christian term, and used very infrequently in Jewish scripture. As such, the Christians developed the term to mean largely a gift from God, of grace or some talent. Eventually the *Holy Spirit* came to represent God himself, and found its place in the triune God concept.

The Way – The epistles of Paulus mention *The Way,* a term he devised to represent either the journey Christians were on in their pursuit of eternal life through Jehoshua, or the discipline required of Christians in leading a good life so as to merit a place with God the Father and Jehoshua. The concept of *The Way* did not take hold with other Christian communities, perhaps because there were so many Christian communities which did not necessarily follow the teachings of Paulus. As a consequence, use of the term **The Way** did not long survive Paulus' death/disappearance.

The Christos – Early followers of Jehoshua were uncertain whether he viewed himself as a healer, prophet, or the promised one, the *Meshiach* (Messiah). Jehoshua, according to the gospels, implied to some of his apostles he might be a prophet like Elijah, or the *Son of Man* (a prophet figure) mentioned in the Book of Daniel. Neither of these titles exclude the use of the term *Meshiach* to describe Jehoshua, because the term meant *Anointed One*, and referred to a priest or king who would be anointed with holy chrism, and serve as a leader to unite all Jews. It is quite possible, therefore, that Jehoshua was hesitant publicly to declare himself the *Meshiach*, but did not object if his followers so described him. After his death, the term was used more frequently by his followers. Paulus, translating it to the Greek, used the term *Christos*, which developed in *Jehoshua the Christos* (Jesus the Anointed One), and eventually *Jesus Christ*. The first two Greek letters of the word *Christos* are Chi and Rho – X and P – and when placed on top of each other they produced a commonly used symbol for Christian. It should be mentioned that none of these titles discussed here implied Jehoshua was divine, a god, or God. That designation was to come a century later, though Paulus initiated the process by insisting that Jehoshua was already sitting at the right hand of God the Father.

Faith – The term *faith* does not show up frequently in the early gospels, but it was frequently used by Paulus in his epistles. By the time John was writing his gospel in the early second century, it was in common usage in many Christian communities. Paulus used it largely as a quality a Christian must have to accept the rationally unexplainable, like the resurrection of Jehoshua. He also used it to imply steadfastness, which became especially important when Christians began to suffer persecution under Nero.

Churches and Assemblies – Within the first few decades after the death of Jehoshua, Christians met privately in homes, or in secluded natural places. There were no churches as we understand them. Eventually larger communities such as those in Jerusalem or Antioch found warehouses or other large buildings to serve as community centers, but if repression was imposed by authorities, Christian worshippers would retreat again to homes, or in the case of the Roman communities, to the catacombs (caves) south of the city. Paulus used the term *Assembly* to describe community groups of followers, and for the first century of Christianity, *Assembly* is the most appropriate term to use to describe Christian worship. To this day, some Christian denominations label themselves as Assemblies (the Assembly of God, for example – a U.S. Pentecostal denomination).

Temples and Synagogues – There are only two Temples in Judaism – the First Temple built in Jerusalem by Solomon, and the Second Temple built as a replacement by Herod the Great. No other city may have a Temple, and Jews were required to visit the Temple once in their life in pilgrimage. The question of building a Third Temple has become a matter of religious, political, and even eschatological (end times) considerations for Judaism and Israel. Certain Christian sects hold the belief that rebuilding the Temple in Jerusalem is a sign that the End Times are near and the Last Judgment is at hand. Jews outside of Jerusalem worshipped at a local synagogue, which did not provide burnt offerings as were commonly done at the Temple in Jerusalem. Major cities had an especially large and elaborate synagogue serving as the central focal point for Jews in that city, and these structures were called Great Synagogues.

Zealots, Essenes, and other Groups

The Zealots have been mentioned in considerable detail in this book. They were loose bands of insurrectionists intent on forcing the Romans out of the Jewish provinces. The movement, while loosely federated, arose in Gadala in Galilee through the leadership of Judas of Gadala in the first century BCE. They seem to have had some political influence, as Josephus mentions them as one of four quasi-political parties in first century Judea, the others being the Pharisees, the Sadducees, and the Essenes. The first two of these groups have been discussed extensively in Book One. The Essenes were devoted to purity of action and thought, on very strict terms, to the point where some scholars feel they were celibate. They lived in poverty and eschewed worldly possessions. Josephus says they were resident in the deserts near the Dead Sea, but clearly some leaders lived in Jerusalem and undertook political or judicial offices, such as membership on the Sanhedrin. A "non-official" group at the time were the Iscarii, or Iscariots. The word is Latin for dagger (*scarius*), and members were called dagger-men, for their practice of sneaking up on their victims, knifing them, and then blending in with the crowd afterward. The Iscarii were assumed to be Zealots who used particularly violent tactics against not only the Romans, but prominent Jewish political, business or religious figures whom they considered too close to Rome. They are noted, for example, for stabbing to death the High Priest Yonathan in the streets of Jerusalem. There is some indication that Yohan of Gischala was one of their leaders. Judas, the betrayer of Jehoshua, was called an Iscariot, but since the group was neither ethnically nor geographically based, it is possible Judas was posthumously given this appellation to reflect his role as a traitor.

Appendix G

Bibliography

Asimov, Isaac. *Asimov's Guide to the Bible: The Old and New Testaments.* New York: Avenel, 1981.

Bütz, Jeffrey J. *The Brother of Jesus and the Lost Teachings of Christianity.* Rochester, Vt.: Inner Traditions, 2005.

Bütz, Jeffrey J. *The Secret Legacy of Jesus: The Judaic Teachings that Passed from James the Just to the Founding Fathers.* Rochester, Vt.: Inner Traditions, 2010.

Carlson, Stephen C. *The Gospel Hoax: Morton Smith's Invention of Secret Mark.* Waco, Texas: Baylor University Press, 2005.

Crossan, John Dominic. *The Birth of Christianity: Discovering What Happened in the Years Immediately After the Execution of Jesus.* San Francisco: Harper, 1998.

Crossan, John Dominic and Marcus J. Borg. *The First Christmas: What the Gospels Really Teach About Jesus' Birth.* New York: Harper, 2007.

Crossan, John Dominic. *The First Paul: Reclaiming the Radical Visionary Behind the Church's Conservative Icon.* New York: Harper, 2009.

Crossan, John Dominic. *God and Empire: Jesus Against Rome, Then and Now.* San Francisco: Harper, 2007.

Crossan, John Dominic. *The Greatest Prayer: Rediscovering the Revolutionary Message of the Lord's Prayer.* New York: Harper, 2010.

Crossan, John Dominic. *The Historical Jesus: The Life of a Mediterranean Jewish Peasant.* San Francisco: Harper, 1991.

Crossan, John Dominic and Jonathan L. Reed. *In Search of Paul: How Jesus' Apostle Opposed Rome's Empire with God's Kingdom: A New Vision of Paul's Words & World.* San Francisco: Harper, 2004.

Crossan, John Dominic. *Jesus: A Revolutionary Biography.* San Francisco: Harper, 1994.

Crossan, John Dominic and Marcus J. Borg. *The Last Week: The Day-By-Day Account of Jesus' Final Week in Jerusalem.* San Francisco: Harper, 2006.

Crossan, John Dominic. *The Power of Parable: How Fiction By Jesus Became Fiction About Jesus.* New York: Harper 2012.

Crossan, John Dominic and Jonathan L. Reed. *Excavating Jesus: Beneath the Stones, Behind the Texts.* San Francisco: Harper, 2001.

Eisenman, Robert. *James, the Brother of Jesus: The Key to Unlocking the Secrets of Early Christianity and the Dead Sea Scrolls.* New York: Viking, 1997.

Ehrman, Bart D. *Forged: Writing in the Name of God: Why the Bible's Authors are Not Who We Think They Are.* New York: Harper, 2011.

Ehrman, Bart D. *Jesus, Interrupted: Revealing the Hidden Contradictions in the Bible (and Why We Don't Know about Them).* New York: Harper, 2009.

Ehrman, Bart D. *Misquoting Jesus : the story behind who changed the Bible and why.* New York: Harper, 2005.

Funk, Robert Walter, and the Jesus Seminar, ed. *The Acts of Jesus: The Search for the Authentic Deeds of Jesus.* San Francisco: Harper, 1998.

Funk, Robert Walter, Roy W. Hoover, and the Jesus Seminar, ed. *The Five Gospels: The Search for the Authentic Words of Jesus: A New Translation and Commentary.* New York: Macmillan, 1993.

Funk, Robert Walter and the Jesus Seminar, ed. *The Gospel of Jesus: According to the Jesus Seminar.* Santa Rosa, Calif.: Polebridge Press, 1999.

Funk, Robert Walter, trans. *A Greek Grammar of the New Testament and Other Early Christian Literature* [by] F. Blass and A. Debrunner. A translation and revision of the 9th-10th German ed., incorporating supplementary notes of A. Debrunner, by Robert W. Funk. Chicago: University of Chicago Press, 1961.

Funk, Robert Walter. *Honest to Jesus: Jesus for a New Millennium.* San Francisco: Harper, 1996.

Goodspeed, Edgar J. *The Apocrypha, an American Translation.* Chicago: University of Chicago, 1938.

Jacobovici, Simcha and Charles Pellegrino. *The Jesus Family Tomb: The Discovery, the Investigation, and the Evidence that Could Change History.* San Francisco: Harper, 2007.

King, Karen L. *The Gospel of Mary of Magdala: Jesus and the First Woman Apostle*. Santa Rosa, Calif.: Polebridge Press, 2003.

Kloppenborg, John S. *Excavating Q: The History and Setting of the Sayings Gospel*. Minneapolis: Fortress Press, 2000.

Mack, Burton L. *The Lost Gospel: The Book of Q and Christian Origins*. San Francisco: Harper, 1993.

Mack, Burton L. *Who Wrote the New Testament? : The Making of the Christian Myth*. San Francisco: Harper, 1995.

Meier, John P. *A Marginal Jew: Rethinking the Historical Jesus*. New York: Doubleday, 1991.

Meyer, Marvin W., trans. *The Gospel of Thomas: The Hidden Sayings of Jesus*. San Francisco: Harper, 1992.

Meyer, Marvin W., ed. *The Nag Hammadi Scriptures*. New York: Harper, 2007.

Meyers, Robin R. *Saving Jesus from the Church: How to Stop Worshiping Christ and Start Following Jesus*. New York: Harper, 2009.

Meyers, Robin R. *The Underground Church: Reclaiming the Subversive Way of Jesus*. San Francisco: Jossey-Bass, 2012.

Meyers, Robin R. *Why the Christian Right is Wrong: A Minister's Manifesto for Taking Back Your Faith, Your Flag, Your Future*. San Francisco: Jossey-Bass, 2006.

Pagels, Elaine H. *Adam, Eve, and the Serpent*. New York: Random, 1988.

Pagels, Elaine H. *Beyond Belief: The Secret Gospel of Thomas*. New York: Random, 2003.

Pagels, Elaine H. *The Gnostic Gospels*. New York: Random, 1979.

Pagels, Elaine H. *The Origin of Satan*. New York: Random, 1995.

Pagels, Elaine H. *Reading Judas: The Gospel of Judas and the Shaping of Christianity*. New York: Viking, 2007.

Pagels, Elaine H. *Revelations: Visions, Prophecy, and Politics in the Book of Revelation*. New York: Viking, 2012.

Robinson, James M., Paul Hoffman, and John S. Kloppenborg, ed. *The Critical Edition of Q: Synopsis Including the Gospels of Matthew and Luke, Mark and Thomas with English, German, and French Translations of Q and Thomas*. Minneapolis: Fortress Press, 2000.

Smith, Morton and R. Joseph Hoffman, ed. *What the Bible Really Says*. Buffalo: Prometheus, 1989.

Smith, Morton. *Jesus the Magician: Charlatan or Son of God?* San Francisco: Harper, 1978.

Smith, Morton. *The Secret Gospel: The Discovery and Interpretation of the Secret Gospel According to Mark*. New York: Harper, 1973.

Spong, John Shelby. *Eternal Life: Pious Dream or Realistic Hope?* New York: Harper, 2009.

Spong, John Shelby. *Jesus for the Non-Religious: Recovering the Divine at the Heart of the Human*. New York: Harper, 2007.

Spong, John Shelby. *Liberating the Gospels: Reading the Bible with Jewish Eyes: Freeing Jesus from 2,000 Years of Misunderstanding*. San Francisco: Harper, 1996.

Spong, John Shelby. *Re-Claiming the Bible for a Non-Religious World*. New York: Harper, 2011.

Spong, John Shelby. *Rescuing the Bible from Fundamentalism: A Bishop Rethinks the Meaning of Scripture*. San Francisco: Harper, 1991.

Tabor, James D. and Simcha Jacobovici. *The Jesus Discovery: The New Archaeological Find that Reveals the Birth of Christianity*. New York: Simon & Schuster, 2012.

Tabor, James D. *The Jesus Dynasty: The Hidden History of Jesus, His Royal Family, and the Birth of Christianity*. New York: Simon & Schuster, 2006.

Appendix H

Discussion Questions for Book Clubs

1. What would you say are two or three overarching themes that were developed in the book?

2. Historians contend that one secret to the success of the Romans in maintaining their empire was their tolerance of different religions. Yet the Romans had ongoing problems dealing with the Jews when it came to religion. What else might have caused tension? The monotheistic nature of Judaism? The strict dietary, clothing, and other rules Jews lived by? A different set of moral standards under Judaism?

3. How well depicted were the principal characters in the book? Did they seem realistic to you? Did you understand their motivations for the actions they took and the philosophies they espoused?

4. The book depicts a pronounced split developing between Jews and Christians, leading to fighting and mistrust. This sets the two religions on a path that leads ultimately to anti-Semitism infesting the Christian church for two millennia. If you could alter history in the first century, what would you do to prevent anti-Semitism from finding a foothold among Christian communities?

5. The first serious persecutions of Christians began under Nero in the 60's. These and later repressions obviously had a profound effect on Christians, because a cult of martyrdom rose among Christians and persisted for 250 years. If you were a Christian during the time described in this book, what would motivate you to give up your life for Jehoshua the Christos? In other words, how did the desire for martyrdom arise?

6. The Romans refused to allow the Temple of Jerusalem to be rebuilt, and all that remains of the Temple Mount today is the

Wailing Wall. What is preventing Israel from rebuilding the Temple today, either where it used to be, or somewhere else?

7. The depiction of the Zealots and the Iscarii suggests that they prevented Jerusalem from surrendering to Titus and avoiding destruction. This depiction is based on the writings of Josephus, though we should remember that he too did not surrender Jotapata to the Romans. Might there be another story here? Were there religious or other forces that motivated the Jews to hold out to the end? Seeing all this destruction, what logical conclusion might the first generation Christians of Jerusalem reach?

8. Paulus never married and promoted a theology that might be called prudish for its time, since attitudes toward sex were very relaxed, and even prostitution was legal throughout the Empire. Why would the early Christian communities accept Paulus' view of sex, when the alternative was to participate in the very open culture when it came to sex. Bear in mind that some of Paulus' epistles chastise certain communities for encouraging sexual freedom, so not every Christian Assembly accepted his teachings on this. Why, then, did some communities do so and not others?

9. It was said in the book that one-third of the population of the Empire were slaves. Why was slavery so important to Roman culture? What were the economic and political factors that promoted the practice? Why was it so universally accepted, even by Jehoshua, as part of the natural order? Do you think when Jehoshua talked about the "Kingdom of God", he was talking just to fellow Jews who understood the term in the scripture, or did he include slaves as well?

10. The Pharisees had a concept of the resurrection of the body at the Last Judgment. Paulus was a Pharisee, and he was also familiar with pagan traditions of gods rising from the dead. This book suggests that these were the reasons that the idea of Jehoshua's resurrection in the flesh began to circulate. How plausible is that suggestion?

11. If Paulus had not existed, what would have happened to Christianity? Would it even exist?

Appendix I

About the Author

Garrett Glass is the prize-winning author of *Who Cut God's Hair*, and the *Jehoshua* series of historical fiction. *Who Cut God's Hair* is a non-fiction survey of God-belief in the light of recent advances in neurobiology, psychiatry, psychology, anthropology, and related scientific fields. Glass develops a five-stage model that applies to all humans, from birth to pre-adult years, in which we are to an infant all-knowing, all-powerful, all-loving, always-present, and capable of creating and providing all of our needs. Glass postulates that belief in God is nurtured in all of us at our most susceptible ages, and as such is the default belief of mankind. But God-belief is not genetically ordained; nor is it necessarily a permanent belief. Many people move away from God belief and religious practice, but if they do, like religious people, they continue to search for meaning in their life. Issued in 2018, *Who Cut God's Hair* won that year's Bronze Medal for religious and spiritual writing, issued by the Independent Publishers Association.

The *Jehoshua* fictional series follows the development of Christianity after the death of Jesus Christ. *Jehoshua: Signs and Wonders* features the first 25 years after Christ's death, and focuses on early church leaders, such as Simon Petros (St. Peter), Miriam of Magdala (Mary Magdalen), Paulus of Tarsus (St. Paul), and the brother of Jehoshua, Yakov of Nazareth (St. James the Just). These figures interact with Jewish leaders in

Jerusalem, and Roman rulers in different
parts of the Roman Empire.   Kirkus
Reviews said the author "skillfully fleshes
out the characters and illustrates the
theological issues without confusing
the reader...well researched and highly
informative." *Signs and Wonders* was the
first self-published book to be included
in the prestigious Patheos Book Club,
devoted to religious literature.

Jehoshua: Conflagration follows the same
figures through the tragic years of the Jewish
Wars, which led to the destruction of Jerusalem in 70 CE, and the
dispersion of the Jews throughout the Empire. In this critical
period, the small section of Jews known as Christians create
an identity separate from the Jews, allowing then to establish
a base in Rome once Jerusalem was destroyed. The third book
in the series, *Jehoshua: Blood Relatives*, is due to be released in
2025. This book is centered around the short reign of Emperor
Titus, with the background provided by the inauguration of the
Colosseum, the terrible fire in Rome in 81 CE, and the eruption
of Mount Vesuvius.

www.whocutgodshair.com

www.ingramcontent.com/pod-product-compliance
Lightning Source LLC
Chambersburg PA
CBHW051528250626
47156CB00001B/273